Metro Winds

ISOBELLE CARMODY

Metro Winds

ALLEN&UNWIN

SYDNEY·MELBOURNE·AUCKLAND·LONDON

First published in 2012

Allen & Unwin
83 Alexander Street
Crows Nest NSW 2065
Australia
Phone: (61 2) 8425 0100
Fax: (61 2) 9906 2218
Email: info@allenandunwin.com
Web: www.allenandunwin.com

A Cataloguing-in-Publication entry is available from the National Library of Australia
www.trove.nla.gov.au

ISBN 978 1 86508 444 2

Cover and text design by Zoë Sadokierski
Set in 11/16 Adobe Caslon Pro by Midland Typesetters, Australia
Printed and bound in Australia by Griffin Press

10 9 8 7 6 5 4 3 2 1

MIX
Paper from
responsible sources
FSC® C009448

The paper in this book is FSC® certified.
FSC® promotes environmentally responsible,
socially beneficial and economically viable
management of the world's forests.

For Stephen,
who shared his passionate love of music with me

CONTENTS

METRO WINDS

So there was a girl. Young but not too young. A face as unformed as an egg, so that one could not tell if she would turn out to be fair or astonishingly ugly. She was to be sent to a city in another land by a mother and father in the midst of a divorce. The one thing they could agree upon was that the girl should not be exposed to the violence they meant to commit on their life. There was a quality in her that made it impossible to do the ravening that the end of love required.

'She must be sent away,' the father had said in civil but forbidding tones.

'For her own good,' the mother agreed. 'My sister will have her.'

The girl stood between them, wordless and passive as a bolster, as it was arranged that she be sent to the city where her mother had spent her childhood, this girl who had lived on a remote coast of a remote land in a solitary yellow house listening to the chilly grey sea that rushed straight from the ice pole to pound on the shore beside her bedroom window.

Red-nosed and blue-lipped, bare-armed and bare-legged in a faded shift, she had played amongst rocks where crabs scuttled through pools of clouded sky, but on the day of the departure, she wore a navy blue dress and jacket lined with grey silk, dark stockings and patent leather shoes, all of which had been purchased from a catalogue. The heavy mass of silken hair had been wetted and bound tightly into two braids. She watched her white night shift being folded into a dark boxy suitcase, although the mother and aunt had agreed that once she arrived she would be provided with a wardrobe befitting her life in the city.

'She can't go with nothing,' the mother murmured to herself as she closed the mouth of the case. There was little enough in it, yet how could she be blamed for the lack of clothes or beloved toys to pack, or much-read books? The girl could not be forced to accumulate such things.

The mother glanced at the girl with a pang of unease as she straightened, but reminded herself that the child's destination was a very old and sophisticated city, and not some dangerous wilderness, so what need was there for anxiety? She wanted to cup the girl's face and kiss the cheeks and eyelids tenderly, but only rested her hands lightly on her shoulders; felt the fragility of them; noted absently that her own fingers were stiff as dried twigs.

'You will see,' she said vaguely.

There was no need to invoke good behaviour, for the girl was calm and biddable and, remarkably, did not practise deceits. When a question was asked, she saw only that information was required. The consequences of her answer or the uses to which the information she gave might be put did not concern her. Being asked, she told. If she did not know, she said. This might have made her blunt and tactless, but she seldom spoke unless asked a direct question.

What would the girl's aunt make of her? the mother wondered. Rather than leaving her plump sister embittered, the lack of a husband or children had softened the centre of her until she was sweet enough to ache your teeth. She had been full of delight at the thought of having a vessel into which she could pour the rich syrup of her emotions.

'I shall adore her and she will be happy,' she had written.

The mother frowned at the memory, for it seemed to her the girl was too deep and odd to be content with mere happiness. Once, seeing a storm brooding, she had gone seeking the girl, only to find her standing at the edgy rim of the sea, hands lifted to the bruised clouds like a child wishing to be taken up. What sort of child is it who wishes to embrace a storm? she had wondered in appalled awe. The girl's lips had been drawn back from her teeth in a rictus that looked at first to be an expression of pain, but was only what laughter had made of her.

Even so, one could not say to one's sister that the child had a capacity for rare and frightening joy, and so she had simply agreed that they were bound to get along. That, at least, might be true.

Stowing the case in the boot of her car, the mother thought how often over the years she had tried to convey her disappointment in the girl in letters to her sister, who had only congratulated her on her good fortune with an extravagant wistfulness that left no room for a confession of the fear that she had borne, not a flesh-and-blood child with fits of ill temper that must be humoured and fears that must be soothed, but a sort of angel. And not the soft fat promiscuous angels of Italian frescoes, but a wild untameable creature of dry feathers and blazing sunlight and high wailing winds.

Neither the mother nor the father thought of the girl with intimate possessiveness. It was not the man's nature to wish to possess anything other than abstract ideas, for he was a doctor and medical researcher. And the woman found it impossible to love a child who required neither forgiveness nor tolerance. A mother needs needing, she told herself, to excuse the guilt that churned her belly from time to time.

The girl sat docilely in the car on the way to the airport, hands folded loosely in her lap. 'Are you afraid?' her mother asked after they had checked the bag in and learned the seat allocation.

'No,' the girl said simply.

The mother swallowed an aimless spurt of anger, knowing that for anyone else, being sent into the unknown would be reason enough for fear. Perhaps the girl had nothing with which to people her nightmares because she lacked imagination. The mother felt a shamed relief when the time came to say goodbye, yet at the same time it seemed to her there were words that should be said.

I should understand something, she thought urgently.

When the girl turned to pass through the door to international departures, the woman found herself remembering with sudden shocking clarity the lumpy slipperiness as the midwife pulled the child from her womb and swung it up onto her flaccid belly; the rank animal stench of the fluids that flowed out of her, and the purplish swollen look of skin smeared with white foam and strings of bloody slime; that black hair and the dark bottomless eyes that looked through her skin and into her soul.

The airport doors closed with a smooth hiss, severing them from one another. The woman stood for a time looking at the ambiguous smear of her face in the dull metal surface, feeling grief, longing, fear.

The girl spent much of the journey gazing out at the sky, surprised at how substantial the clouds appeared from above. For of course she had only ever seen their undersides, which must have been grazed to flatness by the mountains they passed over. When the sky darkened as the plane entered the long night, a steward asked if she wanted chicken or beef. She never ate meat but the travel agent hadn't thought to ask when booking the ticket. It did not matter. She liked the way hunger gnawed at her belly from the inside with sharp little teeth.

When she slept, it was to dream an old dream of wandering in dark tunnels searching for something she could not name.

The girl's aunt had been tremulous and moist with emotion before her niece came at last into the arrivals foyer, yet the first sight of the girl caused the older woman to draw a swift breath. A moment later she could not have explained her reaction; she had seen photographs so the child's appearance was no surprise. In the taxicab she fussed and tutted over the late flight and told herself it was pity that had made her gasp, for the girl's clothes were so severe they only accentuated the vagueness of her features.

The aunt's apartment was large but managed to be cramped as well, being filled with fringed lamps, occasional tables, plump tasselled cushions, painted china ornaments, little enamel boxes, carved animals, winged armchairs, frilled curtains, and vases of stiff dried flowers. The floors were carpeted in dove grey, but exotic rugs coloured henna red, turquoise and emerald were laid here and there atop it to form gorgeous pools of colour. The sound of movement was altogether smothered.

The girl slipped off her shoes and wiggled her toes, searching for the bones of the place under its fat pelt. She thought of the hard wooden floors of the house by the sea, which had been limed the icy hue of a winter sky. Noticing the pale slender feet, the aunt assumed she had removed her shoes out of consideration for the carpets.

She ushered the girl to a bedroom where rose-coloured lamps gave off tiny pools of blushing light. The walls were covered in a velveted indigo paper and the window and four-poster bed were draped in thick folds of violet lace surmounted by an overdress through which gold ribbon had been intricately threaded.

Having noted the lightness of the case, the aunt left the girl to unpack to avoid embarrassing them both by witnessing the paucity of her possessions. Her sister had clearly made a worse marriage than she had feared. She smiled in pity at the girl over a late supper laid out on gold-rimmed plates. There was a silver pot of hot chocolate, rich cream puffs, jam horns, sugary slices and little sandwiches. The girl ate one corner of a cucumber and lettuce sandwich, and when pressed to try a paste sandwich, explained politely that she did not eat meat.

'But these are only fish,' the aunt said, taking a bite from one of the sandwiches. She was discomfited to be so frankly watched, but the girl made no comment, other than to ask if she might go to bed soon. In a gush of guilty relief, her aunt promised a shopping expedition on the morrow.

In the bedroom, the girl removed her outer clothes and laid them aside. She was wide awake, for her body told her that it was early morning. Wanting to taste the air of the city, she struggled until she opened the window, which had been painted shut. Gazing through it, she stared at the city beyond, blanketed in shadows and pricked here and there by light. There was a breeze and she watched her hair float up in tendrils that seemed to quest as blindly and voraciously as the tentacles of a sea anemone. She thought of the icy wind that slipped up through the cracks in the bone-pale floorboards of her old bedroom, shuddering the window glass in the frame as it tried to get out again. Sometimes it was so strong that when you opened the drawers in the kitchen, the wind blew out into your face, so loud that people telephoning would ask who was screaming. If one looked through the windows at night, there were not the thousand and one lights visible from this lean window, but only darkness laid like a film over shadowy trees, and beyond them the lines of foam that trimmed the relentless waves. If she opened a window, the air would fly like a dervish into her room, smelling of icebergs and open grey seas.

There was nothing green or wet or wild in the air of this city. It was heavy with the odours of people and their machines. She imagined it as weary and sour as the breath of an old man who had lived too long. She thought that she would find it hard to breathe or move quickly in this dense air with so many people and their lives pressed up against her, but she was not afraid. If she felt anything, it was curiosity to see how she would manage it.

The following day, the aunt came bustling into the room and shut the open window at once in a fluster of incoherent warnings. She did not believe in fresh air. In fact, moving air of any kind troubled her. She bade the girl rise, for she meant to keep her promise: they were to go shopping. First they caught a taxi to a market of little stalls to buy food. This expedition was undertaken with great seriousness. The girl had never seen fruit laid out with such reverence. Apples gleamed a wicked, tempting red, and each flawless cherry seemed to have been polished to gleaming crimson. Pears and mangoes glowed gold, and there was a mound of queer intricately spiked green orbs she had never seen before. The aunt discussed everything with the stallholder and they seemed to come to a joint decision about what should be bought. They went to a bread stall and a cheese stall, and again the aunt spoke with the proprietors, who were assertive but courteous. They carried nothing from the stalls, for their purchases were to be delivered to the apartment where the maid, D'lo, waited to put them away.

They ate lunch at a restaurant where, the aunt said, a man had once come with a gun to shoot his lover's wife. She relished the details of the anecdote in the same way she had enjoyed dissecting the composition of her favourite dishes on the menu. The girl listened solemnly but asked no questions, to the aunt's regret, for she had withheld several salacious details she would have alluded to if pressed.

The room they were in was decorated with huge vases of lilies and on the spotless white tablecloths, which the tables wore as if they were ball dresses, were small vases of violets. The girl chose a clear vegetable soup and bread, a lemon sorbet and strawberries drizzled with Armagnac. The aunt was disappointed by her poor appetite, and enjoyed her own food less as a consequence.

Afterwards they walked along a boulevard of shops with wide windows. In one, lights converged to worship a single stiletto shoe with a transparent icicle for a heel; in others were a red dress, a baroque pearl and a diamond dog-collar. The girl was led from one dress shop to another where skeletally thin women with white china complexions and slick red mouths discussed cut and fabric. The aunt was puzzled by the girl's passivity. One would think she was being dressed in a bazaar for all the interest she showed in the clothes. Perhaps she was mildly retarded. Her sister had not said so, yet in looking back, hadn't there been something unspoken in the letters she had sent over the years? Something struggling to be revealed?

The girl was unaware that the clothes were more important than the people who sold them. She was fascinated by the languid gestures of one woman ordering this or that dress to be brought out, with a ferocious smile that reminded the girl of a panther she had seen once in a cage, lying perfectly still with a bored expression in its lovely eyes. Only the flick of its tail had revealed its savagery. Pale, pastel-clad acolytes scurried to do the woman's bidding. The girl saw that despite the identical pastel smocks and neat buns, they were quite different. One had a saucy look and quick nimble fingers, another smelled of cigarettes, and yet another had red-rimmed eyes which she had tried to mask with powder.

The aunt's taste for frills and beading and what she called dramatic colours was gently but firmly directed towards more delicate fabrics, paler hues and plainer styles. The only thing she resisted was a white voile dress.

'Not white,' the aunt had said. Could they not see how it increased the insipidity of the girl's features? Besides, white was the colour of confirmation dresses and shrouds. Privately she thought the use of white for brides was unfortunate; if she had ever wed she would have worn violet and peacock blue.

Like the foodstuffs, the clothes were to be delivered, so they made their way unhampered to an open-air restaurant within the main park in the city for afternoon tea.

'I thought you would like the wildness of it,' the aunt said, pleased by her own generosity, since open-air restaurants were not to her taste. She fancied the girl might be missing the primitive beauty of her home. She spotted an acquaintance who was invited to join them, a thin woman with glistening eyes snuggled on either side of a long sharp nose, who proceeded to whisper an interminable story about a man and his doctor wife.

The girl gazed around. It was the hottest part of the day and she could feel the dampness forming in the curve of her upper lip and along her spine, pricking at her palms. Beyond the awning roof of the restaurant, the park shimmered. There were green hedges manicured into animal shapes but they cast no shade. Carefully edged rose beds surrounded a small marble fountain where a woman with bare stone breasts endlessly poured water from a jug into a bowl. The paths were made from crushed white gravel that radiated a bright, white heat. Grass grew only in circles marked off by chains from which were suspended signs forbidding feet. Wrought-iron chairs stood about the edge of these pools of dazzling green and a few people sat in them and stared at the grass as if it were a pond where their faces looked back at them or fish swam.

There were not many other customers in the restaurant at that hour: a table of businessmen stabbing fingers at a map and an elegant woman in a grey pantsuit talking animatedly to a poodle seated on a chair opposite. After a time, a group of people converged on the restaurant talking loudly in foreign accents punctuated with expansive gestures and bird cries of delight.

'Tourists,' the acquaintance murmured regretfully.

A waiter approached the group and they opened their lips to display huge white smiles. Pink gums showed around the edges of their teeth. The waiter herded them gently but firmly into an arbour where their cries were muted and their bright clothes could not disturb the other diners.

An elderly man in a perfectly tailored cream suit and panama hat entered and made his way to the next table. He sat down, drawing out a long slim cigar. The waiter approached and lit it deferentially after snipping off its end, then, without being asked, a second waiter brought a coffee and a small glass of green liquid on a little tray. The girl watched him pour some of the green liquid into a spoonful of sugar and set a match to it. An emerald flame swelled and hovered above the spoon. When it had burned itself out the man dribbled the thick dark residue into his coffee, stirred and drank it.

At length, the aunt pronounced it time to go, refusing the offer of a lift home in the acquaintance's car. They were going by metro, she explained, for the girl must learn to use the subterranean train system in case she wanted to attend the theatre or visit a gallery when her aunt was otherwise occupied. 'But the metro,' the acquaintance said doubtfully, 'she should never use the metro after dark . . .'

'I will explain all that needs to be explained in good time,' the aunt said in a mildly peevish tone, and then the two women smiled acidly at one another and agreed to take tea together again very soon.

The girl had a photograph taken in a booth for her metro pass, and this was snipped out and slid into a laminated case which she slipped obediently into her purse. Inside the metro station, which was only a sort of corrugated tin shed with turnstiles and a ticket machine, there were windows where men and woman sat looking bored and annoyed. The metro platforms themselves were deep underground, the aunt explained, pointing to an escalator that would carry them down to the platforms where one boarded the electric trains.

It was a steep descent and the girl seemed to lean into the air that swelled out of the tunnel.

'Hold tightly to the handrail,' her aunt said sternly. 'You could fall.' The girl rested her hand on it and found it moved slightly faster than the steps, so that she kept adjusting her grip. The ascending escalator was alongside and the girl looked into the faces of people riding on it: a tired man cradling a briefcase as if it were a baby; a young couple twined and kissing voluptuously; two nuns; a group of drunk men singing an obscene song and leaning on one another; a swarthy man with a surly expression; a big woman with a beautiful wide-mouthed face and a stained ecru bodice; a young woman muttering rapidly to herself. The girl was entranced. She had not seen such people in the restaurant or shops or in the park.

The aunt murmured discreetly that one should not stare because aside from being a mark of ill-breeding, it virtually obliged some sort of intercourse. The girl did not see how any sort of exchange could be conducted with people going decisively in opposite directions, but she looked away obediently.

A short hall between two opposing platforms came into view at the end of the escalator. One went left or right through little archways to the platforms, the aunt explained, one side for metro trains going east and south, one side for those going north and west. Just before they reached the bottom where the silver teeth of a grille swallowed the escalator, an enormous gust of cold wind blew up into their faces from the depths, as if the earth itself had sighed. The girl gasped as it tugged her hair from its braids and licked the sweat from her upper lip.

'I smell the sea,' she said in wonderment.

The aunt sniffed surreptitiously but could smell only the oily escalator reek, under which lay an unpleasant tang of urine. She pursed her lips; her notion that the girl was mentally afflicted strengthened, for the city was far from the sea.

When they reached their platform there were only a few people waiting down the far end. Between them and the aunt and the girl, a lone man stood in a niche unwrapping an instrument. He wore corduroy pants with threadbare knees, a greasy blue shirt and an embroidered cloth cap from beneath which hung a narrow plait. A black dog with a faded bandana knotted around its neck sat by his feet. The girl felt a thrill when it looked at her with the same startled recognition as her aunt's ebony maid.

'I told you, it is better not to look at anyone,' the aunt admonished. 'Men like that call themselves musicians but they are beggars, or worse.' She flushed slightly.

The ghostly subterranean wind blew again, and the girl's

hair and clothes fluttered wildly. Her aunt was glad that her own coiffure was firmly lacquered, and that her clothes had substance enough not to be trifled with by the draft. She tried to take shallow breaths, certain the air was laden with the germs of these odd and unsavoury people who lingered between the arches. Thinking of her acquaintance, the aunt told the girl never to go beyond the end of the platforms, which narrowed into ledges that ran away down the dark tunnels.

'The workmen use them when they repair the rails or the signals. The metro is very old and there are disused stations and tunnels and bricked-up stairways and goodness knows what else where you could easily lose your way,' she said. It had been many years since she had used the metro and it seemed to have been allowed to lapse into a queer sort of anarchy. If only the girl had the wit to be afraid, but clearly she did not.

A moment later, the metro train, a sleek snake of silver, burst from the tunnel and sighed to a halt beside the platform, where its doors glided open with a soft hiss. The girl and the aunt entered the nearest carriage and found a seat. 'Never make the mistake of entering the metro when people are going to work in the morning or leaving work in the evening, for it is impossibly crowded,' the older woman warned. She spoke of pickpockets, but in her eyes there was something more than hands feeling for a purse. 'You must also avoid the metro when there are too few people around,' she added.

When they reached the correct stop, they stepped out onto the platform and mounted the moving stair to return to the surface, where the aunt explained they were within walking distance of their apartment. At the top of the escalator there was an old beggar woman gazing downward.

'A storm is coming!' she cried. 'See how it has turned my soup sour!' She pointed accusingly to a battered metal boiler sitting squatly and incongruously in a tattered pram upon which hung a multitude of bulging plastic bags. The crowd split smoothly into two streams which passed either side of the old harridan, everyone averting their eyes. But several young men with army greens and shaven heads stopped to jeer. One had a swastika tattooed on his scalp, the aunt noted, wondering if the girl knew what it was, what it meant.

They made to pass the old beggar woman who, without warning, plunged forward and caught the girl by the wrist. The aunt gave a little shriek and batted uselessly at the clutching hand, the blackened fingers reminding her of the dark, leathery paw of an ape.

The old woman had eyes only for her pale young captive. 'Do you know what it means when soup goes sour?' she demanded.

The girl shook her head in wonderment.

The old woman leaned close enough that the girl could smell her earthy reek. 'It is a sign,' she said, eyes aglitter.

The aunt wrenched her free with a strength born of indignation, and hustled her firmly away, before taking out a tiny lace-edged handkerchief and rubbing hard at the girl's wrist. The old beggar woman's fingers had left a perfect print of grime on her pale skin, but the mark seemed indelible as a bruise.

'Never mind,' she comforted herself. 'I have carbolic soap that will remove it.'

It was night when they came out of the station and the girl was surprised, for they had entered the metro in daylight. Their underground journey had not seemed so long, but of course time might move differently with the weight of so much earth pressing down on it.

They made their way past shops and restaurants and houses behind neat little wrought-iron fences with lace-curtained windows through which she could see people laughing, talking, reading and smoking. She thought of the web of metro tunnels deep down in the chill dark earth beneath all this, and wondered if what had been wild and untamed in this land had not been destroyed, but had retreated and leaked or crept down into the metro. She thought of the old man in the cream suit conjuring his green flame with its dark residue and imagined that what lay below the city might sometimes rise up in spectral threads or strange furtive flames.

That night, she dreamed the tunnel dream again, but this time it was the metro and the old beggar woman with her pram had found her way into it.

'What are you looking for?' she asked the girl in a raw crackle, clutching her wrist.

'I don't know.'

The woman shook her grizzled head. 'Then you must learn or you will never find the shape of your heart's desire.'

'I don't understand,' the girl said.

The woman looked sad. 'Then all is lost.'

The following day, the aunt chose which of the stiff new dresses the girl was to wear with which shoes and which cardigan to carry in which bag. The girl let herself be turned this way and that by the aunt and by D'lo, who said, 'She fine. She sho' lookin' fine.' D'lo had a voice than flowed as thick and golden viscous as warmed sap. The girl liked to hear her talk, and wondered what might be imparted in that voice, in the absence of her aunt.

They had been invited to luncheon and the aunt suggested they walk, since their destination was in the neighbourhood. They passed through a small park and the aunt reminisced about her poodle, Mikoláš, who had been walked there. He had died, but the aunt said *passed away*, dabbing at her eyes sentimentally and interpreting the girl's silence as respect for Mikoláš. She told herself the child was perhaps only a little slow, and that was not so detrimental in a girl as in a boy. Indeed, looking at the mess her sister had made of her life, it might be said that cleverness was more of a disadvantage to a woman than anything else.

The girl was thinking about her dream, for it seemed to her that she had seen something in the tunnels just before the old beggar woman appeared. Something huge and white.

Their hosts' apartment was stylish, with blond leather furniture and chilly, gleaming, marble floors. There were clear vases of yellow irises, heavy cream silk curtains and paintings in muted colours, but also many blank walls which had their own beauty. Most of all, there was empty space filled with shafts of sunlight.

Privately the aunt thought the apartment ostentatiously bare, though of course she admired her hosts' exquisite taste. She preened when they insisted that her own apartment was much nicer, for this was exactly her own opinion.

Their host appeared with the daughter of the house and the girl was introduced to them both. As the man took her hand, an odour arose from him as if he carried something old and musky in his pocket. Instinctively the girl pulled her hand from his fingers when he made to press it to his lips. The other girl reached out a slender white hand and bobbed slightly, her eyes amused.

'My daughter is just returning from her piano lesson,' their hostess explained. The daughter smiled at the aunt and her niece and asked questions prettily, tossing a head of radiant honey curls adorned with a pink ribbon. The three adults smiled.

It became clear that the visit had been arranged in order that the two girls, who were the same age, could become friends, but though the girl answered the daughter of the house gravely, both understood at once that they had nothing in common. Under different circumstances, one would become the victim of the other.

The aunt regretfully compared the pink and gold feminine flirtatiousness of her friend's daughter with her sister's solemn child. Out of loyalty, she murmured to her hosts that the girl was very shy, having lived in isolation with only her parents for company.

As they ate a crumbly dark fruitcake and drank raspberry sirop, the girl was subjected to a smiling inquisition by their hosts. Her responses dissatisfied because she would only answer what she was asked. She could not be persuaded to elaborate on the one thing the adults wished to know but could not openly ask: what had caused her parents to part.

'She is delightfully unspoiled,' the friend murmured to the

aunt when they were preparing to leave. The aunt smiled but took this as the criticism it was, and on the way home spoke disapprovingly about her friend's husband, who was the president of a firm that had lately been accused in the newspapers of bribing a politician to secure a government contract. *She* might acknowledge the girl's deficiencies, she thought to herself wrathfully, as was her familial right, but other people should be more restrained. She was now glad she had not followed her initial impulse and issued an invitation to the small party she had planned in honour of the girl's birthday, which was two weeks away. Given the girl's limitations, a party could only be a social disaster.

A fortnight later, a box arrived from the girl's father and also a parcel from her mother. They had been sent separately, but perversely, the same carrier brought them to the apartment. They were a day early, but the aunt suggested the girl open them in case they contained something perishable.

The parcel contained a sleeveless shift of white silk with small leaves sewn in white satin thread around the hem and neckline, beaded with seed pearls. It was far too young, the aunt thought. Worse, the card from her sister specifically bade the girl wear the dress on her birthday because the mother had dreamed of her in it. The aunt thought this a ludicrous and even irresponsible thing to confide, but only admired the needlework in a lukewarm voice.

The girl fingered the dress, wondering what her mother had dreamed.

The box from her father contained roses. Not long-stemmed roses with tender pink buds, which the aunt would have deemed appropriate for a young girl, but a dense tangle of crimson buds nestled amongst dark green leaves, with stems that curled impossibly in on themselves and fairly bristled with thorns. The colour of them as well as their barbaric confusion confirmed the foolishness of her sister's choice in a husband.

At first the roses seemed to have no scent, but that afternoon, when they returned from an exhibition at a gallery, the whole apartment was filled with their perfume.

The following morning, the aunt woke in fright from a dream in which she had been running naked through a forest of wild red roses, pursued by some sort of animal. Wrapped in a soft lace nightgown under chaste pink linen, she patted her plump belly and told herself she ought not to have drunk coffee so late in the evening. But when she opened her bedroom door, the smell of the roses was so powerful that she blamed them for her dreams. Panting, she broke her own rules and struggled to open some windows.

Later, as she set a dainty birthday breakfast table, she glanced from time to time with real loathing at the roses, which had opened during the night and now gaped in a way that struck her as frankly carnal. She nibbled at the haunch of a marzipan mouse as she set its companions on a small glass platter, consoling herself that at this rate the petals would be dropping by midday and the flowers could reasonably be disposed of by evening. Beheading the mouse with a neat, sharp bite, she thought of the pictures she had seen of her sister's husband and reflected that she had always known there was something wrong with him. A doctor should look ascetic and have slender, white pianist's fingers and soft, limp, blond hair, but the man was swarthy and his hands were as big and rough as those of a village butcher.

She shuddered to think of such hands on her body and wondered how her sister had borne it. She folded pale green napkins, and remembered her own birthday at this age. There had been an elegant party to which silver-edged invitations had gone out. She had worn lavender taffeta and a matching chiffon scarf in her hair, and she had met her guests with skin as pink and cool as ice-cream waiting to be licked. But the boy she had hoped would kiss her had gone to the garden to wait, and when she had been delayed, had embraced another girl instead. The aunt had come out into the moonlight in time to understand that her moment of romance had been stolen. It seemed to her now that there was an inexorable current flowing from that night to this apartment and this day, where she stood as virginal as the girl for whom she was sugaring pink grapefruit slices.

Her eyes misted at the thought of the life of connubial bliss that had passed her by, but then the stairs creaked and the girl appeared in a sea-green nightgown. The aunt could only gape, for the pale, dull girl had become a ravishing sylph with high, flushed cheekbones and heavy slumberous eyelids fringed in sooty black lashes that drooped over eyes so dark they appeared to be all pupil. Her lips were red and swollen, as if she had spent a night of bruising passion.

'You . . . you look . . .' the aunt began, then stopped in confusion.

'I dreamed I was lost,' the girl murmured, rubbing at her eyes with hands balled into childish fists.

Remembering her own dream, the aunt wondered if it was possible for a dream to have wrought this astonishing change. Then common sense prevailed and she told herself the girl had a fever, that was all. Illness produced such hectic beauty; she ought not to have opened the windows.

The girl was thinking about her dream in which she had run along a wind-scoured, sea-scented tunnel. She had glimpsed a white beast running ahead of her and had followed it until she had lost herself. She had come quite suddenly to a place where all of the metro tunnels converged in one huge, barrel-vaulted cavern with many entrances and exits and much graffiti. The cold ground had been clammy under her bare toes, the walls stained by seepage that oozed from cracks and congealed on the floor in overlapping circles of sulphur yellow and livid purple. The smell of the sea had been overpowering there, and then came a drumming as if the cavern were actually under the ocean.

The man with the black dog had been standing against one of the walls, playing a mournful saxophone pitted with green warts of verdigris. The girl had listened to his music from the other side of the cavern, wishing to respect the aunt's fears, even in a dream.

She had felt a prod in the ribs, and found the pram woman behind her. The beggar woman gave a snort that could have been a sneeze or a laugh or something of both and scratched at wiry, fried-looking hair, asking, 'You think you have come so far to obey the forbidding of a frightened aunt?'

The girl knew that she was dreaming, and that the woman and even the saxophone man knew everything she knew because they were all shapes worn by her own mind.

'Dreams are passages,' the old woman had gone on in the manner of one confiding a vital secret. 'The right dreamer can travel anywhere in them.'

'Can I go to the ocean?' the girl had asked. Without warning the cavern plunged into darkness and the dream broke.

After D'lo had cleared the remnants of grapefruit, croissants and coffee, the aunt suggested they dress and go to hear a string trio in the afternoon as a treat. In the evening they had been invited to supper. She hoped the girl would choose one of her stylish new dresses, but obedient to her mother's desire, she donned the white dress that had been sent. When the aunt saw her in it, she felt the blood rise to her cheeks, for far from making the girl look too young, the dress was so soft and pale and sinuous that it caressed and outlined every muscle and curve, giving the impression of nudity.

It might have been made for just such an unearthly

transformation as had occurred in the night, the aunt thought with renewed unease.

The girl noticed the fullness of her lips and the heaviness of her eyes in the hall mirror as they left, and wondered if it meant that the bleeding that she had been warned of was about to begin. Certainly her body felt heavy with some fluid that undulated and lapped inside her. She was not afraid, although when her mother had spoken of it, she had made it clear that girls were expected to fear the blood, and what it heralded: womanhood and all of the pains of heart and soul and body that flesh was heir to. She had wondered if she would be afraid, for she knew she experienced the world differently from the woman and man who were her mother and father, and also from the other people she had encountered.

The thought came to her like a whisper that the raggedy people who prowled the dank metro corridors experienced the world differently too.

In the taxi that brought them to the theatre, the aunt gave her three small, beautifully wrapped packages. The first contained an antique bible with a leather cover and a tiny metal lock, which must be ornamental, for why would one lock a bible? The second held a slender silver torch attached to a key ring which the aunt suggested she use to locate the keyhole in the front door at night, since there was no external light. The last parcel contained a set of exquisite pearl combs which the girl was persuaded to push into her dark locks. It occurred to the aunt that, clad thus, the girl looked like a bride.

It was very hot outside, the culmination of a string of hot days, and a record for the month. They arrived at the concert hall early and stood outside to wait, for there was no air-conditioning in the foyer. The facades opposite looked bleached, and the asphalt gave off a hot black smell. Women around them stood wilting in expensive gowns, while their escorts fanned florid faces. The leaves of a caged tree hung motionless as the sky grew ever more mercilessly and perfectly blue. God might have had eyes that colour when he expelled Adam and Eve from the garden, the aunt thought dizzily, feeling her blood vibrate under her skin and hoping she would not faint.

She decided they should walk a little to escape the press. Around the corner, they came unexpectedly to a church and the aunt led the girl inside. The coolness beyond the arched stone doorway was so profound that she could have wept for the relief of it. They sat in the very last pew until the glimmering stars that had begun to wink before the aunt's eyes had faded. Then she glanced sideways at the girl and wondered if she had not been drawn into the church for a reason. The girl had a dangerously potent look. The aunt uttered a silent prayer that she should be safe, while the girl sat immobile beside her. Of course she was a heathen, her sister having abandoned their religion, but in the eyes of the church it was better to be a heathen than a member of another church. The latter went to hell, while heathens and unbaptised babies went to the grey eternity of limbo.

The aunt didn't believe in limbo anymore. Not exactly.

But she didn't disbelieve either. Her mind was not shaped for such decision-making. She had a nostalgic affection for the innocent rites of her childhood faith, and in old age would be able to draw her religion tightly back around her like a beloved shawl.

The girl liked the cold smell of the church, the cool tobacco-dark shadows striping pictures of dim, tortured saints and the faint humming of the stone under her feet. She liked the little banks of candles and the font of water and the smell of wood polish on the pews.

Finally the aunt touched her and motioned that they should go. If God existed, and the girl was in some sort of danger, perhaps He would see fit to intervene. The aunt could do no more.

The performance they had come to see was merely competent and afterwards the aunt said it was a shame but one could never be sure with violinists. Excellence was as likely as mediocrity. But it was a pity.

Neither had the girl enjoyed the performance, finding the music too consciously intricate. The violin had sounded to her like something begging to be free. She had a sudden profound longing to hear the disordered cadences of the waves and the yearning grew until it hurt the bones in her chest to keep it in. It was the first time in her life that she had consciously desired anything and she wondered if wanting was something that came with the bleeding.

Outside it was hotter than ever and the sun still shone, although it was now early evening.

The aunt wished she had arranged a taxi so they could go immediately and directly to her friend's apartment. With the crowd swelling around them, there was no chance of hailing one, so they walked, searching for a telephone. The aunt's eyes watered at the brightness of the sun and she flinched when sunlight flashed off an opening window and stabbed into her eyes.

The girl was thinking that the heat was a trapped beast prowling the streets with its great, wet, red tongue hanging out, gasping in the exhausted air. If someone did not let it out soon, it would go mad and tear everything to pieces.

At last they saw a passing taxi and the aunt hailed it gratefully. To her irritation, when they arrived at her friend's home, he announced that it was too hot to stay in. He had organised for them to eat in a nearby café, but at least they were borne there in a car with air-conditioning. The friend was very like the aunt in his plump pinkness, although he was somewhat sharper in mind and manner. His eyes were a beautiful transparent aqua that reminded the girl of the sea on certain days when an unexpected beam of light penetrated a dark sky, and they settled on her avidly.

'You did not say she was beautiful,' he said.

The aunt was almost suffocated with all the replies she might have made, from the inappropriateness of giving impressionable young girls such notions, to the strangeness of the fact that she had not been beautiful until this morning. Fortunately a waiter chose that moment to lay a starched napkin in her lap, preventing any response.

'This terrible heat,' she said, when he had departed with their orders.

But her friend ignored the warning tone. Or perhaps he did not notice it, for he was still studying the girl. 'It is interesting to think that with lips a little less full and eyes a tiny bit closer together, you would not be beautiful at all,' he said. 'Such a thin line between ugliness and beauty.'

'Beauty is in the eye of the beholder,' the aunt said firmly. But her friend gave a laugh.

'Yes, and inner beauty is more important than outer fairness. I know all of that and of course it's true, but my dear, the child is exquisite, and her life will be shaped by that because, regardless of what people say, humans revere beauty. Something in us is thrilled by it. Aren't you thrilled by her?'

The aunt glanced involuntarily at the girl and thought that she was more frightened by her impossible radiance, which surely had grown since the morning.

'We who are not and never have been beautiful must be a little envious as well,' the friend went on. 'Few are pure enough to simply worship at the altar of beauty. For the rest of us, there is some cruelty in our makeup that makes us want to shred and smash it even as we adore it. Which is why it is dangerous to be too beautiful.'

The aunt made a business of buttering a roll for herself and offered one to the girl, but her friend would not be diverted. 'You were very pretty and your sister was what one would call handsome,' he said pensively. 'But this girl surpasses all of those lesser forms. Is your father very beautiful?' he asked her directly.

The girl thought a little and then said composedly, 'He is very clever and when he is thinking about his work, he is sometimes beautiful.'

He laughed aloud in delight. 'What a sophisticate! My dear, you must be so pleased.'

This to the aunt who did not know what she was supposed to be pleased about. A certain vexation began to show in the wrinkles rimming her eyes. 'How is your salad, dear?' she asked the girl determinedly.

Over dessert, the friend clutched at his chest and made a strangled noise. The aunt knew he had a heart condition and cried out for the waiter to summon the friend's driver. She did not call an ambulance, knowing that he thought them vulgar, and in any case they were notoriously slow. Waiting, she massaged her friend's wrists and temples and was sorry to have been angry with him. After all, it was true that the girl had by now become almost unbearably exquisite. She noticed that two storm clouds shaped like long-fingered hands were reaching out towards one another, closing the blue sky in a black grip. She had never seen such a thing and, fearing it was an ill omen for her friend, she thrust some notes into the girl's hand and bade her catch a taxi home.

'I may be some time,' she said, climbing into the black car after the friend. Only as the car pulled away and she glanced back, did the aunt see that the dark hands were clasping directly behind the girl, as if the sky itself would pray for her, or crush her. It was too late to stop the car, and she would have been a fool to do so, for of course it was an absurd fancy.

She turned with relief to wipe the brow of her ailing friend.

The girl watched the car until it was out of sight, then she looked around for a taxi. There was none to be seen and the waiter had gone back into the restaurant. She decided to walk until she saw one, since there was no need for haste. No one was expecting her. She walked three blocks, then five. Thirsty, she stopped to have an orange pressé in an outdoor café. Nearby were two young men talking and smoking; one was half lying on his seat and the other was staring into the froth of his beer. An older woman in a red dress batted at the grey ribbons of their smoke winding around her.

The girl felt no desire to talk to anyone. She thought she could find her way back to her aunt's apartment if she only had the river to guide her. She enquired of the waiter, who pointed the way, and set off, trying to imagine how it would be to marry one of the young men in the restaurant and let him hold her. She found it impossible to contemplate. Yet if one did not join with a man, what else was there? The sort of life her aunt led, with its overstuffed cushions, restaurants, the theatre with friends. Neither appealed, but what else was there? Her body seemed to ache, as if it understood its purpose better than she did, and yet all the uses to which it might be put felt wrong. In that moment her longing for the sound and scent of the sea returned with such intensity she felt nauseous and she wished that one could be taken as easily into the arms of the sea as the arms of a man.

Thunder grumbled and she looked up to find the sky filled with surly cloud. A storm had been brewing overhead and she had not noticed. Oddly, the heat had grown more fierce, as though compressed by the dense cloud cover. Thunder rumbled again and even as she remembered the beggar woman's soup, soured by the storm, she saw the open mouth of a metro station at the end of a long narrow street. As she drew closer, she could smell the black skin of the river that glimmered darkly beyond it. There was no illumination at the entrance to the metro, but a light glowed from somewhere deeper down. She entered the station and heard the hum of the escalators. She used the sound to guide her to them and descended. The light increased until she could see the advertisements in their slanted billboards. There were no other people going down or up, and the girl supposed she had chanced on a still moment between the surges of the crowd, for it was still quite early. The aunt's warnings about going into the metro when there were too few people rose in her mind and then faded like one of the unintelligible posters.

The escalator was longer than those she had been on before and she wondered if this particular tunnel was some sort of natural fissure that had been incorporated into the metro web. She thought of Persephone, who had made a bargain to live six months of each year beneath the earth, and wondered how she had felt as she travelled downwards, knowing she would not see the sky or the sun for another six months, and that this was the price she paid for tasting forbidden fruit. Without warning, the metro wind blew and the girl breathed in the briny coolness of it, wondering if it were possible that a dark ocean lay at the heart of the world.

Finally she reached the bottom, and there in an archway stood the man with the greenish-gold saxophone. She was startled to see him, but no doubt he moved about between the stations. He played a long note that strove upwards at the end, then he laid his instrument in its open case, pulled a cigarette from behind his ear and a lighter from his pocket. The flame gave his features a reddish cast as he lit it and took a deep breath, eyes half closed.

As she passed him by, some impulse made the girl fish for a coin to throw into his case. Only then did his eyes open a slit and rest momentarily on her. They were the dull sheeny colour of his saxophone. The platform beyond the arch was empty and she thought of the disused stations her aunt had mentioned. Then a man in a sleeveless singlet stepped through another of the arches. He came towards her brandishing a deformed arm that ended at the wrist and the girl wondered if he wanted money. She had a few coins in her pocket, but the man did not hold out his hand.

'What do you want?' she asked.

'Salvation . . .' the man said so softly she might have misheard, but he withdrew back into the shadows before she could ask him to repeat himself.

The aunt had said many troubled souls gravitated to the metro at night, trying to evade the police who would come to herd them out. One could imagine they might know the maze beneath the city better than the police, and when all of the metro doors to the outside were secured, they would creep out of their hiding places, knowing that they need fear no one except others like themselves.

She thought of the beggar woman with the pram, wondering if the enormous pot of soup had been intended to feed the metro dwellers. She seemed to see her for a moment, wheeling her pram along the platform, a gypsy woman shuffling alongside her in disintegrating slippers, clutching a baby to her chest. The old woman glanced straight at the girl with a level, questioning look which seemed to ask, 'What are you searching for?'

The girl closed her eyes and when she opened them, there was no sign of the two women or the baby, but sitting at the edge of the platform was the black dog that she had seen before with the saxophone man. The dog turned its head to watch her approach, and gave its black tail a single flick that might or might not have been a welcome.

'What are you waiting for?' she asked it softly, not smiling.

The metro wind gusted again and this time it smelled of the storm which must be breaking in the city overhead. The girl's hair flew forward in twin black flags and she turned her face in time to watch a train punch from the tunnel and howl past the platform. The girl glimpsed the driver looking out, his mouth opened in an O of surprise. Then she turned back to the dog, but it had gone. Before she could make anything of this, the metro train had passed without stopping, taking all of the light with it and leaving the girl standing in inky blackness. She did not move, thinking the lights would come back on, but the dark remained, settling like a dust cloth thrown over a couch.

Reaching into her pocket, the girl found the key ring with its slender torch which the aunt had given her. A narrow pencil beam of light sliced the blackness. It was too thin to be useful in such massive darkness. Without knowing why, she turned it on herself, saw the hem of her birthday dress, its winking beads and pale sequins, and wondered if Persephone had been forced to dwell six months in total darkness, or had been allowed a candle.

Turning the light away from her again, she played the narrow beam carefully back and forth to find the archway that would lead her to the escalator. She could no longer hear its asthmatic hum but it might have gone off when the lights went out. She must have gone further along the platform than she had realised, for she could not find the archway openings. She was about to turn when the light illuminated a ghostly white sign. She walked towards it, hearing how her footsteps echoed. There was an illegible word written on it, but the arrow beneath directed her clearly and authoritatively onward. Thinking there must be another part of the platform or perhaps steps that would bring her outside, she set off more briskly. The way narrowed suddenly, and seeing the graffiti-ed wall on one side and the drop to the rails on the other, she understood that she was making her way along one of the narrow ledges that ran inside the metro tunnels.

She stopped, remembering her aunt's warning, and in the silence heard muffled laughter or screams or crying, which her footsteps must have concealed before. She felt cold and wondered if that was fear. She listened again and thought there was not one voice but a babble of them coming from behind her. She turned to face the voices and the metro wind blew so hard she rocked on her feet.

Another train? She glanced back, but turned again because now she could hear a tremendous clattering as if a herd of cows or goats were being driven along the tunnel. But the cacophony resolved into the hoof beats of a single beast, with a loud accompaniment of echoes. Something appeared in the torch beam which could not be contained or encompassed by it. The only certainties were a massive whiteness and a black eye rolling in terror. The girl staggered back against the wall and something huge passed her so closely that she felt the roughness of its pelt on her cheek and the damp heat of its fear.

A horse, she told herself, hearing it gallop away towards the platform. Or maybe a bull, but bigger than any bull or horse she had ever seen. Impossibly big. How had it come down here?

The voices were louder and now she could make out shouting and laugher and grunts and cries and shrieks and even what seemed to be discordant snatches of song. Instinctively she switched off the torch and let them come, pressing herself to the wall. In the light of dull lanterns that barely lit their faces, let alone the way ahead, she saw men and women, ragged and degenerate and shambling, some so hirsute and hunched over that they looked like beasts. As they clamoured along the passage in a narrowing stream, she thought she saw the gypsy woman she had imagined earlier pass by, her mouth open in a soundless scream. Last of all came the saxophone man carrying a great loop of rope over one shoulder and only then did it occur to her that the motley crowd were a hunting party, and the white beast that had thundered by her their quarry.

When they had passed and the noise had faded, the girl

flicked on her torch and shone it after them. Her heart leapt into her throat, for there, looming in its thin stream, was the wild tormented eye of the white beast. Somehow it had evaded the rabble and doubled back. It was trembling and she sensed it was about to plunge away from her into the darkness, perhaps onto the rails below.

'Don't,' she said.

The beast shifted uneasily but stayed as she moved closer with the torch. Its thin beam illuminated an ear pricked forward and, fleetingly, something shining and sharp. She reached out with her free hand and laid it on the coarse white coat. Powerful muscles rippled under her palm as the beast gathered itself to leap away or perhaps trample her to death. Then all at once, it became still and the violence of its terror faded.

'Come,' the girl said, and it went with her. Now that she walked by its head, she could see it was definitely a horse, but its head was deformed. For the first time she wondered if it actually belonged to the metro denizens. It was no less a freak than they, for all its strange beauty. Perhaps she had been mistaken and they were not hunting it but trying to catch their pet. Hadn't there been a tender yearning in the eyes of the saxophone man? Even so, why should the poor beast be kept in the blackness of the metro tunnels?

Her thoughts galloped ahead and she began to run lightly to keep up with them. The beast kept pace so beautifully that it was as if they merged into one animal. The sensation was unlike anything she had ever experienced. Waves of pleasure shuddered through her, and as they ran, her hand on its hot neck, she understood that this was the thing she had sought through all the dreams and all the tunnels, this running, the hot hide under the whorls of her fingertips.

When at last they reached the platform again, she forced herself to stop so that she could look for the arches with her torch. The beast nuzzled her neck tenderly, seeming to draw her smell in, and she shivered with pleasure at the intimate touch of its nostrils on her bare skin. Then she heard the distant clamour of the hunt, if hunt it was. Instinctively she turned to the beast and bade it run, but though it shivered, it would not go. Its eyes pleaded with her. She made herself push it away roughly. It was like trying to push a mountain. She could smell the salt of its sweat.

'I can't protect you from them!' she cried to it. 'Run, can't you?'

But it stayed. It rested its head on her shoulder and leaned against her. The weight of the massive head forced her legs to buckle slowly, and when she had settled on the ground, the beast knelt and laid its lovely deformed head on her knees.

'Oh you poor thing, you must go,' she murmured helplessly, shining the torch down onto it, but the violet sadness of its eyes asked only where it should go, and there was no answer to that.

Then it was too late. There was a great hullaballoo of triumph and the ragged men and women with dirt-streaked faces and crazed eyes were capering around them in the darkness, crowing with glee as they caught hold of the great white beast by its mane and tail and ears. A dozen filthy pairs of hands bore it away and brushed the girl aside without seeming to notice her when she tried to hold onto it. Or so it seemed, until one of the men, a great hulking hunchback with an ash-brown beard, looked over his shoulder at her and said with rough gentleness: 'You found it.'

'Will you take it out of here?' she said.

'Up there?' the man asked, jerking his chin up contemptuously. 'There is no place for its like up there, girl.'

She stood boneless and will-less, as they surged away and were swallowed by the dark, knowing she had stayed the beast for the crowd. Without her, they never would have caught it. Exhaustion deep as a mineshaft opened within her. A surge of the metro wind wrested the torch from her fingers. It rolled away and came to rest against the wall beside a tunnel, its beam reduced to a flickering golden egg. As the girl retrieved it, the wind blew again, gently, a mere sigh, cool and damp with the smell of the sea. She did not know what to do, but it seemed to her that she could not go back up to the city and her aunt. There was no place for creatures such as her there, either. She began to walk in the direction in which the ragged people had taken the beast, uncaring that she did not know where they were going.

The torch light gave a sepia spasm and she was again in darkness. She lifted her hand, groped for the wall, and continued on. She did not know how long she had walked except that her feet hurt. She knew she must be on one of the ledge paths again, and thought she would sit down and rest, but the salt-strong smell of the sea drew her on. The ground under her feet began to slope down and she wondered again if, deeper than the metro, there was a sea, awaiting her. If she could find her way to it, she would surely find the beast and the ragged metro people. Perhaps they had a camp of some kind and she could stay with them and help tend the beast. If it lives, whispered her heart, and oh, she knew what fear was then. There was no mistaking it.

She was still walking an hour later, or perhaps years later. In the darkness, time had become elastic and then liquid. Memories floated around her of the wind and the sea and of her solitary childhood, the way her parents had touched her so rarely. She had never wondered at this, but now it came to her that they had been afraid to touch her.

Ahead she saw a blue light and then the tunnel spilled her into what must be an immense cavern filled with ghostly phosphorescence, but if it was a cavern, then it was big enough that she could not see the walls or roof of it. She walked across pallid sand, cold and soft as powder under her feet, which the blue light turned aquamarine. Beyond it a sea stretched away and away to an invisible horizon. She walked to the edge of it and heard how the waves hissed as they unrolled at her feet. Some distance away, the narrow beach jutted out in a long pale finger, and at the very tip, through a dark jostle of people, she saw the red flare of fire. Beyond them or in their midst stood the white beast, swaying slightly to and fro, its milky coat stained red and pink by the firelight.

Stumbling with relief, she made her way along the beach and out onto the peninsula. When she was close enough to hear the fire crackling, she stopped, for the saxophone man held a knife and so did several others. They wielded them as they danced and the dance was full of stabbing and slashing.

'No,' she choked. 'No!'

'There is nothing else for it,' said a voice and she turned to find the old beggar woman by her side. Her hair shone white in the ghostly light as she went on gently in her cracked voice, 'The beasts come but they cannot stay here in the darkness and they cannot live up there. To let them go running and running in the darkness until they are blinded, until they starve or founder and fall prey to the rats would be too cruel.'

'What is it?' whispered the girl, numb with dread. 'Where did it come from?'

'From dreams, like all of the others,' said the woman. 'They are the shape of our yearning.'

'Why do they come? What do they want?' The girl felt thin and insubstantial, as if she were a dream.

'To be taken in,' said the woman. 'To be known. To be free of those who dreamed them. We let each of them run for as long as we can bear their desperation, and then we hunt and end them. Out of love and mercy. Join us. We saw at once that you were one of us.'

'Is there no way to save this one?' asked the girl.

The old woman looked at her then, squinting as if to see her better, and her eyes widened. 'For most of us, there is no way. But for one who is pure and empty, an unused vessel, there may be a way. If you have the courage for it.'

The girl did not understand what the woman was saying. The wild, deadly dance was coming to a crescendo, and through the faltering movements of the capering figures she saw the beast, white and trembling, foam about its lips and nostrils.

'Tell me,' she said, her heart yearning and yearning towards the beast, till she thought she would die of longing. She was astonished to find she was weeping, for she had never wept before.

The old beggar woman took her cold fingers and squeezed them to draw her eyes from the beast. 'You must go to it and claim it. But there is no going back once you begin.' The girl nodded, and the woman reached into a battered bag and drew out a garland of dried red roses, regarding it with wonder. 'I have carried this for long, long years, ever since I came here as a girl. I had not the courage to wear it, but I could not bear to throw it away.' She set it upon the girl's head. 'Do not baulk or flinch or cry out when you face the beast,' she said. 'Only courage will avail you.'

The scent of the ancient roses was very strong. The girl thought of the flowers sent by her father, his frowning concentration and big bony wrists as he laid the sheaf of roses in their box. She thought of her mother, packing the white dress in layers of fine tissue, singing softly in a darkened room. She pitied them and marvelled at their love for her, despite their frailty, their short, short lives.

The dance ended.

'Go,' the old woman cried. 'Before it is too late.'

The girl moved towards the tattered men and women, who stood panting and sweating and gasping from their exertions. But they drew back and fell silent when she came among them, white as a votive candle in their midst.

'You are mine,' she told the beast.

Hearing the words, it ceased to sway and its gaze fixed upon her. Its eyes glowed like hot coals in the firelight, fierce and terrible and beautiful. They looked through skin and bone and into her essence. Moving closer, she saw herself reflected infinitely in its eyes; the short life that had been and all that might be and her death as well. She did not turn away from it, because she would never see its like again. Whatever it cost to see it, and to save it, she would pay.

She realised it was waiting and that words alone were not enough. She stopped and opened her arms, and at last it came to her. It lowered its head, it pierced her through, white dress, white flesh, red heart. The pain was immense, monstrous, impossible. But she did not scream. She clenched her teeth and closed her arms about the beast's head, embracing it, holding herself up by it as her life and strength flowed away. The world dimmed to grey and she dropped to her knees. The air was full of the smell of blood. Then flames leapt and churned in the air as the beast began to pour itself into her. It burned to take the beast in, for she was only flesh. Then she felt the hot red gush of blood within and without, for she could not contain him. Her back split and blood fountained out, but that scarlet gush was not wet and it was not blood. She was on the ground on her hands and knees, gasping and rocking with the pain.

The old beggar woman knelt before her in the sand, seamed and withered face shining. There was wonder and terror in her eyes. She reached out to touch the girl's cheek with papery reverent hands.

The saxophone man and the hunchback stood either side of

her. They lifted her to her feet, grunting with the effort. Miraculously the blood had ceased to pour from her chest and the skin was smooth and unbroken, though the torn bodice of the dress was drenched and crimson. But there was a dragging heaviness at her back as they released her and bowed. She staggered under an unfamiliar weight as a great softness moved and unfolded behind her. She craned her neck to look over her shoulder and saw what knowledge of the beast had done to her. Wings emerged from the shreds of cloth. Not white but red as the dawn sun, red as fire, red as a beating heart.

'I am changed,' she said.

'How could you not be?' asked the beggar woman. 'There have been others, it is said, who claimed one of the horned beasts, but never did I see it. Never did I speak to anyone who saw such a one. Rare and rare they are. You are.'

'Where did the others go?' asked the girl who was no longer a girl.

'Up,' said the gypsy. 'Out into the world to fly fearless in the sunlight. Alone and complete.'

The girl who was no longer a girl smiled at the beggar woman and at the other poor, dim, ragged people gazing at her, and they lifted their hands before their eyes and reeled back. Knowing she would blind them if she stayed, she spread her wings and the metro wind rose to carry her up and up and out into the dark world where she would haunt the dreams of the fearful, stir secret wings in the hearts of poets, sing lullabies to the dying and reveal herself to those who dared to see her.

The Dove Game

It was hot in Paris.

The minute Daniel stepped from the air-conditioned cool of Charles de Gaulle airport, the sun dropped a hammer on his forehead. The unexpectedness of it stopped him dead, and a woman in a white dress that looked like a silk petticoat wove around him, her thin arms and long neck a glowing pink. He had never imagined people getting sunburned in Paris. The heat seemed wrong here, misplaced, as if he had somehow brought the aridity of the outback with him.

He was to catch a Roissybus to Avenue de l'Opéra in the city, and then take a taxi to his hotel. A queue extended from the closed doors of the bus, through which the driver was visible reading his paper. He took his place behind the elderly couple at the end. It was evident that they were arguing. Daniel thought of the comfortable bickering of his own parents, which had always seemed to him like two old warped boards rubbing together whenever the wind blew from a certain direction.

The woman stabbed a finger towards a mound of baggage and Daniel wondered what could possibly fill so many cases and bags. The rest of the people in the queue also seemed heavily laden. He carried only a half-empty canvas bag. Perhaps it was because he did not need his luggage to anchor him when he was only staying for a few days.

He found himself remembering the look on the face of the travel agent when he said he needed to be in Paris for one day. Her eyes had flickered with faint confusion over his dusty jeans and faded flannel shirt, but she had said nothing, so he pressed on and asked if she could book him a room in a specific quarter.

The girl – she had been little more than that, for all her thin black suit and the slick vermilion smile painted onto her lips – had taken out a map. Daniel could have pointed to the street because he had looked it up to make sure it existed, but she had been absorbed in the mechanics of her own efficiency.

'It must be an important occasion,' she said, pecking at her computer. Her eyes flicked up, inviting him to explain, as if it were part of her job to offer curiosity so that travellers could talk about their plans and be admired for their adventurous spirits; or maybe so that they could be reassured they were doing the right thing.

'It's the right thing to do,' he had said, and been startled to find he had spoken aloud.

'I'm sure it is.' The girl had smiled, offering the possibility of a week in Hong Kong or in Singapore as a stopover. Daniel had shaken his head, saying again that he only needed to go to Paris for one day and would like to return to Australia the next day.

She had regarded him with fleeting severity, as if she thought he was making some sort of joke.

'I'm afraid that is not possible,' she had said finally. She looked at her computer screen and began to type rapidly. Her face grew smooth and her expression bland, as if the computer had consumed her personality. Then the quick, slick smile again. 'The soonest I can get you home is five days from the date you fly. There are already heavy bookings because it will be the European summer, and there is a World Cup game. If you could go on another date . . .'

'No,' he had said softly.

In the end, he had agreed to the extra days, but the decision had made him uneasy because it had been forced on him. The travel agent had explained that countries wanted more tourists, and there were various kinds of inducements and controls. But Daniel had felt that under the little pat of truth were the bones of something harder.

In the Roissybus, he took the back seat because it looked as if his long legs would fit better there. He found himself pressed between a teacher from a Friends school in Baltimore and a German geneticist. He was amazed at how easily and quickly they told their business to one another and to him.

'What about you?' the American teacher on his left asked with friendly insistence.

'What is a jackaroo?' the geneticist asked when Daniel had told them his job. The faint slurring of the edges of words that was her accent made her sound gentle, and she looked like someone's elderly aunt, but Daniel reminded himself not to be taken in by appearances. He knew what a geneticist did.

'Mess with the business of God, they do,' Teatree had said wrathfully one night by the campfire when someone had started talking about the sheep they cloned. 'Scientists think they can do anything. Splitting the atom and cloning Hitler. Growing crops of arms and legs and eyes,' he had said indignantly.

'A sort of Australian cowboy,' the American told the geneticist.

Daniel struggled to think of a question to ask them, because his indifference seemed impolite. A teacher had once written on one of his reports that he had a lazy mind. He didn't know if that was true or not. The geneticist told the American she had been presenting a paper at a conference in Brisbane on the future of corn and regretted there had been no time to visit the outback. *Ouwtbeck*, she said. The American teacher said he had been on a short exchange to an Australian Quaker school in Tasmania.

Daniel said he had a meeting in Paris. 'Not a business meeting,' he added, to short-circuit the questions.

'Personal business.' The geneticist smiled and the teacher fell silent. Abruptly Daniel decided to tell them the truth.

'I'm going to meet someone in place of a man who died. I promised to go in his place and explain.'

'How sad,' the geneticist exclaimed softly. 'He will come to meet his friend and learn that he is dead.' *Det*, she said.

'It's a woman,' he said.

The teacher gave Daniel a look of sober approval. 'You are a good friend. To go all that way, instead of giving her the news over the telephone.'

I was not his friend, Daniel wanted to protest, but the bus lurched to a halt at a huge roundabout where many streams of cars flowed. It was as if someone had decided to tie a knot in a highway. Horns were sounding, brakes screeched and the noise was such that conversation was impossible.

His two companions were gone by the time Daniel emerged from the bus. There were at least thirty taxis lined up along the kerb and people from the Roissybus and other buses were streaming to join the line at one end and climbing into taxis at the other.

On impulse, Daniel turned on his heel and set off in long, loping strides, determined to find a quiet café and check the map, then walk to the hotel. He was soon deep in a maze of streets hemmed on either side by buildings with ornate facades and a multitude of statues. He was struck by their beauty, but also oppressed by the weight of time they represented. No building in Australia was more than two hundred years old, but some of the buildings around him now looked as if they might have been there for many hundreds of years, especially the ones with crumbling, black-streaked stonework.

He had a sudden sharply painful longing for the simplicity of the flat red landscape outside the bedroom window of his parents' home. That particular view of what some would call nothing, framed by limp, flowered curtains.

He crossed the street because there was a car parked on the footpath and realised he was panting like a dog, he who had ridden a hundred boundaries in the outback without raising a sweat. It was something to do with the way the heat was pressed between the stone buildings maybe, compressed so that it was almost solid. In the outback, the heat was light, stretched thin.

There was no café in sight, so finally he stopped in the shade of a building and took out the map. He had not bothered with maps in the outback. The country offered its own landmarks and signs to one who had grown up with Murri jackaroos and trackers.

Cities smothered the land, he reckoned, stopping it communicating with the people who lived on it, though maybe it was more that cities reflected people's desire not to hear the land. Once when the family had come up to the city to plead with the bank to give them more time, his father had said sadly that cities were as confused as the people who lived in them, and that you needed maps for dealing with the people as much as for finding your way around the streets.

A metal sign fixed to the side of a building said Rue Cloche. Daniel took out his map and plotted a course to the street where he would find his hotel, and as he set off again, he looked at his watch and saw that no time had passed since the plane had landed. The watch had stopped, but there was no point in winding it again until he learned the correct local time.

The hotel turned out to be no more than a doorway leading to carpeted stairs, with the name written above a glass door in fancy writing. The bottom floor was a restaurant and, as he climbed the stairs, Daniel smelled coffee. It reminded him of his father so strongly that for a moment he actually seemed to see his father's hands on the rail instead of his own. Bigger, always bigger, soft-furred with golden hair that caught the sunlight, the huge scarred knuckles and the missing index finger.

Some people coming down the stairs eyed him disapprovingly as they passed him, and Daniel realised they thought he was drunk. He felt as lightheaded as he had the time he got sunstroke as a kid. He still remembered how everything had sagged and tilted when he moved, the heaviness of the shadows and the silky feeling of sickness. An older woman in a fitted green dress and smooth bun examined him with shrewd eyes as he approached the reception desk.

Once he had proffered his passport and filled out the papers, the receptionist pressed the lift button for him and explained breakfast was to be eaten in the restaurant below, he had only to show his key to the waitress.

The room when he reached it was tiny. He bumped his elbows on both walls going to the toilet and was forced to shower with the door open, struggling with a single lever that controlled heat, cold, and the force of the jet. At last he lay full-length on the bed, naked, his feet hanging over the end and his head touching the bedhead.

He had slept for hours on the plane, yet his eyes felt gritty the way they did after a long day of riding in the sun, his body jumpy and tense from lack of exercise. He couldn't remember when he had done so little yet felt so tired. He needed to walk, he decided.

He was walking through the fields at dusk, and he saw that there was a pool of light on the horizon where there ought to have been nothing but more night.

'What's that, Dad?' he asked and discovered from the sound of his voice that he was a boy again.

'Circus has come to town,' his father said, squinting his eyes and peering towards the light. He glanced down at Daniel. 'Want to go, son? Don't suppose it'll be anything special, a couple of clowns and a mangy lion with no teeth. A lot of rigged sideshows to draw your money. But we could take a look-see if you want.' That slow, kind smile.

Daniel felt an aching burst of love for his father that made him realise that he was dreaming, and he woke to find the room dark and stiflingly hot, the bedclothes wrapping his limbs like bandages. He padded over to open a window, but it was as if he had merely opened it into a larger room.

Leaning out into the still, hot night air, he stared down into the narrow street below and wondered what time it was. The thought brought him a vivid image of the dead man's watch; the wide silver band and face had matched the overturned silver car and the silvery grey suit the man had worn, which might have been sleek before the crash had hurled him onto the side of the road.

The man had seemed as exotic as a metal spaceman, lying there. His eyes had been a light silvery grey too, when they opened.

'Help me,' the man said. His accent was thick and heavy, but part of the heaviness was pain.

There were visible head injuries and Daniel knew it could be fatal to move him. 'There's a property back about thirty clicks. The Watleys. Tim'll radio the Flying Doctor.'

The man made a strange rattling noise. Was he laughing? 'I fear there is only one creature with wings that will come for me in time.'

Daniel began to shake his head, but the man's blood was puddling in the red dust beneath him, darkening it to black. It looked as if his shadow was swelling around him.

Daniel knelt, but the man's nearest hand twitched in agitation, the silver watch throwing a knife of light into his eyes with accidental, painful precision.

'There is a woman,' he rasped, and Daniel half turned to the crumpled car before he continued. 'You must tell her what has happened.'

'The police . . .' Daniel began.

'Ssst,' the man hissed like a snake. 'Will you help me?' The pale eyes held Daniel's with a strength that seemed hypnotic and he found himself nodding.

'I have . . . have the ticket in my . . . wallet. You must go and meet her in my place. Tell her I was coming. That she was right.'

'Ticket to where?' Daniel had asked.

'Paris,' gasped the man.

How strange the word had sounded, spoken in the hot air, the end of it caught by the harsh flat arc of a crow's cry rising in the spare distance. 'Paris?' Daniel echoed, relieved, because of course no one could expect him to go to Paris.

'I was to meet her on July seven.'

'But you must have a friend who could call to tell her you have had an accident . . .' Again the rattling laugh, this time with a bleak edge. 'I could . . . call her,' Daniel offered at last.

The light eyes fixed on his face. For a moment, Daniel thought there was a radiance behind them, something struggling to blaze out. But perhaps it was no more than a matter of contrasts: the white-hot light and the tanned skin. Even so, he felt the touch of those eyes like a cold draught moving across his face.

When the man answered, the grain of his voice was rougher, as if the smooth surface of it were being sanded away by pain. 'I do not have a telephone number nor any address for her. Only the date and the name of the café where we were to meet.'

Daniel blinked, feeling as if a genie had appeared to grant three wishes. Only it was one wish, and he must grant it. 'Maybe she won't come . . .'

'She will come,' the man said. He had begun to shiver slightly like a snake-bit cat Daniel had once seen. 'We were to meet . . .' the man whispered, 'in the café where I first saw her. Such an absurd . . . name – The Smoking Dog – Rue de Gris. July seven, at dusk. I thought she was mad but she said she would be there, and that knowing this, I would have to come. She was right. Tell her that. I would have come to her.' After a pause he added, 'The café has . . . had a view of Sacré-Cœur.'

Daniel had looked up the French words in a phonetic diction-
ary. Rue de Gris merely meant Grey Street, and Sacré-Cœur was
probably Sacred Heart Basilica. He had looked up the street on
a map of Paris and found that there were seven different Grey
Streets, but only one that would afford a view of the basilica.

Somewhere in the hotel a baby began to cry, and Daniel turned
away from the window. He felt wide awake because back home it
was early afternoon. The thought that his sense of time connected
him to Australia reassured him. He heard men's voices in the
street below, the words unintelligible, a hard blat of some other
language. Daniel took up the television control on the bedside
console, pressed the mute button and channel-surfed. Usually he
found it soothing to see people talking silently, gesticulating and
laughing, cooking and singing or driving along roads. But tonight –
today – for the first time, the images seemed too personal, too full
of meanings he did not want to puzzle out.

He lay back and watched the play of light reflected on the
wall instead, wondering as he had done before if the dead man and
the woman he had promised to meet had been lovers.

'Let sleeping dogs lie,' his mother might have said. A tough,
stocky, practical little farmer's wife, she had performed a staggering

number of daily duties, her favourite being the care of a small beloved flock of hysterical silkies. Yet Daniel had never seen his mother as a domestic slave. She had been a woman with a sharp edge to her tongue and strong opinions, which she did not hesitate to air, and she had ruled the house with an iron will.

Discipline had been the provenance of his mother, too. She had wielded a willow switch with the same determined efficiency she had applied to cleaning the rugs, as if misbehaviour could be beaten out in much the same way as dust. Age had bent and narrowed his father, faded his blue eyes, but his mother had become more and more solid, without ever being fat, more densely energetic.

David fancied that in another life his father might have been a librarian or a scholar in a university, for he loved to read, but his mother could only ever have been a farmer's wife. Daniel had loved his father, and respected him, but it had always seemed a waste of time to bother wading through a lot of words written by someone he didn't know when he could be roaming hills rippling with dry grass, or swimming in the tea-coloured water of the creek. It did not matter to him that he was barely average at school, since he was to inherit and work the farm.

Of course it hadn't turned out that way. His father had over-extended himself to buy some long-overdue farm equipment and then there were a couple of bad drought years, and then a year of floods, and the bank foreclosed. They had gone under with barely a struggle, and Daniel's mind stuttered to the weeks of packing, to watching his mother crating her beloved silkies for sale. Daniel hated everything about the unit in suburbia to which they had moved, but he knew his parents needed his income to help pay the mortgage.

He had gone to work in a trucking company; then, three months after they had moved into town, his father had a heart attack on the way to church, crashing the ute and killing himself and his wife both. She had died on impact, but his father had lingered three days, though he had never become conscious.

Daniel had been glad it had happened so suddenly and unexpectedly, and that they had died together. But missing them was a deep ache that had never eased. Memories kept jumping at him, forcing him to remind himself that his parents were gone and that he would never see them again, never feel his father's gentleness or watch him tamp down the tobacco in his pipe, never see his mother's ferocious energy or taste her golden-syrup dumplings. He had left the city, for the house had been sold up to pay their debts, and so had begun his long drift from job to job, looking for some indefinable thing that would make him feel that same sense of rightness and belonging that he had felt on the old farm. The smell of eggs and bacon on dark winter mornings and the bitter aftertaste of strong sweet tea in the bunkhouse kitchens brought the home breakfasts back to him with such clarity that the present had sometimes seemed a thin, sour dream.

If he was honest, it was his father he missed most, that quiet presence. You never got the feeling he was just waiting for you to finish talking so he could offer advice or an opinion. In fact, he said very little and seldom offered solutions or even suggestions. Mostly he asked mild questions and listened. It seemed little enough, and yet at one time or another practically every one of the neighbours had come to him for advice. People would invariably go away feeling less angry, less desperate, or just plain cheerful. Daniel had consciously modelled himself on his father. He had striven to be patient, gentle, courteous and honest. He was not and never would be his father, yet he believed that he had grown into a man his father would have at least respected.

How many times had he imagined telling his father about seeing the smoke and then the overturned silver Mercedes crumpled against the stand of eucalypts? How many times had he described kneeling beside the big foreigner in his supple steel-dust suit and the strange conversation that followed? The gradual realisation the man was going to die. In his imaginings, as in life, Daniel's father never once interrupted his tale. Nor, when Daniel stopped, had he offered opinions or advice.

Yet Daniel had come to understand he must go to Paris. And so he had flown across the world, violating time. Was it possible to return after coming so far, he suddenly wondered. The thought was like a kidney punch and he stumbled mentally into a vivid memory of the way the dying man's eyes had grown more and more pale.

'It was so hard to trust anyone back then,' the man had said. 'You never knew who would repeat your words, or how they might be used. You could never be high enough to feel safe. That was what made it so extraordinary, that she trusted me. She told me it was because I had offered her an ultimate truth. I do not think you can imagine how rare truth was in that time. I answered that truth was what I wanted from her and she laughed at me. She knew it was a lie. All I told her were lies, but she said that when we met again, she would show me the truth I had shown to her.

'You must go in my place and tell her she was right when she said I would need her . . .' He stifled a groan.

There had been something almost military in that iron control, Daniel thought. The man would have been in considerable pain, the ambulance people had told him after they came, explicit because he was a stranger to the dead man. It was a wonder he had been able to talk at all. Even if they had arrived in time, they could not have saved him, they said, except to administer a mind-obliterating dose of morphine, a little death to ease the bigger death that was looming.

It was the police, when he gave his report several days later, who told him the man's name was Tibor Esterhazy and that he was Hungarian and eighty-five.

Daniel could hardly credit it. He would have taken him for sixty-five at most. The man had been a permanent resident in Australia for over fifty years, and had not once left since his arrival. He had probably been a dissident, given the date of his arrival, a political exile, or so one of the younger police had observed.

Later that same night it had occurred to Daniel that if the man had made an appointment to meet the woman when they had been in Paris, that agreement had to have been made more than fifty years ago; the man would only have been thirty-five. That was the moment when it struck him that the woman might be dead. After all, if she had been thirty when the meeting had been agreed to, she would be eighty now.

The following week, when he had gone into town to sign his deposition, a policeman told him of the ticket found in the man's coat. The destination was Paris, and the date of departure was July 5, two days before the date upon which the dead man had claimed he was to meet the woman. The ticket was proof that his story had not been delirium.

He had asked the man if the woman he was to meet was German too, assuming that was the man's nationality, but instead of answering, the man closed his eyes and died. It seemed to Daniel that he had witnessed that death a thousand times since it happened. It had affected him profoundly, though he did not truly grieve for the dead man. It was the fact that the man had been a stranger, yet witnessing his death had felt so intimate. Perhaps that was why he contacted the police to find out when and where the funeral would take place, wondering if a friend or acquaintance would attend to whom he might confide the dead man's last wish. But no one came other than a policeman who was there for the same reason. The policeman told him the man had left money enough for his funeral. The remainder of his property was bequeathed to a charity that cared for children. It seemed that he had not worked at all, having come to Australia with a collection of antique family jewellery he had sold, investing and living off the proceeds.

'It seems impossible that a man could have lived so long

without making any sort of connections,' Daniel had murmured.

'You would be surprised how many people live that way,' the policeman had responded.

It was as he stood and watched the earth shovelled onto the coffin that Daniel had pictured a woman coming to a café to sit and wait for a man who would never arrive. In the imagining, she was very frail, a female version of his father, emanating patience and gentleness. She was a woman who you could see would wait out the day, hope slowly fading, until she understood that the man she was expecting would not come.

Another thing that the dying man had muttered floated though his mind. 'There is no greater intimacy than truth, boy. Remember that.'

He woke to broad daylight and showered again, thinking of Mick, who was the stocky Irish owner of the small boxing gym which Daniel had joined when he was fifteen. His father had not understood that the attraction was not the violence or the fact that one man triumphed over another. Daniel had liked the gallantry of a sport where two men could drink and slap one another on the back between bouts. Mick symbolised all that was best about boxing, and their relationship, which had begun with respect and admiration, had become, though the word would never be spoken between them, love. Daniel knew he had disappointed Mick when he decided not to go professional, and it was love for Mick that had kept him sparring with young newcomers, trying to teach aggressive young cocks the need to be smart fighters rather than street sluggers. But few of them had the deep gallantry that Daniel considered to be the secret of greatness.

After Daniel's parents died, Mick tried to talk him into working for the gym, but Daniel refused and started drifting from one seasonal job to the next and from property to property. He hadn't seen much of Mick the last couple of years, but he had told the older man of his decision to go to Paris, and why, and asked if he would take care of his quarter horse, Snowy.

'It's like . . . like I picked up a stone when that man died, Mick, and I have to find the place to put it down,' he'd said.

'It's a deep thing to watch a person die,' Mick had murmured, a stern, distant look in his brown eyes. And Daniel had remembered that once, earlier in Mick's career, one of his fighters had died in the ring from a ruptured aneurism. Mick still sent Christmas cards to the widow, though twenty years had passed.

'How will you know who she is?' Mick had asked in the car, having insisted on driving Daniel to the airport.

'She'll be alone and she'll be looking for someone.'

'She might not be alone,' Mick had said. 'And everyone is looking for someone.'

Prophetic words, Daniel thought, walking through the streets, again struck by the age of the city.

Many of the buildings had obviously been sandblasted or repainted in recent times, and though most buildings were crumbling at the edges and grey with filth, on every street there was at least one building undergoing a facelift surrounded by a carapace of scaffolding and billowing plastic. He was startled when asphalt suddenly gave way to smooth, oyster-grey cobbles, but he made no effort to orientate himself using the map. He was beginning to become aware of a flow along the streets, like a hidden current.

He turned a corner and collided with a couple kissing languidly. They seemed oblivious to the impact. You didn't see kissing like that back home, other than at the movies. Young people kissed in the street, but with defiant self-consciousness rather than passion. Not that Daniel knew too much about kissing or passion. He had kissed exactly three women in his life, and one of them had been a whore who had taken pity on his mortification over his youthful inadequacy.

The other boys had not believed his tale, claiming that prostitutes never kiss. Even now he did not know what to make of the fact that a prostitute had broken what seemed to be some sort of cardinal rule and kissed him, or what he had done to deserve it.

He passed through a square and there was a group of black men talking, dressed in expensive suits. They began laughing, flashing confident white teeth, and Daniel found himself wondering what it would be like at home if the Aboriginal men who drifted into town to drink and socialise in the park or the malls dressed in suits like that. There was something so crushed and battered about the old derelicts you saw drinking in the streets, no matter how aggressive or strident they might be about native title and the disputes it had caused in some Aboriginal communities.

Daniel walked for hours, his mind flicking back and forth between life on his parents' farm and his current errand, as if it was trying to weave a tapestry connecting the two. It was only when he entered a street that showed him the sun low in the sky that he looked for his watch and realised he had left it in his room. Twice he asked the time of passersby before someone lifted a wrist to show him their watch face.

It was just past five, so Daniel reached for his map. It was gone; he must have dropped it. Fortunately he had noticed maps under glass at bus stops and busy intersections, but it was six o'clock before he found one that was readable and traced out a path from where he was to Grey Street, near the Sacré-Cœur Basilica. The sky had clouded over, and it seemed as if dusk would come sooner than seven. He walked swiftly, thinking there was something primitive about arranging a meeting at dusk.

The roads had grown busier than before, and people walked purposefully, their faces abstracted by end-of-day thoughts. Daniel found that no matter which way he walked or which side of the pavement he chose, he was moving against the flow of human traffic. Several times he had to step into a doorway to let a group of people pass before he could continue.

When he found that one of the doorways belonged to a small café, he realised he had not eaten for the entire day, though he felt no hunger.

He came to a great square pool of water in a mall. Several mechanical devices were spitting, stirring, ploughing or slashing the water.

'You see that one?' a woman told another woman in English. 'I call it the jealousy machine. See how stupidly it threshes at the water; how ferociously it moves. Yet it goes nowhere.'

The words provoked the memory of a fight Daniel had seen between two Murri men in a camp far from towns and police. He had met them on walkabout during a boundary ride and had been invited to join them. The men had begun by talking but had ended up almost killing one another over a woman they both wanted. They had fought with a ferocity that Daniel had never witnessed between two white men, in the boxing ring or out of it. There had been no sense of display or competition. They had fought almost silently and for nothing, since the woman had chosen another man.

A derelict tapped at his arm, startling him into the present, and he gave the old man the coins in his pocket. His feet were burning and he was thinking he would have to find another illuminated map when he saw a metal sign that read Rue de Gris.

As he entered the street, he noticed two men standing on the corner watching him. Both wore their hair cut so short he could see their scalps shining pinkly through the black stubble and one had HATE tattooed on his upper arm. He nodded to Daniel, a half smile curving thin, soft-looking lips, as if they shared a secret. Daniel's neck prickled as he passed the pair, and he had the sudden absurd notion that they were watching to see where he went.

It was the sun and lack of food that were making him imagine things, he told himself. A headache drilled into the top of his skull like a hot needle.

He came to the end of the street and realised he must have walked right past the café. Only when he retraced his steps did he understand there had been nothing to miss. The street was short and the only thing in it, aside from residences and apartments, was a smart boutique with a hat draped in a swathe of emerald cloth. Standing outside the shop he noticed a small tobacconist on the other side of the road. He was about to turn away when his eyes fell on the sign above the door.

The Smoking Dog.

He crossed the road and went inside. The man behind the counter spoke and when Daniel did not answer, he looked up. He had thinning salt-and-pepper hair combed straight back from a slight widow's peak, but his brows were so thick and black they looked false. He raised them enquiringly as he asked in accented but very good English what Daniel wanted.

'The name of this shop. The Smoking Dog,' Daniel told him. 'I came from Australia to find a restaurant by that name. In this street.'

The owner's eyes slitted, but perhaps it was only that the coiling, heavy-looking smoke from his cheroot had got in his eyes. 'There was a restaurant here before the war,' he said. 'It was burnt out. It was still a mess when I moved here from Estonia and took it over.'

'Burned?' Daniel prompted.

'It was a Resistance stronghold. They were betrayed and the Boche took away everyone they found here, then burned it.' Daniel thought of the policewoman who suggested the dead man had probably been a political refugee. Was it possible that he and the woman had been in the Resistance and had been taken by the Germans for interrogation? If the man had been the informant, and the woman had realised the truth, it would explain why she had issued her strange invitation, talking of truth and lies instead of love. But when could they have had that conversation? At the club when they had been rounded up, or later wherever they had been taken to be interrogated? Or even after they had been freed? The woman might have realised the man had been the traitor and confronted him with it, concluding with her invitation. Which in turn might have caused the man to flee to the other side of the world, fearing vengeance by the Resistance. But why make a date so far in the future? And what was it she had intended to give him at that meeting? Proof of betrayal?

Realising he had been standing there like a fool, his head full of wild speculations, Daniel gathered his wits and said, 'I was supposed to meet a woman in the restaurant this evening.'

'You want a woman?' There was a mocking note in the man's voice.

'I am to meet a specific woman. She made the arrangement,' Daniel said, hoping the man would not ask her name.

'Have you heard the saying about sleeping dogs?' asked the man. 'Forget about a woman who makes an appointment in a place that doesn't exist. Go back where you belong.'

'I'm not sure where I belong anymore,' Daniel murmured, for the man's words reminded him of his mother. He felt a sudden dizziness at the depth of his words, at the unexpected abyss they opened up in him.

The man said, 'You can see the old restaurant, if you want. The shop is only a frontage. I couldn't afford to refurbish the whole place and there was no need. A tobacconist's shop should be cosy.' The man stood up from his stool, becoming in an instant extraordinarily tall. He opened a door behind the counter and Daniel entered the darkness of an enormous warehouse-sized room whose walls retained striped sections of what once might have been some sort of giant mural. There were round tables and a few chairs pushed against one wall, and he had a strange sense that he had stepped back in time, or at least into another dimension.

'The whole place was done up to look like a circus,' the man said, relighting his black cheroot. 'The name of the place comes from a famous sideshow act with a dog. It was a popular place among intellectuals and students, a good cover for secret meetings and the passing on of information and microfilms and all the rest of it. You can still smell the smoke. That's why I got it so cheap.'

'If a woman comes in asking about a man, would you give her a note from me?'

The tobacconist nodded to indicate that Daniel should return to the shop. As he turned, Daniel heard, quite distinctly, a gasp or a cough. He glanced back but there was no movement. The shadows hung like frozen smoke, darkening with every minute that passed. The tobacconist gave him a little push and they went into the shop that had also darkened in their brief absence.

The proprietor closed the door and reached for a panel of switches on the wall while Daniel dug from his wallet the receipt the receptionist had given him. He scrawled his name on the back of it, along with the name of the dead man. He did not know the name of the woman and he told himself he had done all he could. She would come, or she wouldn't. The lights flickered on and the tobacconist brushed a brown-stained forefinger over the words written on the receipt, but he did not read them.

'If she comes, tell her I will come in again tomorrow in the morning,' Daniel said. He thanked the man and went out into the street. He had walked several blocks before he noticed a small boy shadowing him. Clad in scruffy, too-big clothes of the hand-me-down rather than the American-street-cool variety, his skin was the colour of dark honey and his eyes liquid tar, the lashes as long as those of a newborn calf.

'Want to go to circus?' the boy asked, seemingly unabashed. *Sair-coos*, he said.

'Circus?' Daniel echoed, wondering if he had misheard. 'What kind of circus is there in the middle of a city?'

'A ver' zmall sair-coos,' the boy said, and they laughed together.

'Why not?' Daniel said, liking his cheek. The boy looked puzzled, so he added, 'Yes.'

The boy beamed at him. 'Okay!'

Daniel felt suddenly lighter. He had done the best for the dying man, after all. 'Let's go then,' he said.

The boy took the lead, walking quickly. Several streets later, they turned into a lane that sloped down to a small square where, to Daniel's amazement, he could see the dim yet certain shape of a circus tent, though it did not seem to be properly circular. There were lanterns swaying around its uneven rim, but they gave off very little light, so that he could only see the sections of the tent where they hung, blurring away into the growing darkness. The sight of it reminded Daniel of what the tobacconist had said about the decor of the café during the war, and he shivered a little at the coincidence.

The lane became wide, shallow, uneven steps and Daniel came along behind the boy cautiously, forced to concentrate on his footing. When he reached the bottom, he was startled to find his young guide had vanished. He hesitated, and heard music, long sobbing notes that roused in him an unexpected and potent hunger to be home, riding the flat red plains. Moving closer to the tent, he had the unsettling feeling that the longing evoked by the song was the same as his longing for his parents, who were irrevocably lost to him.

'Shall I whisper your future?' a voice asked by his ear, and Daniel started violently.

He turned to see a gypsy woman with a small baby in her arms, sitting cross-legged in an opening in the side of the tent. She seemed to be sitting on a platform, but he could not make out what was behind her.

His silence seemed to anger her, and she sat up stiffly, eyes flashing. 'But you have no time for Calia, have you? You want the main attraction! Another mooncalf come lusting for the Dove Princess. Fool! There is no future in her for any of you.' She was so angry she was almost spitting, and Daniel, taken aback, wondered if she was mad. Yet her words made him curious enough to decide that he would go into the tent.

The gypsy gave an angry grunt when she saw him glance to where a wooden sign had been erected, marking the entrance to the tent. She bared a plump golden breast with a dark nipple. The baby seemed to scent it and butted and struggled until it had the nipple fastened in its mouth, then began to suckle hard. Embarrassed by the bared breast and the derision in the woman's eyes, Daniel made his way to the entrance and pushed the closed flap aside. Light flowed out past him in bright streams as he stepped into a sort of curtained corridor that followed the outer curve of the tent to the left. He tried to push the curtain aside so that he could go into the main part of the tent, but the fabric was heavier than it looked and there was no opening. He gave in and went along the corridor. The outer wall swayed and brushed against him as the wind gusted, and a heavy musty smell puffed out of the cloth. The music he had heard grew steadily louder until he came to an opening in the inner wall of the corridor, through which he could see the main section of the tent. It was smaller than it had looked from the outside, because of the outer corridor that took up a good portion of the space.

Bright lights centred on an empty circle of sandy ground that ran up against the tent wall on the farthest side of the space. On the near side of the circle were curving rows of bench seats, separated from the circular stage by long wooden bolsters wrapped in red satin. There were not more than fifteen people in the audience, most sitting alone. Daniel glanced around, looking for someone to pay, and saw a lean gypsy man approaching with a leather pouch slung about his neck. Daniel paid what he was asked, fumbling at the unfamiliar bills, distracted by a high-wire artist he had just noticed, clad in glittering red and gold, spiralling down on a rope. Obviously she had come to the end of her performance, for when she reached the ground, she stepped away from the rope and bowed to a smattering of applause. Then she ran lightly away and vanished through a slit in the tent wall. The strange, complex tent must have been constructed in this way to allow a backstage area.

Daniel took a seat at one end of the front row of benches as a man in a black cloak lined in gold silk stepped through the slit onto the sandy stage. His long, thick, red-brown hair was drawn tightly into a tail that hung down his back like the brush of a fox. His face was narrow and his teeth flashed white with a hint of gold as he bowed gracefully. The boy who had shown Daniel to the circus pushed through the slit after him, wheeling a glittering gold casket as big as a fridge on wheels. A magician, Daniel thought, as the boy withdrew, and he set himself to watch for sleight of hand.

Cymbals crashed and another boy appeared, so like the first as to be a younger brother, leading a small white goat. There was a burst of violin music and the fox magician began to speak. His words were foreign and incomprehensible to Daniel, but it was clear from his movements that he was describing his prowess as a tamer of the most ferocious sorts of beasts. Then, very slowly and theatrically, he opened the mouth of the goat and pushed the top of his head gently against its teeth.

It ought to have been funny. That music and the seriousness of the cloaked man allied to the symbolic offering of the bright head to the blunt teeth of the goat. Certainly the plump woman nearest Daniel gave a bark of muffled laughter and a young man with a shaven head and ripped T-shirt giggled wildly, hitting his leg and rocking back and forth. But Daniel found that he was not able to laugh or even to smile.

The goat was led away, and the violin music swelled as the man opened the case, unfolding its sides. Gypsy music. Daniel's father had loved classical music, but had said that most of it was like beauty prowling in a cage. This was wild music and Daniel felt a sudden sharp ache that his father would never hear it.

The spotlight split and the music stopped abruptly.

For a long, straining moment, all that could be heard was

the wind and the flapping of the tent walls and roof. Daniel saw
that the opened case had become a red velvet table upon which lay
gleaming rows of daggers.

A pale, strikingly lovely, dark-haired woman clad in a skin-
coloured body suit stepped through the slit in the tent into the
light. Instead of looking naked, the skin suit made her look like a
sexless doll. The boy came darting out after her to fasten about her
slender waist the flexible frame of a crinoline, which reached the
ground, caging her lower body and legs.

A movement drew Daniel's gaze to the fox magician. He took
up one of the daggers, kissed the blade and raised it over his head,
looking all the while at the woman who lifted her arm, a slender
pale stalk. The gypsy violinist began to play a swift, staggering
tune until, without warning, the man threw the dagger straight
at the woman. Even as people in the audience cried out in shock
and alarm, the dagger exploded into feathers and suddenly it was a
bird fluttering to her uplifted hand. A white dove.

The audience applauded in relief and delight as the woman
lowered her arm. The bird hopped from her fingers into one of the
gridded squares of the crinoline and began preening itself. She
lifted her arm again. The music played and another dagger flew
and was transformed into feathers and beak and bird. The music
quickened and slowed and dipped and wailed as dagger after
dagger flew, unerring and deadly, from man to woman, always to
transform into doves until her lower body was hidden in a dress of
living birds. It was an extraordinary sight, but the music went on,
striving ever higher, and the birds began to land on the woman's
torso and on her slender shoulders and along her arms, which she

now held out on either side of her at shoulder height. There must be a net over the body suit, Daniel guessed. The doves flew to her head, too, but their grasp on the silky braids was less secure and occasionally one of the birds slipped and had to claw its way back into place. Daniel noticed a small streak of red on the woman's forehead. He told himself it was only a scratch, a minor accident in a masterly act and nothing more, but there was something in the way the woman stood, the defencelessness of her, the seeming nakedness and the way she offered herself to the man and his daggers, that troubled him.

It had taken only a few moments, his senses told him, but Daniel was sweating hard, as if the performance had lasted an hour. There were more birds and more scratches. None were serious, but the blood on her white skin was very vivid. There was a cruel beauty in the spectacle and the possibility that a knife might not become a dove in time or that the doves were daggers after all. That possibility was provoked by the tiny smears of blood. He was repelled by the thought that the blood should be part of the act. For some reason he found himself remembering the two Murri men engaged in their silent deadly fight, and the savage beauty of their desperate and hopeless desire for a woman who wanted neither of them. The beauty, he thought now, came from the hopelessness; the fact that both had known the fight would make no difference.

Watching the dress of living feathers thicken, he wondered suddenly what his father would say of the performance. But for the first time in his life, Daniel found he could not summon up the older man's face. The conjuring of doves began to seem endless to

Daniel, and yet there was no monotony in it. He would have to be a monster to be bored by something so horribly beautiful.

Outside the tent, the wind was howling, and the roof billowed and heaved in convulsive shudders. There were more than a hundred doves on the woman now, and the weight of the crinoline must have been considerable. Yet she did not buckle or show any sign of strain. The doves gradually covered her arms and her neck and hair until only her face was visible.

The violin changed and the last dagger flew straight at her face, became a final dove that landed there somehow, obscuring her. Daniel thought of claws sinking into white skin, gouging, finding purchase, and he started to his feet, but before he could cry out, the music abruptly ceased. He froze and for a moment there was only the sound of the wind. Everything was in motion – the tent, the air, the shifting, jostling doves. The only fixed point was the black-clad magician with his glimmering foxtail of hair, and so all eyes fixed on him, the eye of the storm.

Slowly his hands lifted until he stood as the woman had stood, mirroring the shuddering, dove-covered mass, and then the doves rose up in a churning coil of feathers, swirling and widening at the top until they formed a spinning funnel, a white whirlwind. Then they exploded outward, and in their midst there was only a falling drift of feathers gleaming in the lights.

The woman had vanished.

The bright lights blinked off as suddenly as the music had stopped, plunging the tent into darkness, then two lanterns were hung, one either side of the entrance which was now, perforce, an exit. After a few forlorn claps, people began to rise and make their way outside. The sudden end of the show had left Daniel feeling off-balance and he remained seated to gather himself. His heart was pounding even as he told himself that it had all been a trick of some kind. But he did not believe it. The blood had been real. He was sure of it. The boy who had brought him to the circus came to sit beside him.

'You like?' he asked, grinning, but his eyes were serious. It was as if the two of them had made a bargain and he was checking the details of their agreement.

'Why does she let him hurt her . . .' Daniel began, and then stopped, not sure what he meant to ask.

'That is what is always being asked,' the boy interrupted gleefully and ambiguously. 'You ask her. Maybe she will answer. You want?'

Daniel realised the boy was offering to bring him to the woman, and found himself nodding. The boy beamed and rose and Daniel did the same. His body ached the way it sometimes did after days of riding. They made their way through the seats and he stumbled a little in the near darkness, for his eyes would not adjust. The pale woman in her dove dress seemed to have imprinted her image on his retina, so that whenever he blinked, he saw her pallid form.

The boy preceded him to one of the exits but instead of leading Daniel outside, he lifted a flap in the blind end of the cloth corridor to reveal a long, narrow chamber furnished with a low table, two battered kitchen chairs and a worn couch. Daniel let himself be ushered through the flap into unexpected warmth. Left alone, he turned to examine the chamber. A half-drunk bottle of red wine stood on the floor, glowing red in the light of a lantern suspended over the table from an old dressing-gown cord. A plastic fast-food container on the table was half filled with cigarette butts and the air smelled of old ash and fumes from a kerosene heater. Daniel was about to sit when a flap at the other end of the space opened and the fox-haired magician entered. He had stripped off his cape and wore dark jeans and a crumpled open-necked blue shirt, the sleeves rolled up to reveal strong forearms and sinewy wrists covered in the same wiry red hairs that showed at his throat.

'You want woman. Sit and we discuss,' he commanded in guttural English.

Belatedly it occurred to Daniel that he had misunderstood what the boy had been suggesting. He had been an idiot. 'I am sorry, I think there has been a mistake,' he said, beginning to rise.

'No mistake, you come to Paris for a woman,' said the fox man, narrowing his eyes.

'No . . . Yes, but to see a specific woman. I have arranged to meet her,' Daniel stammered, hoping the man would not ask her name.

'Arranging with me for time with Dove Princess,' said the fox magician.

Daniel rarely lost his temper and now, feeling it stir, he realised how much he had disliked the performance, how much he disliked this man. The realisation calmed him. 'I would like to meet your assistant,' he said evenly. 'She is very brave.'

'Assistant,' mocked the fox magician. Then he sneered and added, 'She is very beautiful.'

Daniel flushed. Almost he wished the fox magician would attack him so that he could act instead of sitting here tangling up his tongue like a fool. Then he told himself that he was a fool indeed, for whatever was happening here in this strange little circus, it was none of his affair. What was he doing here? He said quietly, 'Perhaps you can pass on my thanks for the performance.'

The other man shrugged and seemed to relax. 'You wan' a wine?'

Daniel hesitated. He wanted to leave but he did not know the words that would release him. He nodded and moved to sit on the couch after the fox man pointed to it and poured wine into two plastic cups he drew out from beneath the table.

'Where is she?' Daniel asked, when he took the cup of wine.

'She vanished.' The fox magician gave him a sly smile before drinking a mouthful of wine. 'Is gift she learned in childhood. Has been ver' useful.'

'It was a trick,' Daniel said slowly, setting down his cup untouched.

The magician put down his cup too and reached out in one smooth gesture to turn Daniel's hand palm up with a quick strong twist. He stared at it intently. 'Here is calloused working hand and yet it is hand of child who knows nothing.' He looked into Daniel's face, and for a moment the cunning in his expression slipped like a mask that had nearly been dislodged, as he murmured, 'Nothing more than a child's pain, perhaps . . . which is far from nothing.'

Suddenly his English was perfect, though accented, and Daniel stared at him, shaken and confused. 'What is all this? Why does she let you hurt her? She must have been half-smothered at the end.'

'Art requires pain,' the fox magician said, but absently, as if his mind were elsewhere. 'Tell me where have you come from, that you seek audience with the Dove Princess?'

'I'm Australian,' Daniel said.

'Ahh. So. A country of children, I think, full of light and thoughtlessness.' His eyes now seemed to glitter and Daniel saw that they were a very light soft green. 'And why did you come here?'

'I came to meet a woman.'

'You do not truly wish to meet the Dove Princess,' said the fox magician, cutting him off. 'She will bring you nothing that you desire.' His voice was very soft, very serious.

'I . . . no,' Daniel stammered.

The magician seemed not to hear him. 'You think to rescue her. But she is not my victim. I am hers. All of us are her instruments, the boys, the doves, you. She designed the Dove Game.'

'The blood is a trick?' Daniel asked.

'The blood is real. The pain is real. That is how she wants it. She sculpts her own pain.'

'But that . . . It's sick . . .' Without realising it, he had taken up the cup and now wine slopped over the brim onto his hand.

'It is monstrous,' the magician agreed wearily. 'But the blood is what gives the game its power. You see that? Even you could see that.'

'But . . . why does she do it? Surely not for money?'

'She says the Dove Game reminds her of a truth she experienced in the camp.'

Daniel found his mouth was dry. 'She . . . she was in a concentration camp? But that was decades ago. It's not possible.'

'She was a child. Children were taken. Not just Jews. Gypsies also. The chosen people prefer to forget that, of course. She was taken from near here. My grandfather was taken, too. That is how she came to join us after the war. He brought her. He said he owed her his life, for she had stolen food for him that kept him from starving. We come here each year on the day that they were taken. She always sends the boy out for men to come and watch her performance, so that she can choose one.' His sighed. 'Her mind is gone, of course. There are brilliant shards left, but not much else. She says that one day a man will come, and she will show him the truth that he revealed to her.'

Daniel thought of a foreign man, dying on a remote outback road, and the pale woman in a dress of living doves, and wondered if it was possible that she was the woman he had been sent to meet. It was too much of a coincidence that he had just happened on the circus, he told himself. But then, he had not just happened on it. The boy had come to find him. He seemed to hear the beating of wings and to feel the full living weight of the doves descending on him, their claws cutting into him.

'The boy who led me here . . .'

'A pretty little monkey she feeds and pets and sends running to do her errands. When we are here, I think her madness worsens, and that is why she sends him for men. They want to meet her, of course, after the show. They offer money and we take their money, but she never meets them. None of them is the man she is seeking.'

'I need to see her,' Daniel said urgently.

'I told you . . .' the magician said.

'You don't understand. The man she is looking for is dead. There was an accident and he asked me to come in his place. To meet her as they had agreed.'

'I suppose it was inevitable that eventually she would summon up a man whose madness matched her own,' the fox magician said in a resigned voice. He rose in a fluid movement. 'Go home, boy. The Dove Princess is not for you.'

'Please, she promised to tell him the truth that she learned . . .' Daniel said, no longer sure of his motives.

'No,' the fox magician said urgently, but he was staring past Daniel.

Daniel felt the air stir behind him. He would have turned but a cool hand descended on the back of his neck, staying the movement. 'Leave us.' The woman spoke in English, her voice husky and accented. The magician bowed and withdrew.

The woman spoke again. 'I have lived only to give back the truth that was given to me.' Daniel felt a knife at his neck, like the tip of a bird's claw, as she asked, 'Do you desire the truth I offer?'

Many things fluttered through Daniel's mind. The sound of madness in the woman's voice like the beating of a bird trapped in a chimney; the way his father's breath had rattled as he died in hospital; the sound of the crow's call on the day the foreign man died; the way the desert air shimmered and transported visions; the velvet touch of Snowy's muzzle against his palm. And then, at last, the sight of a woman wearing a dress of doves, who lived for a truth that was pain.

And he grew old with understanding.

He turned towards her, not caring how the edge of the knife slid shallowly into his skin. The woman was very beautiful but much older than she had looked on the stage, her skin white and finely wrinkled. Her large eyes were dark and full of shadows and he wondered if she would see him through them. He felt the dribble of blood on his collarbone and the sting of the air against the tiny wound.

'He wasn't in the Resistance, was he?' he asked. 'He didn't betray you. He was one of them, the one that tortured you.'

How still her face became, like a skull. 'He asked me over and over for the truth. He said he would use pain to teach it to me,' she rasped. 'He was an artist of pain. I told him that he would one day long for the truth that he had given me, and that he would have to come to me for it, because no one else could give it to him. I told him to meet me where we met. That I would come on the day we had met, every year, until he returned.'

'He was coming,' Daniel said. 'He had an accident. Before he died he asked me to come in his place. To tell you that you were right.'

'Who are you to him?' she asked fiercely. 'His son? His grandson?'

'He had no wife, no children, no friends,' Daniel said. 'I am no one – a stranger he talked to as he was dying.'

'I waited for nothing, then,' the woman said.

'I came,' Daniel said.

She laughed hollowly. 'You want the truth I would have given him?' she hissed. 'You do not want that truth, for once you have had it, there is nothing else.'

'There is nothing else,' Daniel said, feeling that all his life had been leading him to this moment of perfect clarity and purpose.

The Dove Princess gazed down at him and madness and hope and confusion churned in her lustrous eyes, then there was pity and she said, almost lightly, 'But you are only a child.' And swift as a striking bird, she drew the edge of the dagger across her throat. A red mouth widened in a leer as her head fell back.

Daniel heard a scream and knew it was his. He tried to rise, but his legs would not hold him. His head swam and he fell. The world spun and the fox magician appeared in the centre of it, once again the eye of the storm. His mouth moved but Daniel could not hear the words. A dark sea engulfed him.

When he woke he was in hospital, having been found lying uncon-scious on the cobbled pavement, unable to be roused. Two police came and heard his story. They told him he had been the victim of a scam. He had given the gypsies all the information they needed to dupe him. They did not say he had been a fool, but it was in their faces. That he had drunk wine that was drugged, that his wallet had been taken, that it was his own fault. There was no dead woman they assured him when he insisted. No body. No permit had been issued for a small gypsy circus anywhere in the city.

When they released him, Daniel went back to the square where the tent had been. There was no sign of it, of course, only a drift of white feathers in a gutter that might have belonged to any of the hundreds of roosting pigeons in the eaves of buildings around the square.

He sat down on the edge of a fountain. It was very hot. His temples pulsed with the heat as two boys on rollerblades sped by. A woman passed, dragging a screaming, red-faced child; an ambulance clanged past, then another. Or maybe they were fire trucks. Daniel tried to picture his parents and found their faces with difficulty. It seemed to him that they were drawing rapidly away from him, as if they had boarded a train and were leaving him standing on the platform.

He thought about the man who had died in the accident, and wondered if he had truly been a Nazi soldier who had inter-rogated and tortured a child to the point where a sort of madness had fused their lives so that they had made some strange impos-sible pact to die together, or if, somewhere in this city, a woman was mourning the failure of her lover or friend to meet her after a long parting. Perhaps both endings could be encompassed. Or neither.

In the antiseptic hospital night he had dreamed of the woman; dreamed that she had embraced him in her dove dress. He had not been able to tell where her flesh ended and the frantic dove trembling began. He had felt her touch as a cool hand, as claws, as a knife.

Had she cut her throat? Had he dreamed it? Had it been a trick? He would never know the truth.

An elegant old man in a pale suit with a cane came tapping across the square, holding the hand of a boy in a little blue sunsuit. The old man sat carefully on the edge of the fountain, watched by the boy. He sighed and took a crumpled handkerchief from his pocket and unwrapped a crust. He spoke to the boy as he crumbled the crust and threw the crumbs in a pale arc. Pigeons began to land on the cobbles and peck at the crumbs and the boy and the old man watched them gather and squabble. Suddenly the boy darted into the midst of the birds, routing them. They fled, fluttering and shrieking into the air. The old man swayed with laughter and the boy ran at the few birds that had waddled hastily to the sidelines, sending them scrambling into the air too. He glanced at the empty cobbles with satisfaction, and then strutted back to his grandfather, who had turned to rinse knotted fingers in the water.

The boy noticed Daniel watching and gave him a long, solemn, assessing stare. Then he smiled conspiratorially.

Daniel smiled back and felt all at once that the shadows that had come to roost in him had been routed, too. He felt sunlight and a clean soft breeze flowing through him.

THE GIRL WHO
COULD SEE THE WIND

for Rosie

1.

Papa died when I was eight.

The death of a parent pulls away one half of the sky so that a weird light is cast upon all ordinary things. My father's death opened up a vast chasm, setting me apart from all others, but when I said as much to Mama, she answered that I had always been different.

It was true that she had always seemed to think so. Willow, she named me, and as if it were also my name, she always added, The Girl Who Can See the Wind. I had earned the title when I was still in my perambulator, watching a swirl of leaves and grit in the elbow of a building. 'Look,' Mama had cried out to Papa in delight, 'Willow sees the wind!'

He laughed at her but she insisted it was so.

I had heard both my parents tell this tale but I did not think of myself as special. Mama had said, half angry, half laughing, 'Do you imagine a daughter of mine can be like other children?'

I did not argue with her, but I secretly believed that all children saw the things I did, only they kept their seeing secret, while Mama wheedled mine out of me. I might have resented that wheedling when I was older, if Papa had not died and cast Mama into bitterest despair. She tore her hair and raked her face with her nails, shrieking so wildly and incoherently that she might have been speaking another language. Anguish crushed Mama and sapped her spirit, though her beauty was indestructible. Her grief was so monumental and fantastic that my own seemed inconsequential beside it, a peeping chicken beside a screaming eagle. I had loved Papa and I mourned him sincerely, but for me, grief was less a wild thing unleashed within me than a profound misplacement of normality. It was only as I grew older that I understood this distortion was as much the result of Mama's grief as of Papa's death.

It was in one of the rare quiet moments in those grotesque, dreadful first days after Papa's death, that Mama told me how she had watched and fallen in love with him long before he noticed her. I found it hard to believe that any man could be near Mama and remain unaware of her, for aside from her beauty she had great and potent presence. Papa had openly adored her. Indeed, he told me often enough that he had fallen in love with her the moment he set eyes on her. Yet here was Mama telling me she had loved him first.

She said, eyes streaming tears, 'I gave up everything to be with him.' She said this so bleakly I could not doubt it, although I did not know what she could have meant, for Papa had been handsome, wealthy and well-born. But I had learned that it was better to let Mama's talk run on unremarked, until the cataracts of grief ran dry, for each question elicited a new flood of pain. I speculated to myself that Mama must have been even more wealthy, or so nobly born that her family had regarded wedding Papa as a wicked betrayal and had cast her out and forbidden her to mention them. Certainly Mama did not ever speak of her past nor of her own parents or siblings, if she had any. When asked, she always said that her life had begun when she met Papa. I developed the sense, as children do, that this was an area that had been fenced off and forbidden long before I was born.

Only after Papa died did I come to wonder if he had been curious about Mama's past. Had he adored her so much he accepted her silence on the matter as simply part of the bargain? I could almost believe it, for his eyes had rarely shifted from her face and form whenever she was close, and he could not long abide being away from her. Or perhaps she told it all to him in the early days of their loving, and had then sworn him to silence.

One way and another, all that was said and unsaid about love by my parents gave me to understand it was marvellous and intoxicating; but the more wondrous it was, the greater the cost. It was not until after Papa died that it occurred to me he had never spoken of giving up anything or of being forced to pay for his love. Even dying first had meant it was Mama and not he who must bear the cost in pain of that mortal parting. Yet for all her anguish, Mama never wished she had not loved Papa.

For me, the most difficult facet of her grief, aside from the loss of any sense of normality, was the almost morbid fear she developed for my welfare. She hated me to be away from her and would insist she loved me with an intensity that embarrassed and even alarmed me a little, though I tried not to show it, for I did not wish to hurt her further. I told myself such fierce protectiveness was the natural consequence of what had happened, for if a husband could die, then so might a daughter.

But I want to tell you of my stepfather.

A year passed and the dreadful corrupting grief that had assailed Mama since the death of Papa ebbed to a bleakness in the eyes and a twist of pain about the lips. Mama entered a new phase of sorrow, where she began to have nightmares, waking night after night with screams. I knew the nightmares were about me, because the first thing she would do upon waking from them would be to fly to my bedroom to hold me and whisper reassurances to herself that I was safe. Sometimes she would beg my forgiveness, though what I must forgive her for I could neither imagine nor discern from her gabbling hysteria. I wondered if she was asking me to forgive her for having given birth to me, since, being born, I must suffer. Someone honed by grief might have such a conceit.

Papa visited her nightmares too, for sometimes when her cries woke me, I would hear her begging him to forgive her. I wondered what she imagined she had done to harm him. After all, he had not died because of any action or inaction of hers. Even the fever that killed him was from a recurring sickness he had picked up in the tropics years before they had met.

I was wise enough not to reason with fear, any more than I had tried to reason with grief, and eventually the period of nightmares gave way to a sudden spate of journeying abroad. Despite her concern for my welfare, or perhaps because of it, Mama left me behind. Of course I had tutors and chaperones and a house full of servants who clucked around me like mother hens, but they were on the other side of the chasm that Papa's death had opened up, and I was lonely and afraid when Mama was absent, half convinced she meant to disappear, or even, in darker moments, to cast herself from a cliff or the prow of a ship. My imagination was fuelled, you see, by the romantic, ghoulish novels that boredom made me steal from the bedrooms of the chambermaids. But each time, Mama returned safe to smother me with kisses and tell me again and again that I was precious and wondrous and rare, worth the price of pain I cost her. I took this to be an oblique reference to the birth pain she had endured in bearing me, the mention of which I found a little shocking.

Then a day came when Mama returned with flushed cheeks and vivid eyes to announce that we would be moving to the end of the earth. Her face glowed with such delight that I did not dare ask her why and risk causing her to fall back into grieving for my father. I told myself in the flurry of preparations that there was not the time to ask, but when we were on the ship, and there was a sea of time, I floundered and could not think how to ask. Her moodiness and unpredictability, and my habit of being careful and watchful with her, had stifled my ability to converse lightly and easily. Indeed, she told me more than once not to be such a dullard, and seemed, as that journey progressed, to grow ever more gay the further we went from all we had known.

I was ten when I first saw the country that was now to be our home. The ship had sailed into a sparkling blue harbour surrounded by dark, densely forested, grey-green hills, and I could at first see nothing of the town that was our destination. The only thing I could see, I took to be some sort of industry, half veiled in red smoke. The ship brought us here and we came ashore to crooked streets of red-brown earth and houses made of wood and to a bustle of horses and carriages and people whose movements raised the perpetual rust-red blear – a strange, rough factory of life. I breathed in the bloody dust, appalled and stumbling because my feet could not immediately adjust to the lack of cobbles underfoot, but when I said as much, a crewman told me gently that it was only that I had not yet got my land legs back. A carriage awaited us and it carried us away from the dusty town and up into the forested hills I had seen from the deck of the ship. I ought to have been pleased to be in the midst of what was certainly untouched wilderness, but the colours were all wrong, both too drab and too garish, as if exaggerated by the exaggerated sun. It beat down with such relentless fury that I cowered in the shade of the awning, unable to imagine baring my skin to it.

I wondered if it was the sun that made the men and women who inhabited this place so heavy and vague in their movements. Their eyes and expressions seemed to me both exhausted and bewildered. Mama had said many of them came from across the sea, like us, but it was impossible to imagine either of us being so reduced.

I soon took to calling them the clay people, for their skin seemed as rough and muddy as their voices and minds.

All of our furniture and most of the servants had been sent in advance, and were waiting to greet us in a house so similar in dimension and ambiance to the one we had left behind that I had to assume Mama had chosen it for that reason. Yet why had we come here, if nothing was to change?

But of course everything was changed and much that we had brought with us did not fit our new lives. In particular, all of our lovely winter coats and muffs and boots were put into storage, for it never snowed here. That Mama had allowed them to be brought, gave me a nugget of hope that she did not mean us to stay here forever, and in those first days I analysed her words and tried desperately to find in them a confirmation of my hope. I was desperately unhappy. If I had felt estranged before, here I found myself a pale-skinned, over-delicate freak full of irrelevant complexities of manner. I did not like the heat nor the clothes one must wear to endure it. I did not like the light, which stabbed into my eyes like little blades and exposed everything so mercilessly, or the way the heat dried all that was green to brown. I did not like the untidy look of the trees, or the ever-present, ominous hum of insects that rose from the bleached grass. But I did not make any tantrum or protest. Aside from the fact that it was not in my nature, the heat drained me and made me feel exhausted almost the moment I left my bed. I could not imagine undertaking the long journey back home.

Winter, when it came, was only a little better, for all seasons were but variations of summer in this land. But at least there were cool breezes and occasionally dew beaded the morning grass. I took to rising very early, just before sunrise, in that hour when the air would smell clean and fresh and damp and there might be a few veils of violet cloud in the peach-gold sky. All the birds sang at that hour, though later in the day only a few cried out, sounding harsh and exhausted.

Best of all I liked the thunderstorms, which were elemental and thrilling, knives of light slashing through the blackness, with great cracks of sound. Then rain would begin to fall. I loved the intoxicating scent given off by the parched earth when the first drops fell, but, like everything in this new land, there was no gentleness in the rain. It did not fall, save for the first spattering, but hammered the earth so hard that, setting off in it, one felt it might be possible to drown standing up. There was a dry stream-bed that ran by the house and after rain it would suddenly and for a short time become a churning torrent. Once I saw a horse floating in it the morning after a storm, bloated monstrously by death. That violent rain fell only briefly, and then, as if to punish me for the pleasure I took in storms, the heat would always draw a haze of sweaty steam from the earth to sheen the skin and clog the air.

Mama was no more enamoured of the heat than I, and she would often express disgust over how things were done or, more often than not, left undone in it. From time to time I saw her staring at the clay people with incredulity. She became ferociously determined that nothing in our household or our behaviour would be permitted to deviate from what was proper.

But even as I struggled to be formal in a country that lacked any idea of formality or any reason for it, I could not help wondering why Mama had brought us here. Lying on my bed under a canopy of netting to keep out the insects, it came to me one day that, before deciding upon our removal, Mama had been on a quest. Yet what had she sought, that she had found it here? Unless she had truly sought the end of the earth. If that were true, she did not show any particular love for the end of the earth nor its inhabitants. But she smiled often and serenely here, though at her thoughts I fancied more than anything in our surroundings. Even so, her smiles gladdened me after the sombre years of mourning. Perhaps she had brought us here simply to force herself to give away all our dark, smotheringly hot mourning attire, and might therefore cease to grieve. We had come from a place where there were clothes for every eventuality and behaviours to match each garment so that one could not exist without the other. But here, the heat slashed away the connection between fashion and form, though the clay people had tried to cobble together a fashion that allowed for the heat. Descended as many of them were from the middle and servant class of our own land, their notions of good taste were intolerable to Mama.

A few weeks after settling ourselves and our possessions in the new place, Mama said that we must shop for a wardrobe. This was not an indulgence but an absolute necessary, for even the lightest of the clothes we had brought with us were too heavy and ornate for the heat and for the rough simplicity of the society about us.

I enjoyed the shopping expeditions simply because it seemed as if our lives were curving back to some approximation of normality. But the clothing offered to us, even the finest of it, was appalling and the cloth available was unsuitable for anything but the plainest house gowns. My mother ended up sending abroad for a dressmaker and a seamstress as well as a cobbler, who brought with them at her command silk and lace, pearl buttons and other rare and costly fabrics. But she made a point of buying cottons and linens and wool locally, for she said it would not do to alienate the town entirely. It surprised me to hear her speak of local traders as if their feelings mattered, but then I remembered that she had always had the best of everything at home because she had wooed the underlings as much as their masters, knowing who did the true work.

Before Papa died, we had shopped often for gowns and hats and new shoes for this or that occasion, but having spent the last years in black and grey and purple, it was a heady experience to be permitted to think of colour again. Even Mama seemed nearly elated as she chose blues in all shades to complement her lavender eyes and flaxen hair, while I was directed to pale primrose, cream and delicate light greens. I was permitted one moss-green gown, which I adored because it seemed a dramatic adult colour. The endless fittings, which could have been a trial in the sullen heat, were pleasurable because Mama laughed and talked with the designers and cutters in a gay, charming, effortless manner she had not exhibited since Papa's death. Only very occasionally did she fall silent in that preoccupied way that told me she was thinking of Papa. But to my relief, her mouth drooped only for a short time before she began to speak of some new bonnet she had seen, or the settee she was having designed for the large formal parlour.

There were times I felt guilty about my longing to see her smile and be happy, for I knew it could only come if she dwelt less on Papa, and to wish for that seemed a disloyalty to him. Yet with or without my wishing it, Mama was putting off her grief.

Once new furniture had been built, light and limed or painted white, Mama set about establishing a salon in our house that swiftly became the only gathering place for the few people of any elegance or wit. It was a court, and she its queen. It was not hard to establish herself in this way, for Mama's skills in entertaining were formidable, having been instilled in her in a country where there were a thousand rigid rituals and archaic standards to be observed in even the smallest encounters. And of course there was her beauty and her charm. Naturally I did not attend the salons, but I was able to peep down the stairs, and occasionally a guest would be invited back in the daytime for tea, and I would be presented to them.

Then one day, during such a tea when a neighbour had come to call, Mama glanced out a window and the blood ebbed from her cheeks. Mama had the habit of seeing her thoughts more than the world, but her appearance was so altered that I glanced out the window too, half expecting to see nothing. But I saw passing a group of the tall, graceful, shadow-dark folk who were the natural and nomadic inhabitants of this land.

'They have no sense of private property,' I heard the neighbour observe tolerantly. 'They think it odd or funny that we imagine we can own bits of the earth.' I had heard this said before of the velvet people, and could not help but admire their philosophy. If one thought of it, the notion of owning land was no less absurd than the idea of owning a portion of the air.

These were wild velvet folk outside our window, clad only in their warm brown skin and loincloths. One never saw them like this in Dusty Town, as I had named it to myself. I watched the liquid grace of their walk and the light, strong way their feet grasped the parched earth; this close, I seemed to hear a music rising up from the land at their passing. I was so enthralled by this phenomenon that I forgot why I had looked out the window until I heard the neighbour ask Mama if she was unwell. I turned back and saw that she was still staring out at the velvet people with such a bottomless terror in her eyes that my heart began to pound.

'What is it?' I begged, coming to sit by her and take her hand, as the neighbour took an uncertain step away.

'Mama!' I shook her a little when she did not seem to hear me.

She shuddered and put a slender white hand to her throat and whispered, 'It cannot be. Not here at the end of the earth . . .'

'Mama?' I cried, growing really frightened. She turned to look at me and I wished I had not spoken, for here was all the grief I had thought was gone. Then she clutched me to her, holding me so tightly that I could not breathe, and whispered fiercely that she would keep me safe. I struggled to disengage her hands and felt my cheeks flame at the thought of the neighbour observing what must seem to him a sudden fit of madness.

Somehow he was got rid of and Mama went to her bed, forbidding anyone to enter her room. I hovered about her door, frightened and confused by her relapse into grief and possessive terror. When night and a slight coolness came without any sign of her emerging, I went onto the verandah, ignoring the warning of a servant that I would be eaten alive by insects. I did not bother to explain that they did not bite me as they did others, but only troubled me with their irritating whine. It was the same with Mama, and I supposed our blood was too cool or strange for them.

I looked up at the black night and the hard diamond shimmer of stars and tried to fathom what had happened. It seemed to me impossible that Mama could be so upset by the sight of a group of velvet folk, for we had seen many of them since our arrival. Was it the fact that they had been unclothed? Those we saw in town wore the cast-off clothes of the clay people, either by choice or because it was forced upon them by rustic prudishness. It was even possible that Mama had not yet seen the wild velvet people, for I saw them most often in the early mornings when I sat upon the verandah. But no, I could not believe my sophisticated Mama would be troubled by their nakedness, for all her belief in the importance of clothes. It was so obviously the correct attire for them, a symbolic acceptance of the relentless sun and heat.

Was it perhaps the neighbour's remark about the attitude of the velvet people to the possession of land that had scoured Mama? She had a deed to the land upon which our house sat, and for many acres about it, but no, he had spoken as he had after he had seen the look on Mama's face.

What had she said? *Not here at the end of the earth.* The words had rung with incredulity, suggesting that she had seen something she did not expect to see. I remembered how she had then clutched wildly at me and vowed to keep me safe, exactly as she had done during the period of nightmares before she had gone on her quest. The queer notion came to me that Mama had brought us to the end of the earth to keep me safe, only to be reminded by the velvet nomads that we had not escaped.

Mama kept to her room for one week and then a second began. On the thirteenth day of her retreat, I turned eleven. I had looked forward to the day because it seemed the first step out of childhood and that much closer to twenty, which Mama had always said was the age at which one truly became a woman. Papa had laughed at this when Mama said it once in his hearing, saying she was mistaken. One legally became a woman at eighteen. I thought the moment of maturity was not so easy to fix. Some girls were women at fifteen and others still immature at one and twenty.

'Among my people a girl becomes a woman at twenty,' Mama told him almost coolly, and to my surprise there was pain in her eyes. That flash of pain and her coolness had fixed the memory in my mind.

Sitting on the verandah, waiting for the sun to set on my eleventh birthday, it occurred to me that this memory was the only one I had of Mama speaking of her people – her people, I thought, not her family.

And suddenly she was there beside me, standing on the porch in glowing white like a radiant ghost, her eyes fixed on a stand of silver-trunked trees grouped on what was sometimes, for a brief period, a lawn, the same trees around which the velvet people had looped two weeks before. The trees were native to this country and the only thing about which Mama had expressed unqualified approval, saying there was power in them. It was true, there was something about them that attracted the eye. I was about to rise when I noticed that Mama's feet were bare. I gaped at her small perfect toes, struck by the realisation that I had never seen her feet naked before. It seemed a sign of something but I did not know what. I stood up and waited for her to speak.

Mama did not look at me, but when she took my hand, hers felt cool instead of feverishly hot as it had been when I had helped her to her room. I saw with tremendous relief that her expression in the dim light of dusk was tranquil. Whatever storm had seized her had blown away.

'We must have a ball,' she said in a dreamy voice. 'That is how things are managed where I was born.'

I stared at her, arrested by the notion that she was about to speak of her childhood, but she only went on staring at the trees. The next day, she began to make preparations for what was to be the most lavish ball the country had ever beheld.

'A ball is like a summoning spell,' she told our mesmerised housekeeper. 'It must be carefully designed and composed. It must be so magnificent that no person will fail to hear of it or dare decline our invitation.'

The ball was to be held two months hence, in autumn, and everyone of consequence among the clay folk sent an acceptance when they received the thick invitation cards individually embossed with dark red roses by an artist hired to perform the task. None of the velvet people was invited, and when I asked Mama why, she said only that it was of no concern of theirs. As the day approached, supplies began to arrive by ship as well as chefs to cook them and footmen and maids to help guests from carriages, take coats, offer champagne and serve food. Fresh ingredients were brought from all over the country and exotic flowers shipped from nearby islands and kept in the cellar with the rare wines and ports Mama had brought with us.

I did all that I was told. I held open doors and helped to place things and to polish crystal and silverware. Mama even allowed me to help design the flower arrangements and to iron her evening gloves and kerchief, but knowing that I was not to attend, some part of me was inattentive to the preparations. It was this part that now pondered the velvet people. Since my mother's strange behaviour the day the neighbour had called, I had become more aware of them, and I often found myself watching them closely. Indeed, my early mornings were now focused on the moment when a tribe of them would pass by the house every few days, always in those cool hours before dawn. I watched them often enough to be sure that they always took exactly the same route across the paddocks and around obstacles. It even seemed to me they trod in exactly the same places each day. It was as if the strange, exquisite music their feet drew from the land depended upon their treading the same steps, as if any deviation would alter the music. I became convinced that they walked by the house not to go anywhere or to accomplish anything save to practise the making of music, which the clay people utterly ignored.

In Dusty Town, I noted the confused, lumbering movements of the velvet men clad in the ungainly attire of the clay folk, whose steps drew no music from the land. Was it the clothes they wore that stopped them from finding the music, or an inability to find music that made them don the clothes and ape the ways of the clay people? Perhaps in building their great untidy settlement, the clay folk had made it impossible for the velvet people, who had once passed over this place, to walk where they used to walk, so that the music had been irrevocably broken. I had noticed that the same velvet people passed our house, though sometimes there were a few extra people, or one or two fewer. Perhaps the impossibility of walking their own ancient songlines had destroyed those velvet people whose song paths had been built over, trapping them within Dusty Town to wither like leaves caught in a grate. In any case, they seemed to me as different from the wild velvet people as a separate race.

One morning when we had come to the wharves very early so that Mama could supervise the unloading of some hundred-year-old eggs to be served at the ball, I elected to stay in the carriage. I had been sitting for a time, wondering at the fact that even now, when there was no one in the street, the dust hung suspended in the air. A wind blew up. I was startled because I had never known a breeze to blow here, and had supposed that there was something about the shape of the hills surrounding the town on three sides, and the closed nature of the harbour, that prevented the wind from entering. I turned to look in the direction from which it was blowing, and was astonished to see a group of wild velvet men and women and a few children walking down the centre of the street. I could see them quite clearly because the wind had blown a clear passage for them through the haze of dust. Then I heard the sound of music. It was more hesitant than at any other time I had heard it, with unusual dissonances, and the velvet people moved very slowly, almost carefully, though no less gracefully than usual. Listening to the music they were making, I felt instinctively that the discordances

I heard were not mistakes but part of the music, and that it was being delicately and intricately shaped around the obstructions that were the clay people's buildings. It reminded me of trying to play a piece on a piano that had several broken keys, so that you must quickly find alternate keys. It was as if these wild velvet people were striving to create a music that would encompass the obstructions and barriers thrown up by the clay people.

I had never seen nomadic velvet people in the town before, and I wondered if this walk was an attempt to heal the people who had once made music here, by creating new lines of song that might be walked. Two young velvet women appeared in a street ahead of the walkers, clad in the slovenly cast-off shifts of the clay folk. One walked a little ahead of the other, inclining her head as if to listen to something she could barely hear, and the second came behind her, plucking at her dress fretfully. Both stopped and gaped at the sight of the wild velvet people, and after a moment the first girl kicked off her shoes impatiently. Her face was trans-figured by wonder but the other girl merely stared at her in stupid amazement.

The song walkers arrived at the intersection where I sat, and as I looked at them, the oldest of the velvet men looked up and met my gaze, without breaking his slow stride or interrupting the song. He showed no surprise to find me sitting there watching, which gave me the queer feeling that he had known all along that I was there and could see him and the others. The look he gave me was long and searching, as if my face were a book he was reading, then his eyes widened and he smiled, a startling crescent moon of white. He took several swift steps towards me and then away, which gave a peculiar thrilling trill to the song he was walking, and made the other walkers look at him. I held my breath, for it seemed to me that I had just been woven into their music.

The velvet man smiled at me, and pointed to my feet. I looked down at them, clad in their neat, white leather, buttoned boots, and noted the stain of red on them though I had not taken a single step. I thought of the velvet girl who had taken off her shoes, and wondered what I would hear if I took off my boots and stockings and stood barefoot in the dust. But when I looked up, the man and the other velvet people had vanished, and even as I watched, the wind erased their path and whirled away, leaving only the hot, sticky red stillness.

Mama came out then, and I forgot what I had seen in the business of getting the crates of black, gelid eggs into the back of the carriage.

Preparations for the ball had swallowed weeks of time, but suddenly the day dawned and I was watching Mama's maid lace her into her boned petticoat and make up her face, then a hair-dresser spend an hour brushing and pinning and winding her mass of pale yellow hair into a delicate tower of tiny curls and ringlets around sprigs of violets and fastening it with amethyst combs. Last, the dress was held out and Mama slipped her arms into its short lace sleeves. It was made of watered silk and silk chiffon in twenty shades of violet, layered like the petals of a vast flower, and as the hundreds of tiny buttons were fastened all down the back of the gown, another maid powdered Mama's bare white shoulders and long swan's neck, and slipped on her jewel-encrusted slippers. Mama permitted me to spray a mist of exotic scent on each slim wrist and on the little pulse that beat in the hollow at the base of her throat and then she let me help her on with her long gloves. Two maids fastened the thirty buttons on each, and she announced that she was ready.

'Oh madam, you look like a princess!' said the youngest maid, then blushed red as a beet as the others shushed her, but Mama only smiled. Then she dismissed all of them.

When we were alone, she looked into my eyes and said very seriously, 'It matters, how you look and how you move, Willow. Never forget that. There is a power in such things that can be harnessed to transform a girl into a princess.'

I nodded, for these had been my own thoughts about the song walkers I had seen a few days earlier in the town. I was tempted to speak of their music but held my tongue, remembering how the sight of the velvet people had thrown Mama into despair.

The night of the ball passed swiftly for me, for of course I did not attend. I watched the guests arriving from the top of the stairs, admiring their clothes and imagining lives and personalities for the ones I did not know, but once they passed into the main rooms I could see nothing. I fell asleep listening to the muted music, and dreamed of turning and turning to it in a full-length gown.

I woke early, eagerly, and I was not disappointed for, as we breakfasted, Mama told me a thousand tales of the night. That it had been a dazzling success was no surprise to me, yet Mama seemed elated, almost as if she had doubted it.

One week after the ball, Ernst came to call. He was a tall and handsome man with a bristling black beard and splendid large eyes that shone like black pearls dipped in oil. He was so like Papa at first glance that my mouth dropped open foolishly when he was shown into the parlour. When I said so to Mama after he had departed, too shocked to guard my tongue, Mama merely smiled and reminded me tranquilly that he had come to the ball. She said this with such satisfaction that one might have supposed the sole reason for the ball had been the luring of him to it.

Ernst was gentle and courteous in his manner with me from the first, and as the weeks passed he visited many times, becoming more warm and less formal, until at last I realised that he was courting me as well as Mama. I understood this all of a sudden, and rather later than I ought to have done, when Ernst observed one day to Mama with almost startled pleasure that, in appearance, I could be his own daughter. I am tall and lean and dark like Papa was, but instead of explaining this, Mama only smiled with a sort of pleased satisfaction, as if a difficult puzzle had been solved.

'Will you marry Mama?' I asked one evening. I had been given some watered wine to try which had made me bold and a little giddy. It was too soon for such a question, of course, for the cadences of courtship are slow and ornate, though far less slow, I came to discover, because Mama was a widow and not a maiden. Instead of being annoyed or affronted by my pert question, Ernst laughed and did not report my indiscretion to Mama, which made me like him even more. They wed a month later. Only then did I learn that Ernst had two wards, both the children of a distant cousin, who had come under his protection when their parents had died in a fire. Like Mama and me they came from abroad, though they had been here for several years.

The younger was a plump boy called Reynaldo and the older a tall, very handsome, long-faced and rather gloomy boy called Silk. They came to live with us, though Silk was mostly away at school, and when at home, he spent time with various friends or with his nose buried in his books. I loved reading too, and spent a good portion of my time in our library, which doubled in size after Ernst married Mama and became my stepfather. I should have liked to be friends with Silk, for it seemed to me that we shared a common love, and I had never had a friend, but he was like a closed door to me, and in time, I ceased to wonder what might lie behind it.

Reynaldo was as loud as his brother was silent, as bullish and stubborn as Silk was elusive, and although I found him tiresome and tiring I could not help but like his rather thick-headed courage, for I had little boldness in me. He ardently claimed me as his property and declared often that he would marry me when he was grown to manhood. He did not doubt that I shared his desire, so it was fortunate for both of us that he had to spend most of each day with tutors or fencing masters. I did care for him, but I did not love him, and this made me wonder uneasily if I had in me the warmth of heart to love properly. Then, nine months after Mama wed Ernst, she gave birth to a daughter.

2.

'But Rose is such an ephemeral name,' Ernst protested. 'Would it not be prudent to name her Ruby or Adamant, or some such resilient and eternal name?'

A long time later, I remembered those words of his, and wondered if he had some prescient inkling of what was to come.

'Rose,' Mama only repeated very firmly. 'The beauty of a rose lasts forever in the mind, long after the petals have fallen.'

I could tell from Ernst's expression that he doted on her too much to insist upon having his way. Besides, he must have known by now that there were certain matters upon which Mama would never give way; naming was one of them, as was the wearing of clothes appropriate to each occasion, the placement of furniture and flowers, and the composition of gardens and meals.

Once Ernst had nodded his surrender, Mama bade me sit in the chair so that I might hold my sister. My stepfather looked worried, but Mama said almost pointedly that it was best we bond as soon as may be.

So Ernst brought Rose to me, ignoring Reynaldo's jealous demand to hold the baby. I looked into Rose's little flower of a face for the first time. Unlike those of other newborn babies I had seen, it was not red and shrivelled but as soft and pink and delicate as a flower, and the fluff of golden hair atop it made me certain she had inherited our mother's indestructible beauty. Her cloudy eyes cleared to a pure light blue and seemed to focus on me. I knew babies that young could not see, and that the seeming colour change must be the result of clouds glooming over the sun, but I felt her look as a hand that reached into me and touched my very essence. When she withdrew her gaze, I felt it still.

Was that why I loved her so much? I cannot say. I only know that from the beginning I adored her. Reynaldo was fiercely put out by this, and once tipped Rose from her perambulator in a jealous rage. But instead of screaming, she only looked at him with her big blue eyes until he flung his arms about her, begging her to forgive him. After that he became her devoted defender and often argued with me over who should push the perambulator in the garden. I regarded him more affectionately than I had done hitherto, because he shared my worship of my dainty little sister, though his passions were as violent and brief as rainstorms. Even Silk, who came home for one of his brief visits soon after her birth, smiled at Rose and let her be placed in his arms so that he could admire her. I felt a little stab of surprise to see her lift starfish fingers to his face and touch his lips, for I had never seen her do that to anyone but me.

Rose grew to resemble Mama, just as I had guessed she would. But as well as her pink and gold loveliness, she had a nature that was all her own. She was sunny, sweetly generous and utterly open. When Reynaldo wanted something of hers, she let him take it. When he pushed in front of her, she smiled at him and gave way so willingly that it was as if this was her own desire. Later, when she had friends visit, she allowed them to wear all of her clothes and often gave away her favourite toys and garments because she could not bear for anyone to yearn for something that it was in her power to bestow. I felt shamed by her unselfishness but my stepfather worried aloud that she had no discretion. Of course he feared she might grow to be a sweet-faced fool, but I knew already that she was no more a fool nor foolish than I. She was merely good in so thoughtful and intelligent a way that it was impossible to argue with her. Indeed, there were times I found myself giving some favoured trinket of my own away to a worthy child simply because I could not find an argument in favour of keeping it. In her own way, Rose was as difficult to resist as our Mama, but her power lay in her essential sweetness and I never regretted my obedience.

I did not worry that she was lacking in wit, but there were times when it troubled me that she was unable to conceive that the world might mean her harm or do her mischief. When we walked out, she would run down any dark lane to introduce herself to a cat whose sly twinkling eyes she had spotted, never fearing there might be less savoury things than cats awaiting her. Sometimes, when I read to her, I found myself deliberately exaggerating the monsters and evil characters in her books, in the hope of frightening a little wariness into her. But it did not work. Rose only pitied the monsters their wickedness and wondered if a little kindness or something pretty might not shine a light into the darkness of their souls.

When Rose was five and I was seventeen, a clay man came to the house gate. Before I could stop her, Rose went to talk with him and offered him a drink from her mug. I hastened to draw her away, telling the man he might have his own mug and a pie if he went to the kitchen door and said that Miss Rose and Miss Willow had sent him. After my careful speech, which made my face flame, the man responded in a language I did not understand. I shook my head helplessly but he only shrugged and smiled and then he nodded to Rose, who beamed at him and rushed to the gate to wave him away.

'You must not talk to strangers,' I scolded her when he had gone.

'He was not strange,' she said.

'I did not say he was strange. I said he was a stranger. That means someone we do not know. We should not speak to people we do not know.'

'But why not?'

'It is better that some people are left to be strangers.'

'Perhaps some people prefer to be strangers,' Rose conceded. 'Indeed, I think Edgar might like it very much.' Edgar was my stepfather's rude and surly manservant, who had made it clear to Rose and me that he thought his master had complicated his life foolishly by marrying. He was careful to show only his most polite and deferential face to Mama. He was one of the few people who seemed immune to Rose's charm, but he knew where the true power of the household lay.

'A stranger might mean us harm,' I explained, feeling unsettled by Rose's innocent interrogation.

'But we should see if he meant us harm. He was only going to sell ribbons at the fair. He saw me and thought of his own daughter.'

I stared at her. 'How can you know that, Rose? That man spoke another language.'

'I could see it, of course,' she answered simply.

I did not know what to say to that. It must be that she had made up a little history for the ribbon seller, yet she had very little imagination, and sometimes sorely vexed me when I was reading one of my favourite tales to her with her insistence on querying everything that diverged from reality. I shook my head and said we had better go in as Reynaldo, who was now away at school, was due home any moment.

That was just one of many occasions upon which Rose revealed her ability to know things about people without being told, a power I lacked, for all my fabled ability to see things other people did not. Whenever I questioned Rose as to what she saw in this person to elicit her sympathy or to rouse her concern, she merely looked at me, bemused and smiling a little, as if she thought I was playing a joke on her, or setting her a puzzle. I suppose to her it was as if I pointed to a chair and asked how she knew it was a chair. When she finally was able to take in that I could not see the things she saw, she said kindly that perhaps seeing the wind made it hard for me to see people properly. I answered indulgently that it might be so, perceiving that her ability seemed as commonplace to her as my ability to see odd things was to me. Of the two abilities, however, Rose's seemed infinitely more interesting and useful.

Mama had changed since the birth of Rose. All of her moodiness and the last of the stiffness and melancholy of bereavement had been vanquished. She seemed to me both more contented and more steady of temperament than I had ever known her to be, though occasionally she called me in to her at night to tell me with a strange fierce intensity, 'You are both my daughters.'

'We are true sisters,' I would agree, and she would give a brittle laugh as if relieved by my reply. It puzzled me very much that she seemed to need reassurance about my affection for Rose, which would have been apparent to a blind man. In truth I had never for a moment thought of her as anything but my beloved little sister. That the blood of our fathers differed was nothing to me and I told Mama so. Her face softened, revealing a complicated meld of grief and regret and triumph. I found myself wondering if it was concern for Rose that motivated these interrogations, or her own guilt that she did not love her second daughter in the same passionate, possessive way she loved her first. Her love for my little sister seemed to me as extravagant and light and lacking in substance as a great tub of froth, and perhaps she felt it to be so too, and wished to know that someone loved Rose more sincerely. If I was right, then she must have been reassured by my answers.

By the time I turned eighteen and Rose six, Mama began to exhibit some of the strangeness of the days after my father's death. She took to clutching at my hand and pressing it to her cheek, her eyes devouring my face as if she thought I would vanish. She sometimes muttered to herself in a foreign language, even though she was no foreigner, and her habit of focusing on some inconsequential thing she had seen or heard became more pronounced. Once I saw her stare transfixed at a daffodil pushing up through the earth at the foot of one of the ghost trees, and another time she hushed me savagely so that she could listen to a rare breeze soughing through their branches. Another time she watched the passing of one of the velvet nomads with an expression of enchantment mingled with despair. Once I saw her slap the face of a fish monger in Dusty Town because he offered a certain sort of fish, but a moment later she had given him a golden coin to pay for a different fish and his goodwill. She left him smiling toothily after her, one clay cheek still red with the small imprint of her hand.

Ernst did not notice her strangeness, for although he adored Mama as much as ever, it seemed to me that he did not see her so much as the vision he had fallen in love with, and that was unchanging. Nor did Reynaldo notice it whenever he was home. He was now a sturdy youth and attended boarding school during the week. Silk, who might have had a more subtle and discerning eye, had been some years abroad, completing his studies.

One evening, as we came arm in arm to the dining room to find we were the first down, I asked Rose what she saw when she looked at Mama. It had occurred to me that my little sister's perceptive vision might give me some clue about the reason for Mama's oddness of late. Rose answered that Mama was gathering her courage. I was so startled by the kindness and pity in Rose's eyes that I failed to ask what she had meant.

Then one afternoon, Mama came home from a trip with my stepfather to announce that we were moving again. She had found the perfect place: an apartment that faced onto a park in a larger and more sophisticated town. Relieved that we were not to change countries again, for I now thought of the land we had come to as my home, I packed up my treasures and helped Rose pack hers while the household was dismantled about us by servants. Ernst was as eager to move as Mama, as the new town was larger and better established. It was also where Reynaldo went to school, so he would return to live with us. Reynaldo was to inherit my stepfather's business when he had finished school, for he had no aptitude for deep thought and no desire to be further educated. Silk, our stepfather announced, must be the scholar of the family and his brother would mind its business. Silk had finished his education now, and was more like to be enticed home by the prospect of life in a large town.

We had not dwelt a year in our new home, when Mama died and Rose disappeared.

Misadventure, the newspapers called it, an odd, unsatisfactory word.

Mama and Rose had been strolling home through the park after a pantomime when a mist had settled about them. The town was so far south that it caught some of the coolness of the ice pole, and the occasional mists had been one of the first things to delight me about our new home, for they reminded me of my childhood. The mist must have confused Mama, so that she and Rose walked deep into the park and, becoming lost, had wandered in circles. Finally Mama lay down in exhaustion, never knowing that she was only a few steps from the edge of the park. Rose went to find help, but she had gone the wrong way, becoming lost herself.

That was what people said.

I knew it could not be the truth, for upon our arrival in our new home, Mama had brought me to this very window and said I must never, on any account, set foot in the park. It was a wondrous place, and I, who never argued, would have argued about that, but there was such desperate, immoderate terror in Mama's face that I feared for her sanity. She demanded I vow that I would never enter the park, no matter what, and when I promised, she made me pierce my finger with a pin to seal the swear with a drop of blood.

That was how I knew it was impossible that Mama would have entered the park of her own free will. Even confused by the mist, she would have been able to follow the line of ghost trees that marked the borders of the park. One day, sorrow made me forget my reserve and voice my doubts about the popular theory to a neighbour. He assured me earnestly that cold could confuse and dull the wits. I could have argued that Mama would hardly have become cold enough to sap her wit in one step, but Silk laid his long thin hand on my shoulder, rendering me silent.

After the neighbour left, he led me into the library and made me drink a glass of something gold and potent, which he said would steady me. He was taller than ever, but now less thin than lean, and he looked tired, for he had spent the day searching for Rose. He spoke of the park, and like the policemen who had searched for her, he told me he had reached the other side without having seen a thing. But from my window I could see that the park stretched on for miles, a trackless wilderness running as far as the eye could see, and beyond. There was no way it could be crossed in a day or even in a week. When I said this to the senior policeman handling the case, he gave me a look so long and so serious that I guessed he thought me addled with grief. So I did not argue with Silk.

In truth I was touched by his determination to find Rose. He would not listen to Reynaldo or my stepfather's sharp-eyed solicitor when they tried to convince him there was no hope of finding her. There was a strength and weight of grief in him that I had not expected, and I had drunk enough to say as much. He sat beside me, gathering my cold hands into his. 'Willow, if she can be found, I will find her. Do you believe me?'

I wanted to say that he would have to be able to see the true nature and extent of the park that had stolen Rose from us before he could hope to find her, but what would be the use? I did not look into his face, lest his honest expression of sorrow and determination cause me to lose all control. I feared I would blurt out my conviction that he could never find her, for it was only Mama, Rose and I who had been able to see the true nature of the park, although that seeing had done none of us any good. So instead of speaking, I wept and let Silk comfort me.

He stayed three more weeks, seeking Rose. When this produced no result, he offered a substantial reward for information about her disappearance. But once the fakes and liars and the mistaken sightings were weeded out, there was still nothing, and finally Silk agreed to let the solicitor arrange a memorial service for Rose and invest the inheritance that Mama had set aside for her. Silk came to me and held my hands, telling me gently and gravely that he would be a fool if he spent his life searching for a dream. He must accept the facts, however they pained him, and it would be best if I could do the same.

He went abroad again, and I stayed and tended my grief and my stepfather.

You would never have guessed to look at Ernst that something was broken inside him. Outwardly he was the same, spare and handsome, though now there was a little frosting of grey at his temples. He retained his gentleness and maintained his cultured habits after the accepted period of mourning, attending the ballet and plays and accepting invitations to various engagements, but they were empty gestures. He and I had both grieved and come to accept the death of my mother, but the loss of Rose was a wound that would not heal in either of us. My stepfather saw nothing else, and eventually that inner wound slowly turned him blind, so that I was forced to lead him hither and thither through life, making sure he did what a man was supposed to do: brush his hair and teeth, wash his face and tie his laces . . . If I did not, he would have stumbled out of his front door half undone.

Reynaldo, who had all but taken control of the household with the aid of the solicitor, began to speak of an institution, claiming that the reputation of our business must not be compromised. With no interest in higher education, Reynaldo was busy making alliances and had developed an interest in banking, which was rigid and conservative enough to suit his nature. He was contemptuous of what he perceived as weakness in Ernst and had begun to listen to the solicitor's suggestions that a smaller apartment would suit us better, freeing up money for investment. It is true that my poor stepfather had lost his grip on life, but I loved him and I did not wish to lose my companion in sorrow.

I wrote a letter to Silk, asking him to ensure that Reynaldo did not allow the solicitor to put our stepfather into an institution or sell the apartment. I explained that I could not bear to leave it, for although I knew it to be utterly irrational, I could not shake the idea that Rose might one day return, and should there not be someone who loved her waiting to greet her? Was not the greatest proof of love fidelity, even against all rationality? It was unfortunate, I added pragmatically, afraid that Silk might think me romantic and hysterical, that both I and my stepfather were currently reliant upon the solicitor and Reynaldo, but I would gain control of my own fortune when I was twenty and then I would buy the apartment and take upon myself the expense of caring for our stepfather. I added that it was a pity Mama had put control of her estate into the hands of my stepfather's solicitor, for he was not a man to let me have a penny of it a day earlier than he must.

I wrote the letter sitting at the little desk by the window seat in my room. I had chosen that room for the window seat, which had a cosy, secretive feel that had enchanted me, especially when the curtains were drawn. And of course, it had the best view of the park.

3.

Our apartment was in a many-winged building three storeys high and covering an entire town block that on one side faced the great, wild park where it was always winter to my eyes. There were more windows than anyone could possibly need facing the park, and it was said that a madwoman had designed the apartment, forcing the builders to make it so. This was what came of having a woman design a building, people muttered. Mad she may have been, but if mad, it was a kind of madness angels have, for though the park was a strange and fell place, it was also beautiful beyond describing, for those few of us who could perceive its beauty. Our apartment was the one that faced it most squarely, and my own chamber was at the very centre of the apartment, so that its windows only showed the park, making it seem that outside it was truly winter. I knew the servants thought me morbid to keep the room after what had happened, and subtle pressure had been exerted on me to shift to another chamber, but I had resisted.

As I gazed out over the park, I found myself remembering how Rose had always asked to be taken to play on the apron of snow that sometimes blew a little way out from the ghost trees marking the outer border of the winter park. The snow could be fashioned into snow witches and Rose was always urging me to come and help her before it melted in the heat. I would hang back at the edge of the drift of snow, longing to join Rose, but conscious of Mama watching me and wondering when she would demand the same promise of Rose she had extracted from me.

Occasionally, instead of watching over us as we played in the snow, Mama would walk right to the line of ghost trees and peer through them, as if she were searching beyond them for someone or something hidden from her. She never passed through the trees, but occasionally she would stand there for so long that daylight would seep from the world and Rose's lips would turn a soft lilac, since she would not leave the snow until she must. One day when Mama had stood staring into the trees for a long time, I walked over the crisp snow to her side and put my hand into hers. She looked at me and the fear in her face faded into a tender sorrow. She said softly, 'It was snowing the first time I saw your father.'

I do not know what more she would have said, but Rose came running up and threw her arms about Mama's soft waist, saying impulsively, 'Let us go into the park now, all three of us together.' Her little heart-shaped face was flushed with longing and it had astounded me that she, who saw so much, did not see that Mama feared the park.

'It is late,' Mama whispered, seeming to speak more to herself than to Rose.

'It is not so late,' Rose protested. 'By dusk we could be at the tower.'

'Mama does not like the park, Rose,' I told my little sister gently, wondering if Mama had hidden her fear from Rose, having judged her too young for the litany of warnings given to me. Mama never seemed to realise how clever Rose was, perhaps because she did not focus upon her as she did on me. But to see Rose misunderstanding my mother was astonishing and made me wonder if I knew her quite so well as I thought. Before either of us could speak, Mama caught Rose in a quick embrace, smoothed her hair and urged her to run back to the house to see if Papa's carriage had drawn up yet, for he was to come home early today so we could go to the fair.

Rose gave a squeal of delight, for she loved the fair, and went running off. I knew the task was a distraction and looked to see what Mama meant to tell me outside the hearing of my little sister. But she only cupped my chin in her cold hand and stared down at me with such a look of baffled angry love that I felt a queer slipping of fear through my bones.

'Understand that I did not know,' she said, holding my gaze. 'I did not know that what I gave away to win my heart's desire would come to mean everything to me.' She stroked my hair now and looked down at me with a sorrow so striking that even after her death, a long time after, I could summon up that expression of desperation clearly.

'I don't understand,' I told her with perfect honesty.

'No,' she said as Rose came skipping back to report that the carriage was not there. Mama's expression changed and she gave

Rose a brisk warm smile and held out her hand. Rose took it and then reached out as she always did to take my hand, too, giving me her sweet, open-mouthed smile.

Thinking back on those early days in the apartment, I noticed anew the way Mama had always been brisk and cheerful with Rose, rather than tender. She had cared for her and played with her and dressed her up like a doll and sung her songs and tickled her. My mother had needed little enough to fly into a rage with me, but I had never heard her speak a cross word to Rose. Of course, Rose was so good it would have been hard to find a reason for anger, yet I had never felt jealous, because all the overt attention and showy affection Mama bestowed upon Rose had seemed to me a compensation for the fact that she did not love Rose as she loved me. I ought to have felt sad for my little sister, but in truth it had not always been pleasant to be loved so intensely. Indeed, I had sometimes felt Mama's love for me as a rich, lustrous fur blanket that was beautiful and wondrous but too heavy. Now, pondering the difference in Mama's treatment of her two daughters, I found myself wondering if she had loved me more intensely than Rose because she had loved Papa more than she had loved Ernst. Certainly her light, affectionate love for Ernst matched the lightness of her love for their daughter, just as her possessive love of me matched the depth of passion she had borne my father.

For some reason, my thoughts drifted to a night some months after the memorial service for Rose, when the solicitor and some business associates and their wives and daughters whom he wished to introduce to Reynaldo had come to dine. After the meal, when Reynaldo and the men withdrew to the library, they to drink porter and smoke their pipes and he to observe how men of substance deported themselves in the absence of women, I suggested a walk in the garden to the wives and daughters. The older women declined, but urged their daughters to go with me.

'The men go out so they can exchange their secrets, then the older women send their daughters away so that they, too, can tell secrets,' said Bernice, who was the oldest and boldest of the daughters. 'I think that we should make up our own secrets in revenge. Let us talk about which of us should be married off to Reynaldo.'

'You are a terrible cynic to speak of such a thing,' said one of the others, a tiny, dark girl called Magda. 'Besides, my mama said it is Willow who is to be married off.'

Bernice, who was frankly and contentedly ugly, smiled and said she supposed *I* could marry Reynaldo, since he was not related to me by blood and the gap in our ages was not so very great.

'I think of him as a brother,' I said firmly, wondering how long it would be before I could be alone again, wondering too if it was true that Reynaldo was trying to arrange a marriage for me. Certainly he had not spoken of it, and in truth it was my stepfather or Silk who ought to manage the matter, but Reynaldo was never averse to taking control of a situation.

Bernice sighed as if I had taken a tray of sweets away without giving her time to choose one. 'Well then, one of us must certainly be wed to Reynaldo, since we are all daughters of the wealthiest families in the town.'

'Oh, you are such a silly,' said Friday, the fourth of our party. 'First he is too young for any of us, and second, a girl who has a fortune, such as we all will have from our parents, need not marry save for love, and I do not think any of us feels that for Reynaldo.'

'It matters not what man we wed, so long as we will be safe and cared for, since our husbands will not be the love of our lives,' Bernice said calmly, stolidly.

Magda gave a shriek. 'What are you saying, Bernice?'

'Only that women do not give their deepest love to their husbands. Oh, we can love them, and serve them and adore them. We even obey them if we cannot get away from it. But I believe it is the children we will bear who will bind us most deeply. The love of a child is the love that will truly enslave us, for we might leave a husband, but never a child.'

'I do not believe the love of a husband must be lessened by the having of children,' Magda protested.

'I did not say the love was lessened, only that the love of a child will inevitably eclipse the love a woman has for its father. I am sure that is why men stray so, because the pretty princess they fell in love with has inconsiderately become a wife and a mother,' Bernice continued. There was a glimmer of amusement in her eye that made me wonder how serious she was.

'You think a man cannot love the mother of his child?' Magda snapped.

'Some rare man might even love the mother of his children more than when she was a princess, but in general, a man has not the capacity to sacrifice himself for love. Not the love of a woman, anyway. He is all too ready to sacrifice himself and his family for an ideal or for his country.' There was a touch of bitterness here, but none of us remarked upon it, since the voracious political ambitions of Bernice's father, as well as his neglect of her mother for an actress he kept in an apartment on the other side of town, were all too well known.

'Men do not love as women do,' Friday conceded, after a moment. 'But I think there is a reason for it. Men were once the hunters and the protectors of their families, and they could do neither if they were dead. So they must be selfish and keep themselves alive, for the sake of their families. And also in order to hunt, they must be single-minded and ruthless. Those aspects of their character remain even in this day, preventing them from abdicating their souls when they wed, as women do.'

'Oh, what a vile discourse,' Magda cried, looking really repelled. 'Don't you think so, Willow? What of falling in love?'

'I do not think one falls in love in the same way one trips over the edge of a Persian rug,' I answered her composedly. Yet even as I spoke, I could not help but think of Mama, telling me she had fallen in love with Papa before he had even seen her. And Papa had said he had fallen in love the first time he had set eyes on Mama. Even Ernst spoke of falling in love with Mama at the ball, though she had not told me when she first loved him. Perhaps my poor stepfather grieved Mama's loss so because he had not felt he ever had a proper grip on her. Perhaps he blamed himself for not winning from her an undying love. Poor broken Ernst. 'At least,' I amended, 'I do not wish that sort of love for myself.'

'Then what sort do you want? It seems to me we have agreed that there is only romantic love in stories, full of princesses and princes, or the love that comes after, where a woman loves her children and her man is neglected and sulky and goes looking for another princess,' Friday said with interest.

'Perhaps that is it,' I said. 'Perhaps I want some other kind of love than those kinds. I don't want a prince or a ruthless hunter. I don't want someone to fall in love with me at first sight. I want a man who will look more than once before he loves, and when he loves, can love all that I may be as well as all that I am. That probably sounds terribly dull to you,' I added, fearing that I sounded pompous and self-righteous. They all regarded me in silence, and then Friday spoke.

'What I think is this,' she said in her decided way. 'A woman does not fall in love as a man does. A woman must entice a proposal as a flower sends the scent of its honey to draw the bee to it. Therefore she must judge a man and seek out one who suits her purposes. Consciously or unconsciously, she chooses a father for her children.'

Magda gave a dramatic cry and fell back against the garden wall as if Friday had shot an arrow through her heart. But then she stood up and said almost spitefully, 'Have they no say in it then, these brainless men? These breeding bulls? These bees who will fall to the lure of the flower?'

For some reason, I thought of Silk, who was a closed door. Would he someday see a woman and fall in love? Maybe all men were locked rooms until someone opened them, and maybe the opening could only be done with love. But if love opened men, what did women do with what they found inside?

'We can't speak for men,' Bernice was saying now, rather dismissively. 'I am only pointing out that whatever reason we have for loving and wedding a man, we are bound by love to give our whole selves to them, not just our bodies, because of the children we will bear them. And when the children are born, our love is drained off for them and men get what is left, like skimmed milk after the cream has been taken.'

Magda made a face. 'How horrible and bare you make life seem.'

Bernice shot her a look of friendly contempt. Then she said, 'It seems to me that the old romantic ideal of falling in love for love's sake is outmoded simply because it leaves out most of the truth of what it means to wed. That is, all that comes after the wedding.'

The conversation was interesting to me because I had never heard love discussed in this way, as if there were various recipes for it. My idea of love had been shaped by the tales I had read, and by Mama's loves, and it had surprised me to find I had any opinions on the matter, however muddled.

I had got cold, sitting so long and thinking, and I got up stiffly, undressed and put on my nightgown, then climbed into my bed to lie shivering a while before I slept.

I dreamed that Rose was not dead but in a stone chamber lying on a cobweb-draped bed in a gown of pink gold, scaled like the skin of a snake. Her face was pale as ice and still as stone, yet there was a blush of life upon her cheeks and a red bloom on her lips. A great window behind her opened onto a snowy park and I watched tiny flakes drift in and settle on the cobwebs and on Rose's cheeks and lips and eyelashes.

'I must save her,' I thought. Then a wave of helplessness washed over me, for of course if she were a princess it would take a prince to find her and kiss her back to life. The only way to save her, then, was to bring a prince to her, but where was I to find him?

I woke, and the room felt cold, as if the snow had blown from my dream into my bedroom. But it was only the wind from the winter park, flowing towards the apartment block and through my open window. The maid must have crept in and opened it, for of course she did not feel the cold of the park any more than she could see the snow.

Wrapping myself in my shawl, I padded across the room and sank again into the window seat. I stared out at the moonlit park, thinking of my dream. The grey sky sagged over the white ground of the park, and the white trunks of the ghost trees shivered in the wind. Were those trees inside the park or outside it, I found myself wondering. Snow settled in them sometimes, but the next day their leaves would glitter greenly. Then I wondered for the hundredth time what had led Mama to enter the winter park. If I knew the answer to that question, perhaps I would know what had happened to Rose.

The policeman in charge of the case had asked me soon after the tragedy if it was possible that Rose had gone into the park first, and that Mama had followed her, for while their tracks ran side by side to where my mother lay, the two might not actually have gone into the park at the same time.

'But where is Rose, since her tracks stop where my mother's body was found?' I had asked, for despite all the speculation, there had never been a sign of any footprints to support the theory that Rose had gone away seeking help for Mama.

The senior policeman, who was not old so much as weary and crumpled looking, had regarded me solemnly, perhaps waiting to see if I would answer my own question. He had watchful, intelligent grey eyes that offered neither judgement nor expectation. I had noticed that he spoke a good deal less than the other policemen, and yet when he did speak, it was always to mention something that no one else had noticed. After a long moment, he asked if I thought my mother would have lain down because she felt ill. I said I did not think she would have lain down in the snow if she was ill. A younger policeman who had been listening glanced sharply at me, and only then did I realise that I had spoken of snow. No doubt he thought my mind had foundered. The senior policeman merely looked at me, saying nothing.

Now, I watched the moon cross the sky, thinking how many times the senior policeman had come back to the house to ask questions about Rose and Mama of my stepfather and me, and of the servants, and of the way Reynaldo mimicked with vicious accuracy the slow, careful, waiting silences that punctuated these interviews, muttering wrathfully about harassment.

I felt the policeman suspected me of hiding something because he always sought me out in the end, no matter who else he questioned, yet I had been glad of his visits, for he had seemed to be the only other person besides myself and poor Ernst who had not given up on finding Rose.

One day he came upon me in the garden, sitting on a bench in the shade and gazing across at the winter park. I asked him mildly if he suspected me of knowing something about Rose's disappearance.

'The mind is full of secret corners and strange rooms,' he had answered. 'It is possible you know something without being aware of it.'

I wept, surprising myself more than I surprised him. He did not try to comfort me or question me or stop me weeping. But when I stopped of my own accord, he offered me his handkerchief and said in the same quiet, unprovoking voice he always used, 'I thought you did not believe your sister was dead.'

'I did not cry because I think she is dead,' I said. 'I feel as if I am to blame for whatever has happened to her. Mama was always so concerned about what would happen to me, when she ought to have worried about Rose!'

I still felt responsible for what had happened, I realised.

I wondered what the policeman would make of the dream and decided I would tell it to him when he came next. Somehow I did not doubt that he would continue to call, for the mystery of Mama's death and Rose's disappearance had taken hold of his mind. I thought of his earlier suggestion that Rose might have gone into the park first, and wondered what had made him think so. It struck me that he might all along have had some theory he had never voiced. Certainly Rose had never feared the park and sometimes she had spoken as if she was only putting off the pleasure of entering it, like someone leaving the icing on a cake till last. I had imagined she was teasing me, but once she ventured to take a few steps under the trees when Mama had not accompanied us, and I had been forced to show her my fear before she would come out to me. Was it possible that Mama had become distracted by something, allowing Rose to slip away? I did not think so, but nor could I believe that Mama and Rose had accidentally strayed into the winter park.

If only I had gone with them to the pantomime. If I had been there, holding Rose's other hand, I could have kept her from the park, or if not that, then at least we would have been lost together.

I heard a strain of music that reminded me of the velvet song walkers, and I glanced out of the window to see that dawn had come. I looked this way and that along the street, trying to see one of the rare velvet men who passed through the town, but instead I saw a flash of colour, red as blood, vivid and unmistakeable at the edge of all that black and grey and white that was the winter park. I watched until the flash of red resolved into a woman in a scarlet cloak and hood. Then I realised it was not a hooded cloak but a wild mass of red hair. I could not see her face, for she looked down at a great shaggy beast that walked beside her. A dog it must be, yet my first impression had been that it was a bear. She went along the other side of the line of ghost trees and then passed out of view. I wrapped my shawl tighter and flew along to Rose's old room, which offered a view from one of its windows of the road and the nether end of the park, but there was no sign of the woman.

Deciding I had probably dreamed her, I returned to my room to bathe and dress and went down to breakfast. I had told cook not to come in early, for my stepfather ate almost nothing and I liked to break my fast very lightly and only when I was hungry.

But being awake so long had given me an appetite, and I decided to make pancakes the way they had been made in the country of my birth. Once the batter was resting, I melted butter and opened a bottle of preserved cherries. The smell of them was sweet and rich and red and made me think of Mama who had supervised the cooks as they boiled them in sugar syrup, sweat shining on her forehead and making little golden curls riot about her pink cheeks. She had sung as she worked, and I had sat listening to her, rocking Rose in her cradle and waiting for her to spoon a taste into my mouth.

The door bell rang and I heard my stepfather's voice. A few moments later he entered, accompanied by the policeman I had been thinking of earlier. He guided my stepfather gently, and nodded to me in his characteristic grave, courteous way. I dropped an awkward curtsey, conscious that I was red-faced with the heat and had a splodge of cherry juice on the bib of my apron.

'Inspector Grey has a question,' my stepfather said, then he sniffed the air and sorrow washed the slight colour from his face. His dark eyes clouded and he stooped, as if he were under an intolerable burden, and ran a long-fingered hand over his face and left it smudged with a bruise-like weariness.

'I have made pancakes for breakfast,' I stammered.

My stepfather flinched, as if I had tried to strike him a blow from behind, then he turned and made his way to the door, hands outstretched, saying not a word as he closed the door behind him.

'They smell very good,' said the policeman kindly.

'Would you like some? I am afraid I have made too much for one and I find that I have no appetite.' I gulped out the words, striving to control myself. Then I sank gracelessly into the chair my stepfather had grasped, my face streaming with tears.

'You must eat,' said the policeman. 'You must keep up your strength, for hope is the hardest work.'

'Hope?' I wondered incredulously if he mocked me. 'Hope will not save Rose.' Then I told him my dream, adding, 'So you see, it is a prince who is needed.'

'There is truth of a sort in dreams, and in tales as well, but when it comes to life, if there are no princes, well, we must make do,' said the policeman.

I looked at him, half marvelling. 'It is surprising to hear a policeman speak in such a poetic way,' I said.

'Perhaps it is not as uncommon as you think. We are men as well as policemen, and once we were children. A good policeman must keep his mind open.'

He began dishing out the pancakes efficiently, adding melted butter and warmed cherries, then pouring the coffee I had made into fine china mugs and fetching cream and sugar from the cool closet and pantry. Finally he brought us knives and forks. He seemed to have an unerring instinct for the whereabouts of things and he smiled a little when he caught the expression on my face. 'I do not have a wife and so I am accustomed to cook for myself. Contrary to popular belief, I am a man who likes to cook and all good cooks have similar habits. So as well as being a policeman and a man who was once a boy, I am also a cook.'

I said nothing, distracted by imagining him going to his solitary bachelor apartment or maybe to a small brown cottage where he would do his own laundry and cook for himself with only a servant to come in and clean for him, not because he lacked wealth, though that might also be true, but because he liked his solitude. He would read poetry, I decided, while he waited for his eggs to cook. But how did such a man fit into the philosophies of Bernice, Magda and Friday? Or mine, come to that?

He put a fork into my hand and began to eat his own pancakes, lifting his brows at the taste of the cherries. I told him that the recipe for preserving them had been Mama's and a secret she had guarded jealously, supervising the cook and undertaking the final part of the process herself.

'Your mother had many secrets,' he said.

I looked up into his grey eyes and thought that in a certain light they had the sheen of moonlit water. 'I can find out nothing about her before she married your father. I wrote to the country where you were born but the authorities can find no records of her birth. She must have come from somewhere else.'

I thought of the occasional foreign words and sentences she had uttered, usually under stress, and of her saying that among her people a girl became a woman at twenty. 'She never spoke of her past,' I said.

The policeman said nothing, but his eyes were searching.

'Mama loved Rose,' I said, and heard the defiance in my voice.

He put down his fork, looking genuinely surprised. 'How did you know I was wondering about that?'

I shrugged. 'Mama used to say I could see things no one else saw. When I was small she called me The Girl Who Could See the Wind.' I laughed sadly. 'It was Rose, really, who saw things about people, but she didn't see that Mama was afraid of the winter park . . .' I stopped.

'Did Rose see what you saw, in the park?' he asked carefully, treading the tightrope between accusing me of delusion and wanting to understand.

I did not answer.

'If your sister went into the park after something no one else could see, then it follows that a girl who can see the wind might be able to find clues hidden from the rest of us,' he said. 'Might even see what her sister saw.'

'I promised Mama I would never go into the park. She made me prick my finger with a needle and draw blood to make the swear.' I stopped, hearing how peculiar that sounded. But the policeman only carried his plate to the sink to rinse it.

'It was just a thought,' he said, and he bowed and thanked me for the pancakes before turning to the door.

'Inspector Grey,' I called. 'My stepfather said you had a question.'

'Ah,' the policeman said. 'As to that, you told me a while ago that your mother had sometimes seemed to fear for your safety, yet she did not exhibit the same fear for your sister. I merely wondered if you had any thoughts about what she feared.'

I shook my head and he nodded politely and let himself out.

After he had gone, I sat looking into my cherry-stained pancakes for a long time. Then I wept a few tears of confusion before pushing away my uneaten food and going back upstairs. Sitting in my window seat, I looked out at the park, now striped with sunlight. There was no sign of the woman in red.

Once I had heard the servants speak of the disappearance of Rose. One of the maids whispered that a gang of criminals had captured her, having struck Mama dead, but neither they nor the newspapers that later printed a similar story mentioned that there had been only two sets of footprints, both ending at my mother's body, which made it impossible for Rose to have been taken by kidnappers. Inspector Grey told me it had been decided to keep the footprints secret as a means of disqualifying the few madmen and women ready to confess to any crime, for while the coroner found Mama had died by misadventure, Rose's disappearance had given rise to a slew of lurid blackmail and kidnap theories that resulted in several confessional calls. I had asked if it would not be better to reveal the two sets of footprints ending at Mama's body, making it clear Rose could not have been kidnapped, but the inspector had explained that the callers would then advance occult theories instead. He had given me an odd look then, as if he expected me to offer my own theory, but I had none.

I looked out at the park and summoned up a picture in my mind of Rose holding Mama's hand as they walked home from the pantomime. She would have been chattering about the performance, no doubt asking questions that would have called from Mama the irritated little cough she always developed when she was asked too many questions. Eventually, she would have snapped at Rose, but then what? In some way that I could not conceive, Rose and Mama had gone into the park together or one after the other. It seemed most likely that Rose would have gone first, Mama following unwillingly. But what happened then to make Mama lie down, and what of Rose? Tests had shown that no footprints had been obscured, deliberately or by chance, nor had Rose's prints leading to the body been false. The evidence of the footprints showed quite clearly that mother and daughter had entered the park, whether alone or together, and that Mama had lain down of her own volition and died, though no one could determine the cause of death, since it had been a mild night and there was not a mark upon her.

Of cold, I thought, but what had become of Rose?

Nothing, my mind told me. She entered the winter park and she is still there.

Two days later, Inspector Grey called again and asked the servant who answered the door if I would come out to the yard to speak with him. It was odd that he did not come inside, but I took my parasol, for the sun blazed down, and went out. To my considerable surprise, the policeman was standing under the jacaranda tree with one of the velvet nomads.

'This is Nullah,' said Inspector Grey. 'He is a native tracker who works for us sometimes. I brought him to look at the place where your sister disappeared. I thought you would like to hear what he has to say.' He nodded at the velvet man, who was watching me closely.

'I am Willow,' I told him and I held out my hand.

Nullah took my hand in his own enormous warm grasp, and seemed to weigh it more than shake it. Then he smiled at me with the very same familiarity as the song walker in Dusty Town had done long ago. He released my hand, and said something to the inspector.

'He wants me to tell you he greets you as an equal and invites you to walk about the land with him,' said the policeman. 'It is an unusual compliment because Nullah is considered a leader among his people, a spirit guide.'

'Please ask him whether he saw anything that will help us find Rose.'

But the policeman shook his head. 'You misunderstand. I brought Nullah here to look at the footprints, but as soon as he set eyes on the park he stopped and said there was no point because the land there will not sing to him. He would have to learn to hear it and that would take many years.' The velvet man said something, and the policeman nodded and said, 'He asks now why I summoned him when I have you to guide me.'

'Tell him that he is mistaken about me. I am not a guide.'

The velvet man seemed to understand and shook his head. He spoke at length to the policeman, who asked several questions and was answered before turning back to me.

'He says the park is not part of his land. It is a place where another land is pushing through. He says he cannot walk there because he has no link to that place, but that you do. He says he can feel it.' The inspector shook his head, looking suddenly younger in his puzzlement. 'Maybe I am misinterpreting. Maybe he is just trying to tell me that he thinks you will be able to discover what happened to your sister.'

The velvet nomad spoke again, a few words, looking at me.

'He asks if you love your sister,' the policeman said, then he answered without waiting for me to speak. The nomad nodded, pointed to me and then pointed towards the park.

'I swore I would not go there,' I said, and heard fear in my voice.

The velvet man spoke again, his eyes holding mine. The policeman exchanged a few words with him and then said, 'He asked why your mother demanded such a promise. I told him that she feared for you, and he said that the mastering of fear is the first step a child must take away from its mother and father. He said if you are able to master your fear, he could teach you to hear the song of this land.'

'What do you want of me?' I asked the policeman.

He sighed. 'I did not know that Nullah would react as he did. I've never heard him talk this way before. To be honest, I wanted to see what you would make of his words, because he seems to see something in that park that I don't, just as you do.'

'You want me to go there,' I said dully. 'Perhaps I will disappear too. Then instead of solving one mystery, you will have another.'

'I will come too,' said the policeman. 'I will let no harm come to you.'

'How can you go there?'

'I will go with you. I need to understand what it is that this park meant to your family – at least to you and your mother and sister. Maybe then I can work out what happened to Rose.'

4.

I went to the kitchen and bade the cook prepare food for a journey, while the policeman took Nullah to the train station. I ordered a maid to find the trunk of winter clothes we had brought with us. Mine were too small, but I took out a heavy gown and a cloak of Mama's, as well as boots, muff and hat, weeping a little when I saw how well they fitted me. Upon his return, the inspector accepted one of the heavy coats that had belonged to my father, for Mama had kept these as well. How strange it was to see them inhabited again. I sat down to write a letter to my stepfather, explaining what I meant to do.

'Love will lead me to Rose or to death,' I wrote baldly, then I sent my love to my stepfather and signed my name, sealing the silky sheet of writing paper into an envelope upon which I wrote his name. I propped it alongside my stepfather's pipe stand so that he would find it when he reached for the pipe before supper that evening. He would have to summon a maid to read it to him.

I felt numb with fear of what I meant to do, but I was resolved. Suddenly it seemed to me that my whole life had been shaped in order that I might enter the winter park. The policeman was not forcing me; he was merely an instrument of fate. I felt the heat of the day beating on my back as we crossed from the apartment to the line of ghost trees, but the cold from the winter park raked my bare cheeks.

'Do you believe what Nullah said?' I asked the inspector when we stood at the edge of the park. 'Do you believe the park is not part of this land?'

'I believe this will bring us to the place where your mother's body was found,' he said.

I followed him through the ghost trees and the moment we were on the other side of them, the heat and noise of the town was cut off and a thick, soft silence fell about me. I looked at the police-man, but his expression had not changed so I knew he did not feel the cold as I felt it. Indeed, his forehead shone with perspiration, for he had no need of the coat he wore.

I looked down and saw two sets of footprints in the snow, one belonging to an adult and the other to a child. They were as fresh as if Mama and Rose had just walked there, and yet the policeman did not look at them. He was clearly finding his way by memory. I turned my attention back to the footprints that progressed side by side into the winter park, and knew that Rose had not come in first after all, nor Mama. They had walked side by side, almost keeping pace, save for the additional skip Rose had made every few steps to keep up. My heart ached at the memory of the jerk she had given my hand whenever she had executed that little skip. And then we were entering a clearing. I stopped, seeing the unmistakeable imprint of Mama's form.

I was not aware of having cried out, but the policeman looked at me sharply. 'What do you see?' he asked.

I pointed to the outline and for a fleeting moment I saw the red earth and the leaf litter among twisting tree roots that the policeman was seeing. I said, 'I can see the outline of where Mama lay, in the snow. I see Rose's footprints leading away!'

'In the snow,' he repeated. 'Can you see the two sets of foot-prints leading to where the body lay?'

I nodded. 'And I see Rose's footprints going away there.' I pointed deeper into the park.

'You can see her footprints in the snow?' he asked and I nodded. 'My people saw scuff marks and footprints in the dust when the body was first found, but those have long since faded.' He gave me a considering look and then pointed some way to the left of the prints. 'You see where the body lay there?'

'It was there,' I said, pointing to the depression in the snow. Then I saw the look on his face and realised he had been testing me. 'Did you think I would lie?' I asked.

He frowned. 'You would be surprised what people make themselves see when they are desperate. Let's find out where the prints lead.'

I did not move. 'I think if you and the others could not see Rose's footprints leading away from Mama's body, you won't be able to go with me if I follow them.'

He did not look at the ground but into my eyes. 'I see you,' he said. 'I will follow you.'

Very deliberately, he reached out and took my arm. I did not know if he was humouring me, but I was glad he was by my side. I took a deep breath and set off following Rose's footprints, comforted by the weight of his hand.

We had not gone far before it was clear she had walked an erratic zigzag path, which always seemed to change direction at the foot of a tree. Almost all of the trees about us now were pine trees or unfamiliar black-trunked skeletons with complex many-tined branches.

'Could she be playing a game?' said the policeman.

I shook my head. 'I think she is following something. A squirrel maybe.'

'A squirrel?' He shook his head. 'It's hard to imagine a child running after some small animal if her mother had just died.

Maybe your mother didn't lie down until after Rose left the clearing.

I said nothing. The policeman was still trying to fit what we were doing and learning here into his world, and yet he was with me as we went on, following the steps that continued their erratic progress until they came to a stream running black as ink through the whiteness. I stopped.

'The footsteps stop at the edge of the stream,' I said.

'There is a stream?' asked the policeman. He was gazing about in the same vague, groping way as my stepfather. I noticed that the sweat had dried on his forehead and he was holding the edges of the coat together.

'What do you see?' I asked him curiously.

'Only the mist,' he said.

I stared at him. Then I looked around at the glowing white snow, radiant in the sun whose light reached us but not its heat. The pine trees wore shapeless hoods of glistening snow, and the black-trunked trees were sugar frosted. The park ran away out of sight, still and snowy, seemingly empty of life. I could hear nothing save the trickle of the stream whose current must be swift enough to keep it from icing over, and the occasional creak of a branch or the huffing sigh of snow slipping to the ground. There was no birdcall, nor the chatter of squirrels foraging, nor the delicate nibbling of deer grazing. But I could hear the faint soughing made by the wind in the bare branches of the highest trees. I sniffed, but my nose was too cold to smell anything.

'I think,' the policeman said presently, 'that I can hear water, but it sounds far away.'

I said nothing, for I had remembered something. Once, when Rose had spoken of entering the park, she had mentioned a tower. I had taken no notice of it at the time, but I ought to have done, for Rose was not in the habit of inventing things. I concentrated upon the memory and it grew clearer.

'It is not so late,' Rose had said. 'By dusk we could be at the tower.'

'There is a tower,' I said. 'I can't see it, but I have just remembered that Rose once mentioned it. She wanted to go there.'

I began to walk, and the policeman followed, still holding my elbow.

We walked for several hours, always moving uphill and mostly in silence, then the policeman stopped. 'I still can't see snow, but my blood is turning to ice,' he said. He sounded shaken but not afraid. I reminded myself that he had summoned Nullah, which told me his mind was not limited by reason and logic; even so, I hesitated a moment before drawing my elbow from his grasp. He did not vanish as I had half expected. He slipped off the pack he carried and got out the thermos of hot chocolate that the cook had made. His hands shook as he poured it into the enamelled cups and I saw that his fingers were white as marble. When he drank, his teeth chattered a little against the rim of the mug.

'Why aren't you married?' I asked.

He smiled. 'I never married because as far as I could see, marriage was the end of the mystery of love. Or the beginning of the end. And I like mysteries.'

'But you are a policeman, so you must like solving mysteries, which ends them. That is a paradox.'

'I like paradoxes even better than mysteries,' he said.

We packed away the mugs and the thermos, then as we continued, he asked me to tell him exactly what Rose had said of the tower. Somehow he was able to be a policeman in the midst of all the strangeness he was encountering, or perhaps he became his policeman self in order to cope with it. Either way, I liked how seriously he asked questions and listened to my answers, never telling me this or that was impossible, and how he sometimes smiled reassuringly at me. I explained that Mama had often told me stories when I was a little girl, and that I had passed them on to Rose. 'Her stories were full of towers and princesses and princes.'

'And wicked witches?' he guessed.

I laughed a little. 'Of course! The witch was the most important character. It was she who gave something and then demanded a terrible price, or who was offended and cursed the hero or heroine or locked them up. Without the witch there would be no story.'

'Do you think this story has a witch?' he asked.

I frowned, sobering. 'I don't know . . .' I stopped, because the policeman was looking past me, his eyes widening with surprise. I turned to see that we had come to the top of the snowy incline we had been following. Now the land fell away sharply to a deep valley, which was white with snow at the upper edges but green and undulating at its base. Rising above one of the hills was a roof.

'The tower,' I said, my heart quickening.

But it was not a tower. An hour later, when we had got down into the valley, we saw that the steep-pitched roof we had seen belonged to a solitary little hovel, half built into a hill. It was sheer chance that we had been at the right angle to catch sight of it. We could see smoke drifting out of its crooked chimney.

'What should we do?' I asked, whispering.

'Knock at the door and ask for directions to the tower,' the policeman suggested. 'Unless you think it might be the witch's cottage.' He sounded almost giddy and I wondered if he was telling himself that he was dreaming. But when I looked at him properly, his eyes were alight with determination and curiosity.

We made our way to the cottage door and banged its heavy knocker. The door opened after a long moment, and a wizened little woman peeped out, squinting short-sightedly at us.

'We are seeking directions to the tower,' said the policeman courteously.

'I will ask my mistress,' offered the crone and hobbled away, leaving us standing on her doorstep.

'There is our witch,' he said.

'You must not joke,' I said sternly, for I had the idea it might be dangerous to disbelieve the story you were in.

'I have surrendered to mystery,' he said. 'That is when I began to see what you see.'

The old woman returned and bade us enter. We followed her down a dim, ornately carved corridor that seemed too long and grand to be contained by the little cottage. The policeman made a ghastly face at me as we entered and I had such an urge to pinch him in vexation that I was shocked. The hall brought us to a door where a carved fox leered at us, baring its teeth in a knowing smile. Then the door opened and though the room ought to be deep inside the hill against which the hut leaned its stolid rear, the first thing that met my eye was a large bay window with an arresting view of a forest that blazed with autumn colour. A fire crackling energetically on a wide hearth echoed the bright shades of the leaves, as did the red hair of the woman seated in a chair facing the fire.

'I saw you!' I blurted. 'You were walking on the edge of the park. You had a bear with you!'

'That was Godred. He has gone hunting but he will return before morning,' said the woman, who might have been five and thirty or fifty. The only certain thing about her face was its beauty. Even her expression was ambiguous: an enigmatic smile below piercing, almond-shaped green eyes and frowning brows.

'Who are you?' asked the policeman.

'You have the look and manners of an inquisitor,' the woman observed disapprovingly. She looked at me expectantly, and without thinking I curtseyed and spoke my name as I had been taught to do as a child. Indeed, though I was only days from becoming a woman, she made me feel a child.

She nodded her approval. 'You have pretty manners as well as a pretty face, I see. Well, Willow, I am Madame Torquemada. And you?' She turned her eyes to the policeman.

'I am Inspector Grey,' he said calmly. 'We have come to find a girl who was lost. She is the sister of this young lady.'

'I have never seen any young lady here who was lost,' said Madame Torquemada. 'Why don't you both sit down? I have asked Griselda to bring us some coffee and after that she will show you to your rooms. You can freshen yourselves before supper.'

'Our rooms?' I echoed.

She smiled, showing white even teeth and, despite her beauty, there seemed to me something dangerous in that baring of teeth. 'Night is coming, my dear child, and Godred is not the only thing that will hunt when the moon rises, nor is he the most dangerous. We will dine together tonight and we will talk, and then if you wish I will direct you to the tower.'

Questions bubbled up in my throat and pressed against my lips. Before I could speak, however, the policeman rested a warning hand on my wrist. We sat in silence until Griselda came in staggering under the weight of a great carved tray laden with a heavy silver coffee jug, delicate porcelain mugs, several plates of dainty sandwiches and tiny iced cakes. The policeman got up and took it from her, and she set about serving us. We had given our coats and boots to Griselda to hang in an alcove by the front door, yet the slightly old-fashioned winter gown I wore was still too hot, for the fire threw out a surprising heat. The policeman's cheeks were slightly flushed but he gave no other sign of discomfort as he sipped the delicious coffee, nor did he ask any questions, and when at last the old servant withdrew, Madame Torquemada gave him a faint smile.

'There is more to you than meets the eye,' she said. Without giving him the chance to respond, she swung her head and looked at me. 'So, you seek your sister, who is lost to you. Are you so certain she wants to be found? Young ladies often don't, you know.'

'My sister is a child and I love her,' I said. She lifted one brow as if to ask what that had to do with anything, so I added, 'I fear it is my fault she is here.'

She inclined her head. 'It is true you are the reason your sister is here, but it is not your fault. It is your mother's fault. She made a bargain with me, and then tried to cheat.'

'A . . . a bargain?' I stammered.

She nodded. 'She found a place where the curtain between our worlds was thin, and looked through – always a foolish thing to do, since of course one will inevitably see a mortal man and fall in love with him. Do not ask me why that is, but it always seems to work that way. It might even be that there is some law which governs such things.' She said this to herself rather school-marmishly and suddenly I noticed that her red tresses were shot with silver.

'You are the witch,' I said.

'Of course I am, child. What did you suppose? And no doubt in that childish world where you were born, all witches are wicked.'

'Most of them,' I admitted apologetically.

'Of course. And those who seek us out are always innocent, never foolish or avaricious or covetous. Pah! Your mother came and begged me to help her. She wanted me to open the way to the world she had seen, and she wanted the man she had seen to fall in love with her. I tried to reason with her. You have only seen him, I told her. He might be a fool or a boor, or cruel, or worst of all, dull. But no, she must have him and no other. And nothing would do but that he must fall in love the minute he sets eyes on her. Now why would any girl want a man whose love can be bought by nothing more wondrous than a pretty face and shapely form? But she would not listen, of course. The young are so conservative in their desires. It is the desires of the old that are marvellous and difficult, except for those fools who want only to be young again. Well, I tried to talk her out of it, but she would not be swayed, so still seeking to daunt her, I named such a high price I could not believe she would agree to it. Her immortality must be given up to open the way and her firstborn daughter must be surrendered to me before she became a woman, in payment for the charm to ensure the man would love her when he set eyes on her. She did not even try to bargain, the little fool. And having made the offer, I had no choice but to go ahead with it. There are rules that govern such bargains and even witches are subject to them.'

She looked out the window and, seeing that the sun had set over the autumn forest, she rang a bell at her elbow. Griselda came hobbling in to lead us to our chambers. I went meekly, bathed in the copper bowl of lukewarm water, then I donned the gown that had been laid out, a gorgeous dress of citrine silk that fell from my shoulders and brushed the floor. Griselda came to help me fix my hair and I let her do as she wished, gazing into the mirror and thinking that Rose had been taken by the witch instead of me, and somehow it must be put right.

When I was led to a vast dining room an hour or so later, the policeman was there alone, clad, to my surprise, in his own dark trousers and grey shirt. He stared at me and I felt the blood heat my cheeks.

'You look like a princess,' he said.

'Of course she is a princess,' said Madame Torquemada, entering resplendent in a gown of peacock purple and brilliant turquoise, though there was now a good deal more grey than red in her hair. 'So was her mother, for all her silliness and deceits. A faerie princess, I mean, as opposed to the princesses of your land. There, all young women are princesses, but here or there, only a few have what it takes to be queens.'

'A prince?' I asked rather stupidly, for I was somewhat confounded at being told I was a faerie princess.

'Growing up,' Madame Torquemada said tartly. 'Learning to think as well as feel. Girls who think are rare in any world.' She went to the long, polished, wooden dining table and waited pointedly until the policeman came to pull out her chair for her. Then he came to seat me, before taking the other chair. Only then did I notice there was a fourth setting. Was it for Griselda? Somehow I could not imagine the doddering old servant sitting down with us. Rose then? I felt a thrill of excitement at the thought.

'You were telling us about Willow's mother,' prompted the policeman, as he obeyed Madame Torquemada's instruction to fill our first glasses with a pale topaz-coloured wine. I noticed with slight dismay that there were five glasses before me, ranging from the small one we held now, to a very large balloon and ending in a tiny glass thimble. I sipped frugally at the light yellow wine, delighted at the flowery taste, but warning myself that I must not finish it.

The witch began her story again.

'Charledine was adamant, as I have said, and so I opened the way and she left with the love charm. I did not have to look to see if it worked. She wed your father and in due course she bore you. But then she discovered what all women learn who bear a child. She loved you. She had not bargained on that, else she might have barred her heart against you. Naturally she did not wish to give you up to me, especially after her husband died. You were yourself, but you were also all she had left of her prince, for of course all men who are loved are transformed into princes.'

The tale was interrupted again as Griselda came to serve the first course. It was a clear, delicious soup and I realised that I was hungry, for although we had drunk chocolate, we had not stopped to eat any of the picnic packed by the cook. The witch did not resume until the plates were cleared away, and the policeman had poured a glass apiece of the next bottle, a butterscotch-coloured wine with a tart bite that refreshed my mouth. It was so delicious I had trouble leaving even a little of it.

'The bargain was that Charledine must bring her firstborn daughter to me before she was grown, whereupon the way that had been opened would close and she would be left to live her mortal life. Of course I expected you would not be delivered to me until the very eve of womanhood so I did not think of the matter, save occasionally, when I looked into my scrying mirror to see how you were coming along. When I saw your father had died, I knew there would be trouble, and sure enough, your mother fled to the end of the earth, as far from the way I had opened as she could. Typical and pointless, for naturally there was magic even at the end of the earth. A very different order of magic, to be sure, than that of this world, but a power that a witch could use. When your mama realised it, she knew that it was only a matter of time before I opened another way to fetch you. There was no need to hurry, for you were still far from womanhood as we count it.'

Another course was served and eaten in silence but I had lost my appetite because I was beginning to see what was coming, and to dread it. A rich red wine was poured, and this time I drank it all.

The witch sipped her wine appreciatively, then went on. 'Charledine used a rather old-fashioned form of magic to summon a man who looked like your father, and she wed him and bore him a child. Of course, he was not a true prince because she did not truly love him. The child she conceived by him was named Rose. This daughter, also a firstborn child, she was careful not to love, for it was to be sacrificed in place of the daughter she had borne to her dead prince. She began to search for the gate that she knew I would construct, and when she found it, she influenced her husband to purchase an apartment beside it.

'Then, when Rose was old enough to walk and understand instructions, she brought her here and sent her to find me.'

'No,' I whispered. 'Mama couldn't have meant to sacrifice Rose . . .'

'She offered her to me, in settlement of our bargain. She realised I would know Rose was not her true firstborn, but she also knew how I would value the child's youth. And Rose fitted the bargain, being born of Charledine's blood and, if the meaning can be stretched a little, she was the true firstborn daughter of her father, if not her mother. So I accepted the child. Only later did I discover that I could not close the way I had opened because of the link of love that bound Rose to you. It was not the gauzy, inconsistent love of a princess for a prince, but the real, earthly love of one sister for another.

'So, I had no choice but to leave the way open, knowing that eventually you would be drawn through it. And now here you are. Willow and her protector and champion, the Inquisitor.'

'What happened to Willow's mother, Charledine?' asked the policeman.

The witch gave him a glimmering look, then she sighed and turned her gaze to me. 'Your mother did not tell Rose what was happening. She had prepared her in a way, by filling her head with stories of towers and princesses and sacrifice. She had told Rose that a special destiny awaited her. She was to go to faerie and there face a wicked witch, and of course there was to be a prince.

'But as she prepared to go, Rose turned back to her mother and said, "I love Willow and I don't mind. Will you tell her that?" And Charledine saw then that Rose knew everything. It was not her faerie blood but her innocence that made her so wise. Rose knew that she had been born to save you. If she had cursed your mother and wept and begged to be spared, Charledine would not have been moved, but Rose gave herself willingly, because of her love for you.

'I do not know what was in Charledine's heart after Rose left her. Perhaps, at the very last, she loved the child, or maybe Rose's words made her realise how you would feel when your beloved sister vanished, and she could not face it. She may even have feared that you would know what she had done, just as Rose did. Or maybe it is simply that, having freed you, she did not wish to go on without her prince, and so she lay down and gave up her spirit to the land.'

There was a long silence, and I felt the tears streaming down my face. I did not know if I wept more for my mother's betrayal and death or for Rose's sacrifice.

'And Rose?' asked the policeman.

But Griselda entered the room, this time with dessert. She put the small, eggshell-thin chocolate dishes of tiny forest strawberries in front of us, and I ate without tasting, certain the witch would say no more until the food was finished. Only as I put the last strawberry to my mouth did I notice the tips of my fingers were stained red. Something occurred to me. 'In stories, when you eat a person's food, you are in their power.' There was a dull accusation in my voice.

'My dear Willow, you were in my power from the moment you stepped into this land, for I am its queen,' said the witch. She sighed a little and made an impatient gesture for Griselda to clear the table. In her haste to obey, the old woman dropped several of the strawberries, which rolled under the table. Seeing the poor old thing's distress, I slipped from my seat to help her. When I put the berries into her gnarled hands, she gave me a toothless smile.

'Your sister was kind too,' she whispered, and scuttled out.

I turned to see Madame Torquemada watching me. She nodded. 'Your sister came here, of course. Godred led her here. He took her the long way, for the tests. Her visit to me was the next-to-last test, and in being kind to my dear faithful Griselda, Rose showed her sweetness of nature. There remains only one test and it is the most dangerous. If she succeeds in it, she will become queen in my place. If she fails, she will be eaten by a dragon.'

'I will take her place,' I said at once.

Madam Torquemada laughed. 'I have seen the passing of a thousand princesses and I have waited a thousand years for a worthy successor, though not always impatiently.' She gave a secretive and rather sensuous smile, and glanced at the empty setting. Then her expression became weary and I saw that the red in her hair was now a mere burnish of gold on silver. 'I will not release your sister, for none has ever come so close to winning my place.'

'What is the test?' asked the policeman.

The witch gave him her sharp-toothed smile. 'She must make the queen's choice, and not the choice of a princess.'

5.

The tower lay three hills further on from the hut, which had become a palace from the inside out, so that we only saw its true magnificence when we were departing. Madame Torquemada's hair had reddened again, and she rode elegantly side-saddle on a beautiful horse, white as sugar, which had taken a liking to the policeman and kept nibbling his ear. Once, it nipped him, drawing blood, but he only mopped it with his handkerchief, saying the love of a horse was a terrible thing. The witch laughed a good deal at that, for some obscure reason. She had offered us horses to ride as well, but I had never ridden and the policeman said he needed to walk off his dinner of the previous night.

So we walked alongside the slow, high-stepping horse, the policeman keeping a light hold of my arm, though he no longer needed it.

'I was wondering,' I said, when we stopped beside a stream

to let the horse drink, 'why Mama was so afraid to have me come here if you meant me no harm.'

'There are two parts to the answer,' said the witch queen. 'First, being a princess, Charledine did not ask herself what I meant to do with the child. She assumed the worst without even deciding what the worse would be. She was unable to imagine that I might have some less wicked purpose for the child than a mother who was prepared to give it up in order to ensure love at first sight. The second part to the answer is that of course I mean harm. Is not the bestowing of a world the greatest harm I could do to your sister? For I will be giving her pomp and ceremony and back-breaking, heart-wrenching, endless responsibility for all who dwell here, for all the princes and princesses who will see her as a witch just as they see me as a witch, and misjudge and malign and fear her. Indeed, you ought to wish she will fail her final test. It would be a kinder fate to be eaten by a dragon.' She glanced up at the sun and nodded. 'Let us make haste now, for we must reach the tower before he does.'

'He?' I echoed.

'The prince,' said the witch.

Less than an hour later, we came to the green slope facing the tower. The witch dismounted and commanded Griselda, who was travelling with us in a little trap pulled by a doe-eyed donkey, to climb down. I stood looking at the tower, which was a narrow grey tube of stone rising high to a needle-point shingled roof. There was no door and only a single window under the eave of the roof. Looking at the window, I thought I saw a flash of gold.

'Rose,' I murmured, and drew breath to shout, but the witch laid a hand on my arm.

'She will not hear you,' said a deep scratchy voice. I turned to find the great shaggy black bear I had seen with the witch. Godred apologised for his failure to return the previous night, saying things had taken longer than expected. I would have been frightened, but Godred had such a mild eye and a gentle manner that it was impossible to fear him. Besides all else, there was a good deal of grey about his muzzle and ears that made me realise he was quite old.

Madame Torquemada came to stand beside the bear, shading her eyes to look at the tower window, now where I saw clearly a white hand on the sill, and a skein of golden hair. 'The princess looks for her prince. And here he comes,' said the witch. She turned around. I turned too, and was stunned to see Silk hurrying across the hillside. His usual immaculate attire was shredded and his face scratched and bleeding. He carried a short sword in one hand and a mirror in the other, and, to my astonishment, my step-father came stumbling along beside him, leaning on his arm.

'Well, that is unexpected,' murmured the witch.

'Silk is not a prince,' I said.

'Not yet, but he has done better than any of the others, considering he came from the other world. And bringing the old man is very unexpected. Indeed, it makes me think he might even be worthy of her. Most young men can think only of possessing the princess. All of their sense and morality is contained within that quest, but not so this one. Of course he started out to rescue a child, but I made sure he learned she is no longer a child, for he must make his choices in the face of the knowledge that he is seeking a princess.'

'What has happened to him?' I asked.

The witch gave me a sharp-toothed, knowing smile that seemed to sneer at the secret fantasies I had once had of Silk. 'He looks a bit the worse for wear because of the tests. Godred said he did quite well. Just goes to show scholars are adaptable and intelligence serves as well as brawn,' said Madame Torquemada, looking with teasing fondness at the bear, who nodded sagely.

'He passed the last test only because of the old man's blindness,' said Godred.

'He sees her,' said the policeman as Silk ran past us, oblivious. His eyes were wild and passionate, but he stopped to help the older man when he stumbled. Then they were at the foot of the incline and he began to shout up to Rose.

'They always do that,' sighed Madame Torquemada. 'Why do they never imagine I might be close enough to hear and come gnashing my teeth to murder the pair of them?'

'She must have told him to be quiet,' said the policeman, for now Silk had ceased shouting and was trying to climb the tower.

'It's glass, of course,' murmured the witch.

Something was flung from the tower, a long golden rope of what looked like hair, that ran all the way down to Silk. He gave his sword to my stepfather and began to climb it.

'But Rose does not have so much hair!' I cried.

'Not when you saw her. She would have been, what? Eight or so then? But time here runs differently than in your world. After all, she would hardly have been a fitting prize for a prince if she was a little girl with no bosom to bury his face in. A bosom is essential to a prince. But that is the beauty of her coming to me bosomless, as it were, for it meant I had more time to train her and influence her. And of course to encourage her to grow her hair. I never spent so much time with the other princesses. Such is the sweetness of her nature that it was impossible not to love her and hope for her more than I hoped for all the others.' Madame Torquemada spoke without taking her eyes from the tower, riveted as the rest of us to Silk, slowly scaling the golden rope. 'It is hair woven with silk thread. She always had a way with the enchanted silkworms, but I am afraid her skills at weaving are never going to be more than merely adequate. Still, you can't have everything. The main thing is that it will hold his weight. Such a disappoint-ment if he plummets to his death now.'

Silk had managed to get himself halfway up the tower, and the rope was holding firm. I told myself that it would have given way by now if it was going to. But even if the rope held, Silk was clearly growing tired and I knew the rope must be burning and blistering his soft scholar's hands.

'That is the worst bit,' murmured Godred, and I noticed Madame Torquemada rest a hand on his neck.

'He's up,' said the policeman. 'But he left his sword on the ground and you can bet he will regret that.'

Madame Torquemada gave him a wicked look. Then she turned into a raven. One minute she was a striking, red-haired woman, and the next she was a gleaming black bird with blood-red eyes, launching itself into the air. I closed my mouth with difficulty.

'I always hate it when she does that,' grumbled Godred.

'It is disconcerting,' said the policeman.

'There she goes,' said Godred, as the raven swooped down through the window into the chamber.

'What will happen?' I asked the bear.

'It depends, but mostly it is about choices. And about sacrifice. And love, of course. Right now you can be sure that the young man can hardly think for drinking in the beauty of the princess, and she can hardly breathe for admiring his courage. It is all desperation and wonder.' Godred had been speaking more to himself than us and suddenly I had a revelation.

'Godred . . . are you . . . were you a prince?' I asked.

'Of course.' He gave a rumbling laugh. 'I completed the three tasks that allowed me to reach the tower, and I climbed it, though I did not forget my sword. Still, you can manage without it, I think. I figured out later how it could be done. This one is clever and he might think of it. The important thing is that he remembered the mirror.'

'The queen is being the witch now?' I guessed.

'The wicked witch,' specified Godred, tiny black eyes twinkling.

'But won't Rose recognise her as the one who trained her to be a princess?'

'To be honest, the queen looked rather like Griselda when your sister lived with her. Except she had a hump and a squint. I thought she was overdoing it having both, but she always likes to see if a princess will be repelled by ugliness. Yet she was not training your sister to be a princess, you see, she was training Rose to be good and clever and wise and strong and compassionate and tricky. She was training her to be a queen, just in case she passed the tests.'

'And she can't be a queen until she . . . what? Defeats the wicked witch?'

'That is how it seems,' said Godred. 'But the true test is what she will choose after the prince destroys the wicked witch. There is a final test for the prince too, of course.'

'I wish we could see.'

'We will. That is why we are waiting here. This is The Hill of True Love Declared.'

There was the sound of an explosion and we turned to see purple smoke puff from the tower, and several black feathers spiral down. A good deal of time passed suspensefully and then Silk was climbing down the golden rope and a young woman was climbing after him. I gaped, for it was clear that Rose was almost my age and no longer a little girl. As the couple reached the ground and embraced one another passionately, I saw that Rose had indeed inherited my mother's blazing, indomitable beauty.

'She is very lovely,' murmured the policeman thoughtfully.

This gave me a pang, but now they were coming up the hill towards my stepfather, none of them showing any sign of seeing us. They pulled poor Ernst to his feet and Rose embraced him and he wept and kissed her and laughed aloud. Then they came further up the slope and I saw how Silk gazed over the older man's head at Rose in astonished wonder. At the top of the hill, where the rest of us stood unnoticed, they stopped to let the older man rest and Rose and Silk drew a little apart. I took a step towards them.

'The strange thing is that I have been happy here,' said Rose. 'I learned so much about the forest and the animals, and about magic and herbs from my mother.'

'She was not your real mother,' said Silk.

Rose sighed. 'My real mother. It was hard to know she never loved me, but she never treated me ill, and there was always Willow. But I did not know what it was to be loved by a mother until old Agathe took me in. I think, in truth, that mothering is a thing you do rather than a thing you are. A woman may have a child, but that does not make her a mother.'

'You will be a true mother,' Silk said, and he gathered her into his arms and kissed her so passionately that my insides felt hot and molten. Then suddenly Silk fell back with a groan, and clutched his head. 'I forgot. The curse!'

'Perhaps it will not work,' said Rose.

'Somehow I think it will turn out to be very efficient,' Silk said with a little of the cool sense of humour that had made me nervous of him.

But Rose embraced him impulsively, and they kissed again. This kiss went on for a long time and there was more longing in it than passion.

'That's the best bit,' murmured Godred.

'I don't really understand what is going on,' I whispered, though clearly they could no more hear us than see us.

'The wicked witch cursed the princess to be a beast and the prince threw himself in the way. The curse is legendary and the only way to escape it is for him to go back where he came from,' Godred explained obligingly. 'If he was from this land, the prince would have to go back to his own kingdom and never leave it. The princess can go with him, but in order to do so, she must give up all of her powers. But the princess knows that in defeating the witch queen, she is supposed to take her place, and she cannot do that if she goes back with the prince to his own land. To have her prince, she must abandon all the people and creatures who have helped her and have come to count on her.' I was about to protest that Rose didn't have any powers, but of course she had been here long enough to learn a great number of things.

The kiss ended and the lovers gazed at one another.

'Here it comes,' said Godred, as the raven landed on his shoulder, unnoticed by the lovers.

Silk became a cat.

'I knew it,' croaked the raven. 'I knew there had to be cat in him, for him to have been so cool and clever.'

Rose was on her knees now, and weeping, and the cat was winding about her and butting its neat head against her forehead.

'You saved my life,' said Silk the cat.

'And you saved mine, but look what it has cost you. Oh Silk.'

'We can go back. If we hurry, we can get there before the way closes. Then I will be myself again and we can be married.'

'But . . .' Rose stopped, and I saw her realising all the things that Godred had said. 'I . . . promised to rule in her place. To be wise and good and . . . to be queen here.'

'You made the promise under duress,' said Silk. 'You didn't mean it.'

'I did mean it,' said Rose. 'Because without a queen this place will diminish. All the beauty and wonder that leaks out from it to enliven all the worlds would be lost. It can't be left to die for the sake of a love between two people, no matter how wonderful.' Her expression was anguished.

'I can't stay and be a beast,' Silk said.

Now it was Rose's turn to plead. 'It would not be all of the time. If you stay, we will be lovers when you are a man and friends and confidants when you are a beast.'

'I can't,' said Silk with finality, and then he turned his green eyes on her and said, 'What of your father? He can't stay here. And what of your sister? She thinks you are dead these many months. She sits in her window seat and looks endlessly at the park, and what will she do when it vanishes and takes her stepfather as well as her sister and mother, all swallowed up by mystery?'

'Clever cat,' hissed the raven.

Rose was silent for a long moment, and her face was white, but at last she shook her head and said, 'You must lead my father back and give Willow a message from me. She must know that I have never forgotten her and that I will always love her and think of her, and wish her happiness.'

'You have made up your mind?' asked the cat, coldly now.

Rose wept, but her voice was steady. 'I must stay. It is the right thing to do and I cannot do the wrong thing, not even for love, for how should love survive in the aftermath? Can't you understand?'

There was a long silence. Then the cat lost its rigidity. It sighed and came to wind about her, putting its small nose against hers. 'Of course I understand. But I . . . I cannot be an animal, Rose. Not when neither of us knows how much time I would be a man and how much a beast.'

'No,' Rose said, brushing away her tears. 'Of course you can't stay like this. Oh, this is such a cruel ending. I waited so long for you.'

'And I spent my life in reading books, dreaming of a world that was better than the one I inhabited. Sweeter and stronger and more pure. A world that wanted courage and daring and intelligence, a world of wonder. And here it is, but I never imagined that to remain in it I must become Puss in Boots.'

She gave a weepy laugh and cuddled the cat to her. Then she rose with Silk in her arms and taking hold of her father's arm she said, 'We have to go, before the gate closes.'

'A pity,' said the raven and became Madame Torquemada, clad in gleaming black, her hair a blaze of red fire. 'Well, at least he was kind in saying no. He did not blame her for her choice. He was truthful about his own reasons and this parting had sweetness enough in it to comfort them both in the days to come.'

'She to be a queen without love, then?' asked the policeman. 'That is a sad ending.'

The witch shrugged. 'Sometimes endings are sad, though I do not think Rose will live without love. There is too much of it in her not to draw it to her, and this is a world full of princes and heroes. But the cat man was her first love and there is only one of those,' said the queen. 'And now, I must see about my own ending.' She smiled at Godred, then she looked at me as if she had heard the questions surging in my mind. 'Princess Rose made a queen's choice when she decided to stay, for she understood that love cannot last if wrong is done in its name, that sometimes the cost of love is too great. But she cannot become Queen Rose until I am gone, for there can only be one queen here. Now let us make haste, for our lovers believe the gate will close at dusk and we must try to live up to their expectations. In truth, the gate will not close until I choose, but it will be best if your sister sees it close so that she will know the way is ever barred between her and her cat man. And all must be done before I abdicate and make your sister queen.'

We travelled back across the green hills and up into the snowy peaks, then Madame Torquemada summoned up a sled drawn by a pair of reindeer with bright yellow eyes and twelve enormous golden tines each.

'An ending should always have a flourish, I think,' she said as she climbed into the seat.

It was a thrilling ride that took us a different and much longer way than we had walked, and we saw many wonders. Once the queen indicated a distant spire and said this was the Palace of the Moon, where my sister would live. I realised, then, that this journey by sleigh was a gift from her to me, a way of showing me what my sister's life would be.

'This could have been yours to rule,' said the policeman.

'It is enchanting here, but I think that things have a way of working out as they were meant to. Rose will make a wonderful queen. I am only sorry that Silk did not choose to stay. I wonder if I would have had the courage to stay, too, if the man I loved had to go. Rose was always a better person than me.'

The old queen gave me a flashing look. 'I think you would have surprised yourself, though in truth, you are something more

complicated than a princess and I suspect you will have an interesting life back there in that other world, for it is no less complex
than this one, and no less magical, in its own way.'

Time passed. We stopped to eat at an inn amidst trees with
leaves of silver and gold and bronze, where jovial dwarves served
us green wine and a badger sang a song, but I was wondering
about time.

'I have made the way long enough that Rose and her prince
might have a little time to love before they part,' said the queen,
who had been growing gradually older as the long day unfolded.

'Liar! Romantic!' cackled Griselda who now seemed less
servant than crotchety old aunt to the queen. 'You hope he will
change his mind!'

The witch queen pretended not to hear.

When we set off again, it was only a little while before we saw
ahead of us the line of ghost trees that marked the border of the
world where I had been born. And there was Rose, alone alongside
one of the ghost trees, gazing across at our apartment. There was
no sign of Silk or my stepfather, and I realised they must already
have gone into the house. I saw her straighten her back slowly, and
then she moved away through the trees. I watched until she was
out of sight.

'Do not fear for your sister. Her life will be full and good
and she will be much loved and revered here. Your world would
have had little use for one whose goodness was so pure. I wish her
prince had stayed, but it is better that he went than stayed and
blamed her for it. And he would blame her, for he proved at the
last to be more a creature of thought than feeling. I should have

guessed it from the cat he became, for there is always a bit of them that remains aloof.'

'I don't really understand how Silk came into it,' I said, drying my eyes.

'Young men are often a good deal more than they seem to princesses and even to queens,' said the witch. 'He loved the goodness and sweetness of your sister before she became a woman, and there was a yearning in him that the world did not satisfy. Not for adventure or power or even for a princess, but for wonder. Then your letter summoned him home.' She smiled, and it was exactly the same smile that the velvet song walker had given to me, a smile of respect and familiarity. 'You showed all your faerie blood in writing that letter, for no words could have pierced him more deeply.'

'My words?' I echoed.

In answer she looked expectantly at me, and I remembered. I had written asking Silk to come home to stop his brother selling the apartment and putting my stepfather into an institution. I had told him that, although I knew it to be utterly irrational, I could not shake the idea that Rose might one day return, and should there not be someone who loved her waiting to greet her? 'Was not the greatest proof of love fidelity, even against all rationality?'

The witch laughed. 'He had given up on finding Rose, even though his heart told him she was not dead. But your words brought him back in all haste, and he found your stepfather weeping over the letter you had left him. Silk was galvanised and he decided he must follow you. Your stepfather insisted on coming too, and for a time it was truly the blind leading the blind. Well, you know the rest and my weariness grows heavy. I must go and prepare myself.

Griselda will help me and then I will lay my head in Godred's lap, and sleep. Fare you well, Willow. Do not let your mind or your heart limit you.'

She touched the lead reindeer and it and the other reindeer vanished along with the sleigh, leaving only the little trap and mule that Griselda had ridden in from the hut to the tower. The witch hobbled away arm in arm with Griselda, but the bear remained.

'You were her prince, weren't you?' I asked him gently.

He smiled. 'I am her prince. Unlike your sister's prince, I thought her worthy of any sacrifice. And in the end, it was no sacrifice at all.'

'Did you never regret being a bear?' I asked.

He gave a rumbling laugh. 'I am only a bear some of the time, and mostly by my own choosing, though there were times in my long life as consort to my queen when the beast in me caused the transformation at a time I did not wish it. Once I was a bear for a hundred years. I could be a man now, but somehow, at the end of it all, it is comforting to take this form. She could be a beautiful young woman if she chose, but it comforts her to allow herself to be old and bent and wrinkled.'

There was the sound of running footsteps and we turned to see Griselda returning, but transformed into a plump pretty girl with bouncing brown ringlets. I would not have known her save that she was bursting out of the dress she had worn before. Ignoring us, she ran to the soft grey mule that had pulled her trap, and when she stroked it, it became a stocky, beaming young man in rich clothes and golden boots. The pair embraced and ran off without a second look.

The bear shook his head. 'She always did like happy endings and it was a nice way to reward Griselda. After all this time, Prince Peter might have learned a little humility.' He sighed. 'I must go to her now, for we have a final journey to make together. And you had better go, unless you mean to stay, for the gateway will soon be closed.'

He gave a bearish bow and lumbered off.

I looked at the policeman, who said soberly, 'If you stayed there is bound to be a prince for you.'

'You heard the witch,' I answered. 'I am too complicated to be a proper princess.' He offered me his arm, and as we walked towards the ghost trees, I found myself wondering what beast lay inside him. A lone wolf, perhaps, something grey and reserved and very clever.

We stepped back into the real world where it was now a hot moonless night, and the policeman stopped and turned to look down at me. It was very dark but there was a faint luminescence from the ghost trees that let me see his expression. 'I never loved any woman because I wanted mystery and I thought love must be the end of mystery. But now it seems to me that love is a land in which things might be very different from the way they had seemed at first sight, and full of the unexpected. Not so much mysteries as paradoxes within which all the mysteries and contradictions between a man and woman may be contained. The right man and the right complicated woman.'

I opened my mouth to say that I was not a woman, and then I realised I was wrong. I smiled up at him, and said, 'Inspector Grey, remember the part that Godred said was the best bit of the story?'

He nodded, eyes glimmering. 'My name is Alasdair,' he said, and he kissed me for a long, lovely time.

Then it began to rain very hard. I gasped and as we turned to run across to the house, I thought I saw someone running past me. I stopped, squinting and blinking, and turned in time to see a cat, leaping into the dissolving park.

The Stranger

What is it about airports? Case thought. There was something almost mythical about the level of boredom and stagnation he felt, trapped in these mazes of shining glass and plastic laid out over acres of bilious-looking carpet. Yet in movies airports were always represented as glamorous, slightly dangerous places, where pursuit scenes erupted violently in the midst of all that coming and going, the protagonist racing along moving walkways waving a gun, elbowing extras aside as he pursued the plot. Someday he would write a script that captured it all, from the dewy awe you felt at first, primed by all those movies to see airports as portals to worlds of sophistication and mystery, to the disenchantment of the jaded frequent flier who knew an airport was no more than a tatty waiting room for journeys to the same end.

Yet despite all the travelling he had done, there were times when he still experienced a furtive stab of hope that this trip would take him somewhere he had never been before. That sly bit of hope was like the cat in a story he had once read that is always getting its master to open this door and that door during winter, but refusing to go out any of them to its master's baffled irritation. Then one day the master realises the cat is looking for the door to summer, and he keeps opening doors into winter.

He kept travelling, looking not for the door to summer, but for a gateway to somewhere or something that would stop him feeling like a stranger in his own life.

He pictured the scene: a cat stalking from door to door, tail in the air as its master turns one doorknob and then another. It would be a nice opening device for a movie without a linear structure. He imagined trying to pitch his airport movie to the money men and grimaced. Why were they always money men? Was it that women did not invest in movies? Maybe that was why the movie world was so full of men as boys. Was he a man or a boy, he wondered? Sometimes he felt as if he was some other category altogether.

Certainly he had not been man enough for his ex-wife, Stephanie. He sighed and looked at his watch without taking in the numbers. Then, as he habitually did, he thought about that as directions in a script.

Man checks time.

I am losing the plot, he thought.
What plot is that? he enquired of himself drily.

Man mutters to self, then smiles.

If life were a movie, his would be one of those European movies where everything took too long and even the smallest event was invested with a mysterious meaning that never divulged itself. Most people in the New World did not 'get' European movies because they saw them as metaphor. They could not imagine a level of alienation from other people so profound that almost no words or interaction were necessary or indeed possible. The first time he travelled to Europe, he had discovered that a lot of the things he regarded as metaphor were no more than simple descriptions of an unfamiliar reality. Like the way people in Russian novels lived, several different generations crammed into a two-room apartment with bookshelves and thin dividers set up to create an illusion of privacy. He had thought that a metaphor for emotional oppression, only to find that it was just how it had been behind the Iron Curtain during communism, or communism disguised as socialism, or state capitalism disguised as socialism. Privacy and space had been as unreachable as freedom.

His Czech friend Ivana had said languidly that in those times, entire sagas evolved around the attempt to get an apartment. People schemed and planned and paid bribes so they could leave home, where their grandparents, parents and siblings still lived together, sometimes even their in-laws. She herself had slept with the brother of a dead woman in order to get him to sublet his sister's squalid bedsit. It had been illegal, of course, in a place where, for a long time, almost everything anyone could want had been illegal. Her occupation of the apartment had lasted a year before the man had evicted her for fear of being reported. And that had been in the aftermath of the fall of communism. After the aftermath.

The thing was that people like Ivana had a reason for feeling disconnected from the people around them. But he had never been poor, or politically oppressed, or even in much physical discomfort. He had never experienced the extremes of fear or anger or sorrow. His childhood had been pleasant, and when his parents died he had felt sad rather than grief-stricken, before burying them and going on to live a pleasant, even rather lucky life. He had no excuse for feeling alienated.

He glanced around the airport, feeling weary and slightly dehydrated. But not suicidal. Not over an apartment or an airport or because of being left by his wife. Not even because he was living a life in which he had taken hundreds of trips without ever feeling he had arrived. Once, years ago, he had told a guy at a party that he had never contemplated committing suicide. The guy had looked at him incredulously. How could anyone see the state of the world and not feel like killing themselves? he asked. Obviously the man thought him shallow, and Case had felt disturbed in some way he could not articulate, but when he told the story to Ivana, she laughed uproariously.

'Petr is Hungarian! What can you expect? Hungarian is not a language in which to conduct normal conversations. It is a language only for suicide and poetry.'

Case had been fascinated by the idea of a language so tortured it could express only suicidal or poetic thoughts. He saw it as a poetic notion, until he overheard someone at a rap party say that the suicide rate among Hungarians was the fifth-highest in the world. That was the thing he liked about parties. The way you heard or misheard intriguing scraps. The way certain words got

stuck in your head; this piquant phrase or that evocative awkward-
ness. He loved conversation – not taking part in it but witnessing
it. Parties were perfect for that, because everyone wanted to talk
and no one listened. He could be a stranger among them, listening and taking mental notes, and no one cared. He saw himself as
a natural and instinctive witness of the world, which was perhaps
why he'd been so troubled by the comment that a person who truly
saw the world would be suicidal. Because Case felt like he saw far
more than people who were deeply engaged in life. It was only
that he did not feel suicide to be the natural or necessary consequence of his observations.

He thought of his ex-wife's disgust at his passivity, and
found himself looking at his watch. He did not want to know
the time; it was a pose he often struck in an airport. It's like I
am performing for an unseen audience, he thought. He often had
the feeling his life was some sort of performance. It even worked
as a metaphor. You came out of the darkness of the womb into
the limelight, and so began the performance that was life, which
invariably ended with the curtain falling. Curtains. The only bit
that really bothered him was the idea of coming to the end of the
performance, without ever knowing what it was for. Maybe that
was why he had so much trouble with endings in scripts. They felt
contrived, because life did not come with full stops. Everything
bled into everything else.

His problem with endings was why he had never made it to
the big time, despite all the young playwright prizes and grants
and the preliminary excitement of studios. He was known for
being a very good scriptwriter who had trouble ending his scripts,

to the frustration of his agent. Studios that took him on these days knew they would have to wait and wait and maybe call in another writer to finish his script or rewrite the end. The fact that he did not object to someone putting the tail on his script was why he was still working. The truth was that he was content for someone else to finish his stories.

'So what do you want, Case?' one of his tutors at the Binger had asked irritably a few months before in a coffee shop in Amsterdam, halfway through a three-month grant stay where he had been trying yet again to resolve the end of a script. 'You want to just go on and on and what? Bore the audience to death?' One woman in a session had said outright that maybe his inability to finish – to close – was tied up with his unresolved sexuality. He grimaced at the obvious circumlocution for 'his repressed homo-sexuality'. Well, it was Amsterdam where window-peeping was a tourist industry and you ordered grass off a menu after discussing it with the waiter. There had been a lot of talk about performance as exhibitionism and audience voyeurism. He had kept silent because, for him, any audience that would see the movie arising from his script was irrelevant. He did not think about other people when he wrote. For him writing was an articulation of his observations, and an attempt to lay them out in a way that would make some sense of the world. The reason he had never produced a play that satisfied him, despite the credits to his name, might be the same reason he had never found an ending that felt right.

There was an announcement and he freeze-framed to listen, but could not tell whether the disembodied announcement was in English or Greek or Esperanto, much less whether the speaker was male or female. Fortunately, he could see the departure boards from where he was sitting, and make out the destinations and gate numbers if he squinted. He was searching for the Aegean Airlines flight when a tall woman stopped in front of him, blocking his view.

She was wearing a perfectly fitted, perfectly pressed, parchment-coloured sleeveless suit and a panama hat of the sort that he associated with *Casablanca*, tilted very slightly over one eye. Her long, thin, bare arms hung loosely by her side, the slender fingers slightly furled. She wore no varnish on her short, square-cut nails, and she was carrying nothing. That struck him as unusual, because you never saw a woman without a bag of some kind, especially now bags were as big a status symbol as cars, some of them costing almost as much. The fabric of the woman's suit was so fine and smooth you could tell she did not have so much as a coin in a pocket. Was it possible she was carrying no more than her boarding pass and passport? She didn't even have a book. Could anyone travel that light?

He was interested in how, by simply standing so long with her back to him, she was building dramatic tension in him. It was not so much that he felt curiosity about her face, but the relaxed fluidity of her waiting roused his interest, for she would not stand so long merely to read something that was already there. Like him, she must be waiting for her gate number to be announced. But people did not normally wait without any sign of impatience. She did not fidget or adjust her clothes or shift her weight from one slender, booted foot to the other, nor did she look away from the board. Case had never seen anyone wait so compellingly.

How could anyone surrender with such grace to the necessity of waiting?

> *Woman in perfectly white silk suit and panama hat stands relaxed with her back to the camera as she studies departure boards. Camera watches her from point of view of man seated. She stands unmoving.*

Adequate lines, but how to recast them so that they would express the profound patience evoked by her stillness? Directions should evoke mood without wasting a word in explaining it. No adjectives. A film script like *Taxi Driver* was the perfect example of dynamic poetry – how a violent, dark, gritty movie could be expressed so lyrically as a script! He had no desire to write that sort of film, but he would have liked his scripts to have the spare beauty that arose from real precision.

Of course, most film moguls and agents would not even notice beauty in a script. Spectacular action and an accelerated plot were the qualities that sold a movie into the cinema chains. It was all about formula and box-office take during the first week. That's why the films being churned out were so bad. They were made to make money and that was the whole reason for their existence. No one making the movie pretended anything else. The incredible thing was that people kept going to see them.

He sighed, realising he was on the verge of an irritable inner diatribe of the sort that had irked him in his father when he was young. He had seen that edgy, impatient crabbiness settle into the lines in the faces of older people. It seemed to him that intolerance, rigidity and irritability were all signs of decay, and when he noticed the tendency in himself, first with wry amusement and then with distaste, he had vowed to guard against such rants because, aside from being a surrender to ageing, they formed a metaphorical cataract that clouded your vision. He had the feeling that ageing was not a matter of getting old physically, so much as accepting the habits of ageing.

'Maybe if we could be distracted from going through the motions of ageing we'd be immortal,' he muttered aloud.

The woman in the pale silk turned and looked at him.

Her eyes were pale blue diamonds and her hair was black and blunt-cut to jaw length with sharp wings that brushed her cheeks. Were there such things as blue diamonds, he wondered dazedly, unable to turn his eyes politely away. Common sense told him that she was too far away to have heard his soft words. But why would she look at him like that if she had not heard him? And even if she had heard, what had he said that had so caught her attention? Or was it merely that he had spoken in English or with an Australian accent? She was looking at him with an expression that might, in a face that lacked the strange blandness of extreme beauty, have been surprise. Her stare had the same quality of intensity as her waiting. That polar gaze was so compellingly focused that it was as if she reached across the distance separating them and touched one finger to his lips. Yet there was no intimacy in her look. She might have been studying a fascinating bug under a microscope.

She turned and walked away without haste, but she was gone from his sight in an instant. It was as if several frames had been cut from a reel of film. One minute she was walking away from him – gliding away, his mind insisted – then she was gone.

People do not vanish, he told himself, groping for balance, for her glance had been so heavy that its withdrawal had made him feel less substantial. He licked his lips and found them dry. You are half out of your head from lack of sleep, he told himself sternly. He was. He had flown non-stop from Australia to Athens, and right now it was about two in the afternoon in his head, even though it was only five in the morning in Greece. He would have got a later flight except there were only two airlines that went to Santorini, and the Olympic Airlines flight was in the evening, which would have meant hanging around all day. So he had opted for the Aegean flight, which had meant waiting four hours in transit.

He got up, slung his bag over his shoulder and strolled across to the duty-free shop, letting his eyes run over the displays: gleaming bottles of Chanel, of Glenfiddich whisky with black and gold labels, of dark red French wines, and then the stuffed children's toys, chocolates, books and more books – three for the price of two, two for the price of one. There were long lines of bestsellers from number ten to number one, with a disproportionate number about vampires. Ostensibly he was passing time but in fact he was looking for the woman. He wanted to see her again. Or, to be more exact, he wanted to feel the weight of her gaze. There was something about how it had made him feel that he needed to experience once more, in order to understand it. It was absurd, but the desire to find her kept pulsing though his mind so that even when his legs were tired he could not bring himself to sit down.

He forced himself to stop at last, only after he had twice all but accosted tall slender women. Somehow he had failed to notice that one had been close to sixty, with white hair, and the other a redhead in a grey trouser suit. All he had noticed was that both had exhibited an echo of the remoteness and stillness that he had sensed in the woman in the white suit.

Striving for humour, he reminded himself that obsession was when everyone started looking like the person you were searching for. But he was astonished by the strength of his desire to find the woman. He was struggling against the impulse to get up and go hunting again when he heard his name announced.

'Will passenger Casey Heath please come immediately to boarding gate six. This is a final call for Mr Casey Heath for A3 flight 54 to Santorini.'

He was shocked, because he had never heard his name announced at an airport before. He looked at his watch and saw he had fifteen minutes before the gate closed, but by the time he reached the final length of concourse, he was moving too fast and sweating heavily, his heart racing unpleasantly. He told himself to cool it. He did not normally get flustered. It was the woman.

Stepping onto one of the moving walkways, he imagined a tracking shot following him from one walkway to another until he reached his gate. He calmed down when he saw there were still people lined up. He concentrated on sliding his laptop out of his backpack before the security checkpoint, removing coat, belt and shoes in the prescribed order. Then he waited until the airport official waved him through the metal detector. It beeped as he passed through, and the official ran a portable detector over him before waving him on. He repacked his stuff, put on his shoes and passed into the waiting room where there were a few people still waiting to board.

It was only as he joined the queue that he noticed the woman in the white suit was standing at the front.

Seated on the plane as it taxied to the runway, he wondered what was the matter with him. It was not as if he had not seen his share of glowing people. The film industry was full of them. The truth was that what most people called beauty was so often really just youth and the health that naturally went with it, combined with regular features. That was why all gorgeous people looked more alike than ordinary people. On screen you had to find a way to contrast beauty, to surround it with ugliness and irregularity so that it would stand out. That was probably why, he suspected, beautiful people often chose plain or even ugly partners.

The woman had been beautiful in that same way, and yet her face had burned into his memory. It seemed to him that he could still see her when he blinked, like the afterimage of a firework. The detail of the memory was amazing. He could summon up the startling pallor of her skin, the slightly heavy, crow-black brows and lashes and the sharp angles of the framing hair. She had worn a maroon lipstick that was nearly black. His ex-wife had used a Chanel nail polish called *rouge noir*, the colour of this woman's lips. The eyes in a face like that ought to have been dark and lustrous, but instead they had been twin skylights.

He wondered, bewildered, if this was *l'amour à première vue*. Certainly he had never experienced such intense feelings before for a woman, not even for his ex-wife. But if this was love at first sight, it was not as he had imagined. His heart did not seize with a longing to possess her or even to know her. Indeed, his desire was not so much to see the woman, but to be seen by her.

Once the plane was in the air, he strolled up the aisle, ostensibly to stretch his legs, but he was looking for her. She must have been in the washroom, he thought, disappointed after having lapped the whole plane. Returning to his seat he told himself that he was acting like a schoolboy. He lay back and closed his eyes, but the noise of the plane seemed too loud and the vibrating of the armrest too insistent to allow him to sleep. Even the soft snore of the old Greek woman next to him was too loud. He was not usually so over-sensitive, and he pushed his thumbs against the bony roof of his eye sockets and then pressed the heels of his hands hard against his forehead to ease the stiffness in his neck and shoulders. To stop himself from getting up and searching the plane again, he tried scripting a meeting with the woman on Santorini. He sited the accidental meeting on a walkway so narrow that one of them had to back up.

Man: 'I am a stranger here.'

In his imagination, she did not answer. She only looked at him enigmatically. Maybe she was Greek? He didn't speak the language but surely he could find what he needed in a phrasebook. He thought of her face again and it struck him suddenly that she looked more Slavic than Greek. That white skin, the high almost prominent cheekbones and heavy brows, and the way her eyes narrowed at the outer corners. They were the sort of eyes his grandmother had called sideways tears. 'Never love a woman with eyes like that, for she will steal your soul,' she had once told him. He smiled, but a queer shiver went down his spine.

He thought of something one of the lecturers at the Binger had once said. There was only one basic dramatic circumstance. Someone wanted something very badly and was having trouble getting it. Before this moment, he had never wanted anything much, save to understand why he was the way he was. But now his desire to meet the woman filled his thoughts. He wanted to hear her voice and feel the chilly potency of her eyes on him.

He lapped the plane twice more before the seatbelt sign came on and the flight attendant shooed him back to his seat. Fastening his seatbelt, he wondered how it was possible that he had not set eyes on the woman. He had even, in some desperation, described her to a flight attendant, explaining that he thought he knew her and wished to say hello.

He made up his mind to get off the plane quickly so he could watch the other passengers disembark, but in the end he was trapped in his seat by the old woman sitting beside him, orthodox cross hanging golden on her chest, in no hurry to get up. As passenger after passenger filed past, she conducted a rapid and voluble conversation in Greek with the woman across the aisle. By the time Case managed to get out, most of the other passengers had already disembarked. Just the same, he waited, pretending to be adjusting the strap on his laptop bag, certain that the woman had not passed him, even though she was not among the remaining passengers. She must have been seated in first class.

He headed determinedly for the baggage carousel, passing smoothly through the passport checkpoint, but the woman was not among those collecting luggage. Taking his own bag, he headed out, imagining a scene in which she was being met by the blond guy who played Jason Bourne. What was his name? He frowned, hating not being able to remember an actor's name, but he had been having trouble with names lately. It was absurd, because he could remember that the guy had played in *Good Will Hunting*, and the two Bourne follow-ups, but not his name.

'Damn,' he muttered under his breath, because she was not in the arrivals hall.

He was met outside by the taxi driver he had booked, holding up a piece of paper with his name, and on the way up to the village of Firostefano, he had offered an extravagant but mostly incomprehensible travelogue in a combination of Greek and contorted but enthusiastic English. Case only half listened. He knew from his research that the village was on a steeper part of the island where dazzling white buildings capped rocky cliffs. The slope on one side was so steep that the roofs and terraces of one row of villas were level with the path leading to the doors and gates of the row of villas behind them. His villa had two terraces, one the roof of the outside bathroom and the other the roof of the second and detached bedroom, both offering stunning panoramic views of the caldera. It was this view that he saw from the side window as the taxi pulled up on the stony stretch of ground running from the front of a whitewashed church to the edge of a precipitous drop to the sea.

For a long moment, Case stared out across the satin sea to the distant horizon, seeing several small islands which, along with Santorini, were part of the rim of what had once been a huge volcano, while the caldera in their midst had once been the fiery cauldron atop the volcano. Now the sea filled the caldera, save for two small volcanic islands that rose up like jagged teeth.

'Caldera!' the taxi driver shouted, then tapped the front window of the taxi. Case looked obediently ahead and saw a line of whitewashed buildings on level ground broken by a narrow path. Gesticulating and talking in swift Greek and picturesque, fragmented English, the taxi driver went on until Case understood that the villa he had rented was to be found along this path, but that the taxi was too wide to take him further. He paid the driver and received a set of keys with the name of the villa on the tag, before the yellow Mercedes rattled away. Turning to face the view, he picked up his bag and walked towards the low stone wall that ran along the edge of the drop. The view from it was impressive, and yet it was so exactly the same view as he had seen on hundreds of postcards and coffee-table books that it was impossible to be properly impressed. What drew him to the edge was not the view, but the tall, ragged gumtrees flanking it.

The smell of eucalyptus was sharply – almost unbearably – familiar as he came to the wall, and he was filled with a fierce nostalgia that bewildered him with its intensity, for how could he experience such longing for a place to which he had only ever felt himself mildly attached? Sitting on the top of the wall, he felt as if he had never truly smelled gumtrees before, and he sat half dumbfounded until the sun had risen well above the horizon, stealing the last soft trace of dampness from the air.

Simple thirst made him stir, and as he picked up his bag and turned his back on the view, he saw the church. He had noticed it vaguely when the taxi pulled up from the steep street leading into the square, but now he saw that it was a small, whitewashed building with stained-glass windows set either side of an unusually wide timber door protected by a gilt metal security gate. The gate was locked, but the door was very slightly ajar. The ambiguity of a church that was both shut and open drew him closer, and he put his bag down and reached through the gap between the bars to push his fingertips against the door. It was very heavy and pitted with age. Indeed the door seemed older by far than the church, but beyond it he saw nothing but impenetrable darkness. Turning back to the path, he wondered what he had expected to see, and then his mind swerved convulsively back to the woman in the white suit, as he wondered where she was staying.

Dimly he noticed he had not thought of her since smelling the gumtrees, and recognised that both the woman and the gumtrees had evoked a level of feeling in him unusual enough to make him wonder if he was becoming ill. Some kinds of fever made you extremely vulnerable to sensation.

He followed the path through the oblique walls of whitewashed buildings until he came to a shop, its window crowded with groceries too mysterious and foreign to be appealing. Soon after, just as he had been told, there were steep steps leading down from the path. The name of the villa had been painted onto the wall alongside the steps, with a small arrow pointing down. He knew that the first path to the left leading away from the steps would bring him to the gated wall beyond which lay his villa.

Descending the steps, he found himself facing another dizzying view of the caldera, and that was when he heard, for the first time, the deep mournful call of a cruise ship coming to dock.

He had been told when he had first conceived of coming to Santorini that the tourist season finished at the end of August, and by the second week in September there would be almost no tourists staying on the island. But most restaurants and shops would remain open for the month of September and even some of October, because of the tour ships. These leviathans would continue to glide across the caldera and dock at the island until late in the month, because if weather was inclement they could merely adjust their course and stop elsewhere. An amount of uncertainty was, he had vaguely supposed, part of the romance of a sea journey. Unpacking his few clothes that first day in the slightly dank coolness of the main bedroom of the villa, built into the hill like many dwellings on that steep slope, he thought about the possibility of a conference. There had been so many people on the plane, and companies did stage such events in lavish locations as a perk. Except that none of the passengers on the plane had looked like delegates bound for a conference. The woman in the white suit had been the only person who had dressed well enough; the rest had been utterly nondescript. In fact, now that he thought about it, he did not think he had ever been on a plane with so many unremarkable people. He could not remember a single face. That in itself was remarkable.

His thoughts returned to the woman as he removed his clothes to sleep off his jetlag, having set his alarm for early evening. He had given himself time enough for a shower before heading out for dinner. He would walk around the area and maybe see the woman dining somewhere. He drifted to the edge of sleep and hovered there.

He dreamed of his ex-wife.

'I love you,' he had told her, when she announced she wanted a divorce.

'You don't listen. You don't hear. How can you love? Half the time you don't even see me. You're like one of those people at a party who spends the whole time they're talking to you looking over your shoulder waiting for someone else to come in. You've spent all of the time we have had together keeping most of yourself in reserve, and for what? For who?'

'There is no one else!'

She had laughed scornfully. 'I'm not accusing you of infidelity or having a roving eye, for Christ's sake! I'm telling you that you live like you're in a waiting room. You treat me like I am someone else in that waiting room.'

The dream changed and he saw again the woman in white, standing with her back to him for a long time, and at last, she was turning to him. Her pale eyes stabbed him and he gasped, for the pain defined him and gave him substance.

'You looked at me,' he whispered, and somehow the words were not absurd.

'I had to be sure,' she said. 'You would not have known I looked at you, unless you were the one. You would have been blind to me, like all the rest.'

'Who are you?' he asked, feeling this dream was too real to be a dream.

The dream changed again and he was moving towards the

white church with its strangely wide door, slightly ajar. It was not day now, but deep night, and when he touched the gate, instead of being locked, it swung open. A stinging joy rose up in him as he pushed the heavy door. It opened, and a wave of darkness flowed out at him.

He woke to his alarm, the smell of eucalyptus in his nostrils.

On his first full day on Santorini, he went for a long walk. He had decided to allow himself three days of being a tourist, not wanting to begin work when he was jetlagged. He also wanted some of the place to seep into him. All the research in the world could not tell you how it felt to be in a place, after all. But instead of unwinding or thinking about his work, he spent the whole day looking for the woman.

He walked to most of the tourist destinations and even took a trip to Ancient Thera. Every wide-brimmed hat or tall woman or woman in a suit or woman with short dark hair jolted his pulse. He could not sit more than a short time in a restaurant without feeling that this was the moment when, if he were walking the streets, he would encounter her.

That night, again he dreamed of her, turning to look at him, but now they were somewhere dark and cold, and the smell of earth and stone was strong about them. She held a candle, and instead of a white suit she wore a black robe.

'You looked at me,' he said again.

'I had to be sure before I could tell the others,' she said.

'Others?'

'We are the Undimmed,' she said. 'Come to us.'

He woke again to the alarm and the scent of eucalyptus, determined to find the woman and speak to her. He told himself it was the only way to defuse his growing obsession, but as he walked through the day, the dream still whispered, *Come to us.*

He did not see her, and that night, he dreamed of the church facing the caldera.

The third and fourth days were the same as the first and second, but although the weather continued bright and hot the wind grew stronger, and at night in the restaurants, the blue and white table-cloths had to be pegged to prevent them flying away. There was a chill in the air which reminded him that summer had ended.

It was the seventh day before common sense forced him to accept that the woman had probably left the island. Few people would stay on a place like Santorini as long as he intended to remain. Even in the week he had been there, the number of people in restaurants in the evenings had dropped steadily, with a corresponding rise in friendliness on the part of waiters. No longer run off their feet by the tourist hordes of mid-season, they were pleased to stop and talk, happy to answer questions, especially after he bought them a Metaxa or two.

He played his usual role in these moments, asking them about themselves and their lives, listening intently, because he was genuinely interested, so that they failed to notice he had told them nothing about himself. But no one had seen the woman in white, and no matter how circuitously he brought up the question, Case got the same response: a frown, a slight look of confusion and then a shrug or shake of the head. Some would suggest she must have left on a tour ship. That did occasionally happen when a person was rich enough to pay the exorbitant price of a ticket and set off on such a journey on a whim. It was possible, for each day new tour ships came, and the town would fill up from midmorning till evening, then the liner would sound its mournful call, and gradually the shops and restaurants and streets would empty out as the visitors returned to their ship.

It was the second day of the second week, and late afternoon when he was returning from an early meal through the empty streets to the villa. He was walking across the open ground before the church and there was a strong wind. He was so busy leaning into it that he was almost on top of an old woman in black before he noticed her, standing in the centre of the stony square and looking at the church. He glanced at the church, too, and found it was stained red by the sunset. Its gate was closed, and the heavy timber door behind it as well, as on every occasion he had passed by since that first morning. He felt the eyes of the old woman on him and on impulse he turned to speak to her. She watched him come closer with black eyes set in a nest of wrinkles so thick that they hid the whites of her eyes. Her knotty fingers were working a rosary and the cross swinging from it was polished gilt and flashed sharply when it moved from her shadow into the bloody blaze of light from the dusky sky. Case asked her in a mixture of Greek and English, pointing to the church and himself, when it was open, but he might have been a stone for all she reacted. She simply went on watching him with her shiny black eyes, her sunken mouth moving slightly as if she were chewing something.

He found himself looking down at the swinging cross, flinching at the stab of red light flaring from it. Backing away from the
old woman, who shook her head slightly at him, he continued to
the villa on unsteady legs. That night, he drank a bottle of Boutári
wine someone had left, and slept very heavily, not waking until
midday the following day. He felt weary. He had dreamed all
night, and yet he could remember none of it save a fleeting image
of the woman in black, only instead of a swinging cross flashing
with reflected sunlight, there had been a small golden knife.

He had planned to begin work that day, but having wasted
part of the morning anyway, he decided to take a boat tour to
the larger of the volcanic islands in the caldera, telling himself
the opportunity would not exist once the weather turned. He had
bought an open ticket the first day and so he had only to take the
funicular straight down to the pier, and wander along it until he
found the right boat. Case did not admit to himself his hope that
he would see the woman, until he saw the boat and the family
group who were the only other passengers. Then he realised he
had been a fool. A woman who could wait like that and look at a
man like that was not the sort to take cheap daytrips.

This has to be the end of it, he told himself sternly, and as a
punishment, he climbed aboard the boat after handing over his
ticket to the swarthy man at the little gangway, and sat down
heavily on a pitted bench.

The boat had not long cast off when the matron in the group,
a plump, pleasant-faced woman with abundant freckles, leaned
over to speak to him. He assumed she was asking his name, or
where he was from. Or maybe she was merely asking how long

the tour would take, but he did not understand her. She was speaking English and he recognised the individual words she was saying, yet he could not make out what she was saying. This was so peculiar that he simply stared at her stupidly, wondering if he was the butt of some sort of joke. The woman was clearly taken aback by his response, and repeated herself. Again he did not understand what she was saying, but he forced a smile and a noncommittal shrug because he was afraid that if he spoke to her, she would hear gibberish, or some sort of animal noises. The woman's smile vanished, for of course she had seen him address the boat attendant in English.

When they came to the larger of the volcanic islands, he took the option of walking up the hill from the beach to the top of the island in order to escape conversation with the other passengers. They were already changing into bathing clothes when he set off, removing his jacket and rolling up his sleeves. He was accustomed to feeling a stranger even among people he knew, but he had always been able to pass as normal. On the stony ascent, however, he wondered if what had just happened meant he was degenerating; becoming more and more of a stranger was really only another way of becoming mad.

It was a steep, surprisingly hot walk to the top of the island, though the day was cooler than the preceding days. Several small fumaroles on the way confirmed this was not an extinct volcano. He ought to have felt afraid, he supposed, but he was preoccupied by what had happened on the boat. His mind swayed like the old woman's crucifix. He was careful on the return journey to the island not to meet the eyes of the other passengers, and he disembarked with no more than a brusque nod to the captain and crew.

It was just before dusk and he decided to eat dinner earlier rather than return to the villa and come out later, for he had been told that none of the restaurants remained open after dark. He chose an empty restaurant he had eaten in before, and tensed when the waiter approached and spoke to him in careful English, clearly remembering him. Relieved to understand the boy, he asked for a glass of wine. The waiter frowned and leaned closer, his expression puzzled.

'Excuse?' he said.

Case licked his lips and pointed to a wine bottle on the drinks menu, then indicated the Kleftiko on the food menu. The waiter looked confused and slightly sullen, but he collected both menus and sauntered away to fulfil his duty. Case sat there feeling shaken to his bones by the realisation that the boy had been unable to understand him.

Man in restaurant looks at hands. They are trembling.

There was a stiff breeze blowing as he left the restaurant, and by the time he walked the forty minutes to the villa, the sun had set and it was cold. He was shivering and his face tingled as if he were sunburnt. The air was clammy in the room, and the smell of the earth seemed to press on him from all sides. He had intended to shower, but he was too cold. He piled blankets on the bed and forced himself to drink some tea, reassured by the sudden certainty that he was ill. Wasn't it possible he had been getting sick when he left Australia? The long plane trip always exacerbated any incubating illness, and it would explain his delirium.

Under a mound of blankets, he fell asleep and into a dream of walking up the stony slope to the top of the volcano. The sky was a bleared red and sulphur hung in the air, burning his nostrils and throat and making his eyes water. The heat was terrific yet he was shivering with cold because he was naked save for his shoes. This did not strike him as incongruous so much as inconvenient. He hoped he would not slip and graze himself on the black rocks. When he reached the top of the slope he saw that there was a swirl of magma turning in a slow spiral in the upturned bowl that was the top of the volcano. The woman in white stood there with her back to him, gazing into the fire. Instead of a suit, she wore a robe of cream wool with a long, pointed hood falling down the centre of her elegant back, but he knew her stillness. After a long while, she turned to look at him, and her eyes were a cool touch on his fevered brow.

'We have been waiting for you,' she said. Her voice was soft and deeply accented, and although the words were not English, he understood them. 'We live among you, but we are no longer seen by you.' She smiled and he saw that her teeth were small and sharp and very white as they pressed against the scarlet plush of her lower lip. 'All that you know of us are dark myths and distorted tales of long ago, when we were young and savage because we were too close to human.'

'I don't understand,' he murmured.

'You are the one and the way,' she said, and there was reverence and a profound formality in the words and her speaking of them that made him know they were ancient words of ritual.

'The way to what?' he asked, marvelling that such a fantasti-
cal conversation on the edge of a volcano in a dream could feel
more real than all of the conversations he had heard and taken
part in during his life.

But he saw that he should have no more answer than that.

He woke suddenly to impenetrable darkness, with the feeling that
someone had called his name. He sat up and turned on the bedside
light. He rubbed his face. It felt stiff and sore and he cursed himself
for failing to think of sunscreen, especially given the country he
came from.

He would have gone back to sleep but he was terribly thirsty.
He realised that he no longer felt ill. The fever, if that's what it was,
had broken. His skin felt sticky with sweat, and he was repulsed
at the thought of returning to the tumble of stale bedding. He
rose and went to sit in a creaking wicker chair, drinking the water
slowly. He finished the glass and poured himself another water,
drank it off, then walked to the door and opened it. Moonlight
flooded down into the yard and the bent olive tree was limned
silver. As he stood there, soaking up the eldritch beauty of the
little scene, he heard the woody pop of a falling olive.

The wind had dropped. He dressed and went up onto the
terrace overlooking the sea. The view was bathed in the blaze of
light falling from a full moon.

He recalled the sentence, all those years back, in a musty
yellow guidebook to Greece he had found in the attic of his parents'

house. That weird, inexplicable sentence had been the seed for the script that had ultimately brought him to Santorini.

'. . . bringing vampires to Santorini is as bringing coals to Newcastle . . .'

'But what has Santorini to do with vampires?' asked his agent impatiently, after reading a draft. 'I have never heard anything about vampires in Greece.'

'I know,' Case had told her eagerly. 'That's what struck me. It was such a strange thing to write, and I started wondering what would cause vampires to go there.'

'But you don't tell us in this,' she'd said, shaking the script. 'It's not finished.'

He rose and went down to put on his sandals and a coat, and walked out onto the path and up the steps. Despite the chill of the night, he could feel the heat of the day through the soles of his sandals.

He remembered the way the old woman had shaken her head at him, and then as he was coming to the square where he had seen her. He drew a startled breath because he saw that the gate and the wooden door to the church were now wide open, and there were people inside. There were others arriving, wrapped in cloaks and gliding across the moonlit ground. He was standing in the shadows at the end of the path, his heart beating very fast.

Then he saw her sitting on the low stone wall under the eucalyptus trees, the woman in white. She now wore a long white coat belted at the waist and a scarf tied over her black hair. She beckoned to him, and even from so far away, he felt her eyes on his hot, tight skin. He sighed and moved towards her, hardly aware of his own will. As he approached, the night perfume of eucalyptus filled the air and he breathed it in, relishing the pungency of it.

She held out her hand to him, and when he took it, expecting her to draw him down beside her, she rose to look into his eyes.

'I dreamed of you,' he said. Some of the cloaked figures gliding into the church glanced over as if they heard his soft words, but he could not see their faces or expressions.

'A seed was planted,' she said. 'Many seeds were planted, but only one will summon the stranger who will be the way and the gate.'

A shiver ran through Case. 'What will happen to me?'

'Once our kind was closer to humanity, but we are immortal and in all the long years began to diverge. We learned how to do without blood, and to live unnoticed among humanity. We became the guardians of humanity, but as we continue to live, so we continue to diverge, and humanity becomes ever more alien to us. Once a century, a human is consumed so that we may understand humanity well enough to care what becomes of it. That human is the stranger who, once consumed, is known, and through that one, all humanity.'

'I am the stranger?' he asked, but he knew. Here was the answer to his long searching and all of his journeys. He had been a witness all his life, and here at last was his audience. An ecstasy of terror and exaltation welled up in him.

'Come,' she said. 'They are waiting.' She took his hand and

led him across the stony yard towards the church, where he could see people sitting facing the altar.

'A church?' he murmured, thinking of all the stories he had researched of vampires being repelled by crosses and holy water.

'Where else do immortals belong but in a house built for an immortal who was killed by humans,' said the woman, 'an immortal whose blood is symbolically drunk again and again?'

His mouth was dry as she brought him into the church and to the front, where a man stood, facing the altar. He had the same quality of stillness as the woman, before he turned to face them.

'I am Gabriel,' said the man, and his eyes were the same pale, dazzling blue as the woman's.

'Are you an angel?' asked Case.

'I am as an angel,' answered Gabriel. 'And now, you must choose.'

'Choose?' asked Case. His lips felt stiff and cold.

'What we would have of you is a gift and it is yours alone to give. But this is a dark gifting, for it will end the life of the giver. I think you have guessed that. And so now, you must decide if you can give.'

'There were others?' Case said, after what seemed a long time.

The figure nodded. 'There were, and in each case, they gave their gift freely.'

'If I decide I don't want to die . . .'

'You will leave this place unharmed,' said Gabriel. 'You will never see any of us again. You will not be hunted. Think on it, but you must decide before dawn, and that is near.'

Case blinked rapidly, and felt a strange desire to weep. He turned to a looming marble statue of a saint at whose feet lay a sheaf of flowers. The scent was heavy and sickening. Case realised that he was terribly frightened, but he also felt that he had been waiting his whole life for this moment, even if he had not known it consciously. And if he turned from it, what was he to do with what remained of his life? Would he go mad looking for pale eyes to make him feel real?

'Have you made your decision?' asked Gabriel gently.

Case looked at him, realising there was no choice. Not really. That must have been what the others like him had understood. His life for the future of humankind. It was an exchange any fool could understand. And wasn't this the moment towards which he had been travelling, all unknowing, all these long years? Wasn't this the consummation he had been seeking in all those script endings he had tried to write?

He did not need to tell the immortal his decision. He saw comprehension in those clear, blue eyes. He did not know what he expected, but Gabriel nodded and the rows of seated, cloaked people rose with a soft collective movement and gooseflesh broke out on his neck as the woman in white stepped forward and laid back his collar to bare his neck.

He saw through the open door of the church that the sun was beginning to rise. A fiery crimson light lanced across the sea and in through the door to strike knives of light from every shining surface. Gabriel moved forward, bathed in red, darkness fluttering at his back in great shadowy wings. He laid his long, cold hands on Case's shoulders. His eyes were a blaze of pale light, and

Case closed his own eyes. Then he felt the lips of the immortal against his throat. For a moment, he thought that there would be only this kiss, and death, but not all of the old dark stories were false, for he felt the sharp teeth as they punctured his skin and the pain was so intense that he had to clench his teeth to prevent himself crying out. Then the immortal began to draw his life from him, and there was a terrible dragging anguish as if his heart were being torn out. The light of the dawn grew so that he could see the redness through his eyelids. The hands released him, and other hands clasped him, and again he felt the teeth in his throat. All of them, he thought. They will feed on me, and he screamed and felt himself falling away from the sound into the hot burning heart of the volcano.

His last living dream was of the moonlit gumtrees, their sharp scent piercing the alien air.

The end, he thought.

'Wake,' said a voice.

He opened his eyes. He was outside and it was morning. The woman in white was bending over him, and for the first time, he saw that she was little more than a girl with light, bright eyes.

His throat felt sore but when he lifted his hand to the place where they had bitten him, he could feel that his skin was smooth and unbroken.

'Our kind heals swiftly,' she said.

'Our kind?' he asked.

'You gave your life to bestow the gift of your knowledge. But you were bitten thrice. Once is for the death of a mortal, twice is for the release of the spirit, and thrice is for the birth of an immortal.' A tear fell down her cheek and onto his and he touched it wonderingly. She said, 'I weep for the human who gave his life for his people. But I rejoice, too, for you are the first new immortal in a century, as I was the first in the last. That is why I was sent.'

He stared at her, and saw the diamond blue of his own eyes reflected in hers. He said, 'I thought that was the end.'

'It was the end of endings,' she said, and she held out her hand to him, and he took it, immortal to immortal.

The Wolf Prince
for Heather

My son howls.

Hearing it, I start to my feet, the weight of the tapestry I have been working on pulling it from my fingers.

Cloud-Marie gargles thickly in dismay and begins to gather the fabric up from the floor. It is densely embroidered and difficult to handle. When she has managed to heave it onto the rack, she turns her big pale face to me and I wonder if she heard what I heard. One of her eyes regards me with great intensity while the other turns slowly away. I have always seen the drift of that wayward eye as an omen, and more than one decision has been dictated by its movement.

I think of the colour of the sky when I woke this morning: bruise-coloured with tinges of unhealthy yellow; an autumn sky. It used to be my favourite season. I loved the way the thick light soaked any wall in a slow buttery radiance, the rustling susurrus of dried brown leaves sliding along the pavement. Now it seems to me a season of fading sorrow.

It was the very end of autumn when first I came to that city which is the gateway to this place. I had a practical reason for my journey, but my true reason was something less rational, less definable and all but hidden from myself. Simply put, the city had seemed to suggest something that stirred my deepest longings. I do not doubt many people who visit it are drawn by the wonder of an impossible idea translated into a real and miraculously beautiful city.

Yet few who travel to that city, which is fantasy made real, discover that it is the gateway to this labyrinthine land of islands and canals it merely mirrors imprecisely. Despite their longings, the majority will keep to the tourist trails, for the city is a maze designed not to trap victims but to keep them from its secret heart. Most tourists will buy maps and rely upon them to discover what the city has to offer. Seeming to document every tortuous alley as they do, the very complexity of the maps is a glamour designed to ensure that those following them will never wander far from well-travelled paths. Those sensitive or wise enough to suspect the truth and lay aside their maps may still baulk at crossing unknown bridges or following strange paths. Some instinct of caution will remind them of all the stories in which those who choose to leave proper paths come to enigmatic and unsettling ends.

That city keeps its secret well, for this is its entire purpose, the reason for its existence.

Suddenly I want the comfort of my own chamber. I sign

to Cloud-Marie that I have finished with the tapestry and, leaving her to return the room to order, I rise and go into the hall. Touching a wall, I find it damp. It is always damp in this realm. In autumn the air is wet because the fallen leaves exude a fermenting steam that intoxicates all who breathe it. In spring, rain falls and falls in grey and slanting curtains that render the grass soggy enough to take a handprint. The air grows so wet that one feels breathing to be little more than a slow drowning. Even in summer, when building surfaces blaze white-hot and the cobbles burn through the soles of your shoes, it is damp, for the heat sucks a haze of water from the canals into the air. It forms a brackish sticky vapour that slicks all flesh and renders all cloth limp. Winter is worse, though. Icy mists rise up as slow and nacreous wraiths, seeping from the cracked black earth to hang almost immobile in the frozen air, breathing a chill, deadly film over the stone walls.

Last winter I caught pneumonia. I remember little of the illness except the way the light cut into my eyes, igniting a headache so astoundingly painful that it made me feel as if my head would explode. You can always tell a mortal who has dwelt here too many seasons, for they breathe as if the sea has entered into their lungs.

I remember the chilly delicacy of the air as it settled on me the first time I came here, how my skin rose into gooseflesh. Now it prickles at the memory. Or maybe a goose walks on my grave, for I suppose there must be a grave, somewhere in the future, waiting to receive me.

Disliking the tenor of my thoughts, I stop at a window on

the side of the palace that overlooks the city and the canal rather than its sprawling grounds. I run my eyes over the ruddy carapace formed by the roofs below. Only a myriad of dark lanes and the glimmering threads of smaller canals show through it, except where the carapace splits wide open to allow the Grand Canal to pass between this palace and the one on the opposite bank. Between them, the gleaming silver surface of the water is ruffled with white and a cold wind slaps at me.

I feel Cloud-Marie's warmth as she comes to stand beside me. She grunts softly but I lift a finger to quell her, for underneath the ebb and flow of my thoughts, I am still listening.

Did I imagine the howl? Such an imagining would require hope to give it force. The knowledge that I might still be capable of hope forces me to hope and, like a man made to walk on long-withered limbs, I stumble a few astonished steps, then fall. Because even if he howled, what salvation can there be for him?

'It's not possible,' I say, speaking aloud without meaning to.

The dry croak of my voice startles me and, continuing along the passage, I discover that I cannot remember when last I spoke. I have not been out in many weeks. No one comes to visit, of course; they would as soon enter Dracula's castle. I can guess that thorny rumours and barbed stories have grown around this palace and its inhabitants in a great wild thicket. If I were younger, they would make me a trapped princess and dream a prince to rescue me, but I am a queen and the prince is a king.

My husband did not change at all after he became a king. Of course, his kind can be any age once they have reached maturity, simply by willing it. Naturally enough he chose to be a young man in his prime most often, except occasionally as a whim when he fancied that wisdom is more compelling when it issues from withered greybeards.

Perhaps he takes that form now, or maybe he has grown weary of the demands of manhood and has made himself into a boy. I do not know, for he has gone a-questing these long years, and even before that, he left me and took to residing in the Queen's Palace, often called the Summer Palace because it is always summer there.

When first he announced that he would go and live there, he used the weather as an excuse, telling me he preferred summer to the eternal autumn shrouding the King's Palace. Ironically, it is the queen whose moods dictate the weather above the King's Palace, but she can control it only so far as she can control her moods. Yet though my moods wrought stormy squalls and chilly rain, I do not believe he left me because of the weather.

The Queen's Palace is prettier than the King's Palace, and stands on the opposite bank of the great canal from it, being a rambling building of pale pink stone with a multitude of balconies and airy flying buttresses. A small, elaborately designed park surrounds it, full of complex and, to me, disturbingly lifelike topiary. Vast flowerbeds are laid out around the leafy beasts in geometric designs of abstract flowers that play sly tricks on your eyes. I have sometimes heard The Queen's Palace referred to as the Palace of Tears, for this is where queens must go when their sons take wives.

She is not dead, of course, *his* mother, my mother-in-law. She dwells even now in the Queen's Palace with all of the other mothers-in-law, though not her great-great-grandmother-in-law, who was human like me, and mortal. What a torture she must have found it to grow old and die among these evergreen faerie queens. But they were kind to her after their own fashion, for my husband told me once that they made themselves age with her, until she died.

So, my husband went to dwell with his mother and all those grandmothers, and for a time he played the prodigal son for them. In those days, the Summer Palace scintillated with unexpected life and self-importance and no one would have dreamed of calling it the Palace of Tears, for its halls rang with music and merriment. The queens adored my husband for the brightness he brought with him, and no doubt he dallied with some of them. Faerie folk are sensuous and there is no such thing as incest for them. They are monogamous only when they are in love. Love, for them, cannot be what it is for mortals, since love for us is mortal and therefore intensified with a bittersweet despair. Immortal love is something entirely different after the first heat; it is a slow relishing, a cool playfulness, an endless game of chess. Desire, too, is different for my husband's kind, for there is no real urgency to have anything, no sense that time is running out. It was only when my husband went to live in the Queen's Palace that I came to truly understand the nature of the difference between human and faerie desire.

My husband would summon me to the Summer Palace to attend sumptuous balls. He would not deliver the invitation himself, but send his courtiers got up as faerie godmothers or as cats in boots to deliver his invitations. His messengers would produce astonishing gowns, golden coaches and glass slippers and various spells or tests. One way or another I would be got to the ball. Once I arrived, my husband would claim me lavishly and there would be music and food and wine and dancing. For a little while I was amused if somewhat puzzled by these games, but I was no immortal who could play back and forwards in time eternally. I was a mother, and motherhood more than anything had shown me that time was not a playground but a stern and inexorable master. I became impatient with the games, yet still I went when he sent for me because I was a woman ripe in her life, and for me, that ripeness was not eternal.

My mortal desire transformed the virginal vestments the king had sent me to wear into provocative wisps of silk that barely contained me; they did not prettify or tame. Impatient desire was like a tiger within me, and sometimes my husband would gasp at the sight of me, as he had not done at that pale younger self. Then he would take me into his arms, whirl me into the dance and cover me with kisses as light and cold and insubstantial as snowflakes. But I was no longer a coy girl-woman needing his guidance and faerie tales to help me find the treasure-trove of my own passion. I would pull him with me away from the faerie lanterns and music and into the nearest dark room where we would couple, clasped together as tightly as the two hands of a single man. But the hands belonged to a drowning man, and despite passion, we would go on drowning.

I wonder now if the savagery of my ripe desire revealed in those encounters alarmed my faerie husband. My full woman's passion was not the sweet, confused yearning of a princess, nor was it the ethereal and airy passion of the immortals who know that they have all the time in the world for pleasure. There were peaks and chasms in my desires yet untouched and I felt an urgency that only mortals can feel in striving for them, knowing they will die. I know my husband desired me, fascinated by the combination of hunger and desperation that is mortal loving, yet when he held me, I think there were times when he looked into my face and beheld a corpse.

Coming into my chamber, I cross to the fire and lower myself with a sigh into the deep, comfortable bucket chair that sits before it. For a time, I let myself be hypnotised by the play of the flames on the hearth, but the howl I heard seems to be echoing in my mind.

Cloud-Marie, seeing me shiver despite the fire, drapes a warm shawl solicitously over my legs. Then she begins to unbraid the dark golden syrup of my tresses and it comes to me as a chill foreseeing that, when I am old, she will do the same thing – lay the soft rug over my skinny shanks before unwinding my coarse grey braids.

She begins to brush my hair rhythmically, and I relax into the pull and tug of her ministrations. I watch her in the mirror, seeing how her whole simple wit is focused on grooming my hair. I consider speaking to her but words make her uneasy, and they are unnecessary anyway because she is gifted with a dog-like ability to sniff out my moods. Even the signing is something that she understands and yet never uses. There is no need. She responds happily and devotedly to orders that ask nothing of her but simple obedience. They make her feel safe and she is centred by them.

I have drifted half to sleep when suddenly I sit bolt upright, for it has come to me that the last person I spoke to was my son. A chill runs through me to think it could be so, for the boy ceased to speak over two years ago. Can it really be so long? It seems to me that I have had conversations recently but I cannot recall the details of them. Perhaps they are only memories of speaking long ago.

There were so many conversations when I first came here. Everyone wanted to speak with me and hear my voice. But those same eager supplicants would turn from me now, and my face, once praised for its clever beauty, is regarded as the unlucky loveliness of a mask worn by false hope, to deceive fools.

My son's loss of words was not a complete and sudden binding of his tongue. At first he lost a word here and there and I put it down to the coarsening carelessness of manhood. But his language continued to diminish and anxiety began to prod at me. I noted how he would pause a little too long when searching his mind for the word he wanted, and then he would give an irritated shake of his head and choose another. It would be a good choice, and perhaps I would not have noticed the hesitation if language and my love of it in all forms had not been the gift I chose to bestow upon him, a gift that had seemed to delight him above all the faerie gifts and enchantments he received. I read books to him and spoke of them and made him speak of them to me. I made him strive for precision when he wanted to tell me things; I demanded beauty, originality, wit. It was not long before he was my master and it was bittersweet to see him clench his teeth at some awkward description of mine, or at a word used in a careless way.

I decided that the diminishing of my son's language must be some magical affliction; illnesses and plagues here are strange and unpredictable. Sometimes there are tempests of sorrow, which affect every creature and produce a monsoon of tears. At other times, great fat frogs rain from the sky. Once there was a sleeping sickness and everyone fell where they were and slept for days. How odd it had felt to be walking through a sleeping world suffused with the mysterious reek of red roses. Of course I was immune to the illnesses of my husband's kind, just as he could not catch cold from me. But our son was a halfling and prey to the illnesses and strife of both worlds.

The loss of language went on until my son found he could no longer produce alternatives. He soon became frustrated enough to substitute the odd curse or to shrug lumpishly when a phrase eluded him. His brilliance was declining with the loss of his ability to express it. Even his demeanour lost its fineness. The daintiness of manners that had so delighted me degenerated into rough sprawling movements.

Eventually he came to shout and curse his frustration at me, he who had never raised his voice, for what need had he to do so when his words were soft scalpels that could inflict deadly hurts if he chose to use them as weapons? I longed to help him, but my desperate patience only maddened him by forcing him to acknowledge what he was becoming. When I tried to speak of it he would snarl at me to hold my tongue and lumber away.

I prayed that his intelligence and emotions were only locked up inside him and not extinguished altogether. I had to believe that, but I was becoming frightened. I set aside my pride and called for my husband, using the fragrant summoning mist he had given me in a cut diamond vaporiser. He did not come at once, and so I sent Cloud-Marie to the Summer Palace with a note for the queen-mother asking her to send my husband to me. She sent back that he was away on a quest but she had used her own magic to communicate with him. He would come as soon as he was able.

I will never forgive him for that delay. As it transpired, he could have done nothing, but he might have helped me to bear the weight of my terror. While I waited for him, I ransacked the fusty King's Palace archives, poring over tomes and seeking some clue to my son's affliction, longing for Yssa to comfort me, but my friend and companion had left the palace before I gave birth. I was desperate as a tigress to find a cure for my son, prepared to slay dragons and tear out the tongues of peacocks.

I found nothing.

It may seem strange that I did not discuss my son's condition with my mother-in-law, but I feared what ailed the boy might be my fault. She had told me her son – my husband – had needed to marry a princess to break an inherited curse. She had foreseen that the right bride would end the curse forever, not just in her son, but in his bloodline. She had acclaimed me as that princess, but what if she had been wrong? Certainly the mark of the beast had been on my husband when we met, and so I know that marrying me did save him, for it vanished thereafter. But what if it was only him who I had cured, and not the curse?

My mother-in-law's foreseeing ensured my welcome by her son's people. I had basked in the adulation and gratitude heaped upon me, glad to believe I was what they said. As a repressed and unloved child, had I not felt that some special and important destiny awaited me? Had I not, as a young woman, felt the yoke of ordinariness about my neck as a dreary weight I was not meant to bear? Once I understood where I had come and what I had done, it seemed to me that I had found my destiny. It did not occur to me that even here there are limits to curses and cures and even to love.

I was disappointed quite soon by love, but perhaps it is so with all who love for the first time, whether their lover be mortal or faerie. I do not know the nature of the disappointment an immortal suffers, but it is in the nature of mortals to weave and sew a trousseau of dreams with which to clothe a beloved, though his or her form or nature is unknown. And maybe few men or women fit those glorious vestments or wear them long, willingly.

It was not that my husband ceased to love me, nor I him, but the promises that our heady beginning had seemed to make were not fulfilled. My delirious happiness faded. To begin with, I blamed myself. I was of the mundane world and it must be my fault the glamour of love had dimmed. Hence I did not speak of my disappointment to my husband because he seemed content, and if I complained, might he not learn to despise me? But in my secret heart, I blamed him, too, for if my feet stayed a little too close to the ground, it must be because his love had not wings enough to lift me above myself.

I became fretful and irritable with him and our lives. He did not reproach me or protest or demand what was the matter with me, he simply began to go more and more upon quests, and when he was in the castle, he was distracted and distant. This hurt, for in the beginning he had been enamoured of conversation with me, attentive to all I said and filled with desire to know my thoughts. I had imagined it would always be so, but now he did not question me and beg me to talk of this or that to him, and his eyes no longer followed me when I was within sight. It was not that he did not desire me, but that he desired only certain limited aspects of me. He knew part of me and felt he knew all. Too often, his caresses confined themselves to those that would bring us most directly to coupling. He rode and arrived too swift at his own destination for me to ride beyond irritation and anger and a growing melancholy to my own more distant pleasure. I would pretend fulfilment out of pride and anger and embarrassment and he would roll away with a pleased grunt to fall swiftly to snoring.

Staring at his sleeping form in the dark with longing and loathing intermingled so profoundly that I did not know where one began and the other ended, I felt myself transported to my childhood home with two cool, rational, intellectual parents who had taught me that if I would be loved, I must be considerate, modest, self-effacing, quiet. My marriage had taught me that I could be loved, and be vividly the centre of things, but now it seemed that this was only for a time. Now I must be a good girl again, and withdraw most of myself behind the serene façade of queen, suppressing anger and fear and longing.

Lying back against the pillows, I oft times wrapped myself in my arms and shivered under the slick of mingled sweat and restless desire, pining for him to wake just as fiercely as I had wished him asleep. I told myself I did not know what I wanted; I was perverse and difficult. I wanted tenderness and affection, but when he fell asleep with an arm over me, I would shift to make his arm slide away and then stretch, luxuriantly free of him.

Perhaps I would have coped better if I had been more independent, but I was a non-magical being in a realm where magic was the means to obtain everything. I had to rely upon my husband for all I needed. At first, no whim of mine had been too small to be fulfilled and even anticipated by my prince. But once we were king and queen, I discovered that many of the courtesies he had paid me were no more than part of that initial seduction. He forgot to conjure tea for me in the mornings unless I reminded him. If he slopped his supper wine, he would not wave a languid hand to spell it from the floor. He never thought to smooth our bed or pick up his underwear. I had been startled at first to find that, although he was king, there was no one to make his bed or wash his dishes or cook for him. Magic served here, but he must exert himself and it began to seem that he would rather use me than his magic.

There were times when life was impossibly difficult. I would sometimes have to ask my husband several times to banish dust or clean our clothing or conjure a meal or even the makings of a meal so that I could cook. Each time I must ask once, and then ask again. When he showed his boredom at my nagging, savage anger and bitterest resentment would come to scour me. But I did not express my rage, for I had by now resumed the habit of silence concerning my thoughts and feelings, nurtured by my parents. Certainly my husband had shown his dislike of my thoughts when they were negative or implied any criticism of him, and in the beginning I had been afraid to make myself a shrew in his eyes. A queen ought to have better things to think of than soiled underwear and dust mites, I tried to tell myself loftily. There was no shortage of food or wine, after all, if I would attend the faerie festivities every night. I never had to bother buying clothes, for my husband was all too happy to conjure splendid dresses and jewels for me, yet I could not wear those dresses more than once or twice since there was no way to launder such delicate fabrics without damaging them.

But gradually, perforce, I learned to fend for myself. Sometimes I would smile grimly at my reflection as, clad in my elaborate finery, I would pass a looking glass bearing a bowl of slops from the dishes. I felt powerless and furious at my powerlessness. I made our bed and picked up my husband's discarded clothes if he had forgotten to banish them, because someone must do it.

'I would have done it,' he would laugh if he caught me.

Then why didn't you? I would think angrily, and outside, thunder would rumble ominously among gathering clouds.

On days when I did not wish to attend a ball in order to break my fast, I would walk to the garden beyond the farthest wing of the palace, and there I would forage for wild tomatoes and potatoes, mushrooms and berries and quail eggs. I learned to set snares for rabbits and wild pigeons which I then roasted in clay balls on a campfire. When winter came I would bring the clay balls home and bake them in the embers of the fire. I might have gone in a carriage to the peasant farmers dwelling about the palace grounds, or even to the little villages to shop, but I was humiliated by the thought that all Faerie would guess how ill my king cared for me.

Better to endure in private. The pride I felt in managing was a hard, cold, wounded pride. Once, in a moment of weakness, I asked my husband to conjure rubber gloves to protect my hands when I scrubbed pots, but he laughed at me and asked if he was a tyrant to make his queen undertake such work. He waved a languid finger and conjured my hands smooth, saying lightly that he did not like the coarse feel of them on his silky, milky skin. I wondered incredulously if he was malicious in his refusal to ask how my hands came to be that way, but now I think he lacked all curiosity. His laziness was only faerie self-centredness and a lack of imagination.

I was not so sanguine then, and there was a blizzard that night above the palace. In the morning my husband gave me a baffled, wary look before going on a journey of some weeks. Despite my anger with him, I was lonely in his absence, and perhaps that was why I made a companion of a woman who came begging for some menial job. Certainly Yssa was comely enough, despite her drab attire, but she had a melancholy, wretched air that made it hard to see how fair her face was. She was not good company at all to begin with, for she seldom looked me in the eye, let alone smiled or sang or laughed. She gave so little companionship, in fact, that

I found myself regretting my coldness to my husband and telling myself that it was mad to think that mere selfishness and a lack of imagination lay at the heart of my growing discontent. How could such small faults corrode such a great love story as ours?

I know now that love is not so sturdy and the fault was not so small.

Why did I stay? I asked myself as the years passed, as maybe all women do who endure indifference and carelessness or even cruelty from their husbands, and contrarily, the answer was different every time. I loved my husband, or I remembered loving him, or he could not help himself, or I wanted his hands on me again, or all men were like this, no matter what the world.

But the truth, which I acknowledged to myself only a long time after he left, was that the fading of love was not the fault of either one of us alone. I wanted something more substantial and demanding than I had got in my faerie prince; something harder and more consuming than faerie glamour. I wanted him to want me as a woman and a person, not just as a princess, but it was the princess he had hunted so ardently, who he desired.

It was Yssa who asked one day if I could not get all of the things I sighed for in my own world. My determined efforts to woo her out of the morbid grip of whatever ill fortune or unhappiness lay in her past had effected a subtle change in her so that she was less downcast and self-effacing than she had been, but it did not take much for her to withdraw into her original grim melancholy. Yet, her suggestion that I look for the things I wanted in my old world shone like a beam of sunlight through the murk of resentment that I had stewed for myself. I hugged her, marvelling that I had not thought of it first. Had I not been told a thousand times that there were a multitude of passages between this world and that which I still thought of as the real world?

With Yssa's help, I made a mental list: good brooms and mops and soft cloths and rubber gloves. How I laughed as I made that mundane list and how happy I felt. How strong and purposeful I felt writing the names of toiletries I had not wanted to ask my husband to provide – tampons and roll-on deodorant, mothballs and even a surface spray to keep spiders from my bedchamber went onto the list, though this last proved a waste, for I discovered that human chemicals have no power here where even spiders and dung beetles are magic.

Yssa helped me to decide what to wear on my adventure, for I had explained to her that women in my world no longer wore full-length sweeping gowns with plunging décolletages. In the end we chose the dullest of my gowns, shortening it to knee length and picking off the lace and frills and beading to make it plainer. Then, just in case, I insisted upon Yssa bundling into my basket a cobweb grey cloak into which had been woven an invisibility spell. Of course I could not shop, invisible, but it would keep me safe if what I was to do proved unexpectedly dangerous.

I was about to leave when my husband came in, just returned from a quest. As always, Yssa withdrew when he entered the room, knowing he did not approve of the fact that I had invited her to be my companion without seeking his permission. Seeing me cloaked and carrying a magical hold-all basket over my arm, he regarded me with indulgent amusement. 'What are you doing, my lady love?' he asked, and some part of me melted at his voice as it always had.

But I told myself it was glamour, not love, and answered him coolly. 'I am going to market in my world for food to cook and for new stockings and a winter coat. I will need money.'

I had not meant to speak of my journey to him, but suddenly I wanted to force him to understand that he had neglected me. I thought my admission that I went to shop for food would shame him, but he had that wondrous blindness some folk have which allows them to ignore hints and allusions and deal only with outright attacks. He merely kissed me and called me a funny child before bidding me enjoy myself. Then he conjured a pouch of precious stones for me to trade for coin. I had already prised some stones out of jewellery he had given me, and for a moment indignation near choked me. He spoke as if I wished to labour in my old world out of nostalgia. It did not occur to him that I might oft times be hungry or cold; that I might lack the most basic necessities because he did not provide them. But though accusations surged against my teeth like frogs and snakes, I kept my mouth closed, and took the pouch.

'Just wait,' I had vowed silently as I turned away. 'You will get what you deserve.' I said things like this many times through gritted teeth, without any clear idea of what I was threatening. My husband did not know that darkling well of bitterness existed in me, but I think it poisoned me a little, so that small matters became larger than they were, and I was sometimes cruel to him. I would turn away when he reached for me, even though I had invited his caress. I wanted to hurt him and I found ways to do it.

Women, I have come to believe, are capable of monstrous cruelty if they do not act cleanly. Or cannot.

I put the pouch of stones into my basket and set off. Outside the grounds of the King's Palace it was summer and gloriously bright. The walk in the sunshine with Yssa lifted my spirits immeasurably, and as we approached the nearest bridge that would lead me to my old world, I had to suppress a wild desire to burst into song. It was not the thought of going back to my own world that lifted me, but the fact that I had found a way to act.

I begged Yssa to come with me, but she baulked at the bridge where we were to cross, hanging back and saying that she would come next time. It was ironic that, although there were many ways from this world to my old world, and few in the other direction, faerie folk seldom crossed. Perhaps, like Yssa, they feared it, or feared what might be done to them, or feared mortality might be contagious. Impatient to be gone, I hugged her and promised that I would not be long.

I noticed immediately how few of the people about me seemed to see me, let alone notice the oddness of my clothes. I wondered uneasily if my time in the other world had thinned my essence in my own world, with its solid truths and heavy certainties. Then it came to me that perhaps I had always been less substantial than others of my kind. Might it not be that all the dreams and longings with which I had filled myself had rendered me less solid than other mortals, and so more able to cross between the worlds?

By the time I reached the open market area that was my destination, I was beginning to understand that it was travellers and tourists in particular who were blind to me. The local people saw me, but turned their eyes away. This puzzled me mightily. I did not know then that the denizens of that city, which is a gateway to this world, had been affected by certain residual magic so that they were able to see what outsiders could not. This was not a power they acknowledged or enjoyed. In the deepest part of their minds where all minds join and become mystery, they knew the secret their city hid. Such knowledge is naturally unbearable for most mortals, and so amnesia has become a subtle art in that city straddling the gateway to Faerie. Thus, many who saw turned aside and at once erased that seeing from their mind.

What fascinated me most in the end were the few tourists who showed by their startled looks that they did see me. I was eager to speak to them, but without exception, anyone I tried to approach fled at once with half-shamed faces. I began to wonder uneasily how my time in Faerie had marked me and was glad to reach the open market and give my attention to my list. But when I tried to shop, I soon discovered that although most of the traders could see me, few would acknowledge or serve me. Those who would were invariably the eldest of the traders, and even they would avoid looking directly into my eyes after that first startled glance. They took the jewels I offered without comment and bagged my purchases. They were grimly courteous and the transaction would be so swiftly concluded that it was as if a door had been slammed in my face. I did not know if I was being cheated, but later, when I returned to Faerie, Yssa laughed at my suspicions, saying no mortal would dare to cheat a faerie.

'But I am not a faerie,' I protested.

'You bear the mark of one who has been loved by a faerie,'

Yssa said, and for a moment the old grim grief showed in her eyes.

I wondered, as I often had before, what had been done to her in the past, but I did not ask for I knew she would not answer. Concern for her robbed me of the innocent pleasure I had taken in my purchases and reminded me of the look of pity I had seen in one rheumy mortal eye. No doubt the old man thought I had been stolen, rather than choosing to enter Faerie. It is true that mortal children are sometimes stolen, but my husband told me that usually they are unloved starvelings who have strayed close to Faerie. They are none the worse for their crossing, and probably far better loved and coddled than in their own world, since faerie folk breed so seldom that all children are precious.

But perhaps it is not always so that those stolen children were unloved. As I left the market, an old woman sitting on a stool outside her door had reached out to catch at my hem, asking with tears in her eyes about her little granddaughter, before her husband hushed her.

The old woman's words changed my mind about going straight back to Faerie upon completion of my shopping. Instead, I made my way to the pension in the small lane where I had lived before my first crossing to Faerie. Scarlet geraniums still dangled in an untidy, vivid cluster from the third-floor balcony of my old apartment, but I saw the nose and the paw of a sleeping dog and a white shirt flapped on the line to tell me my room was now occupied.

What would happen if I knocked and made the concierge acknowledge me? Would she have my case stored in her attic or had it been sent home to my parents along with the report of my disappearance? The police had surely guessed what had become of me, for there must be many disappearances in that city, yet I knew they would never speak of it to the mainland police.

I turned away from the pension without knocking and found myself on the wooden bridge I had crossed on the first day I came to Faerie. Then, I had been wearing flat loafers of the sort my mother had favoured because they were comfortable and quiet. Such footwear does not exist in Faerie, but there, fortunately the highest heels are deliciously comfortable. Indeed I wore high heels to market, and it was hearing them tap tap upon the wooden boards that called to mind the loafers I had worn the last time I crossed that bridge, and made me suddenly decide to follow the same route I had taken on the day I had first travelled there.

I would go as far as the Wolfsgate, I decided, though this time I would not pass into Faerie by that route. I knew of a less contrary crossing close by that I would use.

My intended destination when last I crossed that little bridge had been a small private library. I had been granted special permission to enter it for an entire afternoon. I wanted to examine a certain ancient tome, which referred to an obscure incident in history that I hoped would form the centre of a thesis. I had stopped on the other side of the bridge to examine the letter of invitation from the curator, wanting to make sure I had correctly memorised the name of the street in which the private library was situated. I did not have a map because I had always taken pride in eschewing maps in new cities, and I had passed over the bridge several times already and knew it would bring me to the main thoroughfare from which ran the street I sought.

I had folded the letter and tucked it into my pocket, reassured to have remembered the name correctly, but realising I would arrive early if I went directly to the library. The curator had sounded particularly fussy, an old man unlikely to let me in the door until the specified time, so I decided to explore a little before making my way there.

As Cloud-Marie begins to comb my hair, gently teasing out the snags between her fingers, those two journeys over the same ground seem to fuse. I see myself simultaneously at twenty-two and at thirty-two, moving away from the bridge and turning to go along a canal. Two women slow to admire the opaque aqua flow of water lit with sequins of sunlight, the fringe of green moss waving in the currents along the edge of submerged steps in the canal. The older thinks how the water flowing through the canals in Faerie is darker because it is not water but pure forgetfulness.

Both women come to the piazza and the younger hesitates, trying to decide which way to go. The older remembers what the younger chose, plunges immediately into the narrow lane between two yellow buildings and is surprised to discover a small café had been built further along the lane where there was once none. She was surprised because change is rare in Faerie, and almost as rare close to its borders.

That younger self is left behind as I follow my older self along the lane and see how she was forced to stop when a group of noisy tourists suddenly comes pouring from an intersecting lane, chattering and gesticulating wildly. Unable to continue, she turns to watch how they surge past without seeing the café or her. Their attention is fixed on the formidably buxom woman leading them, her standard an upraised umbrella. She listens as their guide marches them back towards the piazza, explaining in a ringing voice that gondola are made crooked so as to be stable in the water.

'Imagine that,' murmurs a woman at the end of the group holding the hand of a small child.

Instead of responding to her mother, the child turns to look at me. That jolted me, I remember, even though I knew some mortal children were capable of seeing faerie until they learned to filter out uncomfortable and inconvenient truths. That thirty-two-year-old self stands staring after the child and its mother until they vanish from sight, then she turns and continues on her way along the lane until it spills into an open area before a cathedral. It is a breathtakingly beautiful building. Her younger self had almost gone inside, but her older self has a wariness of churches and cathedrals, for there is magic of a kind in them inimical to faerie.

I watch my older self turn reluctantly away from the cathedral, then gaze at the building opposite, which had so struck my younger self when she turned from the church.

I had been astonished, I remember, because it seemed so utterly familiar to me. I had never passed that way before. I knew the red-painted sill on the lower front window, the lion-shaped knocker on the front door, the broken shutter on the third floor, and wondered in bewilderment if I might have seen the building in a photograph.

That was when I noticed a lane between it and the next building. I shrugged off the queer feeling that it had not been there a moment past, for how could a lane suddenly appear? I had smiled, then, realising the red sill and lion-shaped knocker and the other things that I had seemed to recognise were only visual clichés I had encountered a dozen times in films and novels featuring that city.

I had gone to peer along the lane, wondering if it would bring me through to the main streets where I would find the library, but it was too shadowy to see properly when I was standing in the sunlight, so I stepped into it.

Thus did my younger self step unwittingly and perilously into the shadowy space where the realms of faerie and mortal reality overlap.

A man sat smoking on a stoop a little way down the shadowy lane. He had a dark, sculpted beard and a mass of coal-black curls flowing over his shoulders. His long legs were stretched out in front of him and the end of the black cigarillo in his fingers was a burning eye in the shadows as he drew on it. He expelled the smoke from his lungs in a long sighing breath and then turned his head to look at me.

I caught my own breath then, having never seen a man so profoundly handsome and so singularly wild looking. He had a long, beautiful, angular face, a straight nose and bright, almond-shaped turquoise eyes flecked with gold that reminded me of the canal water. Dark hairs curled above his collar and showed at his wrists, which were muscular and strong, but instead of his skin being swarthy to match, he was pale as milk. Unabashed by my stare, he held my gaze as he took another long pull at the cigarillo. I had drawn closer without intending it and heard the sound of dry tobacco crackling. Then he took the cigarillo from his lips and sent it spinning away into the shadows further along the lane.

I felt a fool as I realised how I must appear, standing there gawping at him as if he were a statue in a gallery. I said in a brisk voice, 'I am sorry to disturb you, but I wonder if this lane will bring me to the main streets along the Grand Canal.'

He uncoiled and rose in a single movement, but instead of stepping towards me, he merely leaned back against the wall and slid his hands into his pockets, asking languidly, 'I am not sorry that you disturb me, lovely lady. Are you lost?' His voice was low and soft and seemed to insinuate itself against my skin like an affectionate cat.

'I don't mind being a little lost,' I said.

As Cloud-Marie combs my hair, I blush a little at the boldness of my younger self, though I do not remember myself as bold, this being considered a serious character flaw by my parents.

I went back many times after that first shopping expedition, amass-
ing brooms, dusters, cloths and other domestic and personal items
enough to last a mortal life or two. Eventually the novelty of being
able to buy what I needed palled for me, but I continued to cross
and exchange faerie jewels for the things I needed out of simple
necessity. Then one day my husband invited me to a picnic he had
conjured for his mother's court. It was all laid out upon magical
cloths that would, once spread, offer whatever food and wine were
desired in the thinnest golden plates and crystal goblets. He had
got them on his last quest as a gift from a serpent sorceress whom
he had done a service, he said, fluttering his eyelashes at me.

I scarcely noticed, for I saw at once how useful such cloths
could be and was philistine enough to bundle up the nearest while
my husband conjured for his guests an exquisite ballet of butterflies
complete with orchestral accompaniment. It is amazing how one's
aesthetic senses fail in the face of simple, honest hunger. I meant
to pull the cloth from under the plates and cutlery but discovered to my delight that, at a single deft twitch, all the dishes and
leftover food upon it vanished. When the cloth was later laid out
again on the floor of my bedroom, I was elated to find the dishes
reappeared, gleaming and clean and bearing fresh food.

Yssa said I ought to see if the cloth would give us any food we
wanted, so we tried it again, announcing what we wished before
we opened it out. It did. It was Yssa, too, who discovered that if
you opened the cloth when you were not hungry, it would provide
other things, so long as what you wanted was not animate and
would fit within the bounds of the obliging tablecloth. For the
sake of mischief, she tried wishing for various magical objects,

including another of the cloths, but the cloth was deaf to these requests.

'I was afraid of that,' Yssa sighed.

The cloth did away with the need to travel back to my own world, and this turned out to be very convenient for, soon after, my womb quickened, and I would not cross between the worlds for fear it might harm the baby inside me. In truth I had no interest in such gallivanting about and brooded no more upon my husband's neglect of me. I would go again when the child was safely delivered, I told myself, and this time I would persuade Yssa to come too. But as it transpired, Yssa had gone from the palace before my son was born.

I missed my friend badly, but love for my son filled and absorbed me in a way I had not anticipated, being the victim of my mother's cool boredom over having to tend to a child. Unlike her, I was not oppressed by motherhood. I found myself completely absorbed, which surprised me a little, for even aside from my mother's example, I had never been the sort to yearn for motherhood as some do, nor to plan for it at some convenient moment in the future.

But when my son was born I became a devoted and adoring mother, and for a time concerned myself with little else than my son and poor Cloud-Marie, for by then I had her to care for as well.

As my son grew to boyhood, I was taken up with the nurturing and schooling of his body and mind. Cloud-Marie had no capacity to learn, but she was a sweet, silent companion and adored my son as much as he loved her. Of course she grew more swiftly than the boy, being fully faerie, and she was soon old enough to help me with him. Indeed he preferred her help in bathing and dressing and choosing his clothes. He did not need her help for long, though, and I was glad of it. I had not intended that she should be a servant, but almost without my noticing it, she began to wait upon me with such touching devotion that I could not bring myself to tell her that she need not do so. She got such contentment from her small services and she truly was a help to me, for this was also the time in which my husband began to woo me anew, once again sending invitations and courtiers from the Summer Palace. I suspect he had finally noticed my preoccupation.

I enjoyed his pursuit, even if it seemed rather childish and unreal, because I was sustained and nurtured at some deeper level by my son and daughter, for so I thought of Cloud-Marie. If I sensed my husband did not adore his son enough, I was not deeply troubled, for I had more than enough adoration to lavish on him.

In truth I was profoundly content, until my son's affliction began to manifest itself.

When at last my husband returned at his mother's behest, he did not come to the King's Palace to see what ailed our son, but summoned me to attend him. I knew he was positioning himself for his defence and all of the angers and resentments of the early days of our marriage resurfaced as I was led down long elegant halls to his small formal audience chamber. I realised he meant to meet me here rather than in his private chamber because he wanted the setting to restrain me. Unrestrained, I told him bluntly of his son's affliction, for by now I knew a good deal more than I had done. My husband grew very still for a moment and then he spoke not of curses or cures but of the need for our son to seek a bride. It was then he drew me a little aside and said softly, sadly, that it seemed that our son bore the same curse that had afflicted him.

I had guessed as much, but I felt the blood drain from my face at his confirmation of my fears. 'I thought that I cured the curse by marrying you.'

He nodded. 'You cured me, and I thought you had cured my blood, but the faerie who laid it upon the sons of our house was blood kin and a curse of blood against blood is very powerful.'

I stared at him in disbelief. 'The faerie who cursed your ancestor was a relative?'

'She was the daughter of the king, but she was not the daughter of his wife.'

'She was an illegitimate daughter?'

He nodded, his expression sober. 'I did not speak of the curse before this, because there seemed no reason to dwell upon such dark matters. My mother had a vision as you lay sleeping in the Princess Chamber, which told her that the princess spell you wrought would be very strong, and that you would end the curse upon our blood. I ought to have understood it would not be so simple, for nothing in Faerie is simple. Perhaps it is in the nature of men to always think that they have found the ultimate princess.'

My face and heart flamed with wrath at his cruel words, but he turned from me to announce his decision to quest for a means of ending the curse upon his son and his line once and for all.

'You would go away again, now?' I screamed at him.

He looked down his nose at me, reminding me with his cool eyes and manner that we were in a formal audience chamber. Then he said very gently, 'My love, listen to me. There is truly naught for me to do in what will unfold now. Our son must hunt a girl and bring her to the Wolfsgate Valley where she will be tested as you and other princess brides were tested. This is not a matter for a king, but for mothers and sons.' My husband took my hand and kissed it, and I was so frightened and weary that I allowed his tenderness to soothe me as he told me that I must learn from his mother what was required of me in the bride hunting, for a queen had a vital part to play. There was no time to waste, he said, then he bade a servant lead me to his mother. I had no choice but to go, although I could not face visiting his mother immediately, so I dismissed the servant and went back to the King's Palace to tell my son that he was to wed.

I had expected him to snarl that he did not want a bride, but he blushed and scowled at his feet, and my heart battered against my ribs in grief, for here, all unheralded, was the end of my supremacy in his life. He was ready to become a man when I had not finished having a child. I bit back sorrow and jealousy to say calmly that I would speak with his grandmother in the morning, to learn what was required in the matter of hunting a bride. I said nothing to my son of the curse, but I was determined to have the whole truth of it from my mother-in-law.

She was in the garden training a new falcon the next morning when I returned to the Summer Palace. She was feeding the vicious little creature bloody strips of meat, and the sight of her fingers black with dried blood made me queasy. I was ever shocked and shocked again by the visceral and almost casual brutality in Faerie, yet was it not there, hidden in between the lines of the oldest faerie tales? Is that not why the children of my world woke in terror and screamed after hearing a faerie tale, to the astonishment of their parents?

Seeing me, the queen gave the bird into the hands of one of the other queens, and laved her fingers in a bowl of petal-strewn water to clean them. Then she dismissed everyone and invited me to sit with her in a perfumed arbour.

She began by informing me that her son, the king, had sailed away at dawn and that he would likely not return for some time. I bit back my rage at the thought that he had done what he said he would do, wondering what sort of fool I was to have thought it would be otherwise. Nevertheless, I was angry enough to ask her if faerie kings had no interest in the bride-getting of their sons, even when it must save the boy from a curse conferred upon him by his father's tainted blood. I stabbed the words at her, making them an accusation, though it was not by her choosing that he had left. But I was as angry with her, almost, as with him.

'You said the curse upon my husband's bloodline would be cured by marrying me,' I hissed.

'And so it shall be,' said my husband's mother mildly, and to my complete surprise. 'You have only to find the right bride and test her well to end the curse forever.'

'But I thought that you meant I cured the curse when I married your son,' I said.

She laughed, and for a moment her habitual haughtiness was softened. 'Do you really think that falling in love is an end to anything? It is only the end of the beginning for your kind no less than mine. It is in our children that our endings are written. As for us women, it is not as princesses we have true power, but as queens and mothers. It was as a mother that I scried out the future, and I saw that you would save my son, but more importantly, that you were the means by which the curse might be broken. But what I saw is only a revealed potential, which you must fulfil. I do not know how. It is a pity that you did not inform your husband sooner about the boy's degeneration, though, for he might have bade him seek a bride the sooner. As it is, there is no time to waste.'

I was chilled by her words, but furious too, for how could I have known my son was cursed when no one had ever thought to tell me the symptoms of that curse? As to confiding in my husband, ought he not to have spent time enough with the boy to see for himself what was happening, instead of dallying in the Summer Palace or questing? I wanted to ask her those things and to demand savagely how my son was to catch his bride – was he to be sent out to sit on a stoop in a lane and await a fool, as her son had done? But I only bade her stiffly to tell me what to do.

An echo of the anger I had experienced that day in the flowery arbour with my mother-in-law flows through me, and I have to fight the impulse to dash the brush from Cloud-Marie's patient fingers, for though I do not doubt my husband grieves over what came to pass as much as my mother-in-law, neither of them holds themselves in any way responsible. They do not say it, but I know they blame me, as indeed I blame myself. Yet even now, I do not know what I could have done to prevent what has happened.

The first of many things the queen-mother told me was that her son had spoken the truth; our son must wed a princess bride.

'It would be best if the maid he chooses has some mortal blood,' she told me gravely and reminded me that in Faerie, a true princess was not a mere princess by lineage, as in my world. A girl became a princess in Faerie as the result of a spell brewed up between the prince and his mother, the chosen candidate and a magical chamber such as the one that I had occupied in the King's Palace.

'But I have no magic,' I cried, aghast.

'The instructions you give your son, the way he conducts his hunt for his bride and the way his chosen responds to the tests set for her are the ingredients of the spell. It is the Princess Chamber that will cast the spell, but only if all the ingredients required are present in enough strength,' said my mother-in-law. 'And the better the ingredients, the stronger the spell.'

She summoned the other queens to instruct me in the rituals and practices surrounding a son getting a bride. In sympathy, or perhaps by tradition, all of them came in the guise of elderly faerie godmothers and each bore a gift. I was given advice and old wives' tales, tokens and spells and tomes to aid me. I heard the full history of the curse that afflicted my husband's lineage, which had been brewed up by a powerful faerie maiden who killed the human man she had loved after he betrayed her, as well as his lover, her own half-sister. It was when she tried to close the gates forever between the human world and Faerie that the king intervened, forbidding it. Affronted, she cursed him, though he was her own father, and when she would not undo the curse, the king took her power from her, but he could not break the curse she had laid upon him and the sons of his blood. From that time, the moment a boy first became a man, he turned slowly and inexorably into a beast, until he was fully beast and had not the wit to turn himself into anything. She had known, of course, that without a true king, Faerie would fail and her revenge would be complete. So far, Faerie had not been closed off, but the ways had dwindled as each king sought the princess bride who would save him.

Later, when I returned to the King's Palace, a storm cracked its whip viciously overhead, and lightning clawed at the sky, which responded with a hail of bitter pellets of icy rain. But I ignored the weather and my own fear and grief, for the faerie queens had told me, too, of the mother of that king, a wizened but powerful crone, who had spent herself spelling up the magical Princess Chamber in the King's Palace and devising the rites surrounding it that would produce a princess bride capable of breaking the curse. Many princess brides had come from that chamber and had saved their princes from bestiality, even as I had done, but I was to be the one to save her son and all future sons.

So said my mother-in-law and so I must believe.

I bent my head and heart to this end, examining the strange and sometimes unsavoury tokens I had been given by the queens, and referring to the tomes I had carried off with me. I discovered that there were many rituals as well as rules connected to the getting of a princess bride, and that although I had no choice in the rules, I might alter the rituals or even dispense with them if I chose, that I might brew a more powerful spell. My husband had told me the day before that I must send my son to hunt a bride, but I now understood that it would be the imposition of the help or hindrances I deemed appropriate to test the girl that would give strength to the spell wrought by the chamber.

So, the rules: my son must choose a maid with some mortal blood in her, and she must enter the Wolfsgate Valley and endure three dusks there. He might protect her and aid her as best he could, but the more thoroughly she was tested, the more potent the princess spell would be.

The books made it clear that the prince had no say in anything save that he might choose the maid to be tested and interact with her, within the parameters set by the queen. I was so preoccupied with my research and my preparations that I had failed to note that something had been left unsaid in all the books just as it had not been said in the talk and advice in the garden of the Summer Palace.

None of the queens or books had said what would happen if my son failed to find a bride.

Would it have helped, I wonder now, if I had gone back to my husband's mother, and demanded to know what would happen? Would it have saved my son for me to know the whole truth? But I did not go back, for I believed my mother-in-law when she said that it was my destiny to help my son find a princess bride to save him and his sons.

At length I got up from my bed, put everything neatly away and made a meticulous toilette before going down to supper. My son was there before me, all eagerness to hear how he was to get a bride. No doubt he had some notion of a ball. Would that it was so simple, I thought bitterly. I drew his grandmother's formality about me like a ceremonial cloak and told my son that the reason he must take a bride was because he carried in his blood the same curse that had afflicted his father, which could be cured only by his wedding a princess bride.

His face darkened with anger, and he growled that if a bride was all it wanted, he should get one soon enough, for women were weak and easily caught. Had he not already dallied with several sprites? It was a churlish thing to say, but I comforted myself with the thought that these graceless words were a symptom of his degeneration. Once he had found his bride, he would become again the handsome, charming youth that he had been before the curse began to exert itself.

Ignoring his interruption, I told him sternly that he could not choose just any woman to be his bride. She must have mortal blood and be a worthy candidate for the Princess Chamber. His task would be to bring her to the Wolfsgate Valley, where she must remain for three dusks. He might protect her but he must not speak a word to her, from start to finish. Given his graceless manners, it had seemed wisest to forbid conversation. He should have a token I had prepared to aid him in getting her to the Wolfsgate Valley, and at the end of the three days, he must drive or lure her through the Endgate into the grounds of the King's Palace, before the sun had fully set. She would then be tested by me and, if I deemed her fitting, conducted to the Princess Chamber.

My son's scowl deepened. 'How am I to know if the one I hunt can pass all of these tests?'

'Choose a woman who can love, who is courageous and strong, and worthy of loving,' I told him.

His insolence angered me, but in truth I did not know how he could best choose his bride. Inwardly I cursed my husband for his absence. He might at least have explained his choosing of me more clearly, so that I could better guide our son. But even more than for my husband I longed for Yssa, for being a faerie, she would surely have been able to guide me.

My son broke into my reverie, sullenly demanding to know why the maid must have mortal blood when pure-blood faerie folk were more fair by far and the girl's power would be greater if she was wholly faerie. Was this not a condition I had invented, out of vanity?

I drew myself up and told him coldly that if I had my way, I would send him to hunt a mortal woman, for the wits and courage and will of any such who survived the Wolfsgate Valley would have been truly tested, since she had not magic to smooth her way and protect her. I ought to know, I added, for had I not survived without a skerrick of magic?

His cheeks suffused with angry colour, but something in my expression must have made him wary, for he said nothing. Turning from him, I drew myself up and announced in a formal voice that my son, the prince, was to hunt a princess bride, and that the hunt would begin in an hour. I needed time to complete the spell given me by one of the queens, which I would cast upon a small ring from my jewellery box. It would tell the maid that he who put it upon her finger was a noble young man under a spell that would be broken only if she carried the ring to a certain lady who was mistress of a certain mansion.

My son would have raced off at once, but I bade him wait patiently, and suggested he go and bathe and comb his hair and dress in comely attire before returning to my chamber where I would give him the token I had prepared.

'All of these stupid fucking rules,' my son snarled, and slouched out slamming the doors.

When he set off an hour later, I threw myself into my own preparations. I set Cloud-Marie to scrub and polish the grand parlour as I sought candles enough to fill it with a warm haze of light. Then I went to the gardens and cut great armfuls of long-stemmed, perfumed lilies and sprays of lilac and wisteria, while Cloud-Marie lit and nursed the great stove in the bathing room, and filled and heaved enormous cauldrons of water to boil over the flames. These would boil and be topped up continually now, like the fires, until the period of testing was done.

I laid sheaves of cut flowers on the kitchen bench and went to the mist garden with a feeling of apprehension. Just as the queen had predicted, all of the rose bushes now hung heavy, weighed down by the dense, miraculous crop of white blooms that flowered only when a blood prince of the royal house of Faerie had begun his hunt for a bride. Their appearance meant that my son had truly gone seeking a bride, for if he had merely pretended, the roses would not have bloomed.

The petals from the bushes had to be plucked and strewn upon the floor of the Princess Chamber and on the surface of the bath-water 'so thickly that her nakedness would not be apparent to her own eyes . . .' There they would lie fresh and soft and fragrant as the moment they were plucked, until the morning a true princess bride lay within the chamber.

I tore rose petals off their blooms in handfuls, piled them in my wicker basket and carried it up to the Princess Chamber. Cloud-Marie was on her knees brushing the plush of the green runner on the grand stairs when I reached her with my fragrant burden. She laid down her brush and stood up to follow me, mouth loosely agape, for she understood as well as I that all of the other preparations had been no more than a prelude to this, the reopening and preparation of the Princess Chamber, which I had not entered since my own testing.

Coming to stand before the high double doors with their ornate carvings of roses and thorns, I set down my basket and wiped the palms of my hands on my skirt. Then I closed them about the smooth nestling doves that were the handles and parted them, expecting a resistance that acknowledged the long years that had gone by since I last passed this way, but the doves bowed to one another and the doors opened with the same silky willingness, as if there were no more than a whisper of air between yesteryear and today.

The doors swung inward, revealing the dark maw of the unlit chamber. I could see nothing at all, and I gestured to Cloud-Marie who shuffled down the hall to get two candelabra, one of which she pressed into my hand upon her return. I thrust it before me into the darkness, and after a long, uncanny pause, the profound shadows filling the room ebbed and allowed the light to enter. I stepped through the door, unsettled by the sudden odd feeling that the light had created the room, and before, there had been nothing but a black void.

I had not thought of the Princess Chamber since the night I had slept here, but on its threshold I remembered the almost suffocating intensity of the scent given off by the roses, which had flowed from the room to which my hostess had shown me. And that other smell, which I had fallen asleep trying to name, and now knew very well. It was the scent of magic, of course, and the room was thick with it.

'Tradition,' my hostess had told me, gesturing lightly, dismissively, to the petals that lay on the floor, the absurdity of the bed.

I set the candelabrum on a small table pushed against the white-washed stone wall beside the door, and drew aside the long damask curtains that concealed the door to the small balcony. It seemed but moments since I had first drawn those curtains to discover the exquisite little balcony behind it, and imagined how lovely it would be to go out onto it in the morning and look down on a sunlit garden. I had no way of knowing that it overlooked a mist garden, where sunlight never fell.

A movement in the chamber behind me recalled me to the present and I turned to see Cloud-Marie looking at me with the soft, sucking, bog-brown eyes of a cow. I pointed to the fireplace and she nodded and lurched over to tend to it. There was no need to sweep or dust. All that needed doing, according to the tome my mother-in-law had given me, was to lay down a carpet of petals, heat bathwater, remove the ashes of the old fire, and lay and light a new one, then renew the bed.

'The last and final task is the renewing of the bed . . .'

I had assumed this to mean the bed was to be made up afresh, but it was as perfectly made as a bed with dozens of mattresses piled one upon the other could be. I went over and took the rich fabric of the coverlet between thumb and forefinger, hauled it back and recoiled to find the sheets and the top mattress badly mouse-chewed. The reek of damp and mouse musk made me gag and I wondered why the cover had not been affected when the sheet and mattresses had got into such a state.

Cloud-Marie helped me drag all of the mattresses down and spread those that were intact about the room to air, then she cleaned the hearth and lit a fire that was soon crackling merrily, warming the chamber. Later, I would have her bring lavender and cedar balls and camphor to put between the mattresses. Now we dragged those mattresses that were entirely ruined into the hallway to be disposed of, and those that could be repaired we dragged to my sitting room. The rest we must pile up anew. I did not know how repairs could be managed but even as I pondered it, Cloud-Marie led me to a linen closet where there were silk sheets aplenty that could be sewed together as covers, and great bales of fresh cotton and wool wadding as well as goose down. I was surprised to see them, for even though I had bought them myself long ago at the market in my own world, after I had used them in a frenzy of making new bedding for my chamber and Yssa's, they had vanished. I touched them softly, thinking that Yssa must have put them here. For a moment, my eyes blurred with tears, and I wondered what had become of her, but Cloud-Marie touched my arm and I pulled myself together. Soon we were both sitting back in my tower room, bent over the new mattress cases, our stabbing needles hard at work.

The next day, our eyes red-rimmed and burning with strain and lack of sleep, we carried the new mattress covers back to the chamber and half stuffed them with pure goose down so they would flatten the better. The number of mattresses was the vital thing, according to the books, not their thickness, and I remembered all too clearly my own astonished reaction to an elegant bed made atop a fantastic pile of mattresses that would have me lying closer to the ceiling than the floor.

I had wanted to laugh at the sight of that awkward bed resting amid a sea of white petals, yet the formidable seriousness of the mistress of the mansion precluded it. Besides, I was so overwrought by all I had endured in the past days that I feared I might not be able to stop laughing if I began. What I longed for more than anything was simply to be able to lie down and sleep. I felt sure that I would wake with some sensible understanding of the surreal madness of the previous days. Perhaps even the bed would seem less outlandish in the daylight, after sleep.

I realised my hostess was waiting for me to speak and pulled my wits together to thank her. She nodded and gestured to the bathing room, then withdrew, bidding me sleep well. Her servant closed the door behind them, leaving me alone.

I thought of dragging down a single mattress to sleep on, but the mattresses were set inside the four posts of the bed in such a way that it would require two people to manoeuvre one out. I would have to sleep in the bed or brave the icy stone flags with no more than a blanket under me. I elected for the former; after all, given the things I had endured, it seemed almost decadent to complain about the height of a bed. I entered the gleaming bathing room but was too weary to bathe. Instead, I washed quickly and not very thoroughly and donned the thin nightgown I had been given. Back in the main chamber, I decided I must gather myself before climbing up onto the bed, and I padded about the room exploring, discovering a little balcony overlooking a garden swathed in shadow and mist. There was a chill wind, and before long, I retreated inside to warm myself by the fire.

Drowsy with food and wine and fatigue, my mind drifted to the handsome, dark-haired man in the lane with his canal-green eyes. He had assured me that if I turned back and went this way and that, I would come in a few minutes to the main tourist path along the Grand Canal, but that this was the route for unadventurous tourists, not true travellers, such as I seemed to him. Flattered and intrigued, I had asked if there was some other way. He answered archly that if I took his lane it would bring me to a door in a wall beyond which lay a garden. I could cut through this to another gate that would bring me to a private yard. The lady who owned it did not object to locals passing though to the path alongside the Great Canal. It was a slightly longer route but very beautiful.

Tantalised, I had reluctantly reminded him I was not local.

'If you like, I will give you something to legitimise your trespass,' he had offered, taking from his pocket what looked like a bone armlet. It was only when he gave it me that I realised from its lightness it was made of thin, sun-bleached wood.

'What is it?' I had asked.

'It is the property of the lady. If you would take it to her for me, I would be most grateful. You can tell her Ranulf sends you to her with his regards.'

His words were cryptic and a little suggestive and I had wondered if he was not the lover of the lady who owned the armlet and the garden, and meant to use me as a go-between.

'What if I forget to deliver it?' I had asked, to give myself time to think.

'I do not think you would forget to do something you have said you would do,' he told me, suddenly serious, and he reached out to cup my cheek for a moment in his palm.

'Very well, I will take it, if you are sure,' I had agreed, keeping my voice cool to belie my fast-beating heart. In response, he put the circlet into my hand and used his hands to fold mine about it, bidding me wear it for safety. It was too big to be a bracelet, but I had tried awkwardly to do as he suggested until he reached out to take it from my fingers and slip it gently over my wrist and up my arm as far as it would go above the elbow.

I pressed the place where he had touched my wrist and thought of the way my skin had tingled at his touch, and the look of yearning in his eyes when he released me. It was impossible to think of him as a man playing a nasty trick on a gullible tourist. But when I produced the armlet just an hour past to my hostess, repeating Ranulf's words, determined to deserve his faith in me despite all that had transpired, she had taken the thing from me and seemed to weigh it upon her palm, her expression haughty and at the same time distracted. Certainly it was not the look a woman gave when a precious object had been returned to her. She had eventually thanked me, and invited me in out of the storm-racked night, proposing that I stay as her guest, but there was no warmth in her eyes or words and I had the distinct feeling she thought me a tiresome fool. Yet she had sat with me while I ate and warmed myself by the fire, though she herself ate nothing and said little. In truth she had seemed relieved when I said that I was tired and asked if I might retire.

It was only when she rose, leaving the wooden armlet carelessly on the table, that I noticed there were three exactly like it, threaded with flowers to form a low and intricate flower arrangement. There was a notch in the last, where a fourth ring ought to have fitted, and I realised with mortification that I had returned a bit of a table ornament with ludicrous ceremony. It did not help that I suspected the jape had been played more upon the lady than on me, for I had been the dupe who had enabled it. No wonder she had looked at me with such reserve. What a gullible bumpkin I must seem to her.

My face had burned with shame as I followed her along the hall to the bedchamber, yet now, standing by the fire, I wearily considered the possibility that I might not be the first gulled into performing a fool's errand, given the cool response of the lady of the house. And in the end, what was an unpleasant jest when compared with all that I had endured in the days after meeting him? I frowned, feeling almost dizzy with fatigue as I wondered if days could really have passed as I remembered. Was it not more likely that I had fallen asleep just inside the walled garden, after I had taken shelter from the sudden downpour, that I had dreamed days full of strangeness before waking, fevered and confused, to make my way to the oddly named Endgate?

Surely I had imagined the impossible vastness of the garden, the wolves.

For a moment I was tempted to seek out my hostess to ask what day it was, except that I could not bear to face her again so soon. Besides, I was so exhausted that if I did not lie down, I would simply topple into the flames.

I staggered to the bed and clambered awkwardly up the mattresses, panting and cursing under my breath and wondering what sort of lunatic tradition required a great stack of mattresses and a floor covered in white rose petals. The smell of the roses and some elusive but heady scent under them was very strong and made me feel half intoxicated. I was perspiring freely by the time I reached the top and I thought I ought to have asked someone to take my temperature, but I could not climb back down now.

I drew back the covers and crawled between the cool fragrant sheets with a long sigh at the marvellous softness of them and the pillows, and closed my eyes gratefully. On the inside of my eyelids, I saw again the handsome angular face of Ranulf, the curving lips, the gold-flecked eyes and the wild dark mop of hair. Even the graceful small movements of his hands were clear in my memory, as was the cool silky feel of his fingers against my cheek.

'Fool,' I muttered.

I drifted into a dream in which I vividly relived my encounter with him in the passage. In the dream he suggested the lane would bring me to the thing I wanted most in all the world.

'I have not told you what I want,' I objected.

'You will desire what you find at the end of this passage, I swear it,' he responded fiercely.

'On your mother's soul?' I demanded, deciding he was teasing me.

His eyes widened at my words and he said, 'Oh yes, on my mother's soul. I do swear it.'

Cloud-Marie threw a silken coverlet over the bed and I regarded the result of our labours with some satisfaction. A hundred part-stuffed mattresses still rose high, but now the bed looked merely quirky rather than grotesque.

We went to the kitchen, for I had decided to cook the meal my son's chosen would eat with my own hands. As I worked at kneading dough, I found myself remembering vividly how confused I had been when the handsome stranger in the lane had suddenly ended our conversation by walking away without trying to give me his telephone number so that I could let him know I had delivered the armlet. I had watched him go, wondering if he would glance back, but he had not.

My husband had told me later, when we lay twined and tenderly dissecting the steps that had led me to his bed, that his mother had forbidden him to look back once he had given me her token, saying if he did, I would be lost to him.

'She was right, Ranulf,' I told him, startled. 'If I had seen you look back, I would have suspected you meant to creep down the lane after me and rob me, or worse, I might not have gone along the lane after all.'

His response had been to lick my naked shoulder like a cat. Ignoring the way his tongue roused my senses, I persisted, asking why he had shown himself to me at all, for I might well have gone along the lane of my own accord, rather than turning back.

'I had to be the one to invite you into Faerie,' he'd murmured.

'How could the mere suggestion that I go along the lane be counted an invitation?' I demanded. 'I did not see it as an invitation.'

He tenderly peeled a strand of sweat-stiff hair from my cheek, and kissed me with his cool lips before saying, 'Of course you knew it was an invitation. I offered the ring and you accepted it. You did not understand why I had given it you, but you were curious and so accepted it. Curiosity is a form of courage, my love, and that is one of the essential ingredients for a maid who would enter the Princess Chamber. How else would she dare the spindles and locked doors of the tests leading up to it?'

'What did it show that I chose the central path when the lane split into three?' I had wanted to know then. 'I didn't make my choice out of any special wisdom or instinct. Was it luck that had me choose the right way?'

'There was no right and no wrong choice. All three choices would have brought you to the Wolfsgate. There was only the need to choose. You see, humans generally act according to the ends that they imagine will come of their actions. The Threeways Path strips away the illusion that reason controls destiny. You would be surprised how many people, faced with the knowledge that reason cannot help them, find they cannot act. Many feel that in turning back to known ways, they retain control. A few stand indecisive, realising that even turning back is a choice filled with mysteries. They are the wiser, but if they stand too long, the Cruel Wind will come to drive them back to their own world just as it will blow at the back of those who retreat at once.'

'What if you had chosen a faerie with mortal blood?' I asked, for though I had not been there long enough to meet other mortals who had crossed, I knew they existed.

'I might have done, but it was my mother's advice that I hunt a mortal woman.'

That had surprised me, for I had secretly felt his mother looked down on me because I lacked even a drop of faerie blood. 'She would not have had to face the Threeways Path,' I said.

'Only princess candidates who are mortal face that particular test, but there are other tests for those of faerie blood. Each test, and the response of the candidate to it, is an ingredient in the spell that will be wrought by the Princess Chamber, and there are many ingredients, some stronger than others. There are some deeds done in response to tests that are so potent they require no other ingredient, though that is rare and cannot be predicted or relied upon.'

I set the bread to its first rising and cleaned down the bench, pondering the tests I would set for my son's chosen, and wondering what sort of spell she and I would make between us. This done, I helped Cloud-Marie slice quinces for a pie and cut up wild mushrooms we then doused with spiced marinade. The shared activity and the smells of yeast and sherry and caramelised sugar made me think of Yssa, for it was from her that I learned to enjoy cooking.

She had treated it as if it were an art to delight all the senses, and so it had become for me, under her tutelage. She had been so honestly horrified to hear how I had fed myself before I stole the magic cloth from my husband, that I had become ashamed of my carelessness. In truth I had not known any better, because my own stiff mother had despised cooking as a bourgeois pursuit and cared not at all what she ate.

Yssa had liked the ease of the food conjured by the cloth well enough, but despite being faerie, she had preferred to cook our meals herself. I had not known enough back then to understand how unusual that was, but abashed by her reaction, I had dutifully offered to help her. However, guided by her pleasure in the activity and her skill, I soon began to look forward to those meals we cooked between us. It was Yssa who made me understand that cooking is to eating what painting a picture is to merely looking at it. She made me see that cooking was as wholesome and nourishing to the spirit as good food is to the body.

After her departure, with two children to care for, I had neither time nor patience for cooking and let the art and the love of it slip from me, relying on my magic cloth to nourish us all. It was long since I had cooked, but I had not forgotten what Yssa had taught me. In the midst of the fragrant heat of the kitchen, I felt such a longing for the faerie woman who had been my best friend in this world, in any world.

Yet when she had come to the door of the palace kitchen when I had been there one day early in my marriage, whey-faced and grim, I had no notion of how much she would come to mean to me. Still, I must have sensed what lay in the future, for surely it was not only out of pity that I invited her in, deliberately breaking the protective seal about the King's Palace which prevents anyone or anything entering without royal permission. When he returned from his questing, my husband was annoyed. A queen could ask anyone into the palace, he later explained, but no queen had ever done such a thing without first consulting her husband. I begged his pardon and then teased him for his pomposity. But later, when I mimicked his words for Yssa, she said soberly that the king was right, for the ban was there to protect me.

'I need no protection,' I had laughed, for in those days I was loved well by the people.

I remember Yssa's reply.

'You are a mortal for all you are the queen. Not all in Faerie love mortals.'

As Cloud-Marie set down the comb and began brushing my hair, I told myself that Yssa would have shared my disappointment in the first girl my son hunted, for she turned out to be little more than a coarse child.

She had been born in Faerie of the granddaughter of a mortal woman and a faerie man, peasant farmers who dwelt not far from the palace. I had learned this by smearing onto my mirror a gob of a magical preparation which one of the queens had given me.

I had finished all of my preparations and sat gazing into the mirror at my son, as he embraced his milkmaid with her rosy cheeks and soft round bosom. I saw how her foolish wide blue eyes bulged as he thrust the bespelled ring into her hands and began fumbling at her milky bosom. Seeing him paw her, I felt sorry I had allowed him to take a human shape, yet clearly she was amenable to his rough kisses. But when she tried to slip the bespelled ring on her finger, it would not fit over her thick knuckles.

My son scowled and snatched the ring back, running to the barn to hammer at it. When he brought the poor battered thing back and forced it on her finger, her mouth fell open as she listened to the instructions it offered. I watched my son lead her to the edge of the Wolfsgate Valley closest to the palace and point to the King's Palace, which would appear to her as nothing more than a mansion with spires and turrets. His chosen nodded eagerly and galloped off. Having the use of magic, she suffered no more than a bruise on one knee and a scratch on the nose in the course of the next three days, as my son, now beast-shaped, drove her hither and thither to keep her moving, at the same time making sure she would not be far from the Endgate on the third dusk.

At one point, watching in my mirror as he gawped oafishly

at her washing her plump, filthy feet in a stream, I prayed that my son had chosen her to spite me or even out of laziness rather than that he was so crude as to desire such a bovine mate. I was certain by now that she would never reach the Princess Chamber, let alone spend a night in it.

The girl got as far as the door to the palace, where she took one look at me deliberately tricked up in all the glittering magnificence I could muster and fled gibbering, my ring still jammed upon her swelling finger. My son came raging at me, saying he would not let me tell him what to do. I laughed cruelly and told him if he could do no better in his choices than a trembling mooncalf who ran away in terror, he had better let me hunt for him.

'At least I might choose you a full-grown woman whose desire for a husband will be robust enough to get her through the door,' I said harshly. I dared not show pity or grief or fear. I had to shock awake the subtlety and refinement of taste that I had nurtured in my son, before the curse began to make itself felt.

I saw I had wounded him, and prayed pain would wake his true self, but instead the beast looked from his eyes as he announced arrogantly that he would entice the next one so thoroughly, she would come to me without her drawers. It shocked me that he would say such a thing to me, and I told him with an icy bluntness that he would do better to consider choosing a maid with more mortal blood so that the Wolfsgate Valley would truly test her, else even if she managed to reach the chamber, she would not have what it took to become his princess bride.

The next time he hunted he chose a bold beauty with wit and courage but still no more than a drop of human blood, so she had power enough to pass the three days in the Wolfsgate Valley as if she were in her own garden. My son had bitterly resented my forbidding him a human shape and was glad his chosen had magic enough to protect herself so that he need not reveal himself to her in his beast shape more than twice: once when he had brought the ring to her, tied in his mane, and at the end, when he led her to the Endgate. She sneered openly at Cloud-Marie who brought her to me and gave me an insolent and triumphant smile as she removed the now-battered ring from her finger – it had been removed by a blacksmith from the finger of the last candidate – and gave it to me.

I saw from her behaviour that she had courage enough and poise as well as beauty, but was there any gentleness in her, or self-control?

When she asked to speak to the young man of the house, I told her that he would not come until daybreak and she responded with a request to sleep the night under my roof. She asked prettily enough, but there was no thought in her that I would refuse. When I said she might remain if she was willing to do a service for me, she acquiesced grudgingly. I set her a room full of straw to spin in a chamber suffused with a scented oil that rendered all magic useless, a gift from the queens, then I sent a twisted little man to offer aid. As I had guessed from her reaction to Cloud-Marie, the young woman's beauty made her unforgiving of ugliness, but I had not guessed that ugliness would make her actively cruel. Rather than begging his aid or merely refusing it, the girl had jeered and thrown her shoe at the dwarf. Enraged, he had become invisible, pinched her black and blue, and then sliced off the end of her nose.

I had been sickened to see all the blood and mess, but the

faerie queen who had lent the dwarf refused to command him to set the matter right. She was fond of the little fellow, she said sternly, and he was shaped to meet like with like. I could not argue. There was no denying the beauty my son had chosen had a short temper and a cruel streak and the outcome was her own fault, for had she been kinder and more polite, the dwarf would willingly have helped her. Even so, I could not help feeling sorry for her as she limped away holding a bloody kerchief to her ruined nose.

My son, restored to his true form, came snorting and bellowing to my chamber in fury. I saw that he had been roused to passion by two hunts and longed to slake it, so I let his anger pour itself over me without responding to it until the torrent ran dry. When at last he stood dumb and panting, my heart bled to see him so reduced, but I dared not let him see any softness in me. Instinct told me to be adamantine.

'Did you really think a plump little mooncalf or a strutting strumpet fit to rule this realm?' I asked sharply. 'Or was it that you were not thinking? You were merely following the base and bullish urges of your loins, like any woodchopper or pig butcher? Perhaps in future you might think beyond bed sports when you hunt, since you will be king and will need a princess who can become a queen to help you rule this kingdom of Faerie.'

'I do not want a queen,' he snarled. It was only an unthinking riposte, and yet I thought that there was a bitter general truth in it, for was not I queen, and seemingly tormenter and obstacle to his every desire?

'Do you want a princess bride who will save you, then?' I asked, letting my tone become weary and disdainful. 'For the qualities required by a queen are one and the same as those required for a maid to become a princess bride. Hunt again, my son, and this time choose a maid who will make a good queen, for only such a one will be able to save you.'

Despite his outrage, I saw in his next choice that he had listened, though he said not a word to me about our confrontation following the previous hunt. This time I sent my son out as a cat, hoping some of the subtlety and sly grace of the form would seep into him. I waited for his new chosen to come knocking at my door, and once more cooked and prayed that he had hunted wisely this time. I had forbidden myself to spy, but when the food was done, I went again to my chamber and used the last smear of the seeking salve on my mirror.

The maid my son had hunted this time was a faerie noble's daughter with a goodly dollop of mortal blood from her mortal father, and this made my heart leap, for it meant she would be better tested in the Wolfsgate Valley and so bring more substance to the chamber than any of the others. She was not living with her parents, having run away from their strictness to live with a household of dwarfs. She did well enough in the Wolfsgate Valley, for she had some magic to aid her, but it was weak enough that she needed her wits and courage as well, and those she seemed to have aplenty. My heart soared and I was glad I had given my son the power to turn into a lion in order to protect her. He still resented the fact that I had made him a donkey in a previous hunt, feeling it made mock of him, though in truth he had made a fine, handsome beast and that form had tenacity and patience.

At dusk on the third day, his chosen came safe through the

Endgate and soon was at the door telling me an eager tale of having received a battered gold ring from the mouth of a fish caught by a beautiful orange cat. This had happened, she told me loftily, while she sat watching fish flit back and forth in the depths of a well and thinking deep, pure thoughts.

Accepting the ring and the tale with some scepticism, I invited her in. She lifted her lacy hem fastidiously as she mounted the steps in her dainty shoon. Of course she had used magic to restore her appearance before knocking at the door, and I ran my eyes over her. She was a pretty creature with small, very white teeth, blue eyes, and a long swan's neck, tiny shell-like ears and hair like a river of pale golden fire. But as we ate, I saw that her mouth was small and she seldom used it to smile and only did so sincerely at a mirror hanging on the wall. All of her attention was turned inward and she spoke of her life with the dwarves, explaining with relish how they had worshipped her beauty and lavished jewels and admiration on her. Indeed, her ears and wrists glittered with the gaudy weight of the gold and jewels she wore, and I was sure it had been these she had been admiring in the well rather than fish and philosophy.

She asked about my son, and I told her he would come the next day. She feigned a delicate yawn and asked if she might lie down and sleep awhile. It was cleverer than a request to spend the night, but still I told her that she could lie down under my roof only after locating a golden ball I had lost in a muddy field inhabited by magical frogs.

She agreed impatiently, certain her magic would enable her to find it, but she soon discovered her magic had no power in that field, which had been sowed with a certain herb I had been gifted, and so she must truly search. The unmelodious croaking of the frogs near drove her mad, so I used a magic shawl one of the queens had given me to transform myself into a poor old woman in rags and offered to sing a song that would make the frogs help her find what she sought. She answered pettishly that she did not need the croaking of a useless old woman any more than she needed the croaking of frogs to find the gold ball, which the sour crone of the house required before she could sleep there. She would summon her seven protectors, who would find the golden ball soon enough for her. She had already sent the pet dove they had given her to fetch them. Then she went back to trying to admire her reflection in the water.

Of course I did not allow the dove to deliver its message, having released from its jewelled box a simple confusion spell that would prevent it leaving, so my son's hapless chosen passed the night in the field before stalking away at dawn in a filthy temper, forfeiting her chance to become a princess.

'You are choosing the stupidest tests,' my son snarled. 'What does it matter if she cannot find a gold ball in a field, or turns her back on a beggar woman, if she has passed through the Wolfsgate Valley?'

'You know perfectly well by now that the Wolfsgate Valley does not truly test any but a full mortal,' I snapped. 'That is the reason the queen sets tests, so that the lack may be answered. As to the girl you hunted this time, she was vain and ruthlessly self-centred. I would be surprised if she could tell me the colour of your eyes, for given her nature, the only thing she would have looked for in them was her reflection. There was nothing to her but a crafty cleverness, shallow wit and hollow beauty!'

I bade him hunt again, for time was running out for all of us.

The fourth maid he chose was a mortal who had come to Faerie when she was but a child. She had been adopted by a sweet merchant. She was plump and kind and had a soft full mouth and a gentle heart, which made her promise at once to help the unicorn that dropped the battered golden ring into her lap, but she was also exceedingly simple. She had no magic, being fully mortal, and survived the Wolfsgate Valley only because a faerie godmother had blessed her with luck and because of my son's vigilance and vicious unicorn strength. I had given him that form in the hope that he would be inspired by it.

When she came to the palace to give me the ring, I assayed a test to see if she had even a modicum of common sense. I warned her specifically not to accept food from strangers, though she was hungry, but to walk in the garden, and I would send Cloud-Marie when a meal was ready. Within ten minutes, she took a poisoned apple from me in my old-woman's disguise, and ate it. Loosening her stays and dribbling the antidote for the poison she had eaten into her lovely mouth, I thought it a pity she had not wit enough to temper her sweetness, for a queen cannot rely on luck and sweetness alone.

Still, she had pretty manners, and when I sent her off, saying my son had not really needed rescuing, she went trustfully, woebegone but wearing a bracelet of undying violets, and an instruction from me to her father to bid him wed her to his clerk. She had confessed to me that they had pledged their troth in secret as children, for her father would never permit her to marry so low.

'You sent her away! You can't do that!' my son shouted. 'I wanted her!'

'I told her that your disguise was a trick and that you had no need of rescuing, so she ought to go home, and she went. If she had been wiser, she might have guessed I was lying.'

'You are ruining my life,' shouted my son, but there was fear in his eyes for the first time, and it broke my heart, for I realised that, with this girl, he had truly been trying to find a candidate who would please me.

It had struck me then that part of the problem faced by my son was that the curse had nullified all the grace and cunning of his faerie blood, leaving only the mortal part, and at his age, many mortal men are little more than lumpish boys without subtlety or finesse. How should such a boy be capable of choosing a girl who could become a good woman and a good queen? The next morning over breakfast I tried to talk to the boy about women and their qualities, and about wiving, but he listened with obvious boredom and resentment, tossing the ring up and down in his hand and occasionally letting it fall and roll away to scour my nerves.

Cloud-Marie ceases brushing to bring me honeyed tea, and I sip at it, grateful for its sweetness, its warmth coiling down into me. I close my eyes, but the thought comes nagging and plucking at me that, although I did not bid my son hunt again after the last dreadful hunt years past, I never did officially command him to leave off hunting. And the night before, pity for his diminished state had persuaded me to remove his chain and release him into the Wolfsgate Valley to run there for the night. I had used a bespelled chain my mother-in-law had given me to stop him roaming out of the valley in case he wandered into a village and devoured some hapless peasant with too little magic to stave him off. But it would not have prevented him travelling to the human realm.

What if he had gone there to choose another girl before returning to be chained up again in his yard at dawn? What if the howl I heard earlier was truly a howl signalling the arrival in the Wolfsgate Valley of his chosen, the beginning of a new testing?

Was it possible?

His father had found me there, and perhaps my son retained some dim memory of it, or it might be that my angry words about the worth of mortals tested by the valley had remained even when his human form was lost, to work their way to the surface of his wolf brain. But how could he hunt in the real world where wolves do not routinely run about the streets, and in that city of all cities, where there is no wilderness except the wildness of degeneration? At night he might conceivably pass as a dog, but even if he had managed to find the will to go there and to hunt, what sort of girl would dare accept a battered ring from the neck of a great white wolf? For him to come close enough to bestow it on her, she could not fail to see the savagery in his eyes and know him for a beast. And what of the ring? Certainly I had not taken it from him after what happened to the last candidate, but surely the ribbon had rotted long since, and the ring fallen into a bog or crack. But supposing he still had the ring, and had hunted a girl brave enough to take it from his neck? Would she imagine it could reveal the name of the owner of what she might suppose to be a tame wolf? But what human woman would then obey an eldritch voice issuing from the ring, commanding her to go thence and do this and that in order to free a nobleman's son from a spell?

In the mirror I see that Cloud-Marie's errant eye is turning sideways. My breath catches in my throat as she turns her head so that, for a moment, both eyes regard curtains I have not drawn in two years. I had not thought to ever open them again, for the window behind them looks out on the same mist garden as can be espied from the balcony of the Princess Chamber where, when a hunt begins, white roses bloom in profusion.

I know I must look out, have known it since the howl waked hope in me, yet if no roses have bloomed, my son is lost. But in this moment it is horror that deters me more than the fear of having to abandon hope, for, with all my heart, I do not want to be reminded of what I beheld the last time I entered the mist garden.

Cloud-Marie's good eye turns back and holds my gaze, and I realise that I am not breathing. I release it in a hissing moan as I remember the scarlet beads of blood caught on my son's muzzle. And though my mind shies from it, I remember following the trail of blood to the body of the young woman in the mist garden. She was dead because she had made the mistake of going outside, rather than staying in the Princess Chamber and sleeping as I had bidden her. I suppose my son thought she had failed, or that she meant to leave. Maybe she *had* intended to leave. Whatever the reason, he had torn her throat out.

I shivered, remembering the desolation and anguish and rage of his howls that night and for many terrible long nights to follow. I had wept into my pillow for hours, sick with grief for the girl and despair for my son, who had lost his last chance to save himself. That was when I had given up, for I knew the beast must have gained the ascendant for him to have slain the girl he had hunted for his bride.

Cloud-Marie and I buried her on a grassy knoll just beyond the mist garden, where the sun would fall, and although I told no one but my husband and my mother-in-law what had happened, word of the grisly tragedy got out, and thereafter no one came willingly to the King's Palace. When anyone did come, I would often see them make the sign of horns with their little finger and forefinger, to ward off ill-fortune.

Steadying myself, I drive back horror and gather my courage before signing for Cloud-Marie to take the shawl from my lap. I am chilled to the bone by what I must do and it is not a chill from which any shawl or fire can shield me. She folds it with an oddly graceful and almost ceremonial air, and I feel her uneven eyes on my back as I rise and cross to the curtains. I have to make myself lift my arms, grasp one curtain in each hand and throw them open.

I draw in a breath of chilly wonder, for the garden below glows white with roses that are blooming more thickly than I have ever seen them do before. It might have snowed save for the intoxicating scent the roses give off, even in the clammy air. I draw in a breath and hear the light rasp of the sea in my lungs.

'It is a miracle,' I say, aloud, to the misty night or maybe to the stars. I feel how strange it is to use such a word here. Turning, I see that Cloud-Marie still stands by my empty chair, the rug cradled in her arms as if it were a babe. Instead of looking frightened or relieved or even happy, there is a listening expression on her loose features, and then I hear it.

A wolf, howling.

It is not my son. I know the timbre of his call, and besides, he is chained up. Nor is it the distinctive call of the leader of the wild pack whose demesne is the Wolfsgate Valley. It must be another wolf from the pack, and a picture forms inexorably in my mind of the black wolf.

Then my blood runs cold and I draw in a horrified breath, for I have forgotten the most important thing! If the candidate is a mortal maid, she has entered the Wolfsgate Valley without any magic to protect her or her prince to watch over her.

I turn and run to my son's yard, heart pounding so hard that my ribs hurt. He is straining at the end of his chain to get as close as he can to the side gate, which opens to the short passage leading to the Endgate. His whole body is trembling with electric tension.

I hurry over and release the catch upon his chain. His fur is white and his eyes have the same gold flecks as his father's, but over the paler grey of my own eyes. I cross to the gate and he watches me, pricking his ears. He knows this is the way to the Wolfsgate Valley, but it is only dusk and I have never let him out save at darkest night before. Nor have I made any attempt to fasten about his neck the magic chain that will limit his roaming.

Does he understand what these things mean? Does he understand what he must do now? I pray so, else the blood of another maid will stain his muzzle and my hands. For a moment I hesitate, but love for my son and crippled hope make me unlatch the gate. I do not attempt to give him any instruction. There is only wildness in his eyes now, and the valley will do all the testing that is needed. My son's task is to protect the girl and guide her at the last to the Endgate. Remembering the other howl, I tell myself that though my son might lack a rational mind, he knows in his essence what is unfolding, and I pray that his chosen has not already come to harm.

I open the gate and walk along the short passage to the Endgate, hearing him padding along behind me, panting. When I open the gate in the wall that separates the palace from the Wolfsgate Valley, my son passes through it. For a moment he stops in the clearing and looks back at me, standing in the gateway. I want to see a glimmer of human intelligence in his eyes, of love for me and knowledge of mine for him, but there is only an unfathomable wildness there, and then he turns away from me and looks out into the valley.

At that moment, far away, there is another howl. This time it is the deep throaty howl of the leader of the grey pack, and every hair on my body stands on end as I remember his red maw and ravenous eyes. But my son stretches his neck and gives a long ululating call in reply, then he leaps away and is gone.

Returning to the courtyard, I sign to Cloud-Marie that we must collect the petals for the Princess Chamber. I can see, writ in her body, that she does not want to go into the mist garden, and

I do not blame her. It was always a strange and unsettling place, thick with the smell of magic, but I must go there at once, or I may lose the courage I will need to go there at all, and I have my part to play this one last time.

I steel myself as we make our way down to the mist garden, yet my heart pounds and my gorge rises as a vile picture comes unstoppably into my mind of the last candidate: the bloody gash at her throat and the spray of red so bright against her pale cheeks, the way her eyes stared so horribly and absently at the sky as we sewed her into her shroud.

I bite my lip hard and begin to tear handfuls of petals from the clusters of roses on the bushes and from those climbers trained over decorative frames which display the blooms in cascades and sheaves and coiling swathes. We gather petals for more than an hour, feeding them into my hold-all baskets until I decide we have enough. The scent of the petals is very strong because those on the bottom are being crushed by the weight of those on top.

I am about to signal to Cloud-Marie that we have enough when I notice a spray of shadow flowers beneath one of the bushes. On impulse, I bid Cloud-Marie carry the basket to the top of the stairs and wait there for me. She looks anxious but obeys me. As soon as she has gone out of sight, I pick a few of the tiny lavender-grey blossoms, then hurry through the garden to a gap in the surrounding wall and run lightly up the hill beyond. Being outside the garden, I see the sun has set and the moon shines brilliantly in the dusk, and illuminating the grave atop the knoll. I kneel and lay the flowers where I imagine her breast might be.

I swear to her bones that this new candidate will come to no harm at the hands – nay, the teeth and claws – of my son.

Returning to the palace, I take the petal-filled baskets from Cloud-Marie and we return to the Princess Chamber. As we strew the petals, re-lay the fire and renew the bed, which I never thought to do again, I find myself thinking of all of those maidens for whom I have made this same preparation. Five did not accept the invitation, and of those who did, nine turned back at the Threeways Path and seven of those who went forward did not pass through the Wolfsgate. Of the seventy-eight who passed through it, sixty-two failed the tests there in one way or another. Sixteen passed through the wood and came to my door, but three turned away without knocking. Of the thirteen young women who entered my house, two were convinced by trickery or reason to abandon their quest at once, five failed the tasks they were set by me and two refused to undertake them. One tripped down the stairs and broke her neck. That had been near the beginning and my son had been man-shaped and still soft enough to pity the young woman her fatal clumsiness. He had left her at the bottom of some steps in my own world, where it would appear she had stumbled. Only three had been shown to the Princess Chamber. Only two slept in the bed and neither had brought enough for the princess spell to be woven. The thirteenth was the last, she who walked in the mist garden and died in the teeth of the beast, my son.

I frown, realising the final tally is ninety-nine. I count again, certain I must have miscounted, but I did not. I lick my lips. The current hunt is the hundredth, and I have been too long in Faerie not to recognise an omen when I encounter one. Even the fact that

I have never thought to add up the number of candidates before is significant. All at once I am utterly exhausted. It seems to me that I have not been so tired since I came to the palace seeking refuge after my own three nightmarish days in a walled garden that had turned into a wild valley full of wolves.

I stumble to my own bed, cast myself down and sleep. But there is no escape for, in my dreams, the memories await me.

There were three passages before me, all narrow, all identical, running away out of sight. With nothing to decide between them, for the handsome Ranulf had not told me the way forked, I chose the middle path, and as I stepped into it, a gritty wind whirled up out of nowhere, dragging at my hair and scouring my cheeks. Instead of coming from one direction it seemed perversely to be coming from all directions at once, though I could not see how that was possible in such a narrow alley.

The grit in the wind got into my eyes and they began to water. I felt my way along, eyes streaming, as I steadily cursed my foolishness for taking directions from a stranger.

A *handsome* stranger, my mother's voice sneered, waspish with disapproval, for she distrusted good looks on principle.

I shook her voice from my head, reasoning that the bullying wind was not the fault of the man, though he might have mentioned the fork in the way. I could have turned back, but I went on, wondering at my ill-luck in choosing the one lane in the whole city that seemed to contain not a single doorway that could provide refuge.

After what seemed a very long time, the lane reached a small square. At once, the wind died. Bemused by the sudden silence, I gazed about the empty square in a sort of battered daze. The sun shone through ragged patches in the billowing banks of black cloud overhead and lit up odd details. Instinctively I moved towards the nearest patch of sunlight, my cheeks stinging as if they had been sandpapered. I touched them gingerly, wishing there was a canal running by so that I could wet them. But the square was closed, save for the lane I had come through. This explained why I had not seen any other tourist since entering it. But where were the people who lived in the buildings around the square? Ordinary citizens here appeared to regard the squares adjacent their apartment buildings as extensions of their living rooms or public meeting halls and they would come out on the slightest pretext, bringing chairs to sit on while they took the sun and gossiped or smoked or played cards. Yet here was a square empty of people.

I looked around more carefully, wondering if it was possible that the buildings were deserted. I had heard it said that the whole city was sinking into the water a fraction every year, and my own landlady had told me many first floors in buildings were not used at all. Perhaps these buildings had degenerated so badly they had been condemned, or had been sold to a developer who was yet to decide their fate. I grimaced at the thought of a KFC or a McDonalds or Taco Bell in this ancient place.

Then I noticed that one of the walls of the square was not the exterior of a building, but a high wall above which rose foliage. There was a door set into an alcove, which surely must be the gate Ranulf had mentioned. The stones of the wall had a weathered look that made it appear even older than the beautiful crumbling facades of the buildings around the square, and when I reached the door, for it was truly more door than gate, I saw a tarnished metal plaque affixed to the blackened timber, featuring a murky, heavily furred dog baring his teeth. I thought it might be a warning against a resident dog, but when I set my fist to the door and knocked, no dog came leaping and barking at the other side. The wood was pitted, charred and oiled but there was a small square opening in it crossed by two stubby bars. I stood on tiptoe to look through them and saw a stretch of open ground that ran to a line of trees whose branches flailed and twisted in the wind. I could not feel a breath of wind now, but perhaps the wall was shielding the square.

Though I strained to make out what lay beyond the trees, the clouds cast their shadows too heavily beyond the wall for me to see. I reached for the handle to the door, then noticed there was a lock in the wood under it, a great heavy thing of iron that looked as if it had not been opened in centuries. I was disappointed, for any moving parts would long ago have fused together in the damp sea air that permeated the place, and besides, there was no key. What had the man in the passage been playing at, saying I could use the door? Had it been a joke?

A voice hailed me and I turned to see an old beggar woman sitting on the cobbles by the wall. She must be a good deal more spry than she seemed, to have appeared in the few moments I had my back turned to the square. She was turning and turning a plastic cup in her fingers, her faced tilted in my direction, and feeling the same combination of guilt and pity that beggars always roused in me, I went to her, scooping coins from my pocket. No doubt she would spend the coins on drink or ciga-rettes, but at least I had given her the means to get some food if she chose. I leaned forward to drop them into her cup and she started violently.

'What do you want?' she shrieked, so loudly that I staggered back in shock. She turned her head awkwardly as if her neck was wrongly joined and, seeing her face, I almost gasped at her marvel-lous ugliness. Then it struck me that I might have frightened her, for there was a cloudiness in her eyes that suggested cataracts. Probably I had been no more to her than a dark shape looming over her, and from the way she had bellowed she was deaf, too, and so had not heard my approach.

I bent closer and said clearly, 'I put in some coins. In your cup.' Swift as a striking snake, one of her hands darted out and her dry bony fingers closed on my wrist like a manacle of twigs. I wanted to snatch my hand away, because now that she had moved, her ripe stench had risen to envelop me.

'Don't worry,' I said gently, trying to breathe only through my mouth. 'I just put money into your cup.'

'I am no beggar,' she said. 'I will tell your fortune for the coins.' She gave me a smile that bared stained and broken teeth, and turned my hand to flatten it out. I endured this, thinking the mysterious man in the alley and the old woman must surely be partners in trickery, though to what end I could not guess. But a tiny part of me was also curious to hear what she might say about my future.

Idiot, my mother's voice chided me.

The old beggar looked at me so sharply that for a moment

I thought she must have heard the thought, but she only said, 'When you were a girl, you dreamed a prince would come to claim you.'

As predictions go, it left something to be desired, but just the same, her words roused a queer reckless bitterness as I thought of the married lover for whom my parents had disowned me. 'That is the wish of a girl. I am a woman and I have learned that there are no real princes,' I said.

'Oh, there are princes, but there is a price for the having of them,' she answered.

'What price?' I asked, half mesmerised by her intensity. 'I gave you all the coin I have and I do not have my purse with me.' It was true, but I did not expect her to believe me.

'The price is all that you have,' she said. Then she released my wrist and tapped at the scuffed toe of one of my shoes.

A chill slipped down my spine, because how could she know about my safety money – the little flat foil package of notes I had carried around the world in the toe of my sensible shoe? I had forgotten it myself, but now I found myself imagining taking off the shoe and giving the notes in it to her, and then realised that I was doing just that.

Madness, I thought as she took the packet from me and slipped it into her grubby bodice. I waited to feel humiliated by what I had done, but instead I felt as if I had put down something heavy. It was absurd, but I straightened up, drawing my hand from hers to flex my shoulders.

'Give me your hand again,' the old woman urged, making a little crabbed gesture towards me with her grimy fingers.

'I don't want to know the future,' I said, amazed to discover that this was true. 'I will know it when it comes.'

'So you will, child,' she cackled, seeming pleased by my response.

My hair had begun to whip my cheeks and I realised the weather was about to show its claws again. 'I think there is a storm coming,' I said. 'Do you want me to help you somewhere?'

The old woman cackled again and shooed me away. 'I don't need help, but you might.' She rummaged in her skirts and drew out a length of light rope. She pressed it into my hand and then rummaged again before bringing out a disposable lighter. Bewildered, I told her I did not smoke, but she only grinned and bade me take the things she had given me, for I would have need of them ere the end. To my dismay, rain suddenly began to fall. I had stupidly brought my notebooks in a cloth bag, and I struggled to push it up the front of my coat.

'Will you go through the Wolfsgate?' the old woman asked, nodding towards the rain-lashed wall.

'It is locked,' I told her distractedly, realising the metal plate showed a wolf, not a dog.

'It is?' she asked archly.

I was about to say impatiently that of course it was, then remembered I had not actually turned the handle. I ran to it, hoping to get out of the rain and the wind on the far side of the wall. I was still holding the rope and lighter the old woman had given me and I thrust them into my coat pocket to take hold of the handle. It was slippery with rain and the mechanism shifted slowly as if the gate had not been opened for a long time. Then it gave a distinct click. I pushed, but still the door would not budge. Then I saw weeds and grass had grown in a thick tuft at the bottom of the door, jamming it firmly in place. I leaned my shoulder against the dark, stained wood and pushed hard. It gave with a tearing sound. As the gate opened wide, I turned to tell the old woman she ought to come out of the rain, but she had vanished. I had no idea how, but there was no sense standing in the rain wondering about it. I slipped through the opening and pushed the gate closed behind me. As I had guessed, the wall blocked the wind-driven rain, and I sighed with relief. Some rain was still falling but an overhang atop the wall jutted out to bridge the narrow gap between it and a hedge growing along the inside of the wall, so I slipped into the gap and moved along it until I found a place where there was enough space for me to sit down. Scraping together a pile of crackling brown leaves as a cushion, I settled with my back to the wall and pulled a shawl from my book bag to wrap around my shoulders, hoping the rain would not last for hours.

Too late to wish I had gone straight to the library, but the more I considered the events of the last hour, the stranger they seemed to me, and the more foolish my behaviour. I did not understand what had possessed me to take directions from a stranger, let alone to give my safety money to an old beggar, but it was done and my head was beginning to ache. I leaned forward to rest my forehead on my knees, closed my eyes and watched motes of light dance behind them, trying to let the soft sound of the falling rain fill my mind. I was not aware of falling asleep, but when I woke, the rain had stopped and I was lying stretched out along the base of the wall, my hair full of leaves. Luckily the rain had not seeped into my shelter.

I sat up, grimacing, combed my fingers through my hair and squinted at the illuminated hands of my watch. It had stopped, but it was dark enough that I knew I had missed my appointment with the library curator by several hours. I swore as I crawled out from under the hedge and got to my feet.

I went to the door in the wall and grasped its handle but, to my horror, it moved without engaging. Apparently it could be opened only from the other side. I rattled the bars and stood on tiptoe to look through them, only to see the square was as empty as before. I shouted out for help just the same, in the hope that the old beggar woman was nearby, but if she was, she did not heed my cries, or perhaps she did not hear them. Finally, I shrugged and turned to face the walled garden, thinking that at least I might have the pleasure of crossing it and the interest of an encounter with its owner at the other end, when I gave Ranulf's armlet to her.

Feeling my arm to be sure I still had the armlet pushed above my elbow, I made my way across the grass to the line of trees, curious to see what lay beyond them. As I drew closer, I saw there were several rows of coppiced trees, planted in such a manner that each row prevented me seeing beyond to the next row. Fortunately they were planted far enough apart to allow me to squeeze through, and as I moved forward, I wondered how the trees managed when they were planted so close to one another.

As I wove through line after line of the trees, I began to wonder if I had not entered a tree nursery, for there was nothing aesthetically appealing in the suffocatingly close grid of trees. Then it struck me that the grid must curve, for the long fingers of light that managed to slant through the interlaced foliage were now striking the left sides of the trees where before they had struck the right sides. I turned to look left and saw to my horror that the view was exactly the same as when I looked forward. Or back! In any direction I saw only close-planted lines of trees. Was it possible I had been turning without noticing it as I walked? Or was it that the rows themselves were now marching at a slightly different angle?

I began to feel claustrophobic, but mastered myself. All I had to do was to make sure I was walking straight now and sooner or later I would reach the end of the trees. I set off again and counted fifteen rows of trees before I stepped out into the open. The brief surge of relief I experienced gave way to horror, for I found myself teetering on the edge of a low escarpment. A densely forested valley stretched away from the foot of the escarpment, bordered on one side by a long range of jagged white mountains. I had one brief, astounded glimpse of that long, narrow valley, then the ground crumbled under my feet and I fell.

Even all this time later, I sometimes have nightmares of that fall, from which I wake, heart pounding, half starting up. Of course, I had not entered any ordinary garden. No. I had passed through the Wolfsgate and, in doing so, had come to the very heart of Faerie. As tales and myths tell of the otherworld, the hearts of things are always larger than what contains them, so I had entered a garden only to find it encompassed mountains and a forest and streams and lakes. My husband told me later that there was no settlement in the valley, for the heart of Faerie was truly wild and inhabited only by beasts or to those given over to the beast in their natures. The most ferocious of these were the wolves whose territory it was.

The nearest proper dwelling to the Wolfsgate was the King's Palace and all the rest of Faerie lay beyond that.

'What if I had not come through the Wolfsgate?' I teased my husband the morning after our wedding. His heavy beard had been shaven away along with the pelt of hair covering his body, though in truth it had not troubled me as much as maybe it ought to have done. Now his luxuriant black hair had been combed and trimmed into a handsome mane and he looked urbane and civilised. But his turquoise eyes were the same, save that the savagery in them had gone and they were full of laughter and delight.

He kissed me instead of answering my question, and his clever hands became so busy in so explicit a manner that I blushed despite all that had already been done between us. Satisfied, he held me back from him, examined my flushed cheeks smugly and laughed, a throaty growl that made my skin prickle. 'You could never have resisted, faced with that gate. It blocked your way and it is your nature to refuse deflections and hindrances. Princesses decide their own limits and always transgress in order to discover them. It is part of what drew me to hunt you.'

'So, courage and curiosity and some sort of subversive stubbornness are needed for the princess spell?' I asked.

'They are vital qualities, for those who would make rules must be able to exist beyond them,' my husband murmured, examining a freckle on my breast closely.

'And the old woman?'

'Was my mother got up in that guise,' he said, and he stretched out his pale, slender fingers over my bare breast, as if it were a ripe fruit to be plucked. 'She said that she wanted to give you some tokens to aid you, if you pleased her.'

The sound of cutlery and the smell of toast and coffee brings me pleasantly to the present as Cloud-Marie manoeuvres the tray into my chamber. I sit up and smooth the bedclothes with more appetite than I have had in many a long day. When she has set down her burden, I sign for parchment and a quill, wanting to make a shopping list. I have decided on the meal I will serve my daughter-in-law and I mean to obtain the ingredients from our world, hers and mine.

After I eat and make my list, it strikes me that I can see the mortal girl my son hunts in my scrying bowl. The last thing I saw in it was my son bending over the girl he had slain and I have not looked into it since, but now I dress and eagerly mount the long spiral of stairs leading to the small, circular tower room. There is nothing in the room but the enormous stone scrying bowl filled with water so black and still it might have been a hole full of shadow. The bowl is a strikingly beautiful but sinister object from which power emanates like an electrical current. It was a gift sent by my husband.

I do not know if, when he set out the morning before our son began his first hunt, he intended to return soon, and became distracted, or if he always meant to return once our son found his princess bride, but I have not seen him from that day to this. He occasionally sends gifts. In the early days of his departure, they always arrived after I had sent missives to him using various magical devices he had given me over the years for this purpose, though he never sent any message with them. In recent times they come rarely, and still without a word of his whereabouts, though there have sometimes been small notes accompanying a gift, explaining its use.

My husband's first gift came after I notified him of the failure of our son's first hunt. It was a mechanical nightingale that sang with the tongue of any bird that ever existed. A pretty toy, it sits gleaming on my dresser. The brush and comb Cloud-Marie uses on my hair were a gift too, part of a set that included a magic mirror that would let me see my face at any age. It was a grim sort of gift for a mortal, but one day when I spoke my husband's name to curse him, I noticed his face reflected in the glass. The image moved and I realised that the mirror was showing me him not only as he was but also where he was. He looked handsome and wind-blown, and the sky behind his head was like a sheet of raw grey silk flawed with lighter strands. I spoke his name beseechingly, and though he did not answer, his lips twisted. With longing or regret, I thought, believing in his love of me, for all his neglect. But when the mirror clouded and I saw him no more, I came to wonder if his pained grimace had been no more than the shape made of him by the spell he wrought to stop me spying on him. Or perhaps he had given up hope and did not want me to see it.

The mirror was ruined after that and would not even show my face, but on the verge of smashing it I hesitated, for it struck me that even if I could not see my husband, perhaps he could hear me. Often during the long years of failed hunts and growing despair that followed, I found bitter consolation in whispering curses into the smoky glass.

It was some months after the mirror clouded that the scrying bowl arrived. *It will show you our son and that which he sees*, said the little scroll that accompanied it.

The water in it does not offer a reflection of the shadowed stone walls of the room or of the four windows that look out in four different directions over Faerie, and there is not a fleck of dust upon it. There is no dust on any of the surfaces in the chamber, though I have not been here since my son last hunted. Is it magic that keeps the chamber clean or Cloud-Marie's vigilance?

I cross to the scrying bowl and kneel, leaning over its rim to look down into the liquid blackness within it. That it does not show my reflection makes me feel dizzy, and I take a moment to steady myself and to gather courage enough to reach down into the bowl. I close my eyes, for I have always experienced a childish horror in doing this. Sometimes in nightmares things have reached back to grasp me. Once it was my son leaping out to close his teeth in my throat.

I feel the wetness of the water, if water it is, and stir my hand. Feeling it begin to whirl, I open my eyes and see my son in wolf form loping through the forest at a purposeful speed. But it is not a wolf form, I remind myself. My son is now a wolf in truth, and for a split second I do not see him as degenerate and cursed, but as a creature of breathtaking beauty and terrifying grace, a snow-white wolf prince.

I study the terrain he is speeding through, and understand he is heading towards the mountains. That my son goes this way can only mean that the girl has chosen to go towards the mountains, for there is no doubt he is going to her. I am eager to see her face and to discover if I can judge her character from it, but I cannot do so until he finds her. I withdraw, resolving to return after I have completed my preparations.

I descend from the tower, wondering why the girl went towards the mountains. I, too, had considered going that way when I woke in a bed of moss at the bottom of the escarpment. The fact that there was no way back up the sheer drop behind me meant I had no choice but to go forward one way or another, and my fleeting glimpse of the mountains had shown them to be extraordinarily beautiful. But I was forced to recognise the impossibility of a range of mountains on a muddy island in a lagoon. I settled instead upon climbing the long wooded slope I could see on the other side of the valley, which would offer me a view. I wondered what it said of the maid chosen by my son that she had decided to travel towards the mountains. Was she a fool who would follow any mad vision, or someone capable of holding to a vision despite the lack of concrete evidence?

In my chamber as I prepare myself for the journey to my old world to fetch the ingredients I will need, I focus my thoughts determinedly on the meal I will serve my son's chosen, rather than worrying about what she is doing and why. I have decided upon a simple repast and not the elaborate feasts I have prepared before: sliced fresh tomatoes served with pungent chopped onions on thick slabs of fragrant rough bread, olives and a good parmesan broken into little crumbling pieces, and instead of eating inside, we will sup in the fountain courtyard.

I reach into the basket to ensure I have my pouch of jewels and gasp in pain. Withdrawing my finger, I find I have driven a hidden needle in a small tapestry deep into my thumb. When I withdraw it, blood wells dark and thick, and one drop falls like a ruby bead onto the white linen that is yet to be embroidered.

My hair stirs on my scalp, for surely this is another omen.

Dismissing my fears, I set off for the nearest crossing place. There are only a few ways from that world which was once my own to this one, but there has never been much difficulty or formality about moving from Faerie to the real world. Ever since the first faerie king opened a way to the mortal realm, fell in love and brought a mortal back with him, there have been numerous ways to cross. These are always closing and opening according to the whims of the king whose task it is to weave and renew the ways.

The first two crossing places are obscured by a mist which is nothing to wonder at, for mists of obfuscation are common in Faerie, and I feel only a mild irritation when I cannot find my way through them to the mortal realm. The third time, I use a wooden bridge I have often used before, remembering to check for trolls before setting foot on it. Few things are more tedious than having one of the great brutes grasp your ankle and force you to play their wretched riddling game for hours. Reassured I am not to be waylaid, I climb the steps to the bridge and set off into the thick mist, only to find myself coming back to the same bank I had just left, as on the last two attempts! I turn and try again, with the same result, though I cannot detect myself being turned around.

Only then do I recall reading in one of the tomes bestowed upon me by the old queens that once a prince begins to hunt his bride, the powers of kingship devolve to him, but that he cannot take them into himself until he has wed his bride. That meant there would be a hiatus during which the powers of kingship are inaccessible to the old king or to the one who would be king. At the time I read the words, I barely took them in, but now I am sure the crossing places have been slowly degenerating in the years since my son undertook his first hunt, and that some are now unusable.

Perhaps all.

I have thought little of my old world since the birth of my son, but I feel a stab of something very like terror at the thought of not being able to go home, and it comes to me that perhaps I am less resigned to living out my life in Faerie than I have believed.

When I am back in the palace, I calm myself, for the cure to one problem is the cure to both. If my son can hunt a true princess to be his bride, he will be saved, and then, as king, he can repair and reopen the ways between the two realms.

Forced to abandon my plan to obtain ingredients for the meal I will offer my son's chosen, I find all I need in my garden or with the aid of the magic cloth. The meal itself does not take long. Once I have kneaded the bread and set it to rise, I slice tomatoes and onions and steep them in oil, brown vinegar and basil, and set out several cheeses and a good red wine. I consider going to look in the scrying bowl, but tell myself that too little time has passed. Better to wait a while longer, especially when I can do nothing, no matter what I see. I pace for a time and then go to my sewing chamber and sign for Cloud-Marie to get out my basket of threads. Taking up a needle, I begin to sew, but my thoughts run like a wolf through a shifty wilderness of fears and hopes that have grown up in me. They bring me at length and inexorably to the Wolfsgate Valley, to the moment that I woke at the bottom of the cliff over which I had fallen, utterly bewildered.

After dusting myself off and gathering my wits as best I could, I set off for the rise I could see, but the ground sloped down and I soon lost sight of it. I walked for half an hour using the position of the sun to keep a straight course, trying to figure out what had happened. It was impossible that this wilderness was on an island in the midst of a city. No, somehow I was somewhere else. The only thing I could imagine was that the man, Ranulf, who had given me the stone circlet, found me unconscious at the bottom of the cliff and carried me in a boat to some remote place on the mainland.

It made no sense and yet there was no other explanation.

I noticed that the carved ring had grown tight about my upper arm and I was about to ease it down when I noticed a small track winding through the trees to my right. My heart leapt, for a path meant people and I set off at once upon it. Gradually it wended its way up into a dense copse of trees and though there was no sign of human habitation, it curved in the direction I had originally intended to go, and I felt sure that it would eventually bring me to the bare hill I had seen that would offer a better vantage point from which to study the terrain.

Half an hour later, I spotted a small clearing a little way down one side of the ridge, where there was a rough hut. A subsidiary path split off and ran down to the hut, which seemed as picturesque as an illustration in a children's book as I drew closer. Then I saw a man sitting on a stool by the door, whetting the edge of an axe. This sight was alarming enough that I hesitated, but feeling sure he had already noticed me, I did not feel I could turn tail like a frightened rabbit, so after a slight pause, I continued on. When I came to a halt, I saw the whetting stone still a moment as the old man looked at me, then he went calmly on with his work.

The sound of the stone on the metal set my teeth on edge, but

I was in no position to be finicky. 'Excuse me, but I am lost,' I said. 'I wonder if you have a map and could show me where I am.'

He scowled at me, or maybe it was a smile. It was hard to tell in a face so seamed and leathery and sprouting great feathery tufts of hair from incongruous parts. It occurred to me belatedly that he might not understand English, so haltingly I began to translate my request into the language of the land, but the man wagged his head and said something to me in words that, if they bore any relationship to the language I had just spoken, must be distant. A dialect, I told myself, dismayed. But I smiled reassuringly and tried to convey by hand motions and mime that I needed to find a way out of the wilderness. The man looked suspicious and even offended as I persisted, my cheeks growing redder and redder, but suddenly he laughed uproariously.

Completely taken aback, I stopped and watched him bellow and rock and slap his knee until his mirth had run its course. Then he pointed to me and to a path that ran away from the clearing towards a heavily wooded hill. I tried to ask if the path led to a village, but the best I could get from him was that I must go that way and that I should not stray from the path. He made the latter very clear. I mimed that I was thirsty and hungry, but he shook his head sternly and showed three fingers to me. Then he pointed along the path again. I took the show of fingers to mean I must walk three kilometres to find what I needed, for surely he would not send me off on a three-hour walk without water. In any case there was nothing to do but to go on, since I had no means of making him give me water or food and he was clearly waiting for me to leave.

Mistaking my hesitation for incomprehension, he again pointed insistently along the path and shook three fingers in my face. I nodded wearily and trudged off, consoling myself that it would be better anyway to find a place where I could beg a bed for the night, as it was growing late.

By now I had given up all hope of trying to make any sense of what was happening to me. I must go through it, that was all, and when I came to the end of whatever it was, I would understand it. There were times in life when that was the only thing you could do. The affair with the married man had been just such a thing; an inexplicable and inescapable folly, seen as such only from without. Sometimes you simply could not see properly when you were in the middle of something, no matter how clear-headed and certain you were.

The path narrowed to a mere track as it wound among the trees, which were thick enough that the path grew quite dark in places, certainly dark enough for me to have to slow down to be sure I had not strayed from it. The old man's stern warning had impressed me, and now I thought I understood his insistence. He had been trying to tell me that I must not leave the path lest I lose sight of it and become irrevocably lost. I was uneasily conscious, too, that the day was steadily but surely drawing to a close. Whether or not I had reached a village, I would have to stop once it became too dark to see.

I was terribly thirsty by now, for I had drunk nothing since I had left the pension to seek out the library. Was it really possible this was the same day? If only I could find a stream, but I dared not leave the path. In faerie stories, the worst thing anyone could ever do was to leave the path. A path was like a clear intention that must be followed, but there were always other tempting possibilities trying to draw the hero or heroine away from their original pure purpose.

But I am not a heroine in a story, I thought. I am a historian and the daughter of two pragmatic parents who disliked imaginary games and thought imaginary stories the province of the foolish and uneducated. And I am thirsty. As if conjured by my desire, I saw a gleaming pool of water in a little clearing only two or three steps from the path. Head pounding with thirst, I hurried to the edge and flung myself down on my belly to drink. The water was ice cold and very pure. I drank until my belly ached and then I lifted my head to gasp a breath and saw it: a coal-black wolf sitting on the other side of the pool watching me with eyes that shone like mercury.

I froze, water dripping from my chin and the ends of my hair, but I could not push them back or mop my face without moving, for I was still kneeling forward, resting on my hands. On all fours, I thought, wildly. I could feel gooseflesh rising over my entire body, even on my scalp. I did not want to be eaten by a wolf. Especially I did not want to be eaten in the middle of an inexplicable adventure so that I would never know how it ended.

Except that I would know exactly how it ended.

It is not the end of the story that matters, I think, my needle darting in and out of the tapestry, but understanding the meaning of it, unless the end is the meaning. The memory of the extreme terror I experienced seeing the black wolf gazing at me is dimmed in my mind for a moment by this thought, by the sense of its importance. Then memory floods back, carrying me with it into the past.

The stone armlet suddenly slipped from where it had been lodged about my upper arm and fell down to give the back of my hand a good hard rap. I bit back a cry of pain, but perhaps I made some involuntary sound, for the black wolf suddenly rose.

I sat back onto my heels, lifting my hands to defend myself. The bracelet fell into the crook of my elbow but I ignored it. My attention was all on the wolf, padding to the side of the pool. It was close enough for me to see that it was a she-wolf, and it struck me there was nothing threatening in her demeanour, save that she had come closer. She had not hunkered down or snarled or shown any sign of aggression and she made no attempt to come around the pool, or gather herself to leap over it.

'What then?' I croaked.

She stiffened at my voice and lowered her head slightly, but her hackles stayed down and she did not growl. She only went on staring at me intently. I wondered if she could be a tame wolf that belonged to someone who lived along the path. I could not sit there forever, so very slowly I got to my feet. My knees cracked but the she-wolf only followed my movements with her silver eyes. Then she began to pad softly around the pool towards me.

Heart thudding wildly, I took one panicky step back, and then another.

She stopped and sat back on her haunches. I stared at her indecisively, feeling as if I were involved in some complex negotiation whose rules I did not understand, and which might end with me having my throat torn out. Then some impulse made me glance down and I saw that I was back on the path. When I looked up again, the she-wolf had vanished. Mind reeling, I suddenly became aware how dark it was. The trees about the pool seemed closer than they had been and I had not noticed until now how dead and black they were, branches stretching down towards the water like claws.

I shivered and continued along the path, knowing I would not be able to do so for much longer, for once it was dark, I would not be able to see where I was going. I imagined the black wolf shadowing me in the darkness, biding her time, though for what I did not know, since she had already had the perfect opportunity to attack me. My mind felt as unsteady as my legs, yet there was nothing I could do but walk, my eyes fixed on the vanishing track, my ears listening for the sound of paws.

***

'A black wolf?' my husband had questioned me later, looking sceptical and amused, and my needle slows as I remember the intimacy of that long-ago conversation.

'Black and female,' I answered. I was somewhat indignant about his scepticism, given that he was a faerie prince who had been well on his way to turning into a wolf when I wed him. But at the same time I had been distracted by the coolness of his white faerie flesh against which my body seemed to burn like a brand.

'The wolves of the pack that dwell in the valley are all grey,' he had murmured, taking my fingers from his chest and kissing their tips absentmindedly. 'Perhaps it looked black in the shadows under the trees. Strange that a female was alone though; the pack usually stays together.'

'Maybe she was a lone wolf?'

'Lone wolves are male. More like she had new cubs in a den somewhere close by. You were fortunate she was alone. No wolf will attack a human alone.' Gathering me close, he kissed me on the mouth, and said against my lips, 'Fortunately I got to you before the pack arrived.'

'I was frightened out of my wits when I saw her, but I don't think she wanted to hurt me,' I told him. 'I think now that she was trying to get me back to the path and away from the black strangler trees growing around the pool. She stopped coming towards me the moment I was standing on the path.'

'It was because you were on the path that she had to stop,' my husband had corrected me, shaking me a little. 'All of the wolves in the valley are ferociously wild. You saw that for yourself. They would have killed you if I had not distracted them so that you could get to the cave.'

I was not convinced, but now I was distracted by the memory of my astonishment when an enormous red bird appeared just as the wolf pack surrounded me. To my horror, the big grey wolf that was their leader had stepped right onto the path, which, until that moment, all of the wolves had seemed scrupulously to avoid. It was not until later I worked out that the path repelled the wolves only in daylight hours. The red bird had uttered a piercing scream and dropped towards the leader of the pack, talons outstretched, and the wolves had scattered. After a frozen moment, I had seen my chance and darted for the mouth of a cave.

'I did not see a black she-wolf among the others,' I finally told my husband.

'Because she was not black,' he answered indulgently. 'She was a grey wolf you thought to be black who would have killed and eaten you with relish had she thought she could manage it alone, my pretty morsel.' He slid his hands down my back and cupped my buttocks, and when his lips claimed mine again, I had forgotten about the black she-wolf.

My needle is still for a moment as I remember how it was to be held and cupped and pressed by hands that seemed as if they could never get enough of me. And yet they had ceased to want me. Was I no longer desirable because I had become a mother, or was it because I was human and ageing, if slowly, that caused my husband to turn from me? Or had the chemistry between us faded in the face of our son's affliction? Perhaps all of those things had eroded the lustre of our desire. I resume my sewing, thinking that perhaps it is that the ways and paths to the body are closed one by one, by many things, and all without a person noticing, until a day comes when you discover there is no longer any gateway to the flesh.

I sighed and let my thoughts return to the moment I had entered the cave.

It was pitch dark when I remembered, with a burst of relief, the lighter the old woman had given me. I dug frantically in my pocket until my fingers found it. To my astonishment, when I pulled it out and flicked its flame to life, I found that it was not the cheap disposable lighter the old beggar woman had given me, but a heavy, beautifully engraved silver lighter. How had I not noticed that, I wondered incredulously.

There was no time to ponder it, for I knew it would not be long before the wolves came into the cave after me, and there was nothing I could use to bar the entrance or use as a barrier. The only possibility of safety lay in getting to high ground. Holding the lighter high, I saw a ledge jutting out some way up the side of the cave. I went to the wall beneath it and studied it intensely for a moment, then I extinguished the flame and thrust the lighter in my pocket.

I began to climb in utter darkness, feeling for the nubs and niches I had seen and praying I was not veering away from the ledge. I had not been climbing for more than a minute when I heard the wolves enter the cave. One of them gave a growling snarl, and when I heard it running towards me, I nearly fell from sheer fright. I froze and heard it leap and then fall back with a yelp to scrabble at the face of the rock beneath me. Only then did I know I had climbed high enough to be safe, though not by much, for I had felt the heat of its breath on my ankles. Forcing myself to be calm, I continued to climb slowly and very carefully. It seemed to take forever before I felt the ledge above me and, with a sob of hysterical relief, dragged myself up onto it. I lay there gasping and trembling for a long time before I could bring myself to sit up. Moving so that my back was against the wall, I prayed the wolves had gone, but one flick of the lighter was enough to disabuse me of that fantasy. The pack sat below the ledge, staring up at me with sullen red eyes. I spent an utterly terrifying night on my narrow ledge in the darkness with the smell of wolf all about me, and the knowledge that, if I slept, I would likely roll into the maws of the waiting pack.

Whenever I felt myself drifting off, I would flick the lighter flame on. One glimpse of the vigilant wolves was enough to bring me wide awake, heart banging at my ribs. Yet despite that, I did fall asleep ere morning, and woke with a terrified start only to find that the pale limoncello sunlight of the very early morning lay across the sandy floor of the cave. There was no sign of the wolves save for their criss-crossing spoors, but it took me another hour to get up courage enough to climb down and go outside.

The clearing where the red bird had appeared overhead was empty and wet with dew, which glistened like diamonds scattered on every leaf and blade of grass. It was beautiful, but aside from drinking my fill from a small stream beside the cave and filling the empty water bottle I had in the bottom of my book bag, I felt no urge to linger. I hurried to the path. A long red feather was lying on it and I took it up reverently to marvel at its beauty. That was when it came to me that the path would keep me safe so long as the sun was in the sky. Only later did I understand that the feather had imparted that knowledge. Another of my mother-in-law's clever refinements.

Slipping the feather into my coat pocket, I set off briskly along the path. I paid no heed to the rational part of my mind that insisted a path could not protect a walker, because neither could a valley and a forest be contained within a wall on a mud island in the midst of a city, but here I was. Too many impossible things had happened for me to feel anything was impossible, save perhaps finding a way back to normality.

I kept up a good pace to begin with, but by late morning I was flagging badly. Aside from the fact that I had hardly slept the previous night, my shoes were beginning to disintegrate and I had fallen twice, grazing my knees badly both times. By midday I was so sleepy that I could scarcely keep my eyes open, so when I came to a grassy sunlit clearing, I simply lay down on the path, rested my head on my arms and slept. I had thought dimly that I would not sleep long lying on the hard ground, but I had not taken into account my exhaustion. When I woke I was horrified to find the shadows of the trees around the clearing had grown long and thin. I had slept for hours, and the sun was barely high enough to show above the tops of the trees.

Certain the pack of wolves had not done with me, I scrambled to my feet, wincing at the pain in my knees, and set off at a limping trot, praying I would find another cave or, better still, a house or settlement of some kind before darkness fell. But an hour later, I was still on a path surrounded by trees when I heard the distant howl of a wolf. I began to run, convinced the pack was beginning to assemble for the chase. Soon after, the ground began to rise once more, and as the slope grew steeper, I slipped time and again on the loose scree, opening up the grazes on both

knees. Mopping at the blood trickling from the cuts, I was horrified to think of the scent trail I was leaving for the wolves, but
I told myself that the steepness of the terrain gave me a better
chance of finding another cave.

It was nearing sunset when I reached the top of the hill I had
been climbing. I was bitterly disappointed to find that the trees
were simply too thick to let me see clearly in any direction. Nor had
I seen any cave. I felt like sitting down and weeping, but despair
turned to terror when I heard a wolf howl again and the answering howls of other wolves, nearer to one another and to me than
the wolf I had heard earlier. I got to my feet, quaking with fear,
knowing the only other way I could protect myself was with fire.
As swiftly as I could I began collecting dried twigs and branches
and piling them up in front of a tree growing at the edge of the
path. Once I had amassed a pile, I set a few strong limbs aside and
then pushed a tissue from my bag in amongst a cluster of twigs on
the heap. I took out the heavy, beautiful lighter and stared at it for
a moment in wonder, but another howl made me glance up to see
that the sun was minutes from setting.

I flicked the lighter and there was a little flare of brightness
as the tissue went up, then the wood began to crackle. I unscrewed
the nub at the end of the lighter and tipped a little of the fluid onto
the end of one of the branches I had set to one side, then I screwed
the nub back into place and held the branch into the flames. The
glistening bark caught alight with a roar and a rush of heat, and
not a moment too soon, for its light flared in not one, but many
pairs of eyes, all red as the setting sun, malevolent and hungry, not
cool and watchful as the silvery eyes of the black wolf had been.

I had built the fire in front of me, keeping the tree at my back, but I knew that I was vulnerable to attack from the sides. I meant to use the burning brand to protect my flank, but what if they attacked from both sides at once? The answer was all too obvious. For a moment a fury swept through me at the thought that I might die in such a stupid impossible way, and I brandished the burning branch and shouted, 'Go away! I will not let you eat me! You'll burn if you try!'

The red eyes continued to watch me, and seeing that the branch I was holding was beginning to fail, I bent down, never taking my eyes from the wolves. I groped quickly on the pile beside me for another branch, not daring to set down the one I held to pour more lighter fluid onto its replacement, but fortunately the second branch caught obligingly. I risked a glance at the pile of spare firewood and reckoned I had twenty minutes at best before the fire began to die. That was why the wolves had not tried to attack, I thought with a chill. They were waiting for the fire to go out.

In that moment, I knew I would die if I did nothing but wait. It occurred to me sickeningly that as well as giving off the smell of blood, I was probably stinking of fear.

There was only one thing to do. As surreptitiously as I could, I gathered up the remaining wood and then let it fall onto the fire in one armful. Then I hurled my burning brand towards the enormous wolf I had identified as the alpha male and turned to scramble up the tree. The fire gave a great whoosh and blazed up as I had hoped, but the leader of the pack must have realised what I meant to do and he leapt at me. The flames were too high and he gave a yelp as fire licked his flank. Then he was howling and rolling to quench his burning hide.

I had managed to reach the first branch and I glanced down to see the leader of the wolf pack glaring up at me with undisguised hatred. I climbed up to the next branch, realising that when the fire died completely, they would be able to get closer to the tree and jump higher.

When I reckoned myself high enough to be out of reach, I stopped, clinging to the trunk of the tree and gasping, unable to see anything below because smoke from the dying fire was billowing up and my eyes were streaming.

My husband told me later that he had been perched in a nearby tree as the red bird, poised to rescue me if I needed it. He had not intervened because, by managing alone, I was bringing potency and endurance to the princess spell.

'So you were only to intervene if I was in danger of dying?' I had asked. 'That's why you didn't fly at the wolves when they came upon me the first time, outside the cave?' We had been walking in the garden on the night after our wedding.

He nodded and said soberly, 'It was hard to see your fear and do nothing.'

Remembering the soft gravity of those words, it comes to my mind as I thread my needle with celadon green silk, that if my son fails this last test, and all vestiges of what he was and what he might have been are fled, he will be wholly wild and it may be kinder to allow him to remain in the Wolfsgate Valley, to find whatever destiny he can as a wolf, rather than keeping him chained within the palace grounds. Perhaps he will join the pack. It would be a fine irony if he joined the wolves that had tried so hard to kill his mother.

A picture comes to me of the black she-wolf. Despite what my husband said, I never thought she meant to harm me. I saw her only once more and fleetingly, before I was free of the valley. Or maybe it was only a vision, I have never been able to make up my mind.

I spent another precarious night high above the wolves, this time in the tree I had climbed. Not trusting myself to stay awake, I bound my hands about the trunk of the tree using the rope the old woman had given me. I was wakened just before dawn by the pain in my hand, and was appalled to see that I had slept in such a way that I had cut off the flow of blood to my right hand; it was frighteningly numb and blue. When I finally managed to unbind myself, I suffered fiery pain as the blood flowed back into my fingers, but I welcomed it, knowing I must have come dangerously close to losing a hand.

I cursed my stupidity all the next day, as the hand throbbed and ached, but at least the pain kept me alert. By the afternoon, the sky was cast over with heavy black storm clouds. I worried that the loss of sunlight would render the path powerless to protect me, as at night, but told myself that perhaps I need not be so concerned for I had seen no sign of the wolves during that whole day. It might be that the grey alpha wolf had been more badly hurt than he had seemed, and was now somewhere far away licking his wounds. I hoped so, but I dared not assume it.

The terrain was now flatter and less richly green and fertile. There were still trees either side of me, but they were sparser and the ground under them was stony and barren. This was fortunate, for twice black strangler trees lurched for me, and both times I saw their movement in time to evade them. It was after this that I named them to myself, and kept a wary eye out for them. By mid-afternoon the path had brought me to a clear swath of ground between trees half lost in thick mist. I slowed down, but seeing that the path ran into the mist-bound thicket, I had no choice but to enter.

The path wound through the trees and into a foul-smelling bog where yellowish water lay either side in pools that bubbled and reeked. I poked the stout stick I had been using as a staff into the bog and found there was no bottom that it could reach, and when a droplet of the foul water landed on my hand, it burned like fire. Washing my hand clean with a little spit, I continued, determined not to put a foot wrong.

I had been walking for half an hour or so when I realised that it was getting dark. I could not see the sky because the mist was too thick, but it was too early for nightfall, so it must be the clouds. I did not know whether to wish for rain or not. Rain might wash the cloying, stinking mist from the air, but it might also cause the bog waters to rise, and already they lapped uncomfortably close to my feet either side of the path. I told myself I was a fool for putting so much thought into a wish! Of course I did not know that I had come to a place where wishes might indeed be granted.

Soon, it was so dark that I could see the bog water had a sickly luminescence. Unfortunately it was not the sort of brightness that illuminated anything. It merely diffused in the fog, making it more opaque. Finally, I gave up inching along and sat down where I was to wait till the clouds broke, hoping they would do so before the sun set so that I could get out of the bog. If I had thought the ledge and the tree uncomfortable beds, it would be worse by far to spend a night on this narrow path with glowing, caustic water either side of me.

At length night fell, and I ceased to worry about burning water or storms or wolves because I could hear something moving in the bog. At first it was no more than a flaccid splash. Then I heard the wet sound of something large. Heart beating very fast, I stood up and searched the water on either side of the path for movement with eyes made keen by terror. I could not see into the water for it shone like a mirror, but when a bubble burst, I flinched. I realised as I stood there peering uneasily about me, that it was not the water that glowed but the mist that had risen from it. The water was merely reflecting the glowing mist.

I heard another splash, closer than before. Whatever was moving was coming towards me and it sounded a lot bigger than a fish. I had seen the wolves as the greatest danger I must face, and I had focused all my fear upon the pack, but now I wondered if there were other dangers. What if one of them was even now approaching me in the bog, readying itself to rear up and take me?

If only day would come, but by my calculations, sunrise was hours away. I took out the lighter and flicked it to produce a flame, but it only had the effect of making the mist and the bog shine. Worse, I had the sense that whatever was in the bog had heard the sound, for there was a long, listening silence.

That was when I saw her: the black wolf. She was standing some distance away in the shining mist, visible only because her extreme blackness gave off no reflection, but her eyes seemed to glow silver. She looked at me, then she turned and padded a few steps before stopping and looking back at me again.

Dry-mouthed, I wondered if I was mad to think she was offering to lead me from the bog. She took another step and turned back to look at me again. I took a step towards her, wishing I had kept the branch to use as a staff to test the ground ahead. She took a few more steps, then turned to me again. I took another careful step and then another; now sure she was leading me along the path, I followed more readily, reckoning that anything was better than sitting on the path waiting for whatever was out there to attack.

She brought me to the edge of the bog, but when I found I was treading on a grassy slope of firm ground and turned to see what she would do, she had vanished.

I never spoke to my husband of that second encounter with the black wolf after he mentioned that the bog gave off a vapour that produced hallucinations, remarking how lucky I was to have got through it in my right mind. I asked only where he had been when I was in the bog. He admitted that he had not realised I was trapped there and had been without, waiting impatiently for me to emerge.

I have thought more than once over the years of the black wolf, and not long before my son hunted his ninety-ninth bride, I mentioned her to my mother-in-law. She had given me a swift, dark look, saying there had been a black wolf bitch, but that her hatred of humans was stronger than that of any other wolf in the Wolfsgate Valley because she was the same faerie who had tried to close the gateway between Faerie and the mortal realm, and who had brewed up the very curse that afflicted my husband and my son.

'She became a wolf?' I asked my mother-in-law, wondering why my husband had not told me this when I had mentioned the black wolf. But then, as my mother-in-law related her story, I realised Ranulf would have disliked speaking of her because he had only just got free of her curse. Faerie folk do not like to dwell on unpleasant things, as a rule.

'She was a shape-changer by her mother's blood,' my mother-in-law had told me. 'She had taken that form to kill her lover and her half-sister for their betrayal of her, and she was still in that form when she cursed the king for stopping her closing the gateway to the human realm. So he punished her by trapping her power in that form. For a long time, she killed any human who came to Faerie by way of the Wolfsgate Valley, and the hunting of fully mortal maids became such a deadly business that it went entirely out of favour among princes.

'But then there were no more sightings of the black wolf and it was thought that she had perished,' my mother-in-law concluded.

It struck me that if she was right, I had been incredibly lucky to come safe from the bog. It seemed too much to put down to luck, but maybe I had been due a little good fortune by then.

I forgot the black wolf once I came out of the mist that shrouded the bog, for to my surprise it was dusk and the great bronze disc of the setting sun was casting a dull gold light over the façade of a large and imposing building of several levels behind a high stone wall. My heart leapt at the sight of it, and at that moment I heard the howl of a wolf, very close. I knew it was not the black wolf but a summoning to the kill by the pack leader, and I set off at a run towards a gate in the wall, stumbling and slipping on the stony, tussocky ground.

I heard another howl ahead and to the left and faltered, but then I began to run harder, remembering I was still following the path and would be safe so long as it was daylight.

The wall was further away than I thought and the sun was setting when the path suddenly forked, one side becoming a white paved way that appeared to lead directly towards the gate in the wall, and the other remaining the same worn and pitted track I had been following since the first day. If my husband had not been there, awaiting me in his golden wolf guise, I would have taken the wide pale path, which would have brought me to a pretty meadow full of wildflowers. Their scent would have put me into a sweet sleep from which I would never have woken.

Somehow of all the tribulations I faced during the three days of testing, that lovely, deadly meadow was the worst of them. The thought of it haunted me for some time after I was wed, and once I went into the Wolfsgate Valley to look at it. Standing a safe distance back, I saw the bodies of a dozen girls who had found a dreadful immortality there, and weeping, begged my husband to use his power to save them. He only kissed me, telling me it was my good heart that had won the aid of his mother by the Wolfsgate, in her crone guise. Then he sobered and added that he would have to touch the sleeping girls in order to wake them, and that none could walk on that meadow and stay awake, not even the king of all Faerie. He kissed me again and bade me pity the sleepers not, for they were said to dream endlessly of their heart's desire, and perhaps it was a better fate than for them to wake and find their princes had long ago chosen another.

His words did not comfort me, and even now I sometimes think of that field of immortal sleepers with creeping horror, but this day, sitting with the heavy tapestry on my knee and waiting for my son's chosen to come through the Endgate, it seems to me that it might be a peaceful end to a mortal life, to lie down in a meadow of flowers and dream forever.

Perhaps I will do that when I am old and weary, and see what dreams come to me. Perhaps I will do that if my son fails.

Cloud-Marie gives a soft gurgle, which is her signal that it is time for us to dine. One eye drifts upward and I shake my head, having made up my mind to wait until morning to look at the maid my son has chosen. After all, I must wait two more days before she can come through the Endgate, and better to wait until one of the nights is past. Knowing I cannot sit here for the whole time without eating or sleeping, I rise and Cloud-Marie and I go together to the kitchen to eat the food she has prepared. When the meal is done, I make my way to my chamber, bathe and put on my nightgown. Soon after Cloud-Marie arrives to comb and brush my hair before going yawning to her own little chamber.

I lie wide awake in my bed, staring at the ceiling, my thoughts full of the mortal maid my son has hunted, spending her first night in the Wolfsgate Valley. I pray for her sake that she is strong and clever and lucky, and that my son remembers he summoned her and watches over her well. I refuse to imagine what will happen if the little flame of awareness within him gutters and he becomes wholly wolf. I try to sleep, but I only grow more and more wide awake. Finally, I get out of my bed, dress myself and go up to the tower room.

I kneel beside the scrying bowl and, as usual, struggle with revulsion before I close my eyes and lower my hand into it. The liquid feels icy and my hand aches. It reminds me, for a vivid fleeting moment, of the pain I felt after I untied the rope to release myself from the tree where I had taken refuge from the wolves. I push the memory away, stir the dark water and open my eyes.

My son sits on his haunches amidst trees. He is gazing down

into a clearing where a campfire flickers. Beside it sits a woman, her long blonde hair bound into a tight plait. She is warmly and practically dressed in jeans and a thick sweater and coat, and she is wearing solid hiking boots. There is a small bulging pack beside her as well as a stout, metal-shod walking staff, and I think wryly of the book bag and light coat and the empty plastic water bottle that were all I brought with me. She takes out a small silver knife and deftly slices an apple. I wish she would turn her head so that I can see her face. I note that she is sitting with her back to a great tumble of moss-covered boulders that curve around either side of her, and I feel sure she has chosen this campsite so that nothing can approach her save from the front.

I study her and it seems to me that her form is full and rounded and that her movements are too graceful and certain to be those of a young woman. She is older than is traditional for a maid, and yet what age is my son now, given that beasts age faster than humans or faerie folk and he has long worn his wolf shape.

My son stiffens and begins to growl. He is looking in the other direction and, following his gaze, I see with a chill that the wolf pack has gathered in a hollow and are tearing at some beast they have killed with efficient ferocity; a deer, by the look of it. I have the sense that my son is hungry and longs to join the feast. Perhaps the grey wolves are eating so close in order to tempt him.

He looks back to the woman by the fire, now combing her hair out of its braid, and I see with astonishment that she is not alone. There is a large dog with a soft red coat stretched out beside her. She strokes it and I am so unsettled by the sight that I lose focus and the vision in the scrying bowl fades to blackness again.

There is nothing for it but to return to my room and lie down. I do not know what to think of the air of competence about the girl in the clearing, or of the fact that she has entered Faerie with a dog. Cats and dogs do cross, I know, but seldom, for their instincts tell them there are many things in Faerie that find dog and cat meat as sweet as human flesh.

But this dog did not wander across, I remind myself. The woman is clearly its companion and when I think of the tender way she broke off her grooming to stroke the dog's head, I find I am glad to think that she has it to defend her, in case my son cannot control himself. Dogs have a loyalty that goes deeper even than the pack instinct of wolves, and I do not know if my son will be able to hold to his hunt. And even if he does, I do not know what will happen when the dog beholds him.

My mind drifts to the slight arrogance in my husband's handsome face when he told me it was my trust in him that allowed him to prevent me going along the path that would lead me to the meadow of sleep flowers.

I realise I would not have trusted him in his wolf form, after being terrorised for three days by the pack, save for my encounters with the enigmatic black she-wolf. It was that, like her, he had not been grey as the wolves of the pack, which convinced me to go with him, even when he seemed to be leading me away from the safety of the ornate building behind its high wall. I am sobered to realise that, if not for my meeting with the black wolf, I would never have reached the Endgate before the last rays of the sun were extinguished by night. I would have fallen victim to the pack unless Ranulf had pitied me enough to transport me magically back to the mortal world, though I had failed him.

I slipped into a vivid dream of those last moments of my testing in the Wolfsgate Valley.

I was within sight of the gate which, like the Wolfsgate, was actually a solid door set into the wall, when I saw the grey pack leader burst from some bushes a little distance away, followed by several of his outrunners. I looked around for the golden wolf, but it had vanished.

Terror flooded me, and I broke into a headlong run, praying the gate would not be locked. Slamming into it, I grasped the handle, the hair on my neck standing on end as I imagined the pack leader's fangs sinking into my neck or calf. But the handle turned. I shoved the door open, flung myself through it and slammed it behind me, then I sank to my knees, sobbing and trembling and gasping as the sun set and darkness fell over me like a cloak.

The next morning, when Cloud-Marie brings my tray, she is visibly unsettled to see me dressed and sitting by the fire. She gabbles a little as she dithers over where to set the tray and I sign for her to put it on the table beside me. I have no appetite but I do not want her to be troubled, poor soul. She makes me a coffee and brings it to me and I take it and smile at her. She does not return my smile, and when she gestures at the brush and comb sitting on the dresser, I nod, knowing it will soothe us both. I look into my bloodshot eyes in the mirror hung upon the wall beside my dresser and see how thick the shadows lie under them.

An hour passes and then two and I can restrain myself no longer. I set aside the tapestry I have been working at and rise. Cloud-Marie watches me, and grinds her teeth. Seeing her agitation, I cross to the window and sign her to bring me a hot chocolate, knowing that the making of it is a lengthy process. As soon as she has gone, I hasten across the room and draw aside the curtain that hides the tower-room stair. I make my way swiftly up to the chamber where the scrying bowl awaits me, kneel and plunge my hand in at once, only closing my eyes when I begin to stir.

I open my eyes and see that my son is moving again. I cannot tell where he is, save that the grass is long and dry and bleached blond, and there are no trees. He is in a part of the valley I have never seen before, which must mean his chosen is there, too. I have no idea what tests await her here but there is nothing gentle in the Wolfsgate Valley. I cannot see the girl, but he is clearly moving stealthily and carefully, stopping often to twitch his ears. I push away the thought that he is stalking her and take comfort in the absence of the grey wolves.

Then I remember the dog and wonder if he is wary of it.

'Bring her to me, my son,' I whisper, and the vision dissolves, but not before I see that he has left the high yellow grass for a stony foothill, on which rises what seems to be the ruin of a human dwelling.

Going back down to my chamber, I manage to sit in my chair

before Cloud-Marie arrives and sip meekly at the chocolate she has made, though the sweetness makes me feel sick. I have drunk two-thirds before it occurs to me to check the petals carpeting the Princess Chamber. If my son has ceased to hunt, save for prey, they will be dying.

I sign that I want to go to the Princess Chamber, and Cloud-Marie takes the mug. By the time I reach the door with its dove handles I am calmer, but even so, when I open the door and see the floor is white with petals, I feel weak with relief and near to weeping. I close the door and return to my chamber where Cloud-Marie stands, still holding the cup, a bead of chocolate clinging to the down on her upper lip. I laugh aloud at the realisation she has greedily drained my cup and, taking it from her, I set it down and enfold her in a hug. At first she stiffens but then she hugs me back and burbles with laughter. When I release her she all but capers.

I sit down and look into the fire and think of her mother.

Cloud-Marie looks nothing like Yssa, and yet there is something in her mouth that sometimes reminds me of my friend. Yssa as she was in the end, not as she was when first she came to the palace, dressed in drab clothes with limp hair and dull skin, her back bowed under the weight of some sorrow whose cause she would not name. How wearily and resignedly she asked if she might have a place in the palace. How humbly and drearily she said that she did not mind what work she did. Lonely in the absence of my husband, I had impulsively agreed to take her in, making it my own little quest to drive the melancholy out of her. She did not smile, but only looked grim as she curtseyed and thanked me. Then she asked if I meant she was to be my maid.

I answered that she would be my companion and she nodded, half flinching. Her evident lack of delight in her new appointment piqued me and made me even more determined to win a smile from her.

I was thereafter unfailingly sweet to her, even though she would not meet my gaze and took all of my orders with a sullen glower. Once or twice I wondered if she thought I mocked her with my kindness because I surprised a look of real hatred in her eyes, but that seemed so unlikely that I told myself she only brooded on whatever hurt had been done to her. Whatever she had fled from to come to the palace had scarred her, and whenever her hands were not busy, she chewed her nails down to the quick. This human-like flaw endeared her to me, and I had gone from regarding her as a project to really caring for her. I gave her gifts and stroked her hair and kissed her and made her sing with me, refusing to notice her determined lack of response. I could see that her life at the palace agreed with her. Her skin soon glowed like a pearl and her fiery hair shone and rippled as she lost her thin, hollow-eyed look. It gave me pleasure to discover what a beauty she was, or would have been, I amended wryly, if ever she would smile or look anyone in the eye.

Then one day, we were walking in a field and I stopped to offer the stick of celery I had been nibbling to a rabbit. It was very timid and it could not make up its mind whether it wanted the vegetable enough to overcome its fear of me. It crept forward and shrank back and crept forward again many times until at last it came close enough to snatch a bite before bounding away.

I looked up to find Yssa watching me with a queer expression on her face. 'You are very patient,' she said. It was the first time she had ever said a word to me that I had not had to drag out of her, and I think she was as startled by it as I. It was on that day that I noticed her eyes, which I had thought grey, were a very clear, pale, turquoise blue, like my husband's. It made me realise that I had never looked into her eyes before. She had always prevented it by looking down or away or by keeping her lashes lowered.

She must have regretted her momentary lapse, because she was full of sour grimaces and frowns for a few days, and did no more than grunt when I asked a question of her. But one night when I was struggling to brush my hair, she took the brush from my hand and said brusquely that it would be better to comb out the snarls first. I had been very surprised and a little bashful, for even as a child my mother had insisted I brush my own hair. When I had not managed it quickly enough, she ruthlessly cut it short. I had kept my hair short since, but in Faerie, I had grown it as my husband had desired, and something in the air had made it grow longer and more lustrous than ever it had done in the real world. Princess hair, I thought it, and I had liked to brush it, though there was eventually so much of it that my arms always ached.

That day, Yssa combed and then brushed my hair with long strokes, and as I watched her through half-closed lids, I saw a smile flicker about her lips, as if the act gave her as much pleasure as it gave me. I wanted to say a dozen things, but I held my tongue for the longest time, wanting nothing to disrupt the sweetness of this moment of surrender.

So I saw it and so it was.

I never did learn exactly what had happened to Yssa, for I liked her too much to intrude upon her sorrow by asking open questions. Once she said something that let me guess she had fled from family trouble, but I never probed for more information than she offered. Even when we became close as sisters, Yssa would freeze and withdraw if I asked any question about her past, and I learned never to do so. Yet I was curious and speculated endlessly about what had happened to her whenever she made some comment that seemed to refer to what had hurt her so.

Once, she said fiercely that there was no bond deeper than a blood bond. Another time she asked suddenly and very seriously if I had such a bond with someone in my world. She had to explain that she was asking if I had a sister or brother, and I had shaken my head, saying I was an only child to elderly parents who seemed more than anything else slightly startled to have got me. Certainly they had shown no desire to have another child. I went on to tell her, because she seldom asked me questions or showed any interest in my past, that when I had fallen in love with a married man they had disowned me with such alacrity I felt they welcomed my misbehaviour. I was surprised to see pity in Yssa's eyes, and that night she had insisted on dressing my hair in a special elaborate style that must have made her arms and fingers ache. Yet her hands were very gentle.

I loved Yssa, but it was not until my son was born that I understood what she had meant by a blood bond. Coincidentally she fell pregnant soon after I did, to a faerie lord who had come to visit my husband. She had met him at a ball I had made her attend with me at the Summer Palace, and they had become lovers that same night. The next morning the beauty I had sometimes glimpsed had blazed in her and I guessed at once what had happened.

'You have fallen in love!'

A complex mixture of elation and sorrow crossed her face, but she nodded and a rosy blush suffused her cheeks as she said shyly, 'I understand now why a woman might give up everything for love, and go mad at the loss of it.'

I did not understand her words, but I guessed they alluded to her past and asked no more. Yet it gave me joy to see her so radiant, for all I thought her lord a vapid dandy with an inability to focus on anything save himself, including his wife. Of course he wed her when she told him she was to bear his child, because children are rarely born to pure-blood faerie folk and they are greatly valued.

At first her faerie lord was happy in her pregnancy because he was so pleased to have fathered a child, but his interest in her and in his child waned as the months passed, and when she swelled and became inaccessible to him, he found other pretty portals more appealing.

Yssa was desolate, for unlike me she was not entirely enthralled by the baby growing in her. Then came the night she went into labour. I had given birth a week or so before, and I was nursing my precious son as I waited for her to bear her child. Unlike my labour, which was swift and only briefly painful, hers was long and full of many agonies. This surprised me, for I had thought a faerie would give birth with ethereal decorousness, all flowers and glitter instead of blood and screams. I wondered aloud if all faerie births were so hard, and the faerie crone who tended her said, 'No more than all mortal births are painful.' She was not in awe of me, for it was she who had birthed my son, and suddenly she said, 'It goes deeper with some than others and that can make a difference. You withheld nothing in the birthing of your child, but this one would keep some part of herself separate from it.'

My friend was beyond hearing her words, but our voices must have penetrated the haze of pain, for suddenly she shouted out the name of a woman – Alzbetta – begging her forgiveness and swearing she would find some way to help her. Then she screamed until foam flecked her cheeks and hoarsely willed her body to rid her of the child and of the love she had borne its feckless, fickle father, cursing both. There was a hail of rain against the window glass and I shivered, for in Faerie, curses are not just words.

'Can't you use magic to help her?' I whispered to the crone, hours later, for Yssa was grown pale as milk and there was a greenish shadow about her mouth and a feverish glitter in her eyes that made me fear for her.

The faerie midwife gave me a keen look. 'I could try, but it would be dangerous, for there is a kind of primitive but powerful magic in birthing that will truck no other kind.'

My son stirred at my breast and I looked down at him and felt a fist of love close about my heart. For a moment it seemed that I could not breathe, for the joy I felt was so deep it was akin to pain. Then there was a grunting groan from the bloody birthing bed and I looked up to see the midwife lurch forward and reach for the baby being born.

Few children are born to faerie folk, and many are not fully formed. No one knows why, but the children are loved no less than a complete child. Yet my friend looked at her child only once, and bade the crone take the baby away. I came to Yssa and held her hand and told her I loved her, and promised she would grow to love her babe as I loved my son. I could not conceive that a mother would not love her child as I did and so my concern was all for my friend, rather than for the child. Yssa wept then, as I had never heard her weep, and told me that the child was misconceived. I held her close and called her sister and kissed her and said I would speak to my husband and see what he could do.

She drew back from me so quickly that she wrenched herself from my embrace, breasts heaving above the bodice of her bloodstained nightdress. Her pale blue eyes looked silver as she said, 'Ask him nothing, for he will be no more use to me than my own lord was. I am done with men. I should never have allowed myself to be distracted from my oath. Now I must atone.'

'What oath?' I cried, but she would not answer. I stroked her hair until she slept and then I went to feed my son. I fell asleep with him in my arms and when I woke, I saw a tiny silver feather by my side. It was a magic Yssa had, to limn small objects in silver, and she had done it to many tiny objects to please me. As soon as I saw the feather, I knew she had gone. I could not believe she would go without saying goodbye, and I was not surprised to find that she had left the child behind. It was only when I went to the nursery to look into its cradle that I realised that aside from being physically deformed and mute, Cloud-Marie was a girl. That was a shock, for having a boy I had been unable to envisage any other sort of child.

There was a tiny silver shell on the baby's pillow. I took it up and then I took up the baby. It opened its strange little cloudy mismatched eyes and I was surprised at the strength of the tenderness that I felt for the tiny deserted scrap.

An hour later, the midwife crone came and looked astonished to find me nursing my companion's child, with my own sated son sleeping in his cradle beside me. But then she shrugged and said why not, for I had milk aplenty. No more was said of it, and by the time my husband returned from his latest quest, a long one lasting more than a decade, our son and Cloud-Marie were both twelve, and I told my husband coolly that the girl would replace Yssa as my companion when she was older. I did not tell him that she was Yssa's daughter. In truth, I am not sure he had ever seen her.

That night, when Cloud-Marie has gone to bed, I return to the tower chamber and gaze into the scrying bowl again. My son is lying in long dry grass watching his chosen from the clearing. She is standing with her back to him and me, facing the entire wolf pack arrayed behind the enormous grey alpha wolf. If I had not known him by his size, I would have known him by the bald burn scar on his flank. The girl holds her knife in one hand, point down, and the metal-shod staff in the other. Her arms are bare and strong and her hair, which hangs loose down her back, is not blonde, as I thought, but a silken fall of silver hair. I am close enough to her now to see that I was right; her figure is too ripe to be that of a young girl. I tell myself I care not what her age is; if she is my son's chosen and can save him, I will welcome her. But why is he behind her, instead of defending his princess?

She steps towards the alpha wolf and my heart jerks to see a deep, bloody scratch on one of her arms. The grey leader growls and gathers himself to leap. I bite my lip, willing myself to be still and silent, for a vision is like a bubble that may burst at an ungentle breath.

The grey pack leader, poised, gives a low growl and bares his teeth in a ferocious snarl. There is blood on his muzzle.

He leaps, but the woman, lithe as a girl, spins away with astonishing balletic speed and strikes at him with her staff. Then, hair flying, she spins and strikes again with her knife, but the grey wolf has leapt back.

My son moves his head to follow their movements, and I wonder again at his inactivity. Then I notice the black she-wolf is standing between him and the woman, also facing the pack. I have no doubt it is the same she-wolf who saved me, and when she shifts her weight slightly, moving into a crouch, my heart leaps into my throat, but she does not move. It is the enormous, muscled pack leader who leaps, and it is only when my son whines that I understand he has not moved or attacked because he is wounded.

The grey wolf twists in the air so that his leap brings him past the woman and closer to my son. I see at once that this was intentional, for now the woman is off balance and too far away to strike with knife or staff. But instead of taking advantage of this, the grey wolf lunges towards my son, lips peeled back from his teeth in a terrifying snarl. Before he can reach his quarry, the black wolf attacks him and drives him back with a ferocity that is shocking to see. Clearly the grey wolf did not expect the attack from the she-wolf. Nevertheless, though she is a female, he joins battle with equal ferocity, and for a moment the two wolves are locked in a deadly struggle of jaws and teeth and claws. Neither wolf gives quarter, and the she-wolf is courageous and relentless, but the pack leader has the advantage of weight. Yet, unexpectedly and without warning, the grey breaks away and again leaps for my son. I do not understand why he is so intent on reaching him, for he is clearly badly wounded, and it is the candidate being tested who is his proper quarry during the trials.

My son struggles to rise, seeing the grey wolf coming for him, but he falls back with a high yelp of pain.

Again the black wolf intervenes, tearing at the exposed flank and hind leg of the pack leader. He turns on her and again they engage, biting and clawing at one another, and sending out a bloody spindrift over the pale sandy earth. They break apart and the grey leader attacks again at once, going for the black she-wolf's throat with open maw and murderous determination. She manages to evade him, but instead of attacking her he tries to get past her, and once again she attacks his rear. Snarling with frustration and rage, the enormous grey turns and they circle one another. To my dismay, I see that the she-wolf is limping and dripping blood.

The grey leader leaps once more, and this time the she-wolf moves too slowly to evade him. His teeth close on her throat and she gives a long, strangled howl of pain that is cut off suddenly by a horrible crunch. Even as the black she-wolf falls limply to the ground at the pack leader's feet, a streak of red comes from behind my son, and to my amazement I see the woman's red-gold dog attack the grey wolf. She is far smaller than he, but she is quick and brave and fierce and even as he snarls and snaps at her, the woman is there by the side of her dog. With a ringing battle cry, she strikes hard and accurately with the metal end of the staff, then slashes with the knife, opening a deep wound in the grey wolf's chest. He yelps in pain and hunkers down, snarling at the woman and the dog, but together they are bright and terrible and formidable and the battle with the black she-wolf has clearly taken its toll.

I see his surrender in the loosening of his bunched muscles a split second before he retreats, and in moments he is gone, and the pack with him.

I want desperately to see the woman's face, for there was something familiar in her voice when she cried out. But she has her arms around the red-gold dog, her face buried in its soft thick pelt, and now my son has dragged himself to the black wolf lying on the ground, her red blood soaking into the sand beneath her. The red-gold dog comes to nuzzle at her with him, whining and pawing, but the black wolf is still and silent.

The red dog lifts its head and howls and howls.

I do not know how to understand what I am seeing.

In my agitation, I let a strand of hair fall into the scrying bowl and the vision ends.

I sit on my heels for a long time in the tower room, cursing my clumsiness, for the scrying bowl will offer only one vision between a sunrise and sunset, but there is nothing to do but to go down. I long to go out and find my son, but I dare not, for if I intervene in any way during the testing, save to carry out certain specific tasks, the princess spell will fail. I run my mind over all that I have seen, and decide my son must have been hurt defending the woman against the pack, whereupon the princess candidate and her dog then defended him in a queer reversal of tradition. I cannot imagine how the black she-wolf came into it, and I pray that neither her actions nor the interference of the red dog have weakened or destroyed the princess spell that is being woven.

I think of the black she-wolf's eyes growing dim as her blood rushed out, and tears start fiercely to my eyes, for she saved my life and now she has died defending my son, yet I do not know why she helped us.

My thoughts circle back to my son and I wonder fearfully about the extent of his wounds. It terrifies me that he might now lie near to death, but I cannot allow myself to give way to my longing to find him. I tell myself his attempts to rise were full of energy; I tell myself I would know if my son had died.

Cloud-Marie finds me standing and shivering at the bottom of the steps and she clucks and chortles with dismay and, can it be, irritation? I want to laugh at the thought, for I have never known her to be anything but utterly gentle and patient. She wraps me in a blanket and makes me sit down in my chair. She mops my cheeks and makes me drink water. Finally, helplessly, she begins to stroke my hair.

I watch her in the mirror on the wall. I seem to see her stroking the hair of an old woman whose tear-wet face is pale as snow, her eyes wide and dark with despair. I picture a field of deadly white flowers where I might go and make a bed. But I know I cannot leave Cloud-Marie alone, no matter what has happened to my son.

Angry at my helplessness, I order myself not to be a witless fool. I do not know the boy is dead. Likely he is hurt – even badly hurt, but he will heal and he will return to me. And suddenly I am shocked to discover I do not care if he comes to me as a wolf. I think of his ferocious beauty as he raced through the wilderness and know that he is my son and I love him, whether he be wolf or man. Only let him live!

If he fails in this last hunt, I will set him free in the Wolfsgate Valley and each day come to the tower and evoke the scrying bowl to watch him. I will see him hunt his food and in time he will take a mate and sire cubs. He will join the wild pack and perhaps a day will come when he will challenge its leader and become a wolf king.

I sign to Cloud-Marie that I want to lie down and she helps me to my bed. She takes off my slippers and covers me over. One eye watches me with anxious love while the other floats peacefully towards the window. Its calmness sooths me. All this hot bright pain will pass, it seems to promise.

I close my eyes and will myself to sleep.

I do not sleep.

I find myself remembering the relief and exhaustion I felt when I finally gathered the strength and will to rise unsteadily to my feet inside the Endgate, wondering where I was and who might dwell there.

I had made my unsteady way along the lane to a cobbled yard, where lamps with flickering flames cast enough light for me to see that the imposing building I had seen from afar was a vast, elegant mansion. There was a fountain in the midst of the yard where water fell in an endless glittering cascade from the tilted greenish-gold jug of a greenish-gold woman. This stood directly before a set of wide marble steps leading to a beautiful carved door, and as I gazed at it, I thought of the man Ranulf, telling me locals were permitted to pass through the private grounds of the property owned by the lady from the walled garden.

It was no garden I had trespassed upon, and yet I was suddenly certain that the door in the wall was the Endgate he had spoken of, bidding me find it and pass through. I seemed to feel the pressure of the armlet above my elbow, as if it were the hand of a man encircling my flesh and, ushered forward by that faint pressure, I mounted the steps. It was impossible that the armlet had not been dislodged during all I had endured since passing through the Wolfsgate Valley. I did not then know that my husband's mother had bestowed a magic upon the thing that ensured it could not be removed except by a direct act of will. I reached the top of the steps, wondering if the armlet was like the red dancing shoes in the faerie story, which had to be chopped off along with the feet in them to prevent them dancing their wearer to death. But when I tried to remove it, the carved ring came off easily and sat light and innocuous in my palm.

I shook my head at my foolishness and slipped it into my

pocket, hoping that its return would win me some kindness in the form of food and a chance to wash and tend my grazes and cuts. At the very least I would be free to pass through this property unhampered once I had brought the carved ring to its mistress. There was no question in my mind that it must be done, for the giving of the ring had begun the strangeness that had taken me over, and so to end it the ring must be delivered. This was absurd reasoning, but I was trying to hold belief and unbelief in my mind at the same time. Even as I planned to fulfil my promise to the turquoise-eyed Ranulf, I strove to convince myself that all I had endured was a vivid hallucination brought on by a fall or perhaps some sort of bite or fever that had come on me when I fell asleep under the hedgerow.

Certainly I had no intention of speaking of wolves and mountains or strangler trees and huge red birds to the lady of this house, or to whomever answered her door. I meant only to say I had hurt myself passing through her garden, in an effort to deliver the armlet as I made my way to an appointment. That missed appointment with the fussy archivist seemed to have occurred long ago in another life, and I longed to return to that rational life. I felt that delivering the armlet would deliver me back to it, to normality.

I gazed at the enormous door and hesitated. It was so ornate and imposing that I found myself afraid to knock. I was about to turn away and seek some less intimidating door at which I might humbly present myself when rain began to fall with the same sudden violence as in the moments before I had passed through the Wolfsgate. Even as I wondered at the coincidence, I heard the rumble of thunder. I told myself it would not matter if I got wet.

The rain would wash off the fetid reek of the bog. (What bog, my mind asked fiercely.) But thunder rumbled again and the rain seemed to grow heavier, hammering down on cobbles, walls and roof with a cacophonous racket that extinguished any possibility of thought. I knocked at the door, but no one came, and I was forced to accept that my knock had been too feeble to be heard. Reluctantly I turned my attention to the great beast head that was the door's knocker and discovered that the only way to lift the brutish thing seemed to be to put my hands inside its maw.

I might have baulked at that, but now the wind was blowing icy rain into the alcove. Gritting my teeth, I reached into the maw of the metal knocker and encountered a smooth grip. With a grunt of effort I raised the head of the beast high and withdrew my hand to let it fall. A sharp pain made me gasp as a single dolorous thud shook the door and the step under me. I had a vision of the sound reverberating though endless shadowed halls and tapestry-hung rooms with cold stone fireplaces. Looking down at my hand, I saw several long jagged scratches welling beads of blood. Only when I bent down to peer into the maw of the knocker to see what had cut me did I notice that the beast's teeth had been sharpened to razor points.

Appalled, I stepped back, wondering uneasily what sort of person had a doorknocker with sharpened teeth. It did not occur to me that I had entered a world where it was mandatory to offer blood when one first seeks entry to any house.

I heard a sound from within and imagined a plump, kindly housekeeper who would take pity on my wet and bedraggled state and sympathise in broken English. She would tell me that her mistress was out for the evening, or better still, had gone abroad for some time. Then she would usher me into the kitchen to dry myself. It would be a vast, warm, cavern of a chamber smelling of fresh-baked bread and hot stew and she would press a thick towel into my hands and cluck over my wetness as she sliced bread and bade me eat. So enthralled was I in imagining the housekeeper that I could almost see her plump motherly face creasing into a smile as she insisted I try some lemon tea cake she had made – the sort of face I had wished my own mother had offered to the world and me, instead of her thin intelligent face with its small, wary blue eyes.

The door opened suddenly to reveal a ravishingly beautiful woman in an old-fashioned but clearly ruinously expensive evening gown, under the hem of which bare, pale feet peeped out.

'Yes?' she said languidly.

'Ah . . . it is raining,' I said, stupidly dazed. She was, after all, the first faerie woman I had ever seen and I had not yet learned to defend myself from the natural glamour of her kind. She made no response to my absurd pronouncement, save to open the heavy door enough for me to slip through the gap. I hesitated only a second, and stepped through into an entrance that could have served as a hall for meetings, it was so large. The roof was too high for me to see it, for the only light in the place seemed to be candles in holders set along the walls. Blackout, the rational part of my mind suggested, or perhaps the owner of the mansion was eccentric enough to prefer a less modern form of lighting. Certainly it gave the place atmosphere.

The barefoot beauty led me from the hallway along a passage, the milky white marble floor of which was softened by a beautiful plush oriental runner. Her bare feet made no sound but I did not dare to walk on the rug in my filthy shoes, so I flapped awkwardly along beside her. The hallway brought us to a large chamber where a magnificent tapestry hung. It was the only thing in the room and it was exquisite. I embroidered myself, and despite everything that had befallen me, longed to examine it closely, but my guide had drawn ahead of me, and so I made haste to catch her up.

I had it in my head that she was leading me to a kitchen or perhaps a laundry where I could wash, but instead she opened a door to a small, exquisite parlour where a very beautiful older woman sat working at a tapestry draped over an antique wooden frame. The woman gave me a searching look, and if I had not been shivering with cold, I would have trembled at the way that haughty, pale blue gaze seemed to peel away my skin and look inside me.

'You have come,' she said, peculiarly.

I could only nod and this seemed to be enough, for the older woman turned back to her embroidery, bidding the young beauty bathe my hurts and my person. I thought she meant I should be taken to a bathing room, but the young woman bade me wait, saying that she would return with water and ointments. Then she drifted away leaving me standing there, dripping on the flag-stones. The older woman flicked a look of irritation at me and bade me stand by the fire so that my clothes could dry. I flushed, for her tone told me she had decided I was a fool.

There was a deep, comfortable chair before the hearth, but I could not sit in it, wet and filthy as I was. Instead, I drew out its wooden footstool and sat gingerly on that, facing the flames and trying to marshal my wits so that I could make some sensible responses when she began to demand some answers. But her whole attention was bent on her tapestry. I watched her needle stab in and out swiftly, half hypnotised by the rhythm until my eyes began to close.

I started awake when the other woman returned wheeling a trolley. She set a large bowl on the flagstones by the fire, then began to fill it with steaming water from jug after jug. When the bowl was half full, she bade me bathe and she would go and get me some dry clothing. I ought to have been embarrassed at the discovery that I was expected to strip off my filthy clothes and stand naked in this room, with its mistress working at her tapestry, but since her cold blue eyes had already stripped my skin off, I simply took off my outer clothes, hesitated, and then stripped off my sopping underthings, all the while keeping my eyes on the older woman. She did not lift her head.

I stepped into the hot water with a shiver and used a sponge to lave water over myself. It was not nearly so satisfying as a long hot shower, and yet there was a medieval poetry in the sound of the water trickling into the bowl, the reflection of flames on my wet limbs, the lavender scent of the steam, which soothed me profoundly. Even so, by the time I was drying myself, my knees stung fiercely and my hand had begun to throb again.

The young woman returned with a white lawn nightgown that seemed to me fine and lovely enough to be a bridal dress. She slipped it over my head and the soft whisper of its movements over my skin gave me gooseflesh. When she commanded it, I sat obediently on a stool as my filthy, tangled hair was washed and combed, and finally she put a soothing salve from a little enamelled pot onto all of the cuts and bruises I showed her. The pain of them began to fade at once, making me wonder what was in the miraculous ointment. Some of the gashes were ugly enough that I had feared they ought to have been stitched, but neither woman suggested calling a doctor.

I submitted to all these intimate ministrations with docility, partly out of exhaustion and partly because I sensed they were part of the strangeness I had entered. When the trolley was wheeled away, I was so weary I could have curled up on the chair by the fire and slept, content as a cat, but a shawl was brought and wrapped around my shoulders and the mistress of the house rose to announce in her cold, high voice that supper would be served in the adjoining chamber. She led me there, where a cold repast was laid out on a long, beautiful table made of the same pale wood as the armlet in the pocket of my wet clothes. I sat salivating with hunger while the meal was served, but before I could touch a morsel, my hostess asked if I would go back into the tapestry room and see if I could find a golden needle that she must have dropped by the tapestry stand.

It was a strangely timed request, and menial, but her young companion had withdrawn for the moment so I nodded and went back through the door to the other room. The fire had begun to burn down and, as the candelabra had been carried to the room we were to dine in, the chamber was now full of shadows, which seemed to gather more thickly about the tapestry stand. I searched among my wet clothes for the lighter, at the same time retrieving the carved armlet so I could present it to my hostess, then I set about searching for the needle. It did not take me long to see the flash of gold, but retrieving it from the crack into which it had fallen took some ingenuity. But at last I carried it triumphantly back to my hostess, who still sat at the table, palms flat upon its surface, as when she had asked me to fetch it for her.

When she held out her hand, I laid the needle upon it and then I gave her the carved armlet.

Remembering my own testing has brought me to the very edge of sleep, but all at once a realisation flashes in my mind like a gleam of flame on a golden needle! Heart yammering, I throw back my covers, pull a shawl about my shoulders and hasten out into the halls until I come to the doors of the Princess Chamber. I take the cold doves in my hands, turn them and throw open the doors. The dazzle of white petals fills my eyes, blinds me with relief so overwhelming it is like a blow to the head, and I stagger against the doorjamb and cling to it, trembling and gasping for a long, giddy moment.

He lives and the hunt is still on.

I feel the approach of the third dusk as a quickening in my blood, and in that moment, I decide I will assay no test if my son's chosen comes safe through the Endgate. It is my right and I have no doubt that she has been tested hard and well in the Wolfsgate Valley. But it is less that than the knowledge that she came when my son hunted her, though he is a beast almost wholly now, and she and her dog fought to protect him, that convinces me she is worthy. Unlike my mother-in-law, I will not hide my joy at seeing her come safe through the Endgate, in case she fails to satisfy the Princess Chamber. I will kiss her and call her daughter and daughter she shall be to me, I am suddenly sure of it. In that glad moment all things seem possible.

Cloud-Marie appears at the door, and I see by her expression that she knows the time as well as I. I sign my requirements to her. I do not know what expression is on my face, but she looks at me for a long moment with one curious eye, before she lopes away. It takes time but at last she comes up to my chamber bearing a laden basket and my cloak. I have dressed myself but I turn to let her drape my cloak about my shoulders and turn again so she can reach up to tie it at my throat, panting open-mouthed as she struggles to make her thick fingers perform the delicate task. I do not twitch myself away or sigh impatiently, but simply wait until she has managed it.

Finally she kneels before me to slip on my outdoor shoes and I touch her wiry golden hair and feel a stab of love for her. Perhaps I made some sound, for she looks up at me from that position and gabbles an enquiry. Her words are gibberish, but I know what she wants. I bid her get her own cloak and she gives me a gaping smile of delight before running to fetch it. As often before, I am struck by her capacity for joy in the smallest things. Perhaps the vacancies in her allow more space for joy, while the rest of us have little space for it and less and less as we grow older.

I shall not be like that, I vow. Not now and no matter what happens in the Princess Chamber. Though I grow old I will open

myself to joy. For some reason, I think of Yssa and my heart aches
for her. If only she had stayed and opened herself to the pleasure
of her daughter's sweetness she might, like me, have learned joy
from her.

In my gladness at knowing my son lives, my love for Cloud-
Marie and her mother grows more intense, for aside from my son
and my husband, I have loved no one better in my life than these
two, the sister and daughter of my heart.

Cloud-Marie returns, struggling into her cloak. I tie her
ribbon for her and then I take up the basket and we set off,
hand in hand. We make our way through the palace to the front
door of the west wing, and come out into the beautiful fountain
courtyard. Cloud-Marie gives a crow of excitement as she lollops
alongside me.

My mother-in-law awaited my arrival within the house, but I
will not be niggardly in my welcome. I am too impatient to behold
the face of my son's chosen. I know that I may not speak to her of
the testing she has undergone, or of the Princess Chamber ere she
enters it, but I need not treat her coolly. I will pretend to believe
whatever tale she decides to tell me, until we are free to speak
truthfully to one another.

I glance up and see clouds of darkness gathering overhead.
It is always so at the beginning and end of a testing, I now know.
Cloud-Marie senses my tension, rocks a little, so I take her big
rough hand and kiss it and clasp it in my own. It flutters like a bird
and then is still.

The sun kisses the horizon and we sit on the edge of the
fountain together and wait and wait until the gate from the lane

that leads to the Wolfsgate Valley opens. The silver-haired woman I saw in the scrying bowl comes stumbling into the fountain yard. She does not stop and gaze around her as I did, coming here that first time, for her head is bent low over the body of the red dog she carries in her arms. As she staggers closer, I see that there is red blood all over the hands that hold the beast so closely and tenderly.

My heart aches and I start towards them.

The woman looks up at me and all strength seems to run out of me, for I know her.

It is Yssa, and now I see the few strands of fire amidst the silver grey.

'Quickly, Rose,' she gasps. 'The pack attacked as we were running for the Endgate. She was hurt defending me. We must get her to the Princess Chamber before it is too late.'

I am utterly confounded, but her command is so urgent and authoritative that I can do no more than obey. Instead of bringing her through the doors, I lead her around the house to the mist garden, and up steps that will bring us to the hall outside the Princess Chamber. She knows the way as well as I, but when we reach the closed doors of the Princess Chamber she stops and looks at me expectantly. The dog's blood is dripping through her fingers onto the white marble floor and questions crowd my mind.

'You must open the doors for her!' Yssa cries.

I grasp the doves and throw open the doors and Yssa runs into the room, scattering and crushing white petals that spin in a fragrant blizzard in her wake. Heaving the dog over her shoulder, she climbs awkwardly up on the edge of the bed to lay the dog there as gently as she can. Immediately blood stains the pure white silk of the coverlet.

'What are you doing?' I gasp, but she only leaps down and catches my hand, dragging me after her from the chamber, slamming the door closed behind us. Then she heaves a great sigh and leans back against the doors.

'I don't understand,' I whisper.

But Yssa's eyes have found Cloud-Marie who has come after us, and she answers me almost absently, without taking her eyes from her daughter. 'She is his chosen and we will see soon enough if the princess spell is wide and kind enough to encompass her. If not, she will die.'

'But . . . she is a dog,' I stammer.

'And your son is a wolf,' says my friend.

'My son must wed one with mortal blood,' I say.

'My niece is half mortal like your son, and of royal blood besides,' Yssa answers.

'How . . .' I begin, but now she is holding out a filthy, blood-stained hand to Cloud-Marie. To my astonishment, both of the girl's eyes fix on the woman that she cannot know is her mother and she is smiling, her expression radiant.

'Sweetling,' Yssa sighs, and gathers her daughter to her in her strong brown arms. Cloud-Marie sighs as deeply as her mother, as if some long, hard task is at an end, and closes her eyes.

Tears fill my eyes and spill down my cheeks at the sight of
them clasped together, but I think of my son and I do not understand. How can he have chosen a dog for a bride and how can a
dog be the niece of my faerie friend and royal and half mortal
besides? The questions in my mind pile one upon another until
I cannot stand under the weight of them. I lean against the wall
and then find I must slide down and sit on the floor in a billowing
puddle of silk and satin.

Hearing the rustle of cloth, Yssa looks down at me, and there
is love and regret in her face. 'My dear friend, I knew your kindness
and capacity for love would encompass even my poor girl. Had you
not endured my resentment and bitterness with such patient grace
that they were stilled in me and I came to love you?'

'I don't understand what any of this means,' I say. 'Where is
my son?'

'He is wounded, but not mortally,' Yssa says and kisses her
daughter, who snuggles closer. Then she looks down at me again
and says, 'My sister sent me to the palace because she said you
could end the curse. She had dreamed of you and then you came
stumbling into the Wolfsgate Valley, green and helpless, wolfmeat
for certain sure if she did not help you.'

'Your sister?' I murmur.

'She was cursed,' Yssa tells me gently. 'I do not speak of the
curse that afflicted your husband and son, but the one laid upon she
who cast that curse: Alzbetta, who loved a human that betrayed
her. My half-sister.'

'But that was aeons past,' I stammered, then remembered
that faerie folk are all but immortal and assume whatever age they

desire. 'How can she be your half-sister . . . she killed her half-sister.'

'She killed Thayla who was the other daughter of her father,' says Yssa. 'I am the other daughter of her mother and loved my sister well despite all she had done in rage and passionate despair. Ages past, I went to dwell with her in the Wolfsgate Valley when she was banished there by the king to live trapped forever in the form of a black she-wolf. It was no hardship, for I am solitary by nature and have the gift of understanding the speech of beasts and birds. I was not unhappy and at first Alzbetta and I fared well enough, but she was desperate to find a way to break the curse, not to save herself, but because, when the king banished her by trapping her in her wolf form, she had been with child by the mortal she had slain. She had no magic in her beast form, but I did, and I found a spell that would arrest the course of the child's growth in Alzbetta's belly. Then my sister begged me to find a way to transform her back to her true form so that she might safely bear her child. I strove endlessly to discover what we needed. I read books and spoke to witches and faeries and sorcerers, but in every instance I failed. My sister took her rage and despair out on humans who entered the valley, and especially princess candidates who were lured there to thwart the curse she had laid upon her father and all the sons born of his line, though I begged her not to harm them and did what I could to help them.

'Then one day, Alzbetta came to me and said she had dreamed a human woman would one day come to the Wolfsgate Valley with the means of saving her unborn child from the consequences of her terrible folly. Thereafter she left off harming any human and only waited, with the child she had carried inside her for so long, and I waited with her.' She sighed. 'It is very hard to be unaffected when you live with bitterness and regret and fear. It turned me in upon myself and made me more of a loner than ever, so that I did not regret the lack of love and children in my own life.'

'Yes,' I say, beginning to understand a great deal.

'One day, Alzbetta came to me and said that you had come and had passed the three days of testing, and that you were a candidate for the Princess Chamber. Somehow, neither of us had expected that, for not all humans who blunder here are summoned. Alzbetta told me she had seen you safe to the Endgate, and that we must wait to see what would come of it. I do not know what we expected, for her vision had shown nothing but that you were the key to saving her child. You were made a princess by the chamber and you wed your prince. Years passed until my sister lost patience and bade me go to dwell in the palace and see what I could learn.'

'And what did you learn?' I ask.

She laughs. 'I learned to laugh and sing and to take pleasure in teaching something to another creature. I learned kindness and gentleness and generosity and patience. I learned, my dear sister, to love you, and that enabled me to love a man.' She sighed. 'You at least were worthy of my love, for you had cared for me and called me sister and loved me long before I was able to feel anything but bitter weariness. You gave me room and tenderness enough to grow.'

'But you did not find out how I am to save your niece?'

'I did not know, until I was in the midst of birthing my own child, then all at once I understood that no answer could be found until Alzbetta's child was born. Therefore she must be born. I went back to my sister, leaving my daughter with you, for I knew she would grow well in the warmth of your steady love, as she would not have done in the shadow of the strange desperate anguish of my sister's life in the Wolfsgate Valley. I told Alzbetta that she must bear her daughter and though she feared what would come of it, she let me unknit the spell that had frozen her womb for hundreds of mortal years, and she bore her child at last. A female.'

'The red-gold dog,' I murmur.

She nods. 'My sister was aghast at first, but I bade her be patient, for she was alive and might yet be transformed by some means we had yet to discover, connected to you. I took my niece to the mortal realm then, because if she had remained in the valley the grey king would have killed her. It is a glamour laid upon the wolf pack of that place that they must seek the life of any maid, mortal or faerie, who enters their valley. My sister wept but it was done. She remained in the Wolfsgate Valley, waiting, while I brought her daughter to your world and dwelt there with her. And so we lived these long years since I left the King's Palace. Indeed you may laugh to hear that I dwelt all this time in the very demesne where you had once lived, and each day I brought my niece to the Wolfsgate to run a little in the area before the guardian trees, where Alzbetta could come to her.

'Until the day Alzbetta came and told me she had seen your son, and that he had fallen to the curse and was almost wholly a wolf,' Yssa said. 'I saw it all then and bade my sister drive him through the Wolfsgate to the mortal realm when next she saw him.'

'You thought to mate them?' I ask her.

'I thought to save them, for if he chose her and she entered the Princess Chamber in the King's Palace, she might be transformed into a princess and he, having hunted a true princess bride, would be rescued from Alzbetta's curse. But I could not bring her to him or he to her by any action of my own without disqualifying it as a hunt. Their meeting must come about by your son's doing. I was pondering how it could be managed when one night, very late, I glanced out my apartment window and saw what I first thought was a white dog clawing at the yard where my niece had her kennel. My heart nearly leapt out of my chest when I realised he was a wolf, and must be your son. Later it came to me that the ground both sides of the Wolfsgate must have been saturated with my niece's scent, and being a beast only by magic, your son had scented this same truth in my niece. I saw them touch noses and then my clever niece lifted the latch on the door to go out to him. I gathered up my things and followed as fast as I could, knowing he would bring her through the Wolfsgate where the grey wolves would be gathering just beyond the guardian trees.'

I must have made some small startled sound, for Yssa, who had sat down on the floor beside me with Cloud-Marie still clasped in her arms, looks expectantly at me.

'You think that the Princess Chamber will heal her wounds?' I ask.

'You told me the Princess Chamber completely healed you of all the cuts and bruises you had got in the valley during the testing,' Yssa says. 'But I think it will only heal in the process of transforming a maid into a princess.'

'And if she is not a princess when we open the door?' I ask.

All of the brightness and strength in Yssa's lovely face fades, and for a moment I see in her face all the centuries that she has lived. 'Then my niece will be dead, and your son will remain a wolf. But the mother of your husband foresaw that, through you, Alzbetta's curse upon his line would be broken, and Alzbetta saw it too, so how else can this come to be, save that my niece become a princess bride?'

Later that night it grows very cold and I insist Yssa and Cloud-Marie have my bed, for I know I will not sleep. I tend my friend's hurts and we pick at the supper I prepared for her niece. Yssa praises the bread and we both laugh because it is her recipe I used. When she and Cloud-Marie sleep, clasped in one another's arms, I sit vigil by the fire, wrapped in a blanket, working intermittently at my small tapestry. My mind is full of all that Yssa has told me, and with thoughts of my son, who waits too, wounded, though I do not know if he understands that his fate and that of an innocent girl are dependent entirely on the enigmatic magic of the Princess Chamber.

I think of Alzbetta, the black she-wolf, who saved my life, whose curse had afflicted my husband and my son, who had died protecting him and her daughter. I think of Yssa whom I believed had abandoned her daughter, only to find that she had entrusted her to me, certain that I would love her. I marvel that all of our stories come to this deep, dark, dangerous, impossible valley of love for our children.

We would give our lives for them, I think, all of us mothers.

Yet sometimes all the love in all the worlds might not be enough to save them.

Morning comes, and it is Cloud-Marie who finds me slumped awkwardly in my chair. For a moment I think I must have dreamed it all, but then I see Yssa is behind her.

'Let's go,' she says. 'I can't bear to wait any longer.'

So we walk together, the three of us, Yssa who is the sister of my heart, and Cloud-Marie who is the daughter of my heart, to find out if the Princess Chamber has made a princess of a red dog.

Both Yssa and Cloud-Marie stand back to let me grasp the doves, and when I open the doors, I gasp, for the room is red as blood, red as fire, red as the petals of a million roses, and the scent of them! Oh, I remember, in this moment, the wonder of my own awakening in this same room, in this same sea of intoxicating crimson.

'Look!' whispers Yssa, and I look and see on the bed, where once I lay, a young woman. Long and slender and naked she is, with skin as white as milk and a great wild mop of red-gold hair. There is not a mark on that white skin as she sits up and stares about her in bewilderment. I see her grow still. She is looking towards the fire and I look there, too.

And I see him lying in the petals before the hearth, even as my prince once lay, waiting for his princess to wake, my son the wolf prince, his pelt white save where it is laid open in red wounds, head unmoving upon his paws.

Yssa catches me as I sway.

'Wait. Wait and see,' she hisses, for now the girl slips down from the bed and runs lightly through the red petals towards the white wolf, utterly unselfconscious in her nakedness. She kneels beside him and strokes him from his head to his tail. Her touch is sensuous, and to my everlasting relief, he lifts his head to look at her. She bends to kiss his muzzle and, all at once, he is not a wolf but a man, naked and white and perfect as she. But when she lifts her head he is again a wolf. Yet she does not seem dismayed by his transformations. She strokes his pelt and strokes it and he is a man again and rolls back against her knees, his eyes languorous with desire.

'I don't understand,' I murmur.

'I don't either,' says Yssa. 'But he lives and she lives, and perhaps this is beyond our part in their story. Perhaps the time for the power of mothers and aunts is over. Now they must write their own story and seek their own ending.'

Yssa draws me from the room and closes the doors slowly. I have a last glimpse of the tawny princess reaching again to kiss a wolf and of a powerful young man with hair as dark as his father's reaching up to draw her into his arms. Then the doors are closed.

Yssa puts one arm around Cloud-Marie and another around my shoulders, and she ushers us away from the Princess Chamber. She kisses Cloud-Marie and says to me, 'You have raised my daughter for me, and you have done all you can for your son. Now you must think of yourself.'

'Myself?' I say the word as if I do not know its meaning. Indeed I do not know what I can be, for if I am not wanted as wife or mother anymore, what am I? As if she reads my thoughts, Yssa stops before a mirror and turns me to look at myself. I see a woman who is not young, nor is she old. There are secrets in her eyes, and lines about them, but her mouth is full and warm and softly red and the silver is only a glimmer of the frost on the dark golden tresses that fall over her shoulders.

Yssa says, 'Your story is not only their story. He will be king and she will be his queen. But what of you?'

I think of going to live with those other queens in the palace of tears, growing old as they mirror my ageing back to me. I think of sending word to try to draw my husband back to me. I loved him and love him still, I realise, but he has gone now. I imagine remaining in the King's Palace in my little rooms, working on my tapestry and sometimes walking in the mist garden, and in time, minding the children of my son and his princess bride. I think of laying myself down in a field of flowers where I would sleep forever, and dream. But suddenly that seems a mawkish, morbid vision.

'I need to find a new dream,' I say, and I am surprised by the brisk impatience in my voice.

'I think you ought to go back to your own world for a time,' says Yssa. 'The boy and my niece will need time alone now, and if you do not mind, Cloud-Marie and I will join you after a little. There is much in the lives of mortals that immortals do not know and I would like to study it, and to see more of your world. In truth, I like the idea of a world where being a princess or a queen is not all there is. And Cloud-Marie will not want to be parted from you for long.'

'I could go to the land where I was born and wait for you there,' I say, the words forming on my lips even as they are forming in my mind. 'It is a land surrounded by sea and I once lived on the very edge of it. When I sat up in my bed, I could see the waves rolling in. I always wondered how they did not roll over me.' I fall silent, but the thought of going back crackles through me like an electrical current. I think of a beach where I walked as a girl; the soft, salted scent of the warm air that played over my skin like a caress. I imagine how it will be to lick my lips and find they taste of the sea.

'Cloud-Marie will like the waves,' says Yssa.

Cloud-Marie waves at her mother, and gives a chirrup of excited laughter, and suddenly we are all laughing.

The Man Who Lost
His Shadow

I gaze through the windscreen at the unbroken, ornate facade
of building after building, art nouveau and baroque details
picked out delicately by the buttery gold of the streetlamps. It
occurs to me that the thousands of tourists who travel to this city
would feel they are stepping into the past, yet when this street was
new, it would have looked very different. Night would have been
an all-consuming darkness. The brash electric light that denotes
the modern world and appears to have defeated and driven off that
ancient darkness – from the streets, from corners, from the hearts
of men and women – is an illusion.

Darkness is eternal and it will find its way, its crack, its vein.

The castle appears as the taxi driver promised, seeming to be
lifted above the snarl of old town streets surrounding it on beams
of light, to float in greenish illumination. He glances at me in the
rear-view mirror and tells me in brutish English that the lights are

switched off at the castle just before midnight. I imagine sitting somewhere, in a café perhaps, and waiting to see it swallowed up by the night.

'You have business?' he asks with a touch of irony that suggests he has some inkling of my affliction, though it is virtually unnoticeable at night. I consider telling him that the turbulent history of his country, the stony eroded beauty of this city that is its heart, fascinated me. But in the end I say only, 'Yes, business'.

Thinking: a strange business.

I do not know how I lost my shadow. After the first shock wore off, I told myself it was freak chance. My shadow might not even have known what it was doing when it severed itself from me. I could easily envisage myself walking and hesitating at some slight fork in the street, my shadow going on, sunk in its own thoughts, failing to notice that it did so without me. Seconds later, I would choose the other way. Maybe after a time it realised what had happened and retraced its path, but by then I was long gone.

That was one of my earliest theories – hopes, you might as well say. One does not like to admit the possibility that one's shadow has left on purpose. I consoled myself with a vision of my shadow, slipping frantically along walls and paths searching for me, wailing as forlornly as a lost child, occasionally plunging into pools of shadow and emerging with difficulty because it lacked a form to pull it from the larger shadow.

Now, I can more readily imagine its relief at being cut loose. It may have been a fortuitous accident that freed it, or maybe it saw its chance to be free, and took it. Either way, I blame my passivity for our estrangement. As a child, caught within the roaring machinery of the relationship between my parents, I had learned to defend myself with stillness. But having gained the habit of passivity, I could not rid myself of it, and so as an adult I found it almost impossible to engage with life. I was a fringe dweller of the most meek and timid ilk, and if someone had accused me of being a shadow in the world, I would have admitted it.

But that was before my shadow was lost, and I understood by the gaping void its absence left that it is we who need our shadows, not they us. Without it to anchor me to the earth, I became dangerously detached. I dreamed of the reassurance of its company, its small tug at my heels, its soft movement before me, feeling out my path like a blind man's cane. Without it to bind me to the earth, I was like one of those astronauts whose each step on the moon is so buoyant it seems they might at any second step into infinity. I feared that without my shadow I would soon make just such a step into oblivion. I had understood at last that I was diminishing without its darkness to balance me, and knew that something must be done.

The taxi swerves violently to avoid another taxi that has tried to pull out from a side street and the driver mutters what sounds like a curse.

I note indifferently that I had not felt the slightest fear at our near collision.

That numbing of emotions was as unexpected a side effect of my affliction as my detachment from linear time, and as easily as my grandmother slipped one stitch over another with her delicate, sharp needles, I slip.

I am sitting in a café booth beside floor-to-ceiling windows. Blinding light floods the table and presses against the frozen transparency that divides it from the darkness beyond. Somehow, the glass keeps them separate. Time is like this, I think, but for me there is no wall of glass. The light and dark are converging, consuming one another.

There is a young couple in the booth opposite sitting in such a way that, although they appear to be independent of each other, their bodies touch all along one side from shoulder down through the hip and thigh to the heels, their connection far more intimate than if they had been wound together explicitly. They are not foreign as I am, although even in a no-man's land like this establishment, where success depends upon its rejecting utterly any trace of the culture within which it exists, they belong in a way that I do not. Part of it may be because they are casually dressed, whereas I am wearing my formal but now somewhat crushed travelling clothes. Or maybe it is that they are young and I am not.

The girl is very tall and slender, as all of the women I have seen here seem to be – young women, anyway. The older women are as bulky as bears in their winter coats, their expressions forbidding and surly. The Asian stewardesses on the airline I flew with for the first part of the trip here were as small and fragile as blown-glass blossoms, while the German stewardesses on my second flight were young matrons with thick, competent arms and no-nonsense expressions. Here the faces of the young women are still and remote. One can see it is a general type and the girl opposite fits it. The waiter brings them two drinks – orangeade, perhaps – and a plate with two chocolate-coated cakes. A waiter is an anomaly in a place like this, a sign of the hybridisation of two cultures, perhaps, each trying to consume and subdue the other.

The girl takes up the plate and cuts into the cake, her expression unchanged. Inside the coating of chocolate is a pale, soft sponge or maybe some sort of creamy filling. She offers the laden fork to the boy, and my stomach spasms dully in what might be hunger. He is sitting very erect, although her spine is bent into a delicate bow and curled around the long, flat belly. She eats the remainder of the first cake and all of the second, licking her lips and talking, but never smiling, never showing any emotion. Her companion nods, and watches her with ravenous attention.

The waiter brings them a tall glass of fruit salad topped with a fat, loose whorl of impossibly white cream. The boy's turn, I think, but he gestures at the glass and the girl pushes aside the empty plate and again offers a spoonful of fruit and cream to the young man, who shakes his head. As before, the girl eats the whole parfait with the same dreamy absorption. When she sets the glass down, the boy runs his hand over her belly possessively, and then slides it around to pull her to him to be kissed. When he releases her, I see that her hands have not moved throughout the embrace and her body retracts automatically to its former languid bow.

The boy has become aware of my regard, and gives me a curious look. I do not glance away, embarrassed. I feel almost no self-consciousness. The affliction that brought me to this strange outpost has advanced to the point where I hardly feel any need to pretend to be normal. The boy calls the waiter and pays the bill and, as they leave, the young woman settles her limp, expressionless gaze on me. There is no way of knowing what is going on in her mind. Perhaps nothing. When they have gone, my exhaustion returns and I begin to think of leaving.

Beyond the windows is a utilitarian rank of spotlit petrol bowsers, and beyond the asphalt surrounding them a narrow road curves back to join the highway bounded on either side by a dense pine forest, passing into shadow.

I did not know what it meant to lose my shadow.

After my initial blank disbelief upon discovering it, I sought help. Ironically, I went to a doctor first, a general practitioner more accustomed to removing warts and administering antibiotics and tranquillisers than to treating a man with an ailment as rare and arcane as mine. She offered me a calmative and, seeing her disdain, I told her somewhat haughtily that she need not suppose that anything was wrong with my mind. Could she not accept the evidence of her eyes as I had done? I lacked a shadow. What could be more empirical, more concrete? Yet she simply pretended to be confused by my symptoms.

'What exactly do you want?' she demanded finally.

I asked her coldly to refer me to a specialist in shadows, since her own training seemed to have left her ill-equipped for such exotic conditions. Somewhat maliciously, I suspect, she sent me to a radiologist, whose view of shadows was shaped entirely by his daily quest for the shadows that signified cancers and tumours on his X-rays. I can only say that his mind had been seriously warped by his profession.

When I told him of my problem, his eyes blazed and he clutched my arm hard enough to leave a bruise, proclaiming that I was the first human to have escaped the curse of shadows. He confided his belief that they were not bestowed by God, as was generally supposed, but had been visited upon us by some force which he refused to name. His mania was apparent when I questioned him about the purpose of shadows. He gave me an affronted look and asked what sort of man I thought he was, to ask him such a question, exactly as if I had asked the shade of his pubic hair. He had insisted on taking and developing an X-ray plate, which he examined suspiciously, finally announcing in a slightly resentful tone that he saw no shadow.

After that, I gave up on the medical profession. I was not really ill, I reasoned. Having lost a shadow I was more like a man whose wife leaves him, clearing out their apartment with mysterious speed and efficiency. With this in mind, I consulted a private investigating firm. The man who ran the agency gave his name as Andrews, which might as well be his surname as his first name. It occurred to me that a normal person would immediately be able to tell, but the nuance was too subtle for me so I contrived not to call him anything.

'I've never been asked to shadow a shadow before,' he said when I had laid the matter before him. I can only suppose he meant it as a joke, but I did not laugh. I am not good at humour, and I told him this. He squinted at me, seeming suddenly sobered.

'Perhaps that's the whole point,' he said. 'Your lack of humour. Think of it from the point of view of a shadow having to endure being dragged about, never having a chance to exert its own mind or will or taste. And on top of that, to be forced to live with someone who has no sense of humour. It must be unendurable.' He seemed very sincere, but a certain reticence in my own character prevented me breaking down and confessing my fear of precisely this eventuality – that some profound lack in me had driven away my shadow. That was a matter to be resolved between my shadow and me. 'They're worse than slaves,' he went on, 'because they can only emulate. Nothing they do is original. There must be millions of them constantly plotting a coup, fed by dreams of freedom . . .'

'Can you find it?' I asked him flatly.

He looked through a leather ledger before consulting with his secretary, and after some negotiating, we agreed that he should have a modest retainer for a week. If after that time his enquiries had produced no promising clues, our contract would end. If he did find a lead, I would pay him a hundred dollars a day thereafter, including expenses, until he found my shadow or my money was gone.

I gulped a little at the size of his daily fee, but a modest, hard-working life has enabled me to put aside a very good sum, and to comfort myself, I reckoned that ten thousand dollars spent on finding my shadow would still leave ample for my old age, and perhaps would even run to a restorative trip to the Greek Islands in the off-season after it was all over, so that my shadow and I could re-evaluate our relationship.

Perhaps it seems absurd to go to such lengths, but I was desperate.

Unfortunately, after a week, the investigator could report nothing. He confessed that my inability to remember when I had lost my shadow was a stumbling block. I blushed when he spoke of this, for his words seemed to me to suggest that I had been negligent. Though I continued to argue that the loss could only have happened a little before I noticed it, he clearly doubted me, and made me doubt myself. Brooding over what he'd said, it struck me that I could not remember the last time I had noticed my shadow. I ran my mind over the days before my retirement, and then the weeks and months leading up to it. Finally, frantically, I began to run my mind over the preceding years, but still I could not recall seeing my shadow on any specific occasion. I envisaged all the bright sunny days I had lived through, from forest walks in the autumn to a dip in the blazing summer heat, to no avail.

I could recall seeing my reflection many times, but not my shadow. I told myself at one point that, after all, it was only a shadow, and then was chilled, for perhaps it was just such carelessness that had driven it off. If that were so, I vowed remorsefully, I would show how much I valued it by the fervour of my search.

Fortunately my retirement meant I had no appointments or ties to hold me back. In fact, the investigator had the gall to suggest a link between my retirement and the day I noticed my shadow missing. Ridiculous, especially since he could not substantiate his notion with anything aside from the most simplistic chronological link. Was he suggesting my retirement had provoked the departure of my shadow, I demanded? He bridled at my tone, and though we parted politely, I did not go back to him.

'Behind there, gardens,' the taxi driver said, nodding at a high wall slashed with graffiti. I wondered why the garden was walled. Perhaps it was a zoological garden and some sort of wildlife dwelt in it. I saw the driver watching me.

'Gardens,' I said. But I was thinking of my shadow, the hunt for which had brought me across the world. In my own country the search had come to seem farcical, yet my sense of loss and desperation had grown. Finally it came to me that there was little tolerance for or interest in shadows in my country, with its excess of sunlight and brightness. Even the violent abuses committed upon its shores were like the violence of a depraved toddler, mindless acts motivated by primitive fears and incomprehension; they were devoid of true darkness. My shadow would never have remained there. It would have sought out an older, deeper place with crannies and corners where darkness fermented and ripened.

One evening not long after my last encounter with the detective, I was sitting in the communal television room of my boarding house and the person with the remote control changed channels.

I found myself watching the end of a documentary in which the camera showed a series of views of an ancient city. The last shot was of a cracked wall, where a child's shadow walked along the shadow of another wall, beneath a scrolling list of names. The documentary ended abruptly and I gave a cry of disappointment.

'What is that place? Do you know where it is?' I asked the other residents seated about in the mismatched chairs. A flat-faced, sombre-eyed man grunted that he ought to know, since he had been a child there before the occupation, before his parents had escaped and emigrated. I asked if they understood shadows in that place. It was a risky question, but there was a surreal quality to the light in the room which allowed it.

'There was a time when people had to *be* shadows there,' the man said.

My landlady reproached me for my selfishness when I told her of my intended journey. 'What would your grandmother think?' She had known my grandmother and had taken me in on her account. Now she was affronted by my decision to leave, as only a woman like her can be, a woman whose masochism was so convoluted that she regarded everything that occurred in the world as somehow directed at her. Nothing that happened, not a car crash in another city in which a stranger died, nor the razing of a park to build a racecourse, nor the swearing of a drunk weaving from a pub, was exempt from being gathered into her aggrieved personal worldview. Of course it was a stunningly self-centred, even socio-pathic way to regard the world.

I answered mildly that, if anything, my grandmother would understand best what I was doing, for she had been a woman of incredible wisdom. Spitefully, my landlady observed that it must have been the weight of all that wisdom that cracked her mind open like an egg. She meant to abash me, for it was true that my grand-mother had been quite insane at the end of her life, but instead I remembered with sudden wonder how, not long before the end, she had appeared to become disorientated. She was always imagining she was in the house of her father, no matter where she was; that my home, or the hotel or mental institution or public toilet, were somehow connected to it, if she could just find the right door. She frequently exclaimed over a picture or vase, insisting that it had been moved from the mantelpiece in her father's study, or from the hall table, and worrying that it would trouble him.

'It is very vexing when things are moved around,' she would sigh and scrub at her forehead fretfully with a tiny clenched fist.

Only now, in this moment, did I understand that her apparent confusion was an awareness of links that had been buried under life, hidden from reason. Children see these links between things very clearly, I believe. It is why they weep at one stranger and smile at another. So do the elderly, some of whom slough off reason with the same gusto with which many of them throw off their clothes, welcoming back the Eden-like simplicity and clarity of childhood. My grandmother's confusion had been nothing less than a deeper seeing of the world, and the documen-tary had suggested to me that finding my shadow might require such vision. That frightened me, because such a manner of seeing cannot be learned or simulated, for that which allows one to see such links of necessity blinds one to other things. Nevertheless, I vowed that at least I would follow this one strange clue without question.

The airport was very crowded, or so it seemed to me, but perhaps it is always like that in the international terminal. I presented my ticket and little bag to the departure desk, feeling unexpectedly exhilarated. I thought of a quote I had read on my desk calendar the day I left work. *What does not kill you makes you stronger.* It can only have been a warning, for it had been little more than an hour later, walking to the tram stop in bright afternoon sunlight, when I had noticed the absence of my shadow.

I stared down at the ground in front of me, feeling the sun pouring on the back of my head and shoulders. I turned and looked up, intrigued and puzzled, to find out what other light sources could have erased my shadow. Then I noticed that the shadow of the light pole alongside me fell on the ground and up the wall. With a feeling of unreality, I held up a hand to the wall, but it cast no shadow.

I rushed home, staggering with terror, clutching my briefcase loaded with the paraphernalia from my emptied desk.

Another taxi swerves across in front of us, forcing the driver to run over the tramlines. The cobbles make the wheels drum under the seat, and I close my eyes, remembering intimately the way I was pressed into my seat as the plane left the earth and launched itself into a long, drawn-out, vibrating dusk in which the sun seemed to hang for hours half submerged by the horizon.

I decline the proffered tray of food, despite my hunger, and resolve to treat the long flight as a period of fasting and mental preparation for my search. I accept only water, as if I were on a religious pilgrimage. Night falls, and twelve hours later it is still night. I feel, disembarking into a day so darkly overcast and befogged, as if I have entered an endless night that will not be broken until I am reunited with my shadow.

Inside the terminal all is chaos because of the fog. People exclaim and speculate and there is talk of long delays for connecting flights. When a man from my flight complains, the woman at the transfer desk explains reproachfully that we were lucky to have been permitted to land at all. I step forward and name my destination and there is a flicker of interest in her weary eyes.

'That's becoming very popular. Some say it is the Paris of the 1920s all over again.' Her vowels are so plump they are like fruit waiting to be picked.

Day passes imperceptibly into night and still there is no call to board. I resist suggestions to leave the airport and stay a night or two in a hotel, not wishing to be diverted from my purpose. The smell of food makes me feel faint and I decide to break my fast with a leisurely meal in one of the better restaurants the airport has to offer. The last meal I ate was a dinner of cabbage and boiled potatoes prepared by my tight-lipped landlady the night before I left. I am suddenly so hungry that the thought of even that grudging meal makes my stomach rumble. Nevertheless, I am grimy and sweaty after the long hours of travel and decide to bathe before eating. I exchange my last banknotes for a few English pounds, and manage to locate an attendant to unlock the shower and give me soap and a towel.

In the booth, I undress slowly and take a hot shower, enjoying the water on my tired skin. Another effect of the loss of my shadow has been to render my skin dreadfully dry and itchy. After what seems a very short interlude, the shower attendant hammers on the door and in an indescribable argot gives what can only be a command to make haste. I obey, surrendering the soiled towel and giving her a pound tip to demonstrate both my disapproval and my high-mindedness.

This transaction reminds me that I will need to change a traveller's cheque if I want to eat. Coming out of the shower, I pat my pockets, searching for my wallet. Unable to find it, I decide I must have left it in the shower cubicle. Then it comes to me. I removed my jacket in the plane so it could be hung up, taking out both the wallet and the travel agency pouch containing my passport and travel documents, and sliding both into the seat pocket. On arrival, I had taken out the pouch, but I have no recollection of retrieving the wallet.

I go to the information desk, noting my lack of apprehension. I put the curious deadening of my feelings down to jet lag, but wonder if the atrophy of lesser emotions is a further symptom of my affliction.

'If only you had realised immediately,' the man tells me regretfully, a touch of Jamaica in his tone. Nevertheless he will make some calls. Can I come back in an hour. Not a question. I sit down for a while near his desk, then decide I can simply report the cheques stolen and arrange to have them replaced. My cards and other papers can be dealt with at another time.

I speak to the young woman at the Thomas Cook counter who assures me the cheques can be replaced quickly so long as I have their numbers, which are supposed to be kept separately. I explain that I have inadvertently packed the list in my baggage, which is checked through to my final destination and might even have gone on ahead.

'That is against regulations,' she tells me primly. 'The bags must travel with the clients. Always.'

I say nothing, knowing as she does that bags sometimes travel without their people, just as shadows sometimes travel alone. It isn't meant to happen, but it can. The announcement for my flight to board comes over the air.

'I will get the cheques once I arrive,' I tell her.

'You can't mean to go there without money,' she exclaims. The genuine concern in her tone reminds me of the mysterious nature of my trip, and it comes to me that this mishap is a sign that I am failing to understand.

The young woman mistakes the confusion in my eyes and leans over her smooth counter to explain. 'In a country like that, you must have money. Everything is for sale. Everything costs and you are safe as long as you can afford the price. Safety has a price, just like comfort or food or coffee.'

I sense that under these words she is telling me something important, but I cannot seem to understand. My mind feels numb. I insist that I have decided to go on. Surely this is the most unreasoned response to what has happened, and therefore the most apposite. Maybe it is even a kind of test. At my request, she writes the address of their office, saying there is a cheap bus to the centre. Upon arrival, I can walk to the office from the stop. Alternatively, I could take a courtesy bus to one of the bigger hotels – the Hilton, for instance – where they would quite likely sort out the lost cheques for me.

She is kind, but I have no desire to stay in a hotel like the Hilton. I will get a bus to the centre of the city after changing the little remaining cash I have, and walk about until daybreak. Then I will get the cheques replaced and find some suitable accommodation.

I check back with the airline attendant who reiterates that no one has handed in the wallet, then give him my landlady's number in case it should appear. I dislike doing this, but I have no forwarding address to give and no one else's name to offer other than my previous employer's, and he is not the sort to maintain warm connections. Indeed, he made it abundantly clear that the severance payment was generous to ensure that I would not expect anything more from him.

Boarding the small plane that will carry me on the last leg of my journey, I wonder what my boss would think if he knew I was on my way, without money, to a city full of shadows and danger, where everything has a price.

On the plane I eat the small club sandwich offered, and drink as many cups of coffee as I can manage during the short flight, for I am beginning to feel very empty and it will be some hours before I can eat. The coffee makes my head spin and the sense of disorientation assailing me increases.

The face of the customs official at the airport is flat and severe, but his eyes are the same soulful brown as the man in the television room of my apartment house. As he takes my passport, I wonder absurdly if they could be related.

'Reason for visit?' he asks. His thick finger taps a blank space in the form I filled out. He slides a pen through the small window separating his official niche from me. I take it up and notice my fingers are trembling. I try to focus my thoughts. It is incredibly difficult, for even though I have understood the question I cannot seem to think how to answer it. I look at the official and find him staring hard at me, as if he is cataloguing my features for a report to be added to a file of suspicious foreigners.

I can feel sweat crawling from my armpits. I force myself to write.

'Research,' he reads. 'What kind of research?'

I feel I might be about to faint or have some sort of convulsion. All of my glassy calmness seems to rupture. My heart beats in jerky, arrhythmic spasms. Then suddenly, with a feeling of delirious clarity, I understand that my reaction is a premonition connected to my ailment, and to my arrival in this country. I simply tell him why I am here. I feel as if I have peeled my skin off in front of him. I feel that, having told him my secret, I cannot draw breath without him permitting it. I feel a drowning, tremulous gratitude, as if I have put my life in his hands. I have a powerful urge to kiss his hands.

'Your shadow,' he says, and I realise he has not understood the word. His English must be regulation minimum and solely connected to his job. He stamps the passport and slides it back to me with the visa folded on top. As I take it up, I feel as if I have shown myself naked to a blind man.

By the time I walk out into the night carrying my bag, I understand that this has been a necessary encounter, an emotional procedure to be endured, perhaps no less vital for entry to this country as acquiring a visa. I feel stronger, though more detached than ever.

From the timetable, it seems as if I have missed the last bus to the city. A short, swarthy man sidles over and asks if I want a taxi.

'Special taxi. Very cheap for you.' He has grasped the handle of my bag and is trying to wrest it from me. I hold on and he ceases pulling at it. Perhaps he is surprised at my strength.

'It's impossible,' I tell him. 'I don't want to take a taxi.'

He looks around furtively, and I have a memory of the

Thomas Cook woman warning me about taxis in this city before we parted. She claimed the majority were run by a vicious local mafia and that many of the drivers pimp for gypsy prostitutes. She had told me of a taxi driver leaping out of his cab and beating two American tourists with a truncheon because they had crossed the street too slowly in front of him. Such fearless brutality suggested a level of lawlessness that ought to have made me wary, but the man holding onto my bag does not exude any air of power or malignancy. He looks more desperate than anything else. His clothes are ill-fitting and grubby, the cuffs of his jacket and trousers badly frayed. In fact, I wonder if he really has a taxi, or merely seeks to lure me to a discreet corner of the car park to mug me.

'I don't have the money for a taxi,' I tell him. He stares at me in sullen bewilderment and so I make a dumb show of the day's events, reaching for my wallet and discovering its loss.

He releases the bag. 'No crown? You no want taxi?' This possibility appears to confound him.

'Later,' I say, pointing away from myself as if to some distant future. Then it occurs to me that the best way out of my dilemma might simply be to ride about in a taxi until morning, when I can visit a Thomas Cook office, then pay him.

'I would like to make a tour of the city,' I tell him.

'Tour? Now?' He gapes at me.

I nod firmly. 'An all-night tour. Fixed price. No meter.'

'Tour,' he says, sucking the word to decide if he likes the taste of it. He nods judicially. 'Fixed-price tour. Cheap. You come.'

I make him name a price, then let him take my bag. He runs ahead into the misty darkness, and I try to calculate the hours since I last slept, but am defeated by the time difference between my country and this one, and by daylight saving on top of that. Did they bother saving daylight here, or did they save night instead? I realise at some level that I am becoming dangerously light-headed. My nostril hairs seem to be on the verge of freezing and the air is so cold it hurts to breathe it in.

He is standing by a beaten-up blue Skoda. 'No taxi,' he says earnestly. 'Tour car.'

I take off my jacket and climb into the car.

He drives quickly and it seems to me it is uncannily dark outside. There are no lights along the highway, and no moon or stars. I tell myself it is overcast, yet I cannot help but feel the darkness is thicker here than back home, congealing at the edges. He does not slow as we reach the outskirts of the city. I stare out at the streets that flicker by like a jerky old black-and-white movie. Everything looks grimy, as if the night is slowly rubbing off onto the city.

'Metronome,' the driver comments, nodding at a set of dark steps leading up from the roadside and pointing up. 'Up,' he says.

'A metronome?' I ask doubtfully. We have circled the city several times now, and it is very late. We move swiftly because there are few cars on the road, mostly taxis or delivery trucks or great dark multi-country transit buses full of sleeping passengers. The castle is ahead of us again but I can no longer see it, and a vaporous mist is rising along the course of the river. No doubt the driver is weary and beginning to make up sights. I do not blame him.

'Doesn't work,' he says. 'Stops and starts.'

Another car roars past us. It is yellow and a lit sign on its roof proclaims it a taxi. Its red tail-lights burn like coals in the misty air. 'Taxis very bad here,' the driver mutters. 'All criminals.'

All at once we round a sharp bend only to find our way blocked by the taxi that passed us. Or perhaps it is another taxi. It is blocking the road completely. My driver stands on his brakes and tries to turn, but he is going too fast. The car slews around and mounts the pavement with a great thump that at first makes me think we have struck someone. Before I can speak, there is the sound of running footsteps and the front door is wrenched open.

The driver utters a thin scream as two huge men drag him out of the seat and begin punching him savagely. He does not fight back. He merely holds his hands over his face, and when he falls, he curls into a foetal ball. I cannot see what happens next, because another of the assailants is blocking my view. I grope for the door but the lock button has been removed. There is a lot of shouting outside, then an ominous silence filled with heavy breathing.

The big man whose back has blocked my view climbs into the front passenger seat of the Skoda and turns to look at me. His hair is bleached white, but his eyebrows are dark and almost join over the bridge of his nose. A thin man with dark, greasy-looking hair slides into the driver's seat and turns the key. As the car moves off, carefully backing to avoid colliding with the abandoned taxi, the big man continues to stare at me expressionlessly. Then he points solemnly through the window. As I turn to look I catch a glimpse of my old driver lying on the ground, before a blow to the head, and a second, deeper night, consumes me.

I wake to find myself lying full-length along the back seat of the Skoda. My jacket has been thrown over me. From that position, I can see nothing except that it is still night. Gathering my strength, I sit up. Outside the car windows the darkness speeds by. There is no sign of the city or of any buildings. We are on a straight, open highway, driving very fast.

The driver says something and the big man turns and lifts a truncheon. I shake my head.

'There is no need for that,' I tell him.

I do not know if he understands me, but he lowers his arm and studies me as if my calmness interests him, then he says something in his own language to the driver. The other man shakes his head and begins to shout. The big man says nothing until his companion falls silent, then he turns back to me and points through the front windscreen.

'Káva. Coff-ee,' he says.

Looking down the road, I see he is indicating a faint illumination on the horizon. The brightness grows until I see it is an all-night petrol station attached to a fast-food café. The car pulls off into an access road and curves round to come to a grinding halt in the gravel car park. There are only two other cars parked alongside the restaurant. One is very new and red.

'You come,' the big man says. He says something else in his own language that sounds like a warning, and I nod.

They walk either side of me as we approach the door. The driver points at the bowsers and the big man shrugs, steering me deftly through the shining glass doors. The brightness of the light hurts my eyes and I am glad of the thick paw on my shoulder, steering me. He pushes me into a booth, takes out a phone and moves away to make a call.

'I just wish you wouldn't bring up the war,' one of the men in the booth opposite says with an American accent. 'It's a sore point with these guys. They think we betrayed them.'

'You did,' the other man snorts in laconic German-accented English.

The thin driver sits down, and gives the other men a dangerous look, but they are too much involved in their conversation to notice. The big man shakes his head at the thin man.

'All of that is ancient history. It's in the past.' The American's tone is irritated.

'Nothing is past here. Haven't you learned enough to know that?'

Silence falls between them, and I wonder what happened to my original driver. Had he been killed? The driver squints at me and I sense that he is wondering why I do not make an attempt to escape or call for help.

'We could have got coffee closer to the border,' the German says.

'Coffee, sure.' The American's voice is ironic. 'We've got a deadline, Klaus. Why don't you wait until we get somewhere civilised to buy a woman?'

'You don't understand,' the German says with friendly

contempt. 'You don't understand anything but disinfectant and prophylactics. You're afraid of everything, including your own shadow.'

The word *shadow* galvanises me. The thin man opposite notices and narrows his eyes, then he smiles and a gold tooth winks at me. I have the mad desire to laugh, for it seems I have exchanged one sort of farce for another.

'Aren't you afraid of getting a disease?' the American asks, fastidious but curious too. They do not imagine anyone can understand their words. They have not even looked at me, and what would they see if they did?

The German laughs. 'The danger makes the pleasure more intense. Darker. In fact, you might say that darkness is the specialty of this place.'

'This place is no place,' says the American almost plaintively. 'A stretch of godforsaken highway where the snow looks like dirty sperm. And those women. The way they just loom up suddenly in the headlights with their black leather skirts and fishnet tights and fake fur coats, their eyes like petrol bombs about to blow up in your face. They scare the hell out of me. How can anyone stop? How can you get aroused by that?'

'They wouldn't be there if no one stopped,' the German observes almost coyly. 'I've stopped every time I pass this way, and every time I do, I am afraid. Nothing is more terrifying than to stop and invite one of these women into the car. They take me down into the dark so deep I don't know if I'll ever come up, if there is enough light in me to come back.'

'But they're just whores, terrible rough whores with scars and thick thighs. I read in *Time Magazine* that they're the worst, most dangerous prostitutes in the world.' The American's voice is lace-edged with hysteria.

'It is true,' the German murmurs.

'It's the disease that scares me . . .' the American says.

The German calls for the bill. As he pays, the big white-haired man returns, dropping the phone into his pocket. He nods at the two men as they pass, then slides into the booth beside me. It occurs to me that the phone call was about me. Will they now kill me or beat me up and leave me for dead? Will they try to ransom me? Or use me as a hostage? These thoughts flutter distantly though my mind, like leaves blown along a tunnel.

The waiter brings us three espressos. The white-haired man must have ordered them. I drink, enjoying the cruel strength of the dark liquid. I have never tasted such bitter coffee before, like the dregs of the world. The caffeine hits me like a punch to the heart.

An hour passes and the phone rings. The waiter glances at our table in such a way that I see he has recognised my assailants. Or perhaps he has recognised their type. Perhaps he guesses that I have been abducted, but he will do nothing. The big man moves away with the shrilling phone to take the call. He nods. He shakes his head. He shrugs and says a few words. He nods again, then puts the phone away and comes back to the table with an air of purpose. He says two words to the driver, who lights a cigarette. Neither of them speaks to me. Neither of them looks at me.

A strange tension devoid of emotion fills me. 'What do we do now?' I ask.

The big man tilts his head. 'We? There is no we.'

I hear the sound of an engine approaching. Both men look away through the glass towards the approaching vehicle. The noise increases until the headlights loom and fuse with the light from the petrol station. The car has tinted windows so it is impossible to see who is inside. The horn sounds and the big man rises from the seat beside me and nods to the driver, who reaches into his pocket and withdraws the keys to the Skoda. He throws them down on the shining formica in front of me.

'You have your own business to complete now, eh?' the big white-haired man says, nodding away into the darkness, and he goes up to the counter and pays the bill. The two men saunter out the glass door and climb into the waiting car, which sends up a spume of gravel in its wake as it departs.

Another car pulls in. Two young people emerge and stretch. They enter and I watch them slide into the booth where the American and German sat. Their bodies touch all along one side from shoulder down through the hip and thigh to the heels, their connection far more intimate than if they had been wound together explicitly.

I slip and now I am walking into the freezing night. I glance back at the blazing block of cement and glass. It looks like some outstation at the end of the world. It begins to snow lightly, white flakes swirling against the blackness. Climbing into the driver's seat of the Skoda, I insert the key. The strangeness of sitting on the wrong side of the car strikes me dimly. The engine fires the first time, despite the rapidly dropping temperature. I let the engine idle a moment, then put the car smoothly into gear. I feel no impatience or confusion. No fear. My hands are steady as I drive out onto the verge of the highway, remembering to keep to the correct side of the road. I have no idea which way is the way back to the city. Then I realise I am beyond choosing. I drive in the direction the white-haired man nodded, gliding into the unknown with the sudden inexplicable certainty that I am getting closer to my shadow. I shiver, though the heater has warmed up the interior of the car quickly. The snow is still falling, yet blackness presses against the car so hard I fancy it is slowing me down. After several kilometres, I realise that the car *is* slowing. The petrol gauge shows the tank is empty.

The car coasts and I steer to the verge, my mind a blank. I feel nothing. I have come too far to pretend to have control over my life now. Enormous snowflakes fly past the windows like huge moths. I can no longer discern white from black.

The car stops, and at the same time, the snow ceases to fall.

I see her then, a woman standing beside the road against the vast rising mass of the forested hill behind her. She wears a slick black jacket and long black boots. As far as I can tell, she wears neither skirt nor stockings. The blue-tinged white of her bare skin shines. Her hair is so blonde it seems to give off its own radiance.

She turns slowly and looks at me. My heartbeat slows. I tell myself she cannot see me, that it would be impossible to see anything in all the light streaming towards her.

She comes towards the car, approaching the passenger door in a sturdy undulating stride. She taps at the window with nails as long and curved and transparent as a dragonfly's wings.

Aside from her hand splayed against the window, I can see only her torso, the patent leather, a liquescent black, outlining her hips and breasts. The passenger door opens and she enters the car as smoothly as a dancer, letting in an icy blast of air that vanquishes the warmth. She is older than she looked from a distance and more stocky. Her hair glows with a silvery pallor that might be strands of grey. I cannot tell her age. Her skin is like fine velvet, but there are intricate webs of wrinkles at the edges of her eyes. Her mouth is purple-black, as if she has just sucked some dark fruit whose juice has stained her lips, but her eyes are the bright miraculous blue of the skies above my own land, and nothing is more pure or relentless than that.

'You are tired?' she asks in heavily accented English.

'I have not slept for a long time,' I say.

'It is long. The road.'

She reaches out and switches off the headlights. We are plunged into the intimate ghastly green of the dashboard light. The colour makes her look as if she is a corpse, and her eyes seem transparent. Her hair now looks black, as if it has become saturated with the night, or with something seeping out from the heart of all her whiteness. 'What do you want?' She speaks English as if through a mouthful of liquid.

'I am looking for my shadow,' I whisper. My own voice sounds foreign. I have never been so close to a woman before.

'I have what you are seeking,' she says. Then she leans away from me, and draws aside the slick black edges of the coat like the lips of a wound, to reveal the full, smooth curve of her breasts where they are pressed together into a voluptuous cleavage. They are white as milk and downed like a peach. She reaches a pale hand between them and scoops one breast out. It is so soft that her fingers sink into it. She gestures at it in a businesslike way and I recoil.

I shake my head. I want to tell her that I am a man, not a child to be suckled. Not some doddering senile fool returned to infancy. But she reaches out her free hand to grip my neck, and pulls me towards her. Only then, with her hair swept back to bare her throat and bosom fully, do I notice a dark vein snaking from her neck to her breast. It writhes under her skin as if it has its own life and moves towards the tip of her breast.

She is strong as a peasant and a ripe odour flows over me as she lifts the breast and pulls me to it. To drink the shadow in her, to be drunk by it.

Acknowledgements

I would like to thank Erica Wagner and Allen & Unwin for their graceful and almost mythic patience with me throughout the long, slow creation of this book. Thanks also to my editor, Nan McNab, for being unfailingly graceful under fire, and brave enough never to let me get away with less than my best. And finally, thanks to Zoë Sadokierski for her lovely, lovely design.

These four stories were previously published, two in a significantly different form:

'The Man Who Lost His Shadow' in *Dreaming Down-Under Book 1*, edited by Jack Dann, Voyager/HarperCollins, 1999

'The Dove Game' (dedicated to Danny) in *Gathering the Bones*, edited by Jack Dann, Voyager/HarperCollins, 2003

'The Stranger' (dedicated to Danel O) in *Exotic Gothic 3: Strange Visitations*, edited by Danel Olson, Ash-Tree Press, 2009

'Metro Winds' (dedicated to Fernanda) in *Exotic Gothic 4: A Postscripts Anthology*, edited by Danel Olson, PS Publishing, 2012

ABOUT THE AUTHOR

Isobelle Carmody is one of Australia's most loved fantasy writers.

She is best known for her brilliant *Obernewtyn Chronicles* and for her novel *The Gathering* (joint winner of the 1993 *Children's Literature Peace Prize* and the 1994 *CBC Book of the Year Award*). She has written many short stories for both children and adults and was co-editor with Nan McNab of the fairytale anthologies, *The Wilful Eye* and *The Wicked Wood*.

With her partner and daughter, Isobelle divides her time between Prague in the Czech Republic and her home on the Great Ocean Road in Australia.

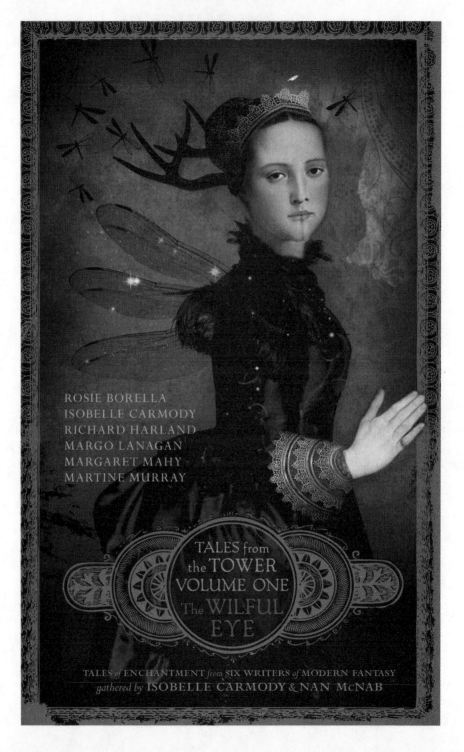

CATHERINE BATESON
VICTOR KELLEHER
CATE KENNEDY
MAUREEN McCARTHY
NAN McNAB
KATE THOMPSON
TALES from the TOWER VOLUME TWO
The WICKED WOOD
TALES of ENCHANTMENT from SIX WRITERS of MODERN FANTASY
gathered by ISOBELLE CARMODY & NAN McNAB

ISOBELLE CARMODY

Green Monkey Dreams